THE STAR CLOCK CHRONICLES

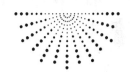

THE STAR CLOCK CHRONICLES

A STEAMPUNK STORY COLLECTION

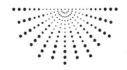

E.J. KITCHENS

Brier Road Press

Scripture quotations are from The ESV Bible (The Holy English Standard Version), copyright 2001 by Crossway, a publishing ministry of Good News Publishers. Used by permission. All rights reserved.

Poetry quotations accessed from PoetryFoundation.com and are in the public domain.

"He Wishes for the Cloths of Heaven" by W. B. Yeats

"Dawn" by Paul Laurence Dunbar

"I See His Blood Upon the Rose" by Joseph Mary Plunkett

"The Jabberwocky" by Lewis Carol

"She Walks in Beauty" by Lord Byron

"Night" by William Blake

"Hey, Diddle, Diddle" by Mother Goose

"The Raven" by Edgar Allan Poe

"Twinkle, Twinkle, Little Star" by Jane Taylor

Cover design by Elementi.Studio@99designs

Scene break image: "Thanks for your Like - donations welcome" @ Pixabay

The Star Clock Chronicles / E.J. Kitchens — 1st edition

Paperback Print ISBN: 978-0-9993509-6-6

Hardback Print ISBN: 978-0-9993509-7-3

CONTENTS

Bertram Orren expected trouble with both the Time Keepers and faeries if he got caught in the faerie woods. He didn't expect to get trapped in an abandoned faerie court deep underground while trying to save airship captain Marianna Bowditch from a will-o'-the-wisp. Nor did he expect he and Marianna to discover an ancient treasure that could help free the world from the Time King's control, one that could bring back the people's ability to navigate for themselves in a world where sun and moon, east and west are myths hidden by the faerie queen's Star Veil. Even if Bertram and Marianna escape the caves, they've no way to navigate themselves to an airship port and safety, and if the Time Keepers find them, the world will never see the dawn.

Airship captain Davy Bowditch wants to build a Star Clock so man won't be dependent on the Time King and his automaton navigators, but to do that, he'll need the help of one very unusual woman—if he can convince her he didn't kidnap her on purpose—and an airship pirate—if he can convince him he didn't kill his son. But in a world where sun and stars are myths, the truth of their existence long hidden behind a faerie veil, trying to build a clock is tantamount to treason.

Former pirate Colin O'Connor swore never to return to his old ways, but when Davy Bowditch goes into hiding and tasks Colin with gaining the iron harpoons needed to destroy the faerie queen's Star Veil, he's forced to go to his smuggler cousins for help gaining the forbidden metal. But neither the smugglers nor the Time Keepers trust Colin now that he's a Sky Keeper, so it's no surprise when a mysterious stowaway warns him he's walking into a trap. But Colin's determined that either he gets the iron or dies trying.

Colin O'Connor may have escaped with the iron needed to destroy the Star Veil, but the Sky Keepers still don't know where the Veil is. Colin heads back to Reydon to find out what he can, and maybe gain the help of the stowaway who saved him from the Time Keepers once before. But Vesper Vanon isn't a typical stowaway—she's a descendent of the Time King himself. Helping Colin could cost Vesper her life, and that's a price Colin isn't willing to let her pay.

Airship captain Kingsley Bowditch is dead. So the world thinks. A slave in the mines where the automaton navigators' crystals grow, he's doomed to labor for the Time King, the man he'd hoped to overthrow. But then Sky Keeper smuggler Caroline Lockley sneaks into the mines and asks for his help to find the crystal that will guide the Sky Keepers to the Star Veil to destroy it—before the Time King arrives for it. Getting the crystal might be easy, but getting it out—with guards, gates, and stray fey creatures between them and the sky—might not. Dusk is coming for the Time King's rule or for the hopes of Sky Keepers in this exciting conclusion to The Star Clock Chronicles.

A FREE NOVELETTE
ABOUT THE AUTHOR
ADDITIONAL WORKS BY THE AUTHOR

To all those who consider the wondrous works of God and who have revealed so many of his mysteries to us eager learners. May you see the greatness of God and his love for you in all his marvelous creation.

PART I
DAWN BRINGER

The heavens declare the glory of God, and the sky above proclaims his handiwork. Day to day pours out speech, and night to night reveals knowledge.
Psalm 19:1-2

CHAPTER ONE

No sun ever rose, no moon ever waxed or waned, no stars ever danced a rhythmic pattern across the night sky. Only faerie crystals brightening and dimming according to one man's will signaled dawn and dusk, month and season. Long ago, the faerie queen Morgan Unseelie cast a veil between heaven and earth, obscuring all heaven's lights, for the pleasure and power of a mortal man, who then fashioned himself the Rí Am, the Time King. From all other mortals, she took away knowledge of time and direction and skill of navigation. Man was dependent on the Rí Am's automaton navigators and fell into the myth that it was the faerie queen, through the Rí Am's intercession, who gave them the sky crystals in the veil for light and the automatons for travel and trade. For this, the queen was hailed as the Giver of Lights, a goddess. And that was a greater offense to some than the Rí Am's cruelty. Those few who kept the true faith—belief in the celestial lights and their Maker—called themselves Sky Keepers and refused to pay homage to the queen and her time king, often at great cost. Some Sky Keepers prayed for the faerie veil to fall, others

merely for a way to circumvent the Rí Am's control. But neither expected the storm of change approaching them.

There were decided disadvantages to being dependent on the Rí Am's automaton navigators, not the least of which was the automatons' indifference to storms.

"The storm's too big, Captain. We can't shift the airship out of it."

Captain Marianna Bowditch slid her gaze from her first mate to the automaton with its captain's coat of fine blue cloth and rows of crystals decorating its chest like soldier's medals. She was tempted to shake her fist at the lifeless navigator. Its impassive, doll-like face was an affront to the lives it endangered. "And the blasted automaton has its course and won't alter it." But her words were lost to the roaring wind. Or was that part of her beloved *Dawn Bringer* ripping away?

Beyond the bridge's myriad windows, the golden glint of brass pierced the churning clouds, a choking curtain spun by night and shadows and raging winds that only parted for slender fingers of blinding white. Was there no end to this storm?

Another golden flash followed the white. The protective shield about the balloon?

The ship lurched, and it wasn't a normal motion, even for a storm.

Marianna yanked up the brass mouthpiece to the intercom system. "Everyone to the Escapers. Now!" Slamming the mouthpiece back into place with one hand, she yanked up her Nor'easter and McIntosh with the other. "Sawyers, have Bates put the Floaters on as much of the cargo as he can—he knows which to look after first. Tell him to set the cargo hold doors to Automatic Open if the fire sensors go off or the altitude drops erratically. I'm going to check the damage to the balloon."

Flinging the rain gear on as she went, she jogged out of the bridge, not bothering to try to run straight as the ship rocked, just letting it toss her and then compensating. Her first mate jogged up behind her as the wind did the work of opening the outer door for her. She grabbed hold of the rope safety line and stepped out in the lashing rain.

"Escapers aren't built to withstand storms like this, Captain," Sawyers yelled as they ran across the wooden deck, slipping and sliding despite the rope guiding them.

"No, but they're less likely to explode." She didn't know what cargo the Rí Am's Time Keepers had forced her to carry along with the paid cargo she'd taken on, but she suspected it wouldn't sit well with fire. But then, few things did.

"But they've no navigator automa—" Sawyers cried out as loose rigging, writhing and striking like a serpent, knocked him away from the line.

She grabbed his hand and jerked him back to the rope. "We've no choice!" They were far enough out on the deck to see what she didn't want to. She risked taking a hand off the line long enough to jab a finger at the bald spot on the balloon's front. The brass shield was gone and the white canvas was rippling like a cloud about to split in two. "Let's get to the hold!"

They battled their way back to the bridge and down to the bottommost hold. Marianna saw all her crew fitted with parachutes and buckled into the Escapers, then released them into the storm one cylindrical, winged ship at a time, praying for their safety. Praying that, somehow, the desperately needed cargo they carried—the smuggled iron and legal food supplies—would get to their destination, Sheffield-on-the-Sea. She strapped herself into the last Escaper, took one final look around at her beloved airship, and hit the release. The floor underneath the Escaper slid away.

The chief advantage of a storm, she thought wryly as she plunged into the wet assault, was that she couldn't see the hated faerie crystals dishonoring the night sky. The second was that the wind could carry the Escapers for miles without guidance, for no conveyance could be guided by a human hand for more than three miles, thanks to the faerie curse. And they were considerably more than three miles from land.

CHAPTER TWO

Bertram Orren was bone weary, but then so was everyone else on the island of Sheffield-on-the-Sea. After spending the wee hours going out in a rough sea as far as they could to salvage what they could of the crew and cargo of the airship *Dawn Bringer*, even the Time Keeper patrols were heading to bed for the few hours remaining until the sky crystals brightened for day.

At least, that was what Bertram was counting on. The Time Keepers might not be mourning the loss of most of the ordered food supplies, but everyone on the island not on the Rí Am's pay was. Something had to be done about the root cause of the impending food shortage, and it was his night to do so. The Rí Am's fish quota was so high the island of fishermen had to rely on crops—and it was easier to do something about the faeries who destroyed those crops than about the Rí Am.

Hoisting his gunnysack over his shoulder, Bertram dragged himself over a low rock wall—a warning more than a barrier—and plodded up the forested hillside. About thirty feet in, he pulled a large ball of twine from his sack and tied one end of the twine to a rowan tree so the faeries couldn't move it. He arranged the ball in its special holster on his belt so it could unwind with ease as he walked, then continued on, walking fast. He had to make it to an area he hadn't already searched before his time and energy gave out.

Not that he would know his time was running short before it was too late. He depended on the Time Keepers to signal the start and end of each school day, and the loudest stomach among his students for the lunch hour. But for roaming forbidden, faerie-infested woods? When the sky crystals brightened. His jaw clenched. One day that would change. But as for knowing when his energy would give out...

He stumbled over a fallen limb he'd missed during a prolonged blink and rubbed his eyes as encouragement for them to stay open. A sudden spike in heart rate did the trick, however.

"Wait! Please!" A woman's voice.

Bertram froze.

Further up the hill, a light held by a dark little figure dodged between trees on a path to the ruins at the summit.

Bertram counted to ten, slowly. So the will-o'-the-wisps were trying the damsel-in-distress tactic now too, were they? Tired of pretending to be lost little children to lure you after them so they could lose you somewhere dangerous?

When the light disappeared, followed by another pleading cry, he continued on, skirting more to the right than he'd originally planned. Would a will-o'-the-wisp be seen far or near to the faerie mound?

About twenty feet later, his heart rate spiked again, this time thanks to the broken glass that nearly went through his boot sole. With a sense of foreboding, Bertram raised his lantern. Broken branches, shards of glass, a busted lantern, the twisted metal body and ripped fabric wings of an Escaper. No bodies.

Stifling a curse, Bertram dashed back through the woods, his twine thankfully reeling itself back in, until he reached the spot where he'd heard the cry, then plunged up the hill.

"Wait! Don't follow that light!" he shouted.

The trees thinned, replaced by jutting rocks as he hit the old path winding up to the ruins of an ancient tower. Was it bad of him to wish the woman wounded? Just enough so she wasn't too far ahead of him. Rain began pelting him, the wind rising for another storm.

He rounded a curve of the hill. About twenty feet ahead, a woman half jogged, half staggered after the faerie light. He winced as she stumbled next to a rocky precipice.

"Stop! I'll help you!" But his cries were drowned out by a crack of thunder.

The will-o'-the-wisp's light disappeared, as did the woman, but her scream lingered.

"Lady!" he cried.

Lightning flashed to his left. Bertram darted right. Into nothing.

"Darn, darn, *darn*." Bertram pushed into a seated position on the damp rock. This was *not* how he'd hoped to find a faerie mound. He didn't have to look up to know the opening he'd fallen through was no longer there. It'd been created by a will-o'-the-wisp in solid rock and was now solid rock again.

Blasted faeries. He wrinkled his nose. Even if he ever escaped, he'd probably never lose that sickeningly sweet, nectar-like odor the creatures favored. At least it was stale here. Not an active faerie mound then. Not what he needed to find, but it was a safer place to be.

"You really must work on your vocabulary, sir."

Bertram startled and glanced around. About ten feet away, leaning against a tree stump that looked suspiciously as if it wanted to be believed a pile of ancient ruins, was the woman he'd failed to save from this fate. She was very pale, except where blood darkened her brow. Her hair, tangled and loose, was at odds with her dress: the smart, tailored skirt and jacket over a corset and blouse of an airship officer. Not surprisingly, a revolver and knife decorated her belt. Pain might currently be adding a few years to her age, but she looked about thirty. Either way, the age looked well on her. She held his lantern, miraculously still lit, close to her chest, seemingly as possessive of its warmth as its light.

"You really must work on your hearing as well as your vocabulary, it seems." She flinched as she shifted. He noted the flash of light against the metal of a PullLine gauntlet strapped about one arm, the one not cradled to her chest. So that was how she'd gotten his lantern—using the PullLine.

Bertram's heart twisted at her pain, but he didn't think it best to express sympathy. He forced a surly tone. "Really, miss—"

"It's 'Captain,' and you should have said, 'Ca-tas-tro-phe!' It has more syllables in which to express your rage."

Bertram tamed a smile and pulled his gunnysack into his lap. Thank heavens he'd packed his medical kit. "The repetition stresses the idea just fine."

"Mayhap, but it's pretentious of a poacher to use such mild exclamations."

"I am *not* a poacher." Bertram pulled out his water

canteen and the medical kit and staggered up, wincing. Bruised but not broken, as the saying went.

"Oh really?" She gave his sack a significant look as he handed her the canteen.

"If you're angling for a brace of pheasants, you're going to be sorely disappointed." Helping her lean forward, he draped his jacket about her shoulders. "I don't share." He knelt beside her and doused a cloth with antiseptic.

"I suspected a selfish nature." She hissed as Bertram gently wiped the blood from her temple.

"Which hurt needs attention, do you think?" he asked.

She indicated her head and arm, and he gently worked her torn, bloodied jacket down her arms and off.

"There's nothing to do about the ribs but wait it out, I fancy," she said as he slid his jacket back over her shoulders.

Agreeing, he quickly cleaned the gashes on her head and arm, noting that her arm was going to need more work than her head: a tight bandage for a sprained wrist and stitching for a gash on her forearm.

He retrieved the needle and thread from the medical kit but paused before sterilizing them, studying the woman's dreadfully pale face and closed eyes. He'd have to approach this delicately. "Catastrophe, catastrophe, ca-*tas*-tro-phe!"

She cracked one eye open, noted the implements in his hand, then shut her eye again, her mouth forming a hard line. "I'm impressed, sir. You're a fast learner."

"There's no one like a hardened smuggler to teach one foul language."

The woman's eyes opened wide in alarm, her gaze raking over his outfit. Searching for the Time Keeper insignia, no doubt. He gave her a roguish grin, and she relaxed back against the ruins with a tired smile. The smile quickly flattened as he handed her a flask of brandy and a packet of pounded wild lettuce seeds for pain relief. He indicated he was about to begin stitching her arm.

"Marianna Bowditch, captain of the *Dawn Bringer*, I presume?"

"At your service." She sipped the brandy. "You're a receiver of smuggled goods then? Almost as nefarious as a poacher." She gritted her teeth but held still as he worked. He had to give her credit for toughness. Not that he should be surprised. The Bowditch captains weren't known for softness. They weren't real smugglers, in truth, but honest captains brave enough to ferry goods for the Sky Keepers, those fighting in big and small ways against the Rí Am and his Time Keepers. Many, but not all, of the Sky Keepers still believed in the Maker and his Word, believed in a sun, moon, and stars beyond the Star Veil that formed their sky.

"Bertram Orren," he answered, "local schoolmaster and unofficial doc ... and nephew to the first mate of your brother Davy's airship." And because of his relationship to one of the Bowditch crew, he helped arrange for the smuggling of needed goods the Time Keepers didn't want them to have, as well as the transport of legal goods.

"I thought I noticed a resemblance in bedside manner. Good old Philip. He's stitched up and played nanny to all of us, my brothers and me and most of our crews." She hissed again and was quiet for a time. "So we made it to Sheffield-on-the-Sea, after all. I'm sorry about your iron. It's probably at the bottom of the sea now, rusting away. ... And your winter food supplies. ... Did any of my crew make it?"

"From what one of the airmen said, all but two of the Escapers are accounted for, yours and another." He gave her hand a gentle squeeze when she bowed her head. "Most of the crew aren't any worse off than you, thank the Maker."

"Yes," she said sincerely but quietly.

"No sign of your airship," he continued. "It must have gone down farther out than we could safely reach. We were able to salvage some of the cargo that floated in. Some sank beyond the reefs. We'll have to choose the divers for those carefully; otherwise, we'll all be in trouble with the faerie-loving Time Keepers if they discover the iron."

"What was the iron for?" she asked, though her voice held more sadness than interest. "Philip mentioned something about it and food, but iron is a tad harsh for my sensitive palate. I don't know about you Sheffielders though."

"Oh, we can eat anything with the right sauce."

Marianna gave a weak laugh and leaned her head back again. She kept her eyes tight shut as he worked the stitches closely together to minimize the scarring. "Pray tell," she said, "which sauce is the proper one for iron? A sauce from red wine, perhaps?"

"Crystal skies, Captain Bowditch! What a suggestion. It could only be a creamy white sauce. No wine-based one would do. That would almost be as bad as a vinegar-based sauce." With a *tsk*, he paused to flex his fingers.

"A white sauce? My mother's chef would never approve —he never approves of any other chefs—but it sounds reasonable to me."

Bertram bent back over her arm. "Since you're reasonable enough to agree with me over a chef—what do they know anyway?—I'll let you in on a Sheffield-on-the-Sea secret: we've a private war going on against the local faeries. In a bold defensive move, the bravest and noblest of us have vowed to take turns hunting for the entrance to the active faerie mound. I know, I know," he added quickly at her look of censure, "night's not the best time to be in a faerie wood, but the Time Keepers are just as troublesome in the day. Anyway, we figured if we found the mound entrance, putting an iron fence reinforced with rowan saplings around it would deter the faeries from interfering with our crops for a while."

Finished with the stitching, he cleaned her other scratches, and a gash not worth mentioning on his leg, before putting the kit away and presenting her with hardtack. Like the child of an airship tycoon that she was, she took the biscuit without question.

He pushed to his feet and stretched a bit of the tension from his back. "Can you walk?"

She looked him up and down, her gaze taking in his shoulders. They weren't the shoulders of a blacksmith, he knew, but he wasn't scrawny by any means, man of letters though he was. "How heroic are you feeling?" she asked.

"I shined up my armor this morning."

As he half expected, she swatted his hand away as he knelt, arms out, to pick her up. "I can make it from the vertical, so if you'll just help me up."

He winked at her. "With pleasure."

He righted her, and they crept along, her clinging to his arm. "Didn't we come into this"—she glanced about at the underground faerie forest, which to some would appear as hewn stone columns and walls, some crumbled, some still upright—"place through the roof? Why is the twine attached to your belt leading deeper into this ruin-in-a-cave?"

"Because it's attached to a rowan tree a ways down the hill from where we came in—the will-o'-the-wisp couldn't snap it, only redirect it by magic. The twine will lead us out. I just don't know what's between us and out."

"How exciting."

"I have an *iron* blade if you feel a need to trim your nails or peel an apple along the way."

"I'll keep that in mind."

CHAPTER THREE

Marianna caught glimpses of the cavern roof and walls as she and Bertram shuffled along, their footfalls the only sound. Scenes of spring and summer feasts, dances, and hunts carved into stone guided them as surely as her escort's twine. Bertram Orren—Philip's nephew. Of all people to come to her rescue. Well, to get himself into a mess trying to rescue her. The thought of Philip brought her back to her crew and ship, and she prayed once again for their safety and healing. And that the iron wasn't discovered by the Time Keepers. Otherwise, her crew would be imprisoned or worse. *Why the storm, Almighty? How long will the innocent be punished and the guilty prosper? The Bowditch family and crews have always, though imperfectly, tried to serve you, despite the risk.* Marianna sighed against a deeper pain than just the physical ones making her steps drag.

"Captain?" Bertram slowed and glanced at her, a trace of concern in his eyes, which were a rather enchanting hue of green.

"Please, call me Marianna, or Miss Orren if you prefer. 'Captain Bowditch' makes me sound like my brothers." Or a confirmed spinster. Which she was not. She was also in pain, and denying the convention gave her a certain amount of pleasure.

His eyebrows rose. Shocking Bertram gave her a certain amount of pleasure as well.

"I command an airship of men and women. You a classroom of juveniles. We are equally brave, I believe."

He smiled at that. "In that case, and since you are the reason for this predicament of mine, I'll call you Marianna. We're not on your ship, so Uncle Philip can't accuse me of supporting insubordination by such an action."

She bit back a groan as they approached a column that had inconsiderately fallen over the path. She allowed herself a sigh, then stiffened her spine and started to climb over it. "Shipboard or not, you can be assured that I shall take great offense at the liberty, which will give me the strength to keep going."

"So that is the true reason for the request, *Marianna*." He gently picked her up and helped her over the column, making her feel like a little child. Rather than protest assistance she needed, however, she used the annoyance of it to help her take another step, then another. The pain medicine was starting to kick in, but it also made her sleepy.

They passed through various chambers and down ancient walkways until slowing at an ornate stone bridge. The bridge was only missing a few stones and looked sturdy enough, which was comforting, for as she stood at the edge of the chasm and looked down, she had a similar feeling as to that when she looked over the side of her airship in flight.

"I never thought of the faeries as stone masons," she said

as she adjusted her PullLine harness and gauntlet for climbing and sent a line to the far wall to serve as a safety rope for them, just in case.

"That's because they're not." Bertram studied the bridge, his expression pensive. She made to walk around him onto the bridge, but he blocked her path. "Please don't think me forward, but"—he scooped her up and stepped onto the bridge, oddly toward the right-hand edge of it.

"Really, Bertram, I can walk," she said after hissing at the sudden movement and the pain it produced.

"I'd prefer you didn't, at the moment." He must have meant it, for he didn't let her down, and as she was in no condition to insist, she didn't.

"Masculine ego," she muttered as she cradled her stitched arm. "I am *not* that badly injured."

He didn't reply, just stretched his neck to see beyond her to the solid stone of the bridge at his feet and took a very careful step onto it. He took another step, placing one foot in front of the other, as if he were walking a tightrope. He repeated the action until about midway across. Then, after a brief study of the bridge again, he took a wide step to the left, swaying a bit as he landed.

Marianna yelped. "If you don't mind, I'd rather walk."

"I'd still rather you didn't," he said, doing another of those tightrope-walk steps.

"I'd still rather I did." They were currently going *toward* the section of bridge that was missing a few stones.

Bertram paused, and for a moment, she thought he was going to put her down, but then he gave a defeated sigh and took a few more of those cautious paces. "It's an arbor, Marianna. It's not a bridge at all. The faeries use trees more often than hewn stone, and they use glamours to deceive those who don't know better. It's much safer for you if I carry you. I'll put you down on the other side."

"You mean—" Her voice rose as her gaze shot to the bridge. It looked like stone to her, even when she wasn't looking at it carefully, more sideways to try to see past the glamour.

"This is the meeting of two tree canopies. I have to follow the right boughs to reach the other side. Your walk is unsteady because of your injuries and the medicine. I was afraid you wouldn't be able to follow my steps, so I'm carrying you."

"But why do I see stone?" she asked, exasperated.

"You're not from the island," he said quickly.

"But that's not—oh." Marianna laughed quietly and relaxed. "Touch of faerie blood in you, is there?" His eyes were very green, after all, so it shouldn't be too surprising.

"I don't know what you're talking about. Now be quiet and let me concentrate."

She bit back a smile. Judging by that tone, he knew exactly what she was talking about and the very respectable schoolmaster did not like to be reminded of the skeleton in his family closet. Oh, she was definitely going to ask Philip about this the next time she saw him and Davy. She'd bet her last bullet the faerie line was from Philip's side of the family too.

When they reached the other side of the arbor-bridge, Bertram put her down as promised, and Marianna retracted the PullLine. Beyond the bridge and its chasm, the carved stone—remnants of a once fine forest of gold and silver trees, Bertram reluctantly informed her—dwindled out. Stalactites and stalagmites took their place, and a gentle *drip drip* added a new rhythm underneath the echo of their steps. A soft glow emanated from the walls, and they dimmed the lantern for a time, relying on the phosphorescence and the twine. Mushrooms dotted the rocks and crevices. Marianna pointed them out. The strange light must be playing with her eyes—or maybe it was the pain—for the fungi seemed to be gaining in size the further they went.

"The faeries were always partial to the things, I've heard," Bertram responded. His gaze as he looked at the three-foot-high mushrooms was almost hungry, Marianna fancied.

"And you?" she asked before she could help herself.

"Only with steak and gravy." Bertram nodded to a low boulder near the twine's path. "Permission to rest, Captain?"

"Granted." With relief.

"Our smooth road is gone. Looks like we'll have to do some clambering about from here on out." He seated her on a boulder next to a parasol-shaped mushroom and dug his water canteen and hardtack from his gunnysack. He offered her the hardtack. Marianna slipped as she leaned forward, her fingers brushing his. His eyes widened, and the tack fell from his fingers.

Marianna bit her lip to stifle a smile. For an average-looking man of about thirty-five, he really was quite charming, not to mention strong and gentlemanly, but pretending to be so affected by a touch of her hand was laying it on a bit thick.

"Um, Marianna?" Bertram's gaze fixed on hers.

"Yes, Bertram?"

"I think I'm going to need a word longer than four syllables."

Marianna stiffened, her gaze darting about the cavern. "Why?"

"Someone just yanked the twine, and I'm pretty sure it wasn't a faerie." He staggered to the left before regaining his balance. "Could be a very large dog playing tug-of-war, but not a faerie."

"Take off the holster. Quick." Marianna stood, motioning to the ball of twine as Bertram worked to remove it from his belt. "Jam it between those two boulders." She checked her revolver: five bullets. She'd not used it since the last pirate attack on her airship, and she'd rather not get in a shootout today. "Who or what do you think would be in a place like this?"

"Pirates, if they bribed Time Keepers for navigators to get here. It'd make a marvelous hideout. Other lost souls. Time Keepers snooping around the woods for your Escaper might have found the twine and traced it inside." He lodged the twine between two rocks. "Unfortunately, the latter is the most likely."

"In that case, they could help us." Her stomach twisted at the thought, but it was possible for Time Keepers to help, she supposed.

Bertram secured the gunnysack on his back, took her arm, and started them walking at a brisk pace, staying about a foot or so from the twine.

"Caves are forbidden here," Bertram said, "as is twine or similar things when used to help you find your way without an automaton, and thus the knowledge and permission of the Time Keepers. I'd rather not meet with one. If it's unavoidable, we'll say you had a nasty bump on the head, were delusional, and insisted on following this *already* placed twine in. I found you some place I'm allowed to be but followed you to the forbidden area to look after you. We can try to convince them someone's been farming mushrooms here illegally and placed the string as their lead. Not a bad idea actually. We're going to be hungry this winter."

The chamber narrowed to a passageway, and they stopped to listen, noticed nothing alarming, and then hurried down it. Marianna set her jaw as her ribs escalated their reminders that they'd been rudely bumped earlier in her landing.

Halfway along its length, Marianna tightened her grip on Bertram's arm and gestured to the twine. It bowed to the right. Ahead, a shaft of light hit the tunnel wall, coming from a side passage.

"Back," Marianna and Bertram whispered together.

Floodlights swayed over the stone at her feet.

"You there! Stop! What are you doing here?"

Bertram picked up speed, Marianna struggling to keep up. They ducked around the corner of the chamber's opening and clambered over boulders and around stalagmites as footsteps echoed up the tunnel.

They dropped behind a wide stalagmite next to the back of the chamber as four Time Keepers followed the twine inside. Their floodlights settled on the reel of twine, then quickly scanned the room before going back to it. But Marianna had no doubt they'd do a thorough search before they left.

"Think one of the mine workers did this on account of the mushrooms?" A Time Keeper poked a dinner plate–sized mushroom cap with his rifle muzzle. His insignia reflected the light, but his uniform was unlike the ones she'd seen around port cities before. It looked more like a prison guard's than an automaton station clerk's or patrol officer's.

And since when did Sheffield-on-the-Sea have a mine?

As if questioning the same thing, Bertram leaned forward, studying him.

"No one would be idiot enough to run a line through the control room." He bent over the twine, rubbed his fingers along it, then sniffed his fingers. "It doesn't smell of gunpowder or other explosive."

"It's attached to a rowan tree on one end and two rocks on this end. Did you expect a bomb?" The taller whipped his light around the chamber, stalking about and illuminating crevices. "Some peasant out on an illegal jaunt with this as his crude form of navigation got waylaid by a will-o'-the-wisp and ended up here. It's happened before."

Marianna lowered her crouch and scooted back as the light swept nearer. One heel touched rock, the other nothing. She twisted around to find that blackness had covered one foot, the blackness of an arched passageway about two feet high and wide enough for Bertram's shoulders.

Marianna tugged on Bertram's sleeve and pointed to the small tunnel. He nodded, motioned for her to put his jacket over her arms and chest to protect them, and signaled for her to go in first.

"And they *never* got out to tell about it," said one with an air of authority. "If they're healthy enough for the mines, take them to the Personnel Supervisor. If not, dispose of them here. But they don't leave. Understood?"

Marianna did, and she crawled faster, ignoring any protests from her body. *Please let the tunnel go where we need to go, and let Bertram get in before they see him.*

Apparently, Bertram wanted to help with that prayer, for Marianna felt three taps on her boot and was then shoved forward a foot over the oddly smooth rock. Then another set of taps and another shove. She slid easily, the surface underneath her feeling of dusty, but polished, stone.

Voices from the chamber flooded into the rounded arc of air above her head, growing more chaotic with each wriggle ahead, which was not comforting with regard to the position of Bertram's feet. Could they see him?

Pausing, she tightened the PullLine harness about her chest and depressed a button on the gauntlet. "Bertram, grab my heels and hold on."

He complied with admirable speed, and she braced the PullLine with her other arm and aimed it down the dark road, for that's what instinct told her it was, a fair folk way from long ago. She released a line, and it extended fully before attaching to something in the dark far ahead. She pressed the Retract button on the gauntlet and held on.

Moist air rushed past, and she struggled to focus on that instead of the agony in her ribs or the strain on her arms or the dig of the harness as they were hauled over the time-worn road. Some sense or a movement of air hinted at cross-passages but no large chambers.

They came to a stop in the same cramped road, the PullLine having attached to the road itself as it went up an incline.

"Did you know there were mines here, Marianna?"

"No, and I don't care for the tone in which you asked that question." Marianna twisted to glare at her companion, not that she could see him, but she heard him rummaging through his pack.

"But you were carrying mining equipment on the *Dawn Bringer*. There are no mines here, so I thought. But, apparently, there's something here worth killing for to keep quiet." The accusation in his tone wore out into anger and concern, but she half wished it'd stayed. She could do with the distraction.

"If you searched the wreckage of my ship, you know more of her contents than I. The Time Keepers regularly commandeer space in my cargo hold but don't make me privy to what I'm carrying."

A greenish glow illuminated Bertram's face, as well as a cylindrical lamp attached to a small box. A Ruhmkorff lamp like miners use?

"Did you steal that from the wreckage and that's why we're running from the Time Keepers?" she snapped between gasps. Wincing, she eased onto her back and closed her eyes. *Okay.* So they were running because the Time Keepers were possessive of their secrets, but Bertram seemed to have extra reasons to add to that.

"How are you feeling?" he asked after a suspiciously long pause.

"Miserable."

"I'm sorry."

"Back to your lamp," she said testily.

He sighed. "The bladders attached to the Rí Am's cargo crates you were carrying worked well—kept them afloat long enough to be dashed on the rocks near the shore. One held these lamps. They're used by miners, I think, so I figured they were for another stop, but something about them didn't feel right. And I'd thought I'd seen Sheffield-on-the-Sea painted on a bit of board floating near them. When the wind kept blowing out our lanterns, the Time Keepers let us use these to help with the cleanup. I didn't turn mine in, figuring I could find out something more about them if I returned it to the Time Keeper Station myself later." He blew out a heavy breath. "I don't like stealing and breaking laws, Marianna, but I've got to help my people in any way I can, and now that means finding out what's going on here."

She was silent for a moment, considering the pleading in his voice. Instinct told her he'd probably never stolen so much as a cookie before getting mixed up with the Sky Keepers. "You sound like my brothers."

She fought a smile. Not quite like her brothers. She'd wager anything he was the nephew Philip had mentioned to her more than once as a respectable, *single* young man. Philip always was a good judge of character.

"And perhaps a certain Sky Keeper smuggler we both know?" he asked.

"And maybe a certain Sky Keeper smuggler we both know."

"One-third of the island is supposedly uninhabited," he continued after a pause, sounding more thoughtful than agitated now, "from the hill we were on over to the rocky coasts. I once saw a map of the island—"

"You do deal in forbidden items, don't you? A map. I envy you. I've always felt like such a fraud as a captain. Seems like we ought to navigate, not simply arrange business deals and keep the crew in line." Thanks to that blasted curse, they couldn't draw a map of anything larger than a small village without ending up with nothing but a senseless swirl of lines.

"It wasn't without cost to the one who shared it, so be careful what you're envious of. The map indicated the island on that side was hilly terrain, rocky, but with a natural bay that could be approached unseen from the other ports on the island. No one's allowed in that section, on account of the faeries, it's said."

"You really should warn people about those creatures. So they don't follow seemingly friendly lights to their doom."

Bertram chuckled. "They don't frequent the docks, and few people willingly come to Sheffield-on-the-Sea to stay, so there didn't seem to be much point. Anyway, there's plenty of land for the Time Keepers to have a secret operation here, though why it would need to be secret I can't guess."

After a moment, she felt Bertram scooting closer, crowding her feet.

"Here." The tip of something dry brushed her fingers. "Have breakfast. Hardtack and a bit more brandy and pounded wild lettuce seed."

"You're joining me in this repast, aren't you?" she asked, leaning up as much as she could to eat.

"I'll wait until after we've finished with this PullLine business. On Uncle Philip's advice, I always carry enough supplies to last a few days when I go on these jaunts, in case I get lost or ... um ... can't return home for some other reason."

The heaviness in his voice indicated such a time had likely come. Even if the Time Keepers didn't find them in the cave, they'd know who was missing from the villages. Especially with a bevy of school children running amuck without their teacher.

CHAPTER FOUR

Bertram permitted a short break, then strapped on the PullLine harness and arranged Marianna's feet on his shoulders, allowing her to ride while he took the brunt of the dragging force. After two more extensions and retractions, the stone above them rose away into a domed chamber.

With a prayer of gratitude, which Marianna echoed, Bertram helped her to her feet. She returned his jacket, did her best to straighten and dust her filthy clothes, then looked around. The ceiling rose to a height even Bertram's purloined lamp couldn't penetrate. In the center of the circular chamber was a throne, once fine, but the fabric of the padded seat had mostly rotted away, leaving a mesh of purple threads. The carved ruins of its stone arms and back were chipped where gems had been reclaimed.

"What do your very special eyes say I'm looking at?" she asked Bertram.

"My very special eyes have nothing special to tell, which I find curious."

Armed with Bertram's lantern, Marianna chuckled as she ran her hand along the angular characters bordering the seat back. "With all this adventure, there ought to be treasure —ancient, fair folk–collected treasure. I must write a letter of complaint to all adventure authors and express my disillusionment." She began easing her way onto the throne. Rotten cushion or not, it was a real seat.

Bertram caught her arm and gently tugged her down the dais. "Sorry, but it's never a good idea to sit on an ancient throne: lingering curses, ancient prophecies, tests of courage, and all that."

Marianna groaned and looked about for a less auspicious seat. "I detest magic." She spotted a stone bench and shuffled over to it.

"Only when it's not working in your favor."

"Which it never is. Don't forget who cast the Star Veil."

"I haven't, don't worry." Bertram wandered around the cavern, tapping his toes against the bottom of a dry fountain; poking at a chest resting on its side, lid open and empty; peeking in a ten-foot-high wooden wardrobe; and finally settling on a large, locked chest with wide metal bands strapped over once fine wood.

"Now," he said, between bites of hardtack, "tell me about your family, your favorite of the places you've visited, and whoever is waiting for you back home."

"My brother Davy and I bunk with my parents at the family estate in Calandra when we're not traveling. My oldest brother, Kingsley, died a few years ago trying to find his own way to navigate. Went to find some rumored tribe in the tropics that still knows the secret of navigation, and never came back. The Time Keepers reported his ship, the *Dusk Crier*, down, all hands lost."

"I'm sorry."

She shrugged, not wanting to deal just then with the ache thinking of Kingsley and his lost crew caused, or of the possibility her family might suffer that same pain on her account now. "He would've called himself a casualty of war and been proud of it. As for a favorite place, I like anywhere that's green, Calandra and Sheffield-on-the-Sea, for instance. All your sheep are adorable."

"You've never had to deal with them."

She laughed. "No, we hardly allow livestock to roam free on airships. Now it's your turn. Tell me about your family. And what you'd be eating for breakfast if you were at home now."

A surprised cry muffled by a mouthful of biscuit was swallowed up by the splintering of wood and the stretching of metal bands as Bertram's trunk collapsed, and he fell into it.

More muffled exclamations followed as he wriggled to extricate himself one-handed. His other hand was occupied in keeping the hardtack free of dust.

Biting back a laugh—only because it would hurt her ribs to release it—Marianna strolled over. The chest had cracked open in the back, spewing its contents as a pillow for Bertram's upper half. His knees on down poked out the front end.

"Comfortable?" she asked.

He finally swallowed. "Ha ha." He waved the hardtack at her. "Take this and put it away. I'm going to need your help."

After much pushing and pulling, scrambling over piled faerie treasure, and shifting of broken wood, they finally decided to dig him out. That is, to remove the pile beneath him and let him ease down backward.

Marianna knelt behind him and, nose scrunched, began shoving the trunk's dusty, nectar-scented, non-gold-and-jewels contents to the side.

Books. She never knew the faeries valued them, and with them smelling so, she could hardly blame the faeries for leaving them. But she couldn't resist noting the titles.

Navigation over Land and Mountain; Basics of Nautical Navigation; Sun, Moon, and Stars and What They Tell Us; Elusive Longitude; The Building and Accurate Functioning of Clocks; Atlas of the Known World; Star Chronometer and Navigation.

Marianna's hands shook. The Time King, who was in charge of education as well as everything else, taught that man couldn't understand such things as navigation and time, that the automatons were the gracious gifts of the faerie queen to a race bound to his own village and the brightening and dimming of the sky crystals in the Star Veil. She'd never really believed that, for the Word—also forbidden—said otherwise and talked of sun, moon, and stars and men traveling on their own, but to see proof...

"Would you mind playing librarian later? This is a very uncomfortable position." Bertram glanced over his shoulder at her. "Are you okay?"

"Bertram, the faeries took their treasures but left ours! Look! What the Word says is true!" She shoved *Star Chronometer and Navigation* in his face and began digging again.

"Marianna!" Holding the book, Bertram scrambled backwards and soon extricated himself and began flipping through the book. "Do you know what this means?"

"Yes, the Time Keepers now have a *really* good reason to want us dead." But it'd be worth it to get this knowledge out, just to have seen proof. Their ancestors' publications on navigation and their equipment must have been collected by force or by magic after the Star Veil was cast, but these few were saved. The hoard of a rival faerie court?

"Yes, no, but—" He stuffed the book into his gunnysack and joined her in digging through the chest.

"The heavens declare the glory of God." He read the epigraph of a book on charting stars. He shut the book softly, a solemnness falling over him that seemed to drape itself over Marianna as well.

"What is it?" she asked, stopping her examination of a strange metal disk with movable arrows over a circular board labeled with numbers and only four letters: N, E, S, W. Was it some sort of code?

Bertram took off his hat and rubbed a hand through his hair. "Even if we make it out with some of these, I fear the Star Veil will block our minds from being able to use them." He gripped the book as if trying to keep it from being dragged away. "All this precious knowledge may be useless."

Marianna covered his hand with hers. "We don't know that."

"Why haven't we figured it all out again, if we could?"

"The curse? No moon or stars to go by? I don't think we came here by chance, Bertram. We were meant to find this and get it out, I'm sure of it. What happens after that may not be up to us."

He huffed, but then squeezed her hand. "You may be right. Perhaps the information could be adjusted to fit the sky crystals."

Marianna shrugged, and they went back to sorting,

making a small pile of loot to take with them. Marianna held up a tiny spyglass, flourishing it in the lamplight. "At least I know what this is. But why is it attached to this wedge-shaped piece of metal with these other lenses and a curved ruler?"

"Beats me, but add it to the pile."

"These books are oddly well-preserved. And maps!"

"Faerie treasures don't disintegrate, even if the faeries have moved their court."

"I take back what I said about magic."

"I thought you mi—what's that?"

Marianna held her breath. Voices? Surely no one had crawled through that tiny tunnel after them? She did a double take on the dim outline of one of the throne room's many exits. Unlike the one they'd come through, this one was at least nine feet high, and it held the glow of a distant light.

"Mother of catastrophes," Bertram spat and jammed a few more books, maps, the metal disk, and the odd spyglass into his bag, while Marianna picked up the only solid piece of wood she could find, tucked it under her arm, and once again checked her revolver. The Time Keepers would know to check the little roads again; they'd have to change tactics.

Tinkering with her PullLine, Bertram dispensed a hook and an adhesion pad from the little storage compartments and quickly attached the hook to the inside of the archway at about neck height. Taking the wooden plank from her, he guided them behind the column flanking the right side of the tall archway, the column granting them concealment from a quick survey of the chamber. They turned off their lights and waited.

And waited.

Marianna's fingers twitched. She missed the flurry of excitement and rush of preparation before a pirate attack. How could Bertram be so still?

What was that whirring?

A light flashed around the chamber as the guards entered. Marianna flattened against the wall.

"Lookie there, boys." Footsteps moved toward the opposite side of the room and the broken chest.

Marianna darted a glance around the column and Bertram. Three guards strode to the broken chest and its treasures. A self-propelled automaton sat in its wheeled box just inside the entrance. Bertram tapped Marianna's hand, confirming her own thoughts—they needed that automaton.

He inched around the edging to the archway, quietly secured the end of one of the PullLine's cords on the opposite frame of the archway, and then passed the line through the hook on their side. That done, he lost himself in the dark passageway beyond. Marianna followed, ducking under the line.

"Take your stand in the first side tunnel," he whispered, maneuvering her in front of him. Marianna nodded and trailed her finger along the wall to guide her. He fell behind, and as soon as she slipped into a side tunnel, he said in a whisper far too loud, "Run!"

But it had the desired effect.

"There they are! Stop!" The guards' lights swept up the passageway. Marianna drew her revolver and backed further into her hiding spot as Bertram zigzagged his way up the tunnel.

Another yell from the guards was followed by two strangled cries, two thuds of fallen men, and one loud curse. The report of a gunshot echoing through the tunnel nearly caused her to drop her own weapon to cover her ears. *Don't let him hurt Bertram.*

"Stop!"

The wobbling beam of light streaming past her tunnel grew larger, the incoming footsteps louder. A lantern, a revolver, a guard passed her.

Marianna leaned out and connected the butt of her gun to the guard's head. He hit the floor with a delightful thump.

"Good work." Bertram dashed past her going back to the chamber. She followed slowly, arriving in time to see that the other two guards would be unconscious for a while.

Not wanting the guards to find and destroy the books they couldn't carry out with them, they hid the remaining treasure in a narrow passageway concealed, but not to Bertram, by a faerie glamour. That done, Bertram stripped the coat and hat off the guard closest to him in size and stuffed his own items in the bulging gunnysack. "Do I pass?" he asked as he buttoned the jacket.

"Not with those pants and shoes."

"I was afraid you'd say that." He twirled his finger, and she turned away to study the automaton. It had the same eerie child-like porcelain face as her ship's navigator, but instead of a full body, this one's torso disappeared into a rounded wood-and-metal box set on wheels. Its jacket was a foreboding black to match the guards' uniforms and was studded with the crystals the Rí Am marked all his belongings with.

The clear, identical crystals set against the black reminded her of the crystals of the Star Veil, but where they formed a tedious checkerboard of light against dark, these outlined a twisted tree, the Rí Am's emblem. She didn't know which pattern she loathed the most.

Shaking herself, she returned her focus to the task at hand. How did the guards activate the automaton to get it to take them to the next stop on their route? And eventually to the exit?

Her gaze passed over the automaton and its mechanized chair again, then fell to the still-clothed guard slumped beside it. A crystal-studded band peeked from beneath his cuff.

Could it...?

Marianna unbuckled the three-inch-wide leather band from his wrist. Inside the outlined tree's canopy, the crystals formed a ring with one crystal at the center. A pattern of movable gears overlaying small brass arms connected to the crystals bordered both sides of the ring.

She guessed the gears could be slid or used to turn other gears in a complicated pattern to unlock the center crystal and move another to its place. To direct the automaton?

"They mean for only the select few to operate those things." Bertram leaned over her shoulder.

"While I'm becoming one of The Select, why don't you shove each of our guests up a different little road? It'll give them something to think about other than us when they wake up."

Bertram grinned. "No wonder the pirates fear the Bowditch name."

Marianna shot him a look, but he saluted her, then jogged off with an "Aye, Captain," to retrieve the guard left in the passageway.

"I do have the traditional rope as well," he called over his shoulder.

Bertram had just stowed all the bound guards, one of whom was already moaning, when Marianna, sweat beginning to bead on her brow, twisted a gear that nudged another that pumped an arm that shifted a crystal.

The automaton whirred into motion down the passageway.

CHAPTER FIVE

Bertram had the distinct feeling he was going to be late for school. It happened often in his nightmares, but never, either in real life or his dreams, because he was following a beautiful smuggler through a forbidden cave carrying ancient, priceless books destined to help overthrow a cruel regime.

Well, at least he was sure he could get an excuse from the teacher. He wasn't so certain he'd get one from the students though.

He barely stopped a chuckle from escaping. He really needed sleep, or more excitement than the indeterminable-thanks-to-the-faerie-curse length of time they'd been plodding after the automaton on the guards' route had provided.

"Whatever you're wishing for, stop it." Marianna shook him gently by the shoulder.

"What?" He rubbed his eyes.

"You were mumbling to yourself, and now we're approaching a lighted hallway."

"What's bad about that? It could be the way out."

"It could also be occupied by guards."

"There you go, spoiling my dreams." He gave Marianna a sideways glance. He'd collected a guard's jacket and hat for her, and she wore them now. The disguise probably wouldn't fool anyone, but it made him feel better to have tried. "Slow your pace. Let's let the machine go ahead. Remember, *we* are the guards occupying the hallway."

The automaton's constant whir picked up a notch as it crossed the raised boundary between their dark cave path and the polished floor of a mining operation station.

Bertram paused at the threshold. *Walk like you belong here*, he told himself, and stepped across it.

It didn't prove too difficult a task, that walk, as the only guard they passed was more interested in hiding the flask he'd been drinking from than in noticing the woman doing her best to hide between Bertram and the wall without appearing to do so.

"You enjoyed that," Marianna whispered as soon as it was safe.

"What?" Bertram asked innocently.

"Glaring at the man as if you were considering turning him in."

Bertram grinned. "Oh, that. That wasn't fun: it was purely a distraction technique."

"Uh huh." Marianna's mouth curved into a charming half smile, one Bertram found more than a little distracting.

"Let's argue the point over dinner some time, shall we? And return your face to its appropriate stoicism, or else we'll never pass ourselves off as guards," he said.

Then, he—Bertram Orren, the calm, confident, level-headed schoolmaster—nearly walked into the tunnel wall. Had he just asked *Captain* Marianna *Bowditch* to dinner?

A woman above his station? Whom he'd known mere hours?

It had to be the sleep deprivation.

Or was it figuring out in a few hours what Uncle Philip had been telling him for years—how wonderful and beautiful and brave Captain Marianna Bowditch was?

No, he'd not take it back. But did Marianna wish it unsaid? He dared a glance at her.

Marianna's eyes were wide. But then that half smile converted into a grin she appeared to have difficulty stifling. It wasn't until they spotted a windowed room ahead that the grin fully disappeared.

Their hallway slanted into a large central space. The automaton motored onward without a care for whether or not they were following it. They stopped just shy of the tunnel's end, and Bertram peered after the automaton. Marianna tugged on his sleeve.

"We've reached the main chamber. It's about the size of the students' playing field, maybe larger, and semi-circular," he whispered back to her.

Three lifts, spaced about ten feet apart, punctured the floor to his left. Metal pulleys rose above the empty docks to the ceiling. The lift platforms themselves were concealed in the belly of the cave. Waiting for the miners to return?

Across were three large doors, two of them sturdy metal doors fitted with small windows. Like prison doors. His stomach twisted. Opposite the lifts, to his right, jutting from what he assumed was the outer wall and taking up a third of the chamber's depth, was the windowed room. Through the glass, beyond the room, he could just see bins attached to the cave wall, likely emptying into a room behind. On their side of the control room was a heavy set of barred double doors, the supply entrance, he assumed. The exit?

The automaton whirred confidently to a side door in the control room, bumped against it, paused, retreated, bumped against it again, and repeated the process once more. With a pathetic whir Bertram took to be confusion as to why no human was opening the door for it, it stationed itself outside like a loyal pup.

Bertram almost felt sorry for it, locked out of its home. For the control room—glass from about three feet up to the twenty-foot-high cave roof—must be the Time Keeper Station and guard station for the mine. Behind the glass were instrument panels, additional rooms, and a dozen Time Keepers, some dressed as guards but others fitting in with the paper-strewn desks and filing cabinets. All wore weapons. One looked up from his desk, pointed to the orphaned automaton, and got up to let it in.

Bertram's pulse spiked. They'd know the automaton didn't go out alone, and they'd know where to search for its lost guards. He looked frantically around the room. Where could they go other than back?

Sure enough, the Time Keepers' questions floated out the open doorway as the automaton glided in. Then the automaton halted, spun around, and glided back out the door. Afraid of the large guns the guards were strapping on? He could understand that.

Unfortunately, the automaton headed toward them like the faithful pup he'd called it earlier.

He grabbed Marianna's wrist and was about to beat a retreat when Marianna slapped his hand. The automaton changed direction, to the confusion of the Time Keepers following it.

"Did I ever tell you you're my favorite smuggler?" Bertram whispered in her ear.

"You can tell me at that dinner you promised," she whispered back, the crystal-studded cuff in her hand.

"It's a deal, Captain."

"It must've malfunctioned," a clerk exclaimed. "Keep it here while I get the key."

Bertram's question as to how they were going to keep the stubborn thing there was answered when a burly guard lifted it onto his shoulder, its wheels still whirring away.

Several of the other clerks and guards came out to watch the thwarted navigator. "We still need to find out what happened to its guards," one said. "Those Sheffield yokels are still loose. Program another with this one's route," he yelled to a clerk inside.

Ignoring the slur with effort, Bertram contemplated the chances of blocking the control room door long enough for them to get out the double doors once everyone went back inside. It wasn't promising. He also suspected opening the doors required help from inside.

"I tell you it's not the locals but the lost airship crew," said the clerk, returning with a short key seemingly made of the same crystal as that studding the automaton's jacket. Reaching up to the automaton, he opened a panel in its base. "They found a crashed Escaper near where the will-o'-the-wisps like to play. The locals are too afraid of the faeries to go into the woods there."

Behind him, Marianna sucked in her breath, and he reached back to take her hand.

"Are you forgetting the twine? Only a local would've placed it there," a clerk said.

"Forget it? I'm not the one who ran into it."

The clerk that comment was directed at grew red in the face and started blustering. The guard lowering the no-longer-whirring automaton shushed them both. "It doesn't matter so long as we catch them. Personally, I'm in favor of the airship captain. They say she's a comely woman, and wandering around down here is reason enough to keep her."

Marianna's hand went limp in his, and he tightened his hold, drawing her closer.

A shrill bell made them both duck deeper into the tunnel. When the guards grumbled but didn't charge in their direction, and the creaking of the three lifts announced a shift change, Bertram reclaimed his position near the tunnel's edge.

The clerks had abandoned the automaton to return inside the control room, opening an inner chamber lined with the navigators. They opened a shoot and slid them outside the control room, to the far side of the cavern, where a guard lined them up against the control room wall and a clerk activated them. The left of the two barred doors opposite them opened, revealing guards in front of a line of workers. A low level of chatter filtered out.

A lift full of miners covered in black dust, and an equally dirty automaton, clanked to a halt, and a guard opened its gate. The automaton propelled itself out, whirred over to the control room wall where their forgotten automaton sat, and parked itself there. The miners shuffled out of the lift toward the back wall, each carrying a sack half the size of Bertram's, but from their walk, it must be just as heavy. They deposited the sacks in the bins on the back wall and filed into the second of the two barred passageways, a guard there opening the door for them. The other two lifts arrived, and more miners slipped quietly into the flow. Additional automatons lined up next to the first. The next set of workers were herded onto the lifts along with the recently activated automatons, and the lifts descended.

One returning miner, hunched and walking slower than most, stumbled. The young man next to him grabbed his arm and steadied him, then looked around as if to make sure no one had noticed the older one's weakness.

Bile rose in the back of Bertram's throat. These weren't workers: they were slaves, prisoners of the Time King.

He examined them again. They appeared to be from all over, and instinct warned him they weren't here for crimes against humanity but against the Time King. They were likely Sky Keepers like himself, or men who simply wandered where they didn't mean to, also like him and Marianna.

The young man who'd helped his companion earlier still stood straight and tall, his dirty brown hair tied at the nape of his neck, as if he were trying to maintain some dignity. Many of the others stood hunched with the dazed looks of men who'd given up. There was something familiar about the proud one. Bertram glanced back at Marianna, and she cocked her head. No. His imagination.

Bertram ushered Marianna back a half-dozen feet down the tunnel. "Do we have any brandy left?"

"Yes. Do you have matches?"

"Yes. And extra fabric strips."

"Wonderful. What are we setting fire to?"

Bertram winked at her, then straightened his appropriated jacket. "Nothing yet. Right now, I'm going to invite an old friend for drinks." He looked over his shoulder at her. "Bullets to get gunpowder from?"

She nodded. Taking a deep breath, Bertram marched out

of the tunnel, strode to the line of returned automatons, pulled out their non-functioning one, and, walking close beside it, pushed it down the tunnel to Marianna, who had the brandy, matches, fabric strips, and bullets ready. They worked out a plan, making one solid one out of their two.

The guards, clerks, and slaves were an orderly bunch, and soon the shift change had been completed. The control room crew went about inspecting the returned automatons.

"What about the malfunctioning automaton? Did we send anyone after the missing guards?" one asked.

"I saw Ned and a navigator going toward the old caves."

"I thought he went off duty some time ago."

"Well, maybe Taylor then. Anyway, there are several patrols out they might've joined. Let's get these automatons seen to, then we'll worry about it."

As soon as the control room door shut behind the last of the Time Keepers, Bertram uncorked the brandy, but he hesitated. "I feel rather bad about this. What if those poor men get trapped in the mines?"

"They won't, Bertram. The Time Keepers will have everything they need to repair the two lifts we'll damage. And as soon as we get out, we'll make sure Sky Keepers all over the world know about this place. We'll figure out some way to free these men, just like we'll figure out a Star Clock and navigation."

"Yes," Bertram said, his tone odd as the "we" in her statement, however she meant it, hit him as personal, like a two-letter navigator that might take his life in an unfamiliar direction, one he wasn't sure he wanted to go. But did his "want" or lack of matter? He'd been given the books as much as she. Had the Maker given him the responsibility of them as well?

But first, as she said, they had to get out of the cave.

Bertram shook himself and sprinkled strips of cotton with gunpowder, draped the fabric over the automaton, sprinkled brandy around, and gave Marianna the brandy bottle. She wadded up her borrowed Time Keeper jacket, and after checking to see that the guards and clerks were engaged with their work, crept to the nearest lift, deposited the jacket there, doused the fabric with brandy, and set it alight. Bertram set a match to the automaton and pushed it into the second lift. When Marianna was back in the tunnel and he nearly so, he lit the brandy bottle itself and hurled it at the nearest lift. He ducked into the tunnel. Flames lit up the lifts.

Yelling for more help, guards and clerks rushed out of the control room with fire blankets. Bertram grabbed Marianna's hand and his gunnysack and sprinted into the control room. Marianna ran a quick eye over the instrument panel and flicked a switch for what he assumed was an emergency lock on the control room door and the outer doors.

"The guard said the twine went *through* the control room. So there has to be an exit this way," Bertram said, leading them through the inner doors. But first he needed to find out what was in those bags. He made a sharp left and opened a door marked *Processing*. Three clerks bent over trays of crystals undeniably like the crystals in the automatons' chests and Marianna's wristband.

"Excuse me." He shut the door, grabbed Marianna's hand again, and darted down the right-most corridor, trying doors as they went. They came to the end, to a locked door. Marianna shot the lock, and Bertram finished it off with a good kick. The door opened onto a dark, sandy path. A sea breeze washed over them.

CHAPTER SIX

The joy of freedom lasted about three seconds, long enough for Marianna to feel the pain from all over again and to remember that their exit had been rather noticeable. There was also the small issue of them not knowing how to get to Bertram's home from wherever they were even if Marianna could physically make the trip, which she doubted, and even if they did know and she could hold out, the curse would scramble their sense of direction after three miles, sending them who knew where. And *that* was if the Time Keepers didn't catch up with them first. She really, passionately disliked the Rí Am and the faerie queen.

Marianna stumbled, and Bertram slowed his pace and supported her with an arm about her waist.

The roof of the cave—or a tunnel in a cliff at this point—rose rounded and weathered smooth above them and extended out to a flat face of rock with an opening on either side, creating a noisy, roughly T-shaped tunnel.

They slowed as they reached the rock face, and both glanced over their shoulder. The lock on the control room door and outer doors was still holding, but it wouldn't keep the guards inside long enough for them to disappear out of sight along the beach. To their left, the cave opened out to a flat strip of rock next to a pebbled beach. Judging by the markings it was an airship landing pad. The vehicles used for loading and unloading were likely stored in the small cave just visible beside it, for they hadn't been in the main chamber. To the right, she could see the end of a pier.

Marianna stepped to the left. "We should try for a vehicle. Surely they go to town occasionally and have automatons set to go there."

Bertram stopped her with a gentle pressure to her side and guided her to the right instead. "These don't go to town. It's a small island—we'd know."

Choosing to be grateful for his knowledge rather than argumentative, she let him direct her out to a gravel road leading to the pier. Blinking against the light—the brightening was past but she had no way of knowing how far into the day it was—she spotted two small boats bobbing in the waves next to the pier. Fishing vessels for the amusement of the guards? Each had an automaton in it, so they must go further out than the rim of the sheltered cove they were in.

"No," Bertram said. With a slight pressure to her side, he turned her away from the pier to face the rock cliff behind them. He hurried them along for several yards parallel to it.

Marianna pursed her lips as she trotted to keep up. Bertram would make an excellent dance partner. He was very good at directing without verbal communication. But they were not currently dancing. "I'm not one of your students that you can direct me without explanation and consultation," she said testily as he hid them behind a bulge in the cliff face. He released her and knelt to rummage in his gunnysack.

"I understand that the fishing vessel's automaton will loop the boat back around here eventually," she continued, "but perhaps we could change its course as we did the navigator inside. I can't run along the shore until reaching a village." She scoffed. "I couldn't even if the curse wasn't going to drive us from the shoreline to who knows where after three miles. Even if the Time Keepers weren't likely to catch us first." *We could use some help, Maker. Some patience with each other too.*

Bertram didn't look up at her but began tying knots in a rope, forming loops large enough for footholds. "I'm sorry, Marianna, but you're going to have to trust me for a few more minutes. We're going up. It's the only way."

"Up?" she exclaimed, glancing in that direction. The cave was the belly of a nearly sheer cliff, weathered dark rock at the base transitioning to a green, shrub-covered hill at the top. "But—"

"Trust me. Please." Bertram's look as he stood was apologetic yet firm. Her shoulders sinking, she nodded. He hadn't done anything exceptionally foolish yet. Hopefully, he wouldn't start now. He gave her a brief smile, then gestured to the gunnysack and rope. "Secure the sack while I send a vessel off as a distraction."

As he ran off, Marianna bent to begin work on the sack, her movements hesitant as she tried to spare her ribs. A commotion echoed up the cave tunnel and out to her. She sped her hands and heard Bertram's pace quicken. A moment later she heard the hum of a small engine and a belch of smoke, and then Bertram was back at her side.

"Stand in the other foothold," he ordered as he stood in

one, placing himself just in front of her and her with her back to the rock face. "This isn't going to be pleasant, but I can't risk you fainting from your injuries on the way up and letting go of me. Next time you plan on having adventures, bring a second PullLine."

Resisting the urge to peek around the rock bulge at the sound of running guards, Marianna snorted but let him make a crude harness around her using the rope. He gripped the sack with its precious treasury of books between his knees.

"You didn't pack for the right kind of adventure if you didn't bring your own," she countered as she stood on tiptoe to wrap her arms around his neck.

He extended the PullLine's grappling line, anchoring it far up the cliff. "You may be right about that. Hold tight."

Marianna did, and they shot up. Biting back a whimper, she squeezed her eyes shut and focused on the rush of damp air flowing over her face, cooling some of the flush of heat brought by pain. She felt them slow as they approached the anchor, then heard the slight hiss of the smaller hooks deploying to stabilize them to the cliff side. They shifted slightly as Bertram released the main anchor and reattached it higher up.

"We're off," he whispered, and they shot up again. As they slowed and came to a stop, Marianna felt shrubs brushing against her. The process repeated.

Somehow, they made it over the rounded cliff top, disentangled themselves, and rested a few minutes before Bertram handed her hardtack and the canteen and hauled her to her feet. The view of the blue expanse of sea was stunning, except for the Time Keeper vessel chasing another they'd soon realize was empty. The view of the island was stunning as well—green hills and valleys and inlets of the sea. But no village within three miles and no conveyance.

Bertram grabbed the sack with one hand and took her hand in his other and set them off, following the coastline.

They knew when they had gone three miles when they suddenly veered inland and her head spun if she so much as looked toward the coastline. If they didn't stop now, the curse would send them off in who-knew-what direction or just in circles for as long as they stayed on the move. If there were three people or more in a conveyance, one could sometimes trick the curse into letting one go seven miles, but no more, if one changed human navigators before each three-mile limit. But it was difficult to know when to change, and for two people walking, the curse seemed to consider them both navigators and only allowed three miles and no tricks.

Not far ahead, a rock outcropping formed a mound that was overgrown with some type of fern with long fronds and stemmy shrubs with tiny leaves, the petiteness of the latter's greenery making up for the largeness of the former's.

"Let's rest here. If we sleep, we should be able to reset our three-mile 'scramble distance.'" Marianna headed for the mound, and Bertram wearily followed, settling down a few feet from her.

He offered her more medicine, which she took, and a book as a pillow, which she refused, neither favoring the faerie-tainted smell of the things or the thought of any dampness from the ferns seeping into the pages.

"We'll have to get a shipping schedule from one of the Time Keeper stations somehow," she said as she settled in as comfortably as she could, "and find out where we can rendezvous with Davy and your uncle Philip and give them the book on the Star Clock so Davy can build it. Before or after that, I know a Sky Keeper printer who'll copy the books for us. Darius Lockley and his niece Caroline will also help distribute them to the other Sky Keepers."

Bertram was silent, and Marianna looked over at him, his face barely visible through the greenery. His expression was thoughtful, troubled.

Marianna bit her lip. *We'll have to ... we can ...* What *we?* She was the one on the run now—it was better for the Time Keepers to suspect her of being in the caves and never find her than blame an islander with nowhere to hide. She was the one with Sky Keeper connections all over the world and a reason to keep on the move to see them. Bertram could go back to being a mild-mannered schoolmaster and stay in Sheffield-on-the-Sea getting plump and gray. She'd be selfish to want to change that. She had no ship; she might as well disappear anyway.

"I know Darius and Caroline," Bertram said at last. "They're my brother-in-law's uncle and cousin. Caroline's twin brother was on your brother Kingsley's ship when it disappeared."

Sorrow momentarily eclipsing her surprise at the connection, Marianna closed her eyes, remembering again all the men who'd followed Kingsley on what had turned out to be a foolhardy venture, who'd perished with him. And she wondered which of her own crew had perished in the storm, leaving the ship on her orders. "I'm sorry."

"It was his choice to go."

Marianna was silent for a moment before forcibly dragging her thoughts out of the pit they were digging. She wasn't impulsive, but she was a captain and used to making decisions, big and small, fast. She'd already decided about Bertram and about what she'd give up for the truth in the books to get out, but she couldn't expect Bertram to do the same so quickly, or to choose the same path either. "I had forgotten so many of you from Sheffield-on-the-Sea end up in the Bowditch crews."

"There aren't many opportunities on the island, so a lot of the young men and women leave to seek out work. Your family's known to many here as respected captains and as fellow Sky Keepers, so they go to the Bowditch ships for work first. You could say we trust your family with our own."

She gave a weak smile. "You love Sheffield-on-the-Sea, don't you?" She was certain Bertram could have gone anywhere and done anything he wanted, become wealthy and lived in Reydon, home to glittering theaters and concert halls and art galleries—and even the Rí Am and much of the Vanon family, his descendants—but Bertram had stayed here, a humble schoolmaster and arranger of smuggled goods.

"Yes."

She heard the tension in his voice and fell silent.

Her heart aching along with the rest of her, Marianna fell into a sleep of exhaustion.

CHAPTER SEVEN

ariabbna was awakened sometime later to a very large, whiskery mouth snuffling its way over her face. Forcing herself to stay still despite a sudden urge to dart away, she opened her eyes to look up the muzzle of a thick-furred, light brown horse.

"Don't spook her," Bertram whispered as he quietly rose to his feet, rope in hand, and crept toward the horse.

Marianna let the horse inspect her, then slowly raised her hand and brushed it along the horse's long face.

"Ok," Bertram whispered. Marianna removed her hand, and Bertram eased the rope over the horse's head. As the rope settled around her neck, the mare merely looked at him and shook her mane, as if saying, "That wasn't necessary. I wasn't going to lose you."

They let out a breath of relief, and Marianna struggled up.

"This is Aishling." Bertram lifted her onto the horse, who stood calmly, then handed her the gunnysack. "A man with a farm not far from my cottage owns her, lets her roam loose during the day." His expression as he looked up at her was one of wonder, the kind coupled with gratitude even if the latter wasn't spoken. "She returns home in the evenings." He held her gaze for a moment, then led the horse to a small boulder and used it as a mounting block.

Hugging the sack to her chest, Marianna blinked away a sudden wetness to her eyes. They were going to make it, and she wouldn't have to walk. "So it's true the curse didn't extend to animals." It was forbidden to train animals for guidance, and many animals had been slaughtered and people imprisoned for trying.

Bertram's chuckles as he settled in behind her were decidedly mischievous. "Just wait till Thomas learns his Aishling helped us get around the curse. He'll probably name a child after her. He's trustworthy, and lives near enough to my cottage to take us there without the curse keeping him from being able to get himself home."

"He sounds wonderful."

Aishling began walking, a slow, plodding gait over uneven rock, her thick hide seemingly immune to the limby shrubs poking her. Marianna soon sank into a sleep of exhaustion once more, trusting Bertram to keep her safe.

"Oh, I'm so hungry. Can you cook, Bertram? Airship captains don't cook, so I was never taught." Marianna eased herself into the first available chair in the front room of Bertram's cottage just as the sky crystals began to dim. It was a cozy, tidy little place. There were no servants to wait on one, but it looked like a place where one could be snug and happy.

Upon seeing Bertram's cottage at the edge of a small fishing village, Marianna had gotten a second wind—or probably a twentieth, actually—and felt almost herself again. She found herself smiling as she looked about the cottage, her fingers tracing the embroidery of a pillow that was likely a gift from Bertram's grandmother. She didn't know how she knew that, but she did. Her smile faded, and she clasped her hands in her lap. This was not a place for her to get comfortable in. She'd be on the run again immediately after dinner. Or maybe after dinner and a bath.

Bertram dropped his sack on another chair and gave her a smile that could only be described as fond. "Humble schoolmasters cook, don't worry. But first we're going to change the bandage on your arm."

"First, you're going to tell me what you've been up to." A female sharing Bertram's intelligent green eyes and slightly too large nose stood in the kitchen doorway, brandishing a wooden spoon.

"Lydia, you nearly gave me a heart attack." Bertram wrapped the woman in a hug, then introduced her to Marianna as his younger sister, Lydia Lockley. Marianna liked her at once. "What are you doing here?" he asked.

"Keeping up the appearance that you're here." Lydia gestured to the cheerful fire burning in the hearth.

Bertram, the dark circles under his eyes evident, blinked at it as if just noticing it, then sighed and rubbed a hand through his hair. "The Time Keepers noticed my absence then?"

"They may suspect it, but they don't *know* it." Lydia punched him lightly on the shoulder. "Your clever, resourceful, and loyal niece and nephew, *my* offspring, when they noticed you were late for school, *found* a note from you that had fallen off the door saying school had been canceled due to the disturbance of everyone's sleep last night. I came over here and poked the fire back to life. When the Time Keepers stopped by—they seemed to think someone had been prowling around parts forbidden last night—I pretended to be a good little sister cleaning her bachelor brother's house for him." She gave him a significant look.

"My house is not that dirty. For a bachelor. And I was grading papers all week."

She cocked an eyebrow, but then smiled deviously. "Be that as it may, I convinced them you were still sleeping. Plenty of pillows and Nathan and his brown hair amongst them helped."

With a laugh, Bertram kissed his sister and spun her around. "What did I do to deserve a sister like you? And tell Nathan and Cindy they get an A in Kindness from now on. Where are they?"

"It's the traveling circus's last day, and I said they could go again with Robert's sister. The show's good, and the sharpshooter and his daughter are Sky Keepers and good for information." She winked at Bertram. "How about an A in arithmetic?"

"Nothing doing." Bertram released his sister and settled into a chair. His gaze fell on the bulging sack on the chair beside Marianna, then shifted to her, lingering there a long moment. His smile slipped away, and he turned to the fire.

Marianna's heart twisted. Had she really expected him to run off into danger with her on a mission likely to get them both killed? She hadn't planned on asking him to, but ... Exhaustion and her injuries must be affecting her, for Captain Marianna Bowditch had never needed anyone before. Well, no one but a good crew, but Bertram wasn't a crew she could command. He was something else entirely. He was a commander and an equal in his own right.

"It will be a little while before the stew is ready," Lydia said, glancing between them. "Why don't I see to your arm, Captain Bowditch?"

"Thank you," she said, "but please, call me Marianna."

Lydia gave her the same raised eyebrows Bertram had but nodded and quickly gathered the needed supplies.

"Any news of my crew?" Marianna asked as Lydia knelt beside her.

"Banged up but no worse off than you, from what I've heard. Two more turned up this morning. With you, everyone is accounted for. They were divided up between villages to be looked after until a transport ship arrives to take them off island. They thought you alone were lost..." She let the statement hang, as if, like Marianna, she was unsure whether it was better for her to stay "lost" or not but feared it was. The question eclipsed some of the joy of hearing her crew, all of them, were safe. Lydia glanced at her brother, the same question in her eyes.

Bertram retrieved his pack and began emptying it onto a table, Lydia watching him as she cleaned Marianna's wound with a quietness Marianna knew better than to interrupt. Bertram organized the books into piles, then went through them again, turning each over in his hand and glancing at the title pages. As he placed the last one back on the table, he finally met his sister's gaze. "I'm not staying, Lydia."

"I half expected not," she said quietly. Instead of questioning or crying or even giving Marianna an evil look, she merely squeezed Marianna's hand gently, then returned to bandaging her arm, her brows drawn. Marianna's heart did a wild dance of joy and gratitude. She gave Bertram a soft smile.

"If I don't go with her," he said, returning her smile, "she'll follow a will-o'-the-wisp and end up who knows where."

Marianna wrinkled her nose at him.

"I didn't find the faerie mound entrance," he continued, turning to Lydia, "but we found something else: On the other side of the island, there's a secret mine for the crystals used in the automatons. We think the crystals have something to do with the automaton control systems. I don't know why it's kept a secret, but there's bound to be a reason. It is a slave labor mine, but the Rí Am wouldn't feel a need to hide that." He held up a book and the odd metal disk, his voice growing excited. "And, Lydia, we discovered something more —books on navigation! And old equipment! Maps! The Word is true. The heavens exist. Men could navigate themselves. The Star Veil was a curse and not a blessing to man.

"Marianna's brother Davy—Uncle Philip's captain—is an inventor, and as soon as we find him, we're going to build a Star Clock to rival the Time King's navigators. And we'll get all the books to Darius and the other Sky Keeper printers, and we'll teach man to navigate again."

Lydia's gaze shot between Marianna and Bertram as if trying to make sure they weren't jesting with her. Marianna nodded, and Lydia hastily tied off the bandages and sprang up and over to her brother and began examining the books for herself. The examination ended with her dancing Bertram around the room. "Wait till I tell Robert! I'll get you Darius's address, and I'll hem up some of my dresses for Marianna—she can stay with us until Commodore Bowditch sends a transport for the crew—and with the kids' help, maybe we can get one of the books copied before you leave, and—"

Laughing, Bertram wrapped her in another hug. "How about dinner?"

Wrinkling her nose, Lydia pushed him away. "And a bath. You reek of the faerie ... and more acceptable but still malodorous things."

With another laugh and a shrug, Bertram released her. His expression, like his sister's, was one of happiness and contentment, belonging, and it awakened an ache in Marianna for her own family. But at the moment, her crew was the closest thing to family she had. She needed to *see* them, not just hear they were safe. She needed to get out of Bertram and Lydia's hair for a while. She wasn't their family, and she didn't want to intrude any more than necessary.

"I hate to ask, but would it be too much trouble for me to see one of my crew? Is one being quartered near here? I can walk, if you'll direct me," Marianna asked, rising.

"Not at all." Lydia gave her an understanding smile, and Marianna got the feeling she really did understand. "Bertram, take her to my house. She can bathe and change into one of my dresses there while you come back here. You can take her to the Lawsons' later."

"ARE YOU AVOIDING GOODBYES, BERTRAM?" Marianna asked as the old-fashioned horse-drawn cart lumbered toward the Lawsons' home later that evening. Marianna cautiously adjusted herself on the stack of books she was sitting on to put her more at Lydia's height. They'd thought it best for her to pretend to be Lydia as they drove through the gas lamp–lit village. "I'm an airship captain and a Sky Keeper smuggler," she continued. "I've had a lot of possible last nights with family. You don't have to accompany me tonight. Drop me off, go back, and I'll find my own way back. It's not far, you said."

Bertram chuckled, and it was an almost normal chuckle. "And I'm a Sky Keeper who hunts for faerie mounds in forbidden forests. I've had those too. If I go with you now, my sister will pack for me and clean my house."

Marianna sputtered in surprise, then shook her head, unable to stop a smile. "You're a spoiled big brother, you know that, right?"

Judging by the curve of his mouth, he knew that very well and didn't mind a bit. "She's a spoiled younger sister."

"So was I, but I didn't spoil my brothers that much. Not that I had a chance with us all on different airships. But speaking of sisters," she said as the stack of books wobbled underneath her as they hit a rut, "do I have to sit on this precarious tower? I feel like a six year old unable to reach the dinner table without help."

"Not unless you want my reputation ruined and a forced introduction to all the gossips in the village."

"Surely they can't be that bad," she insisted, looking around at the quiet, sparse homes in the village that swept around an inlet of the sea and rose into the thin woodlands of the hill behind. "It's fairly dark in the streets."

A man with a lantern walked along the lane ahead, coming their way, but he was the only one out and about. Bertram eased the horse and cart toward the opposite edge.

"Silhouettes are easily distinguished, and I, as schoolmaster, am a prominent citizen," he said with mock pride. "The ladies will come out to see us."

Marianna gave a contemptuous huff. "It's the mischief-loving faerie blood coming out in you. That's what it is."

As Bertram sputtered in protest, the man with the lantern darted into the lane and planted himself in the middle of it. Bertram brought the horse to a quick halt, and Marianna drew in a sharp breath as her stack slid and she fell into him.

"Running away with Lydia Lockley again, I see," the man growled as he approached Marianna's side of the wagon. Of course it would be her side when she's biting back a whimper and hanging on to Bertram as if for dear life and Bertram trying to get her re-seated without touching anywhere he shouldn't. "Well," the man continued, and Marianna could have sworn there was amusement in his tone, "if she has to run away with any man, I'm glad it's you." With that, he swung himself up into the bed of the wagon.

Marianna plopped down to the seat as Bertram removed the books.

"Marianna," he said without looking at the man as they both re-seated themselves and moved away from one another, "this is my brother-in-law, Robert Lockley. Robert, this is—"

"Captain Marianna Bowditch." He spoke quietly but with confidence. This time, both Bertram and Marianna swiveled around to face him. Robert's triumphant expression sobered quickly. "Turn the cart around, Bertram. We need to talk in private."

"We already know we're in trouble. At least, that I am," Marianna said.

"Probably not the half of it. Turn it around, Bertie. They found the iron."

Marianna gasped, her hand going to her mouth. Bertram turned the cart around.

"My crew?" Marianna asked.

"Being rounded up from the homes they were just dispersed to. The Time Keepers can't prove the iron was heading for here, since the crate was smashed up and the manifest lost, but they suspect. They'll question the crew. Would any of them know?"

"Just me. I had some new crew members and so didn't want to risk it. A few others knew we had Sky Keeper goods, but not what. I trust those, but the Time Keepers are good at knowing when someone's hiding something."

And hiding something was tantamount to a confession in their eyes. And her crew were almost all Sky Keepers, and that was enough to get them in trouble if the Time Keepers felt like it, which they probably would with iron involved. She had to help them, but how?

"For your sake as well as ours, you'd better not be found." Robert eyed the gunnysack in the rear of the cart, for neither she nor Bertram wanted to be parted with it and had brought it along. His eyes flared wide. "Were you planning on sneaking off island with the captain, Bertie? And why does that sack reek of the faerie?"

"Open it and see. Just keep your exclamations down."

Robert's exclamations were silent, but more from a lack of ability to produce sound in his shock than in obedience. "You've got to get this off island and to the other Sky Keepers," he said as soon as he could talk.

"We are," Bertram said firmly.

"We need to get *my crew* off island to safety," Marianna said with all the fierceness and determination she felt.

"I'm not sure we can, Marianna," Bertram said gently.

"There are a lot of them, and the Time Keepers already have them. We'll be lucky to get ourselves off now."

"*I'm* getting my crew off." Somehow. With or without help.

Bertram and Robert both looked at Marianna, then each other, and sighed.

"We're getting your crew off," Bertram said with another sigh.

Some of the stiffness eased from her shoulders. *Thank you.*

"We might as well," Robert added with a shrug. "The island's in trouble anyway. The crew's in trouble anyway. You know they can't just leave and return to their normal lives, right?"

Marianna cradled her cut arm, already considering who might hide them, how families could be reunited. "Yes. But at least they won't be imprisoned, or worse." Executed or enslaved in the mines.

"But if your crew simply runs away," Bertram said, not in argument, more in the manner of one bringing up something to consider, "that would endanger the entire Bowditch family and shipping line. It would shout complicity and guilt on a large scale."

Marianna didn't respond for a moment, then asked, "Where do you think they'll take them? I don't want to endanger my family, but nor would my father want me to abandon my crew. He would tell me to save them."

Bertram gave her hand a quick squeeze, then urged the horse into a faster pace. "My guess is the warehouses next to the Time Keeper station at the airship port—the official one. The merchant ships are in at the seaport, and those warehouses will be full."

"We'll have to use the bridge—we'll have to let them *die*." Robert's grin was devious, and the gleam in his eyes decidedly malicious.

Marianna's heart leapt to her throat and refused to beat for several seconds. "I'm very tired and in a lot of pain," she said crisply once she could speak again. "You might not want to make jokes like that around me."

She caught a strangled laugh from Bertram and turned briefly to glare at him before shifting that look to Robert.

He cleared his throat, and that gleam disappeared. "Sorry. Forgot. You don't know about the bridge."

"No."

"It's something we rigged up in case the Time King came for a visit," Bertram explained. "There was an old lady who swore he would come, said he was partly the island's fault and it was our responsibility to do something about him. So when it came time to rebuild the bridge going out to the airship port, we designed it to collapse—when desired. But stable otherwise, of course."

Marianna's eyebrows shot up, and then she grinned a wicked grin. "I like you Sheffielders."

CHAPTER EIGHT

The inhabitants of Sheffield-on-the-Sea were prepared for anything. Which is why Bertram was sitting in the sitting room of one of the remotest cottages wearing a bushy fake beard and a borrowed airman's jacket and cap. And why he had two sleeping darts loaded into the gauntlet of the PullLine Philip had given him years before and that he'd loaned to Robert and almost forgotten about, and that, along with a knife and additional darts, hidden under his clothes. The islanders were always prepared, and so now was he.

The airman he was impersonating, Marianna's third mate, was hiding in the shed. Marianna and Robert were off gathering aid for the rescue, Lydia securing their escape with the circus. His niece and nephew were at the circus with their aunt. He'd miss saying goodbye to them.

To keep himself from pacing the room, Bertram propped his bandaged leg—the one with the gash from the fall into the cave—on a chair his understanding hostess set out for him and reminded himself he was supposed to be an injured airman with a missing captain. He adopted a brooding attitude as he stared about him. He affected surprise and alarm when the Time Keepers arrived. And with a genuine thanks for the kindly Mrs. Nells, he grimaced and limped his way to the Time Keepers' truck, a long, broad thing with a long bed covered in a brown canvas top, and which rather reminded him of a brown beetle that smoked.

He hauled himself inside and took a seat on a bench toward the middle. Marianna had a crew of twenty men and women, and they were all crammed into that one truck. He was the last to be picked up. Two Time Keeper guards were in the back with them, and one rode with the automaton in the cab.

The man Bertram shared the exact middle bench with fit the description Marianna had given him of the first mate—even in his sitting choice. From that position, the man could easily see all his crew and be near them all. He looked Bertram up and down, his expression turning from suspicious to downright dangerous. Bertram got the same feeling from all the crew he'd passed getting in. He didn't fool anyone except the Time Keepers. He could relate to men and women who cared for their own, and as he glanced up and down the rows again, meeting those dangerous gazes, he found his thinking shifting from the rescue being something he was doing for Marianna to something he was doing for *them*, these strangers who currently wanted to toss him overboard for impersonating and, for all they knew, harming one of their own.

"Gilded crystals, Sawyers," Bertram said roughly as he inched nearer the man with the deadly glare and the rank of first mate. "Must you take up the entire bench?"

The officer's eyes widened. He looked Bertram up and

down again, and the glare melted away. "Gilded crystals" was apparently a magic phrase to the Bowditch crew. Strange choice, but as long as it got him their loyalty—and kept them from reporting him to the Time Keepers—what did it matter?

The tension in the truck bed dropped to a tolerable level, curiosity taking its place. After checking the attention of the two guards, Bertram sank a little lower in the seat and cautiously tugged up one sleeve to reveal the PullLine gauntlet. Since Philip had given it to him, it had the mark of the Bowditch shipping line on it. He slipped a couple of the sleeping darts from a hidden pocket in his jacket and gave them to Sawyers, indicating one was for the rear guard.

Sawyers nodded curtly and loaded a dart into his Pull-Line, also hidden under his jacket. That done, he looked back to Bertram, his expression cautiously hopeful in the light of the lamps hanging from the metal skeleton giving shape to the canvas. *What of my captain?* he seemed to ask.

"In honor, not memory," Bertram said softly, and at the man's visible relief, Bertram felt a twinge of jealousy. Just what kind of esteem did the first mate have for his captain?

Chagrined at his foolishness, Bertram quietly explained the plan to Sawyers, then settled in to listen and watch. At the waterfall's roar, it would begin.

Before long they were speeding down the winding coastal road to the airship docks. The truck bed was quiet, Sawyers having ordered all his men to silence. They sat alert and ready, though for what they couldn't know. Not with the two Time Keepers sauntering up and down the aisle between the parallel rows of benches, preventing even a wave of whispers from traveling the truck bed.

Over the flapping of a loose end of the canvas cover came the roar of a waterfall. Bertram nudged Sawyer's arm and scooted forward in his seat, addressing the men ahead, leaving a clear path between the first mate and the rear guard. Tugging his own sleeve back enough to expose his gauntlet, Bertram tapped his foot against his companion's and aimed the sleeping dart on his gauntlet to the front guard. *One, two, three!* He fired the sleeping dart.

The guard in front hit the floor as the rear guard fell into a seat. Bertram and Sawyers jumped from their bench, Sawyers directing two nimble airmen to roll back the canvas covering and Bertram collecting the spent darts. The lamps hanging from the truck's frame would light them up perfectly to those above.

"We've got to get the guard in the cab. They must all be unconscious before we leave." Standing next to Sawyers again, Bertram strained to be heard as the crew started to sing to cover the sound of them scrambling about, pairing up, an injured airman with a fit airman.

Sawyers nodded, then tapped two young men on the shoulder and leaned close to talk to them. He gave them his extra sleeping dart, and as the pair started toward the front of the vehicle, Bertram moved to follow. Sawyers caught his arm. "You don't have to do everything yourself, Orren."

Bertram started to protest, then nodded in thanks, common sense and relief washing away the vestiges of pride. "Climbing around on fast-moving vehicles isn't really in my usual line of work," he admitted.

Sawyers gave him an understanding smile. "It's not a job I'd recommend taking up at our age."

"Speak for yourself," Bertram replied in mock gruffness. "I'm still in my prime." He looked to the sky at their rear and pointed to the yellow lights outlining a glider soaring toward them. "Young enough to enjoy flying."

The airman's face lit up with a grin as he followed Bertram's gaze. "I've missed being in the air." He sprang into motion, another officer joining him in lining up the pairs of airmen under the open top, two pairs on the left, two on the right. The officers watched the approaching glider, then signaled the first set of pairs to deploy their PullLines to the wings near the body of the craft, then the next set to the wings near the tips. The ship dipped as the lines attached and the eight men flew up, but the ship rose again, veering away and soon clearing the cliff top ahead. Thanking the Maker for the nearby hanger and the flying club of brave Sky Keepers willing to take a risk, Bertram turned his attention back to the sky behind.

"Here's the next one!" he cried a moment later as the two young airmen climbed back into the bed with the unconscious guard held between them. Bertram collected the stun dart as Sawyers and the other officer directed the exit of eight more men and women. One set of lines missed the wing, and the ship listed to the side, but the airmen fired again, hitting the wing this time and rising up.

Bertram's heart beat faster anyway, knowing the bridge was coming up fast. They couldn't slow or stop the truck without exploding the automaton, for that's what happened when one messed with a navigator.

"Group up, Orren," Sawyers yelled at him as the last three lined up. The lights of the third and final glider grew closer.

"Sorry, Sawyers," Bertram said, watching the narrow

roadside now. A single headlight flashed on ahead. "I've got my own ride." He looked back over at the officers. "The people of my island will take care of you and hide you from the Time Keepers until they can get you all off."

Sawyers's eyebrows rose, and he grinned, a pleased kind of confirmation in his eyes. "Captain's orders?" he inquired as the men rearranged themselves.

"Yes."

"Well, you won't be needing us then." He winked back at Bertram. "Captain Bowditch will take good care of you. May the Maker be with you both."

"We'll take care of one another," Bertram retorted as the three men shot up. He picked up one of the unconscious Time Keepers as the motorcycle neared and dragged him to the side of the truck. He could just hear the roar of the second waterfall ahead, whose torrent poured under the cleverly designed bridge and into the sea. For the sake of the deception—he wasn't sure about his own sake—he hoped Robert and Thomas were ready with the small explosive device that would trigger the bridge's collapse.

Driving the motorcycle with all the confidence he'd expect from her, Marianna pulled up alongside the truck, bringing the small trailer she towed even with him and as close to the truck's side as she dared, and she dared pretty far. Fortunately for him. Grunting, he lifted the Time Keeper onto the railing and dumped him over and onto the trailer.

"Hurry!" Marianna cried. "Bridge coming up!"

Bertram hefted the next one, wondering how much the Maker cared about them caring for their neighbors. He dumped him overboard, figuring it would be best to assume the Maker cared a lot.

"Bertram!" There was panic in Marianna's voice.

Bertram grabbed the last man and threw them both over the railing. He landed on a guard and rolled off the pile of unconscious men as Marianna slammed on the brakes. Bracing his feet against the railing, he used his body to wedge the guards into place as the trailer whipped around faster than he liked and they raced away from the bridge. The truck rattled as it crossed the boundary between road and bridge, then, with a crack and a roar of water, the bridge collapsed. Chunks of metal and stonework hit the rocks below, some catching on the boulders, some breaking away and flowing out to sea. The truck toppled, the bed breaking away and washing further out than the cab. Perfect for losing passengers.

Marianna brought the motorcycle and trailer to a halt and backed them up. Robert and Thomas sprinted from their place of concealment near the waterfall and helped Bertram unload the guards and, after dunking them in the water, place them near enough to the road and watercourse for them to assume, when they woke, that they must have jumped just before reaching the "already collapsed bridge" or had somehow swum to safety from the wreckage. Bertram had convinced a few sailors to give up their hats to be found in the water to further support their story of a bridge that washed out due to the recent storms and all the airmen perishing due to their previous injuries and inability to swim to safety.

That done, Thomas left them on Aishling and Robert took over the motorcycle and headed them toward the circus.

ONE MOTORCYCLE RIDE UP a winding coastal road, one trip on an officially-illegal-but-Time-Keeper-used toll lift up the cliff side, and one wagon ride later, the glittering, many-hued lights of a circus fought the dullness of the sky crystals' uninspiring illumination and won.

They parked behind the circus, and Lydia soon found them. A man a little bigger than Bertram, some fifteen or so years older than he was and well-muscled, with a selection of knives strapped across his chest and guns on his belt, walked beside her. There was a keenness to his gaze and confidence in his expression that suggested his strengths weren't all in muscles and weapons. Bertram wasn't easily intimidated, but he had a feeling this man could do it, if he wanted.

With him was a young, dark-haired woman about twenty, her lithe build and costume suggesting a trapeze artist. Something about the way she carried herself and studied them hinted she took after her father quite a bit. Despite the dim lighting, the girl's eyes were concealed behind dark goggles.

Though he trusted his sister's judgment, Bertram couldn't help reaching out a hand to the stuffed gunnysack resting on the ground between him and Marianna. He found Marianna's hand there too, and she smiled at him in shared laughter at their over-protectiveness.

As the strangers reached them, the man held out his hand with a friendly smile. "Cal Andrews, knife thrower, sharpshooter, Sky Keeper smuggler." He gave the girl beside him a look of affection and pride. "And this is my daughter, Abigail. But we call her Prism because she sees many colors where others see only one."

"And that's not nearly as fun as it sounds," the girl said with a smile as she shook their hands. "But it has its uses."

Bertram caught a hint of a secret in that softly spoken statement and wondered about this pair of entertainers and smugglers.

"So," Cal said meaningfully as he looked them over with a teasing light in his eye, "I'm told the great smuggler captain of the cloud paths needs the help of a landlubber."

Marianna shot Bertram a wicked grin, and he was somehow both enchanted and alarmed. "Why yes. Bertram is afraid of heights."

PART II
STAR VEIL

"Ah, Lord GOD! It is you who have made the heavens and the earth by your great power and by your outstretched arm! Nothing is too hard for you."
Jeremiah 32:17

CHAPTER ONE

A faerie queen once loved a mortal man. He promised her the moon and the stars—she gave them to him, before she tired of him and slipped away into her own realm again, never caring to undo the chaos she'd caused. For she'd cast a crystal-studded veil between heaven and earth, obscuring the lights the Maker created, the sun for the day and the moon and stars for the night. To all but a faithful few, the knowledge of them was blotted out, like the maps and star clocks that allowed men to travel where they wished, sure in their destination, of their place wherever they were. Men's fate she left in the control of her lover, who fashioned himself the Rí Am, the Time King.

Captain Davy Bowditch hated automatons. Hated that he couldn't tinker with them to find out how they worked—without them deliberately exploding on him. Hated being dependent on them to get where he needed to go, assuming the Rí Am's minions approved he could go there. Hated the exorbitant rates charged for them, which tended to make both him and his men explode in anger.

"That's a quarter of the value of the cargo! All we want is a reroute!" The baritone voice of Davy's first mate, Philip Orren, carried through the Dondre Time Keeper Station's marble halls like the cook's dinner bell. It got everyone's attention.

Davy laid a hand on Philip's arm and looked at the clerk. "How much for a navigator automaton for the airship's Escaper?"

"It's not safe to go so far in one of those," Philip insisted. Hale and hearty at about fifty, with dark hair tied back at his neck and a permanently scruffy silver beard, Philip wasn't one to use "not safe" lightly.

Davy clenched his jaw. "I've got to get to Sheffield-on-the-Sea to look for Marianna, but I can't ask the men to give up what little profit they're already getting. I can make it in the Escaper. *We* can if you want to see your family before the current route gets us there in three months." Davy prayed he'd find his sister there alive and well, despite reports of the wreckage of her airship, which had held nearly half the island's winter food supply.

He glared at the clerk. "And we asked for Sheffield-on-the-Sea, not Briney Bay. It's still a long way from there to the island."

The clerk, separated from them by bars in the marble counter, studied the papers in front of him, sliding the bottom memo in and out of the stack. "Briney Bay's a much better place to go," he squeaked out.

The clerk at the next window leaned toward his comrade. "Tell them."

"But—"

"It'll be announced in a little while anyway."

He swallowed. "Sheffield-on-the-Sea has rebelled again, got caught with iron. The Rí Am ordered a rerouting for all vessels, land and air and sea, away from Sheffield-on-the-Sea as punishment. Their Time Keeper Station has already been closed and all automatons removed."

The blood drained from Davy's face. Behind him, Philip gasped.

"Your automaton will have received orders concerning the latter part of your route. You'll be told later what to do with the supplies you were taking there."

"But ... but that's murder." Philip's cracked voice barely reached the clerk's window. "They depend on the food and fuel brought in to last them the winter."

The clerk flinched. "Unless you want the reroute to Briney Bay, pick up your serviced automaton at Window 23. Next please."

Davy and Philip stumbled to Window 23, Davy catching and tossing away every possible way to navigate themselves to Sheffield-on-the-Sea, but every option involved a voyage of no return—like his brother's attempt to be free of the Time King—or death at the hand of the Time Keeper Reconnaissance Teams. No invention of his for telling time or distance traveled had come close to working. The faerie veil obscured such thoughts. *How long, O Lord? How long will you suffer the Star Veil to blot out the heavens mentioned in your Word? The Rí Am to rule our days and nights?* Or was it true what the Rí Am taught, that the Maker was a myth, just like the sun, moon, and stars he supposedly created? Why else would he let the veil linger?

Davy fisted his hands. Anger and doubt would do him no favors.

In front of them, a somber cabby handed over a receipt for a horse-cart navigator—the automaton complete with a rounded derby, goggles, and a great coat—then made way for Davy and Philip as he hurried to the conveyor next to the window.

Beyond this barred window, two clerks slid a five-foot automaton into a wooden crate, fastened the crate, and placed it on the conveyor. With its brown painted hair and eyes, insulting blue captain's jacket, and crystal pins shaping the Rí Am's emblem on its chest, this mechanized doll ruled so many lives. *Whenever you choose to take down the Time Keepers and even the faerie veil itself, Lord, I want to help.*

Two months later

Captain Davy Bowditch hated being mugged. Hated being shushed.

"Calm down, Dovey. Do you want to catch the Time Keepers' attention?"

Hated being called "Dovey" by anyone but his kid sister. But the large pair of hands that had dragged him into an alley on his walk back to the airship after an evening meal with a local friend, and the irritated voice behind him, were decidedly masculine.

Davy launched himself backward. His assailant grunted as he hit the alley's brick wall with Davy pressed against him. Davy spun around and grabbed the man's throat.

"Who are you and why did you call me 'Dovey'?" he growled in the man's face.

"Bertram Orren, Marianna's husband," he rasped, pulling at Davy's fingers.

"Her what!"

"My husband, so don't hurt him."

Davy spun around to face the petite, chestnut-haired woman who'd snuck up beside him. "Marianna!" He pulled her into a hug. "We feared you'd died, and then the ban came on traveling to Sheffield-on-the-Sea and—"

"I know, Davy. I feared I'd never see you again either." She tightened her arms about him, then pulled back. "But we don't have much time. Bertram and I have been in hiding. We escaped Sheffield-on-the-Sea with a circus, with the help of a couple of unusually talented Sky Keepers—a father and daughter. Instinct tells us they have a greater part to play yet, if they're willing. I pray they are. Since leaving them, we've been traveling with different groups trying to meet up with you."

Davy looked over his shoulder at his brother-in-law—it would take time to get used to that—and mouthed an apology as the man rubbed his neck. Well-built with a sensible look, Bertram smiled an acceptance and picked up a gunnysack from the ground beside him. Bertram *Orren*. Was he Philip's favorite nephew? He narrowed his eyes. Or the one Philip didn't trust?

"We found a faerie trove, Davy"—Marianna shook him gently to regain his attention—"full of things they stole from our ancestors: books on navigation, star charts, maps, and even a metal disc with moving needles."

"We think it's called a 'compass,'" Bertram said, "but we haven't figured out how to use it yet. The faerie curse befuddles us or it. Or maybe it's my iron knife that does." He pulled a worn book from the duffle and held it out to Davy, whose heart was beating too fast to say anything. Was his prayer being answered so soon? "While we're working on that and getting Darius and Caroline Lockley to print copies of the books and maps we escaped with, we have something for you to do."

Marianna took the book from her husband and put it in Davy's hands. "You're the best inventor and builder I know, Davy. The compass and something else called a sextant— figure out how they're made and make blueprints. Give them to the Sky Keepers so we can make more." She tapped the book in his hands. "And you've got to build the Star Clock and find a way to calibrate it. Time, distance, direction. For air, land, and sea. We've got to have them all if we hope to be free of the Rí Am's control." She took her husband's hand. "And get supplies to Sheffield-on-the-Sea before winter sets in."

Davy stared at the book, *Star Chronometer and Navigation*, in awe, then his slack mouth curved into a grin. He had a whole lot of parts to acquire without the Time Keepers getting suspicious, but he had their automaton to thank for getting him to the parts stores.

CHAPTER TWO

"You've been to every parts store in every port you've stopped at this voyage, Captain."

Even though an aisle separated her from the accusatory clerk and the unfortunate captain, Abigail "Prism" Andrews flinched.

"Someone's about to be in trouble with the Time Keepers." Beside her, Banger Conrad, newest member of the traveling circus her father was part owner in, smirked.

Prism tilted her hat forward, shadowing her face, and sped her hands as she dug through a barrel of gears, searching for the one her father requested, her heart increasing its pace as well. *Time Keepers don't like people who sneak copies of the Word around to those who need it. As well as sneak wanted Sky Keepers around.*

"Well, I am an inventor—and an airship captain—and I can't be good at either if I don't have parts," a man replied with a humorous lilt to his voice. "Besides, I like to shop around."

The clerk's reply was lost to Conrad's mimic, "I like to shop around." He pulled a bag of peanuts from his pocket, crushed the papery shells of several nuts, and popped the peanuts into his mouth, letting the shells fall to the floor like leaves in autumn. "He must be building something the Time Keepers won't like."

Prism ground her teeth. Why had her father decided to send Conrad with her instead of coming himself? He'd not let her go anywhere alone since a prince of Amezak, one of their most lucrative stops, decided he wanted to add a circus freak to his collection of wives. He hadn't taken Prism's refusal well, and in the chaos that followed, the circus had barely escaped, and they'd been separated from Marianna and Bertram. Fortunately, the pair had been able to contact them later to let them know they were all right and to check on Prism.

Prism suppressed a shudder and held up the supply list to the canon operator. "Help me find these so we can get out of here."

His gaze skimmed over the list on its way to the street-facing door as two Time Keepers entered, revolvers strapped to their belts. "What's the hurry? The clerk and the cap will be busy for a while, I should say. Your father still has to get the automaton programed to navigate our next tour ... since we can't go through Amezak again."

Prism tore the list in half and shoved the lower portion in Conrad's peanut husk–dusted hand. "Parts. Now."

Conrad blinked, glanced from her to his hand, then narrowed his eyes. Prism held his stare, figuring that even though her goggles concealed her eyes, he'd guess she was glaring at him. Finally, he crumpled the paper into his fist and stalked off. Prism let out a breath. There were advantages to having a sharp shooter and knife thrower as a father ... and trainer. And having crazy eyes.

The voices at the register grew louder, but Prism ignored them, noting instead a couple of other unsavory characters entering the store. Slouchy clothes but buttoned cuffs—buttoned to hide the pirate's wrist tattoo?

Prism shook her head. *Port cities.* Her circus usually traveled overland and never had dealings with air pirates. They'd not bother her. Saying a quick prayer for the unknown captain against the Time Keepers, Prism pulled her hat down even further, grateful the fashion allowed for heavily decorated hats that might detract from the darkened goggles she wore when out in public. If the Time Keepers knew what her freakish eyes allowed her to see, she wouldn't be in danger: she'd be dead.

She turned back to the bin. "Aha." She snatched up the flawless, perfectly sized herringbone gear, deposited it in her bag, and searched her half of the list for the next item.

A flash of movement caught her eye. A tiny ball, about two shades darker than the floor—nothing was the same color to Prism—rolled from the direction of the clerk's counter to the wall.

Boom!

A noise that sounded suspiciously like generic gunfire was rapidly followed by the acrid odor and hazy air indicative of exploded gunpowder, then by the crash of breaking glass. Prism ducked behind the barrel and covered her nose and mouth as a breeze from the open window two aisles over smeared gun smoke across the store like fog, the pea soup kind the caravan drivers wouldn't budge in.

Footsteps pounded down the aisle toward her. A blue jacket materialized in the smoke.

"Bowditch!" A cry from the Time Keepers.

"Pardon me," the man in blue yelled back toward the register, "but I must get this young woman to safety. Chivalry of captains and all that. Can't risk her getting hurt in a pirate's revenge."

Before Prism could react, the captain had her over his shoulder and was running toward the open window. He turned a corner sharply, and she swung to the side and caught a glimpse of Conrad kneeling before the open window, hands together, fingers threaded as if about to give someone a boost up.

Conrad was grinning a wicked grin. "Luggage's at the dock, cap."

"No!" Prism screamed as the captain vaulted out the window.

Conrad's smirk, window frame, bricked alley all passed beneath her. The whirring sound of a PullLine being deployed was succeeded by a jerk. The alleyway bricks grew smaller. They swung up and toward whatever building the captain's PullLine attached to. Grunting, the man stopped their collision against the wall with his legs, then began hauling them up, walking along the building's side.

Prism set her jaw as her heart rate slowed, remembering its years of training for performances. So Conrad and the others thought they could ship her off with a captain so they could profit on Amezak, did they? Well, they had another thing coming.

Wishing she were in her acrobatics practice costume instead of her good dress, she arched her back and swung her legs until she caught the PullLine between her ankles. A few twists and a good shove against the captain, and she was scaling the building while the chivalrous captain was exclaiming—not quite cursing, which surprised her—somewhere down below as he struggled to regain control of the PullLine.

Prism hoisted herself onto the rooftop and plotted a course over the next two and down into an alleyway. With a quick glance at the captain—he was gaining fast and yelling in a rather commanding tone for her to wait for him—she sprinted over the slanted roof.

"Look out!" the captain yelled.

A whistle split the air, a dart pierced her arm. Two steps later, darkness clouded her vision. Prism slumped to the rooftop and began to slide.

CHAPTER THREE

"I may have taken the wrong woman." Davy turned from the unconscious, drugged woman in his first mate's bed to his first mate.

"Why is that?" the older man asked. "Other than she nearly died trying to get away from you?"

Davy scowled, but Philip didn't seem perturbed. "Because I spied another father and daughter pair as we left. Marianna spoke of a father and daughter who would help us, as did the note."

"Ah," Philip replied. That did seem to disturb him, a bit.

"And the man I assumed was her father, he's the one who put the dart of sleeping potion in her arm—while she was on a rooftop. Hardly the sort of thing a father does."

"Why didn't you leave her?"

Davy shrugged, then rubbed his forehead. "I couldn't very well leave her to fall off the roof, could I? Once I caught her, it seemed obvious to finish what I started. But now I've got a stranger on board, and I can't let her go. Someone knew about our meeting, Philip. Angry pirates and suspicious

Time Keepers don't converge at obscure parts stores by accident." He would definitely be staying away from parts stores for a while, until the Time Keepers thought they'd scared him into submission.

"You think they meant for you to take the wrong woman?"

"You searched her trunk—left at the dock as the man said —and her jacket and purse. There's nothing there to help me finish the Star Clock." He pulled a revolver from his pocket. "And there was this in her trunk along with a couple more and a case of throwing knives."

"Yes, I remember. Fine weapons those. Not ones for a novice either."

"My thoughts exactly." He returned the gun to his pocket. He'd locked the other items up in the safe in his room. And there was the blank journal. There was something odd about the feel of the pages. And why a completely blank journal? It looked expensive enough to be a gift, yet it wasn't inscribed. Journals seldom filled up just before a journey, making it more likely a person would pack either one partly used journal or one almost-filled one and a blank one. Was it for copying the blueprints to his inventions? Or was he too suspicious now that he had a truly great invention to guard, and that not even of his own design?

It had been three months since Marianna had given him *Star Chronometer and Navigation*, but he'd not finished the clock. He'd taken apart, rebuilt, and created blueprints for the compass and sextant, and he'd passed on the designs to trusted Sky Keepers. Even if the Time Keepers got ahold of them, they likely wouldn't have a clue what they were for. A clock was more obvious, however.

Davy and Philip sat in silence, Philip contemplating the

unconscious woman and Davy the bland afternoon light diffusing through the open window. What would real sunlight look like? The pink of dawn? The multitude of colors at sunset? He'd read of those in forbidden ancient books. But now? Evenly spaced crystals in the Star Veil glowed in the day, creating a sky similar to perpetual cloud cover, then dimmed at night to individual lights, creating a pale imitation of what he believed must be breathtaking.

Davy picked up the woman's goggles, which along with her hat and jacket lay on the table beside her, and rolled them back and forth in the lamplight. "These aren't lenses for correcting vision."

"Ah. I thought you'd get around to noticing that sooner or later. Did you see her eyes?"

"Under these?" Davy answered, noting how the goggles tended to dull colors.

"No. Lift her lids." Philip demonstrated the action on his own eyes.

"Why would I do that?" He paused. "Did you?"

Philip shrugged. "Seen the doctors do it before. Seemed like the thing to do. Anyway, you should take a peek." He cleared his throat. "Before she wakes."

Davy raised a brow but moved to the bed and carefully opened the girl's right eye. A grotesquely large pupil, an iris like a tangle of multi-colored threads, like the back of a brilliantly hued tapestry, stared blankly up at him. Though a shiver escaped his control, Davy managed not to jump back. Feigning indifference, he lowered her eyelid and returned to his seat. "A rare color that."

"Glad I warned you, huh?"

"Yes," Davy admitted, and added a moment later, "We can't take her back and collect the right woman, thanks to pre-programed automatons. When she wakes, we'll see what we can find out about her."

"What about the Star Clock," Philip asked, "since she's no help?"

Instead of answering, Davy frowned and returned to his private study and workroom, Philip following. He and Philip took their accustomed chairs and stared thoughtfully at the incomplete clock, as if it could tell them how to fix its own problems. The all-important timepiece, an unimpressive thing that would resemble a palm-sized locket with a white face and twelve numerals on the front when finished, sat in a padded box on his workbench. The Star Clock really had nothing to do with stars, other than the inventor's claims that it could keep accurate time on land and sea and even among the stars, by which he poetically meant the cloud paths Davy regularly traveled. Davy suspected that wherever the stars were, things were a bit different there than here. Still, they had to have the Star Clock and have it able to keep time accurately despite the motion and temperature of its surroundings, along with the instruments and the few charts Marianna and Bertram had found, in order to precisely determine their position and navigate themselves.

The various unusable cogs, gears, and springs lying about the fragments of the clock itself taunted him. Even if he'd been able to purchase what he'd picked out at the parts store, he'd still be missing some unusual pieces. He couldn't custom order them without suspicion or gain what he needed to make them himself. Blasted Time Keepers and pirates.

Chin in his hands, he studied the twelve Roman numerals and smaller dividing marks, each neatly painted and newly dried, on the clock face. He was still intrigued by the notion of time measurements being based on twelves and sixties rather than the ten-based system of the financial world. But twelve was a nice number, easily divisible. Apparently, clocks made a *tick, tick, tick* or a *ticktock, ticktock* sound. He was inclined to think that might become annoying, or perhaps soothing in its familiarity over time. One tick a second, sixty ticks a minute, three thousand six hundred ticks an hour, and twenty-four of those hours in a day. Were real days equivalent to the sky crystals' brightening and dimming cycles? How long was a second? However long, he'd gladly put up with any amount of *ticktock*-ing to be free of the Time King. If only that were the only cost of what they hoped to achieve.

Davy stilled, then a smile curved his mouth. He was already committing treason. Why not add a little more to it?

"I can't buy parts anymore, it seems," he said, sitting up and meeting Philip's eye, "so we'll have to take a ship."

Philip's eyebrows rose, but then he grinned. "The lads will be disappointed."

CHAPTER FOUR

P rism woke to a ruckus.

"Pirates!" The word screamed into the room through the open window like a chilling breeze.

Her eyes flew open. Colors everywhere. So many hues, dizzying and beautiful and almost deafening in their own way, all crying out for attention, bombarded her along with the repeated cries of pirates and calls to secure the airship.

Airship?

Prism jumped from the bed, noticing but not considering the well-furnished officer's cabin she'd woken in. She snagged her goggles and jacket from the nightstand and started for the door, fumbling to get the lenses over her eyes. Still sluggish from whatever had been in the dart, she tripped over a trunk that was remarkably familiar. More than that, she noted with a dulled surprise, it *was* her trunk. It'd been her present on her fourteenth birthday. It was almost the same glossy ebony all over even without her goggles. She loved it for that reason. The key was in the lock. Had whoever shipped her off packed her guns and knives? Her journal?

She unlocked it and flipped it open. *Thank you, Maker.* The book, the record of her lifetime of travels, lay on top. She stuffed the small book, the ink needed to use it, and her paint brushes into her jacket pocket and tore through the rest of the trunk.

Finding nothing useful in the way of weapons, she lifted her ruffled skirts and pulled the small derringer from her leg holster, then darted out the unlocked door. Had the pirates distracted her captors so much they'd failed to search her or lock the door? Not that she was complaining.

Prism stepped onto the deck, then ducked to the left, away from the loudest sounds of fighting. She couldn't spot the pirate ship, but the air was damp, gray with clouds, the deck to her right filled with fighting men. But not ten yards away to the left the off-white of folded parachutes attached to the deck railing caught her eye. As fast as her wobbly legs would carry her, Prism darted from cover to cover until reaching the parachutes.

Stowing the derringer in her pocket, she pulled a parachute from its holder, but her hands refused to do more than hold it. She stared at the parachute's assortment of straps as her mind considered the fall awaiting her, the unknown landing point.

"Think about the harem in Amezak, Prism," she ground out. Using the book's record, she could at least find her way somewhere far away from there.

She slipped the parachute onto her back and fastened the awkward straps, her hands speeding their work as someone yelled for her to stop. Prism grabbed the railing and began to hoist herself up.

"Stop!" Strong hands jerked her away from the railing, spinning her around toward the ship and divesting her of the parachute in one smooth motion. A motion that sent her barreling into the chest of an irate captain.

"Are you trying to get yourself killed?" he bellowed. The airship lurched with a strong wind, and the sounds of the fight went quiet as the man who'd kidnapped her without a thought yelled at her with a mix of horror and fury in his face so strong it rocked her back on her heels.

"I-I don't understand," Prism stammered. Was that a value for her life in his eyes, not simply fear for the loss of a hostage?

"It's obvious you don't understand parachutes," the man roared. "You could've gotten yourself killed jumping with it strapped like that. And we're over the ocean!"

Prism blanched and looked around, praying for another route of escape, but around them crowded sailors. Only sailors. No pirates. Only sailors and sailors with makeshift pirate costumes, some including a skull and crossbones crudely drawn on their faces. One, blond and taller than most, the one who'd prevented her from jumping, even had a tattoo on his wrist. A tattoo of two close shades, as if he'd tried to cover one by inking over and around it. He looked as anxious and confused as the rest.

Prism took another step back, away from the audience that was too close, away from the yelling, away from the scene that didn't make sense.

The captain's eyes widened. "No!" He lunged forward, and she was once again slung over his shoulder, then hauled below deck and tossed onto a bed.

But somewhere in the bouncing journey she regained

her senses. He didn't want her harmed. Perhaps she could reason with him. Once he quit hauling her about.

"Will you stop that?" she cried as she righted herself on the mattress.

Breathing hard as he leaned on the table beside the bed, the captain shook his head. He jerked up as a breeze blew through the room, smelling oddly of gunpowder and stew. He dashed to the open window and slammed it shut. The captain's look as he turned to face her practically dared her to try to escape. He crossed his arms and leaned against the glass.

"Morning, lass. I'm Philip, the first mate." A man slightly older than her father and looking just as fit and shrewd, entered and locked the door behind him. "And what my captain means by that steely-eyed look of his is 'not if it keeps you from killing yourself.'"

Prism blinked, then crossed her arms. "I have no intention of killing myself."

Both men studied her as if to ascertain the truthfulness of her statement. Prism could think of only one way to confirm it.

She pulled the derringer from her pocket. "Nor do I have any intention of being taken to Amezak. So if you'll kindly drop me off at some other port of call, I would be most obliged."

The two men gaped at her, then turned on one another.

"You didn't search her?"

"Neither did you, apparently."

"Hush!" she cried. The two men snapped around to face her, indignation as well as a healthy dose of surprise clear in their faces. "Put your hands up."

"Now look here, young woman," the captain began, but Prism cut him off.

"I am looking, and I see a room I didn't come to by choice."

He shut his mouth.

"Who are you?" Prism aimed the gun at the captain's shoulder. She couldn't bring herself to point it at his heart, not after she'd seen the horror in his eyes earlier. But that didn't mean she trusted him completely.

He raised his hands, a mask of calm slipping over his features. His expression reminded her of the one she wore before her father commenced sending very sharp blades her way in their act. She put the captain in his early thirties, of an upper middle-class family, and of a respectable upbringing. Except for a propensity for kidnapping, he was likely a good man.

"Davy Bowditch," he said, calmly. "Captain of the *Dawn Singer*. And you are?"

Bowditch? Marianna's brother? The one she and Bertram were so eager to find? "Abigail Andrews," she said, trying not to let her confusion show.

"It's a pleasure to make your acquaintance, Miss Andrews." He bowed. "May I present my first mate, Philip Orren?" He gestured to the other man, who also bowed.

"I won't say it's my pleasure," she retorted. "Why did you kidnap me and where are you taking me? I'll never go to Amezak, so if that's your plan, you might as well give me back the parachute and teach me to use it. I'll do whatever it takes to stay free of the prince."

Davy blanched. "I didn't kidnap you, Miss Andrews ... intentionally. You see, you were—"

"I was not in danger. The pirate attack at the parts shop

was an illusion. Those weren't real shots or breaking glass. Close in sound, but not the same. My father's a sharpshooter, among other things, and I know what all manner of guns sound like. I also know about illusions. Why all that if not to take me? Are you working for Prince Onesu? Or did the troupe decide to cast me off when Papa wasn't looking? Sell me to another circus and you're to deliver me?"

Davy's eyes widened, and he glanced at his companion. He lowered his hands, his expression gaining an unexpected solemnness. "I didn't kidnap you, Miss Andrews ... of the Andrews Brothers' Circus?" When Prism nodded, he continued, "You were a bargaining chip. Your father had something I needed, and to get it, I agreed to keep you safe for a year." His brows drew together. "At least that's what I believed when I took you from the shop."

Her father? Prism's grip on the gun faltered, but she raised it quickly before Davy could take advantage of her lapse, though he didn't seem inclined to do so. "My father would never sell me, and that man in the shop was *not* my father. Even if Papa asked you to keep me safe, bargaining chips are not carried away tossed over shoulders."

The first mate smirked, but Davy frowned, the kind of look designed to make sailors tremble.

It didn't work on her.

"The pirate Cavan O'Connor isn't terribly fond of me," Davy said with a sigh, "so when both his men and the Time Keepers were bearing down on me in the store, the situation became untenable. I had to leave without the conversation I had hoped to have with you and your ... companion. Hence, the GunPoof and the shoulder-carrying."

"The gun what?"

"The GunPoof, an invention of mine. Apparently, I need

to work on its sound quality." Davy indicated his outside jacket pocket. "May I retrieve the message from your father?" When Prism nodded, he pulled out a telegram and handed it to her. "Does this mean anything to you?"

Captain Bowditch—Marianna said to contact you. Have solution. Prism. Yours if care for daughter 1 yr. If agreeable to you, meet July 25. Last Parts Store. Look for father, daughter pair. —Cal Andrews, Andrews Brothers' Circus

Prism's heart plummeted, and as much as she tried to find a safety net, none presented itself. Her father ... Hadn't he been acting strangely since Amezak, where they'd also been separated from Marianna and Bertram? Had the couple left something important with him, and now he was trading it in to get rid of her? So the troupe could travel to profitable Amezak without trouble and he could distribute the banned copies of the Word there? A chill settled in her chest. He could've talked to her about it. Said goodbye. Not abandon her.

Prism handed the message back to the captain. "You're Marianna's brother?"

"Yes."

"What about the pirates?" she whispered.

"We left them in the shop."

"I heard someone yelling about pirates before I went on deck. Can I help in the fight? I'd rather not be locked in a room, simply waiting to see who wins. My..." she swallowed hard, "my father trained me as a sharpshooter and knife thrower."

The captain's brows drew together, and she thought she saw compassion in his eyes. "That's very courageous of you,

Miss Andrews, but the pirates haven't found us yet. I'm sorry you were alarmed by our mock battle. We travel through areas frequented by pirates and train often."

"The greater the risk, the greater the profit—and the fun." Philip winked at her.

"And the people in those areas are in great need of what we can get through, since fewer ships make it," Davy added.

Prism smiled weakly. "In that case, if you don't mind, I'd like a nap."

CHAPTER FIVE

*A*nd the people in those areas are in great need of what we can get through. Davy rolled his eyes. Since when did he need to justify his actions? To strange women at that. He tapped the butt of his dinner knife against the table. As soon as Marianna came out of hiding, he was going to have a talk with her about promising his help without his permission.

"She'll come," Philip said with a smile. "She's got sense, that one."

"Too much sense," Davy said, the edge to his voice drawing Philip's attention.

"What is it?"

"Someone was in my study—with the book and Star Clock."

"The machine—"

"Unharmed as far as I could tell," Davy said, "but a page is missing from the book. I noticed it after the mock attack earlier."

"Surely not the girl—"

"Why not? Who else would've had the opportunity? It was done while we were on deck."

"But if she's working for the Time Keepers, she'd have destroyed the clock and book—probably the whole ship too—not tried to run away."

"She could be working for someone else." Davy rubbed a hand through his hair. He had no doubt the circles under his eyes were darker than usual. "Even if we finish this Star Clock and get it to work, if we're not careful, and the Time Keepers don't kill us first, we'll just set up another dictator. I can think of a number of people who'd kill to get the technology for their gain instead of getting it to the world, that pirate Cavan O'Connor among them."

Philip stared out the window a moment. "Do you think maybe we aren't dreaming—praying—big enough?"

Davy huffed. "I think a clock to challenge the Rí Am and his automatons is pretty bold, and likely to get us killed."

And the people in those areas are in great need of what we can get through. A pit formed in his stomach. If they took down the Star Veil—the bigger dream—and the navigators ceased to function, who would feed those people until they re-established navigation? If they dreamed bigger, the cost would be bigger as well. But what good was half a dream? Was their dream itself, whole or half, worse than none?

"Yes, but—"

"I know," Davy said hastily. "The Star Veil itself should be our target—remove the barrier so we can see the truth for ourselves and break the curse that befuddles us. But, Philip, if we tore down the Veil, even if we could, we'd lose all the navigation we have now. How long would it take us to set it up again? Who would starve before then? We're copying books, making designs and replicates for the compass, sextant, and chronometer, but we have so few charts. Are those even accurate now? What good is knowing where we are if we don't know where we're going? We'd be just as lost. We have to have charts, and we can't make those because of the curse." They couldn't even make a sun dial like the ancients. Their shadows were dull and unmoving under the sky crystals. Would they even understand the things they'd see?

"With the curse in place, maps and clocks and knowledge won't help, Davy. It's still a three-mile limit."

"If we left the Veil, maybe we could use the knowledge and instruments to create our own automatons—"

"Freedom always comes at a price, lad. Remember Sheffield-on-the-Sea. Your own and your sister's trouble for wanting iron to protect crops from the faeries and for trying to tell time for yourself. The slaves in that crystal mine. I don't say ignore the cost, but remember what's to be gained. And the lostness would only be until we could make new maps. We'll plan ahead and work together for that. And I have a suspicion there are charts around, hidden purposefully or hidden by the curse. They'll turn up or we'll make new ones when the time comes." Philip smiled broadly. "When *time* comes, Davy. Think about that!"

Davy held his gaze for a moment, then sighed and raked his hands through his hair again before smoothing it out. "Thanks, Philip," he said ruefully. "I guess I'm just on edge, not knowing what to do about the girl."

"She—" Philip hushed as the door to the officers' mess opened, Prism and the servers on the other side.

Davy and Philip rose as Prism strolled in, looking perfectly composed. Excellent self-control or the confidence of a spy?

Smiling in welcome despite his torn thoughts, Davy seated Prism, noting how she adjusted a rotating dial on her goggles with the same habitual air as she smoothed her napkin over her lap, protecting her elegant dress. Perhaps the goggles had some special photographic capacity and she was to make a facsimile of the Star Clock's design? Or was it simply to compensate for the difference in lighting between the hallway and the dining room?

They sat silently until the first course was served. He'd banished the rest of the officers from the officers' dining room for the night, allowing more time for the lady to adjust and for them to talk freely.

"Miss Andrews—" he began.

"I've searched all my belongings and found no part or hidden message from my father about mechanics or inventions of any kind. The parts my father sent me to get were nothing out of the ordinary, and I lost them during our hasty exit." She smoothed the napkin in her lap once more, then met his gaze, her shoulders straight and stiff. "I'm sorry, Captain Bowditch. I'm afraid we were both deceived."

Davy clenched his jaw against the sympathy for her apparent pain trying to derail his critical thinking abilities. "I'm sorry as well. But you're sure there's nothing? My sister spoke very highly of you and your father and seemed to think you two held some great something, but a vow of secrecy to your father kept her from saying what. She did say she hoped your father would change his mind about keeping it a secret."

An expression of surprise flitted over Prism's face but was quickly swallowed by a determined frown. She shook her head. "That's kind of her, but I know of nothing." She turned her attention to her soup, and Davy felt an odd sense of relief. A spy would seek more information.

"Perhaps," Prism said a few minutes later, "if you tell me more about this invention of yours and its purpose, it might help me figure out what my father meant."

Davy laid his spoon aside, the soup turning sour in his stomach. She'd only been *waiting* to ask. "I'm afraid not, Miss Andrews. You were right earlier. Your father wanted a solution to a problem of his own and called in a favor to my sister."

Prism's spoon stilled halfway to her mouth. Davy just managed to ignore her rapid blinking, barely visible through the darkened goggles. He pushed on, not really liking the heavy feeling in his chest but determined not to give in to it.

"Have no fear, I'll carry out my part of the bargain. However, since I don't imagine you wish to be carted around on an airship through pirate-swarmed cloud paths, I'll see to it that you're taken to my parents' country house. It's not far from our next stop. You can spend the remainder of your year quite comfortably there." And away from his priceless work.

"You may drop me wherever you find convenient, Captain. I'll find another circus or some other work. I don't like to be idle. I doubt anyone will come for me in a year."

Miss Andrews' obvious hurt at learning of her father's bargain gnawed at Davy. She was attractive and, in a sense, in trouble. Two things calculated to make him let down his guard and trust her. He couldn't afford the risk, but nor could he afford to be distracted by an unnecessary level of distrust.

He glanced up from the GunPoof he was tinkering with

to Philip and the group of young men they had been mentoring the last few years, all cloistered with them in his workroom reading or tinkering with other inventions. He trusted Colin, Nick, and Will with his life, and his inventions and the Star Clock.

"Colin," he addressed his second mate, the former pirate who'd become a close friend, a brother to make up for the one he'd lost. "You have a set of throwing knives, don't you?"

Miss Andrews had knives and guns of a high quality. Not suspicious if she were who she claimed to be—a sharpshooter and knife thrower, among other things, for a circus. He could test her in both but didn't care to send bullets flying around on his ship. Knives didn't worry him so much. The book with its blank pages was suspicious, however. He had a hunch those empty pages weren't empty, if one knew how to look at them. He was pretty sure he knew now how to look at them. Would he find a copy of that stolen page there? He had to get her out of her room to find out though.

"Yes," Colin said. As if recognizing that Davy didn't ask the question idly, he put aside the book on force distribution he was reading—research for a bulletproof suit they were working on.

"Good. You, Nick, and Will take Miss Andrews on an uninformative tour of the ship. End up at the gymnasium. If she plans on joining another circus after leaving us, she'll need to keep fit and limber. Offer to set it up for her to practice her acrobatics and schedule her a daily private time to do so. Then challenge her to a knife throwing competition. We'll see what she can do. I don't recommend being terribly friendly, by the way. Not rude, but not too friendly, at least not until we know more about her. If she's overly friendly with you, make note of that. No one is going to charm information out of us. While she's out of her room with you three, Philip and I will investigate something in her chambers."

Colin nodded, and the three young men left. Davy grabbed his manual on steganography, and after a brief double-check, he and Philip set off for the infirmary to grab a Wood's lamp, iodine and a few other chemicals, and a candle.

Some minutes later, after ascertaining Miss Andrews was absent, they snuck into Philip's former quarters, found the book in the trunk, and removed it to the desk. While Philip gathered a few personal items he'd forgotten earlier, Davy opened the book to the fifth page, feeling more than a bit ashamed. If Miss Andrews were a good spy, he'd recognized belatedly on his walk there, any secret messages she had would be hidden within another message or image. So a blank page needn't be suspect. But that was if she were a *good* spy.

"What is it?" Philip asked as he pulled up a chair beside him and sat.

"Nothing." Davy glanced between the chemicals, the candle that could be used as a heat source, and the Wood's lamp. The ultra-violet lamp could reveal without destroying anything or leaving evidence of their intrusion. Best to start with that. Davy pulled his goggles down and switched on the lamp and held it over the book. Lines of light blue stretched and curved across a page of darker blue.

His eyebrows rose. Not a diary and not a blueprint. At least he didn't think it was a blueprint. She'd used fluorescent ink, applying it lightly with a brush to avoid pressure marks, which could imply the pages were intended to be looked at more than once, since the light could be applied multiple times without harming the paper. He skimmed the pages, but they were all similar, until the three-quarters mark, at which point the pages appeared to be truly empty. But on the rest, there were lots of curving lines, groups of triangles, and some small circles and rectangles with words next to them. A sketch of something with a radiating design and many color words and arrows next to it was often featured on the pages.

"You know how I was just grousing about a lack of maps?" Davy said as he leaned back to give Philip a better view of the pages. "Well, if I didn't know better, I'd say these were maps. But that's impossible. I've tried making maps. Every captain has, and they look like a child's attempt at a tree." He studied the pages again. If he could draw a map, this is what he'd expect it to look like. "I don't recognize many of the names either. Granted, except for when I'm home at Calandra, I spend my time traveling between cities large enough for airship ports, but still."

Philip scooted his chair closer and flipped a few pages. "I've tried making maps too. They were about as clear as a flooded river. I doubt these are maps."

Starting at the beginning, they ran over each page with greater care, looking for anything they might have missed. About halfway through, Philip traced his finger from one word to the next over a winding line. "Maybe it's an odd design for a family tree? Many of the names sound a bit like family names. Or maybe it is a map, but of an imaginary land? She could be an author. I don't think the curse would interfere with that."

"Of that many worlds? I doubt it. It could be a family tree though. But that's a lot of families." The book wasn't long or wide—he could hide it under his hand—but it was thick. "Do you think—"

The intercom came on with a click and a brush of air, then Will's voice. "Captain Bowditch, you're wanted on the bridge." He finished the message with a clearing of his throat, which meant *and be quick about it.*

Time to go.

Davy slammed the book shut, slipped it back in the trunk, gathered up the supplies he'd brought, and sprinted for the door.

"Any time you want a rematch, Miss Andrews, you just let us know." Colin's voice boomed through the wall, and Davy winced on behalf of Miss Andrews and any others close to him. For himself and Philip as well. He and Philip spun around and bolted for the windows.

"You go out first," Philip hissed at him when he opened the window and waved at him to go through it. "I at least have a reason to be sneaking about in my own room."

Accepting the wisdom of that, Davy, grateful he always wore his PullLine, leaned out the window and sent an attachment line out to the ship's hull near his own window. He pushed out and let the retracting line haul him to his room. Since Philip followed and no sound of a lady's complaint chased them, he assumed they'd gotten away with their intrusion.

Colin joined them not long after they'd collapsed into their chairs in Davy's workroom.

"Well?" Davy asked as Colin reclaimed his book and sat. Nick and Will were back on duty.

"Seems okay to me," Colin said with a confidence that eased Davy's concern. "I wondered at first if she'd actually go with us. But once she looked us over, she lost that bit of initial wariness. I got the feeling she's met a lot of people, some better than others, and knows how to read people. She seemed comfortable with us, not talkative though. Didn't try to charm us either," he finished with a bit of a smile. He hesitated, then said quickly as he lifted his book in front of his face and settled deeper into his chair, "She's definitely a knife thrower."

Davy quirked a smile. "Good then?"

"If I still bet, I wouldn't bet against her."

Davy considered everything they'd learned about their passenger, then let out a long breath. He wasn't going to be taking Miss Andrews into his confidence any time soon, but he didn't feel a need to keep her under lock and key.

CHAPTER SIX

"We've just gotten a ping, Captain." The airman rushed into the dining room, disturbing their breakfast, which, like the last two weeks, had been quiet. The captain and Philip had been pleasant, though distant, companions. Or rather she and the captain had been distant. Philip tended to be gregarious when he could get either to talk.

The young airman held a hand-sized metal box topped with a horn similar to that on a phonograph. Prism's stomach tightened, something about his manner, a mixture of eagerness and fear, alarming her. Just what was a *ping*?

"How long do we have?" Davy tossed his napkin onto the table as he rose, Philip doing likewise.

"Not long, sir, but not imminent."

"Miss Andrews." Davy turned to her. "I suggest you change into something more suitable for a pirate attack. Philip, please see that the *cargo* is secured, and stay with it."

"What's a *ping*?" Prism asked as she rose, Philip pulling her chair out for her. "What has that to do with pirates?"

Prism barely stopped a gasp as Philip slipped the handle of a throwing knife into her palm. He winked at her, then followed the captain to the door.

"Look after yourself, Davy," Philip said, clapping the captain on the shoulder, distracting him while Prism stowed the knife in her skirt pocket. "And don't neglect our guest." He grinned at her, then left.

Davy turned back to her, and Prism forced a bright smile. His brow furrowed. She toned down the smile. "A ping, Captain?"

He raised an eyebrow, shot a look after Philip, then held out his arm to her. "We send signals through the air; they bounce back to us when they hit something. It's how bats fly and find food. It tells us another ship is hiding in the clouds."

A ping meant pirates.

Where was the closest parachute?

Stiffening her spine, she tossed the idea overboard. She had offered to help, and she would. She took Davy's arm.

Feeling the captain's eyes on her as he escorted her to her quarters, Prism wondered if he was regretting his bargain with her father. She lifted her chin. She was not going to get in the way or faint or go into hysterics. She hoped.

As they reached the door to her quarters, he gave her hand a gentle squeeze and then released her. "We've not lost a fight yet, Miss Andrews. We'll see that you're kept safe, even if in an unconventional manner."

Prism glared up at him, wondering vaguely if her glares would be as effective without the threat of her father to back them up. "You are *not* locking me in my room."

They'd obviously lost their effect, for one corner of the captain's mouth curved. "I wouldn't dream of it. There's a window that opens." He winked at her, a charming twinkle in his brown eyes. Prism's mouth dropped open. He bowed, then strode away, a confidence in his manner that soothed her concerns despite herself. He disappeared around a corner.

Belatedly, Prism huffed. *A window that opens,* indeed.

"Wear something that allows for freedom of movement," he called back to her, making Prism jump. Huffing again, she hurried inside, butterflies of two different kinds swarming in her stomach.

Prism changed into an appropriate costume, collected her small pistol and belted on the knife. It was one of hers. The captain and his men hadn't searched her, but they'd apparently searched her trunks. Had they returned everything to her?

A few minutes later, dressed in boots, loose trousers, a vest and blouse, and a jacket, Prism stepped onto the deck and adjusted her goggles to match the outdoor lighting, dim though it was through the clouds. Down the deck a ways, Davy and his men stood in conference beside a long, cylindrical weapon of some sort. Its horizontally elongated arm was partly covered by a tarp and mounted on a swivel base. A giant coil of rope lay in a bucket beside it. A modified harpoon gun? What did they hope to spear in the air?

"What say you, men?" The captain's cheerful question arrested her attention. "Colin? Shall we employ Chance today?"

While the majority of sailors whooped, Colin, the tall blond with the wrist tattoo and passable knife throwing skills, nodded, a strangely earnest look on his face. At least three others shared that look.

A man's whistle captured the airmen's attention and flung it to Prism, where it stayed. Her jaw tightened. The stares always took a while to get used to, even after a lifetime of performances and wearing goggles everywhere. Despite having been on board two weeks, she hadn't mingled with the crew; they were strangers to each other. She ate with Davy and Philip, sometimes being joined by the three men who'd given her a tour; took her scheduled exercise alone; and occasionally joined Davy and Philip in the evenings. The crew's stares were friendly and kind, but she didn't particularly like being the center of attention, unless it was during her act.

"Gentlemen, Miss Abigail Andrews, our guest until Calandra, is bravely joining our fight today." Davy stepped to her side, not in the protective way her father often had, but in a comforting way, his manner declaring she could trust his men. "Miss Andrews, allow me to formally introduce my men, the crew of the *Dawn Singer*, the fastest, highest flying airship in the skies."

The pride in his voice made her smile. The tightness in her chest eased, until she met his gaze and noted the caution there. Could his men trust her? it asked. What had she done to deserve that look?

Amid the chorus of welcomes, someone cried, "Let her do it. She'd get us a good one. She's a lucky gal, I can tell."

The captain's eyes shuttered, and a shiver raced down Prism's back. "Would you like to do the honors, Miss Andrews? You claimed marksmanship skills earlier. Here's your chance to prove them." He gestured to the harpoon gun.

"What would I be aiming at?" Prism looked past the grinning sailors to the clouds cloaking the ship approaching on the port side. Slight shadows altered the grays and whites of the cloud, its edges growing. An airship was nearing them and fast.

"The pirate's ship, of course, or rather one pirate in particular, whichever one happens to be in the right spot on the deck."

Prism cast a look of horror at the harpoon gun, its merciless tip still hidden. "That's barbaric."

"My dear Miss Andrews, need I remind you that these are pirates? That they're about to attack us? That you agreed to help defend the ship?"

"If we made ourselves easy to find, what does that matter?" An airman laughed.

"But they can't even see you!" Prism protested. "It would be like stabbing a man in the back. And with a harpoon! I repeat, that's barbaric."

"They've been hunting us, Miss Andrews. If we choose to strike first, what of it? It *is* part of my duties as an airship captain to protect the skies." He led her by the elbow toward the harpoon. "Choose your target wisely. Chance hasn't failed us yet."

Prism planted her feet and crossed her arms. "I'll not use that."

He pointed to the darkening area she'd spotted earlier. "The ship's just through the clouds there."

"I'll not use it."

Davy shrugged, and she almost thought a corner of his mouth was trying to twitch up. "The lady refuses Second Chance, lads, though I've always considered it my best invention. Colin, it's up to you. Strike fast, for they'll be upon us soon."

"But, Captain—" she began. Davy took a firm hold of her arm, and she shut her mouth.

Colin lost no time in stepping to the harpoon and sweeping off its cover, but Prism refused to look at its tip, focusing instead on the blond airman. He aimed toward the growing shadow, bent his head as if in prayer, then released the harpoon.

Prism's stomach twisted as the rope uncoiled loop by loop. A man's scream tore through the fog. And grew louder. And full of curses and threats.

"Watch your heads, men," Davy cried as a black mass bound with ropes and netting hurtled over the bow and sank into the starboard clouds.

As the men raced to the side, grumbling that they couldn't see for the clouds and guffawing about something, a moan and a hair-raising screech ripped from the very heart of the airship. Prism gasped and covered her mouth with her hand.

Davy patted her shoulder. "There, there, Miss Andrews. It's nothing for you to worry about, just a Banshee we've tamed." His lips twitched, the earlier caution in his eyes having given way to a teasing twinkle.

"Don't 'there, there,' me." Prism shoved him away. He rocked back on his heels, then took a step back, grinning. "Circus performers aren't the only ones who deal in illusions, I see, Captain Bowditch. That person dangling over the side is alive, I take it? That wasn't a harpoon but a net."

He shrugged. "If one of your fellow pirates vanished from the deck as if grabbed by a spectral hand, and then you heard such a moan and wail through the mist, would you not be tempted to tuck tail and run?" His grin turned smug. "We hardly have to fight at all."

"Yes, but you could have told—"

Boom!

Davy pulled Prism down beside him as a projectile barely missed the port bow.

"Tuck tail and run, Captain?" Prism said shakily as Davy helped her to her feet.

"I did say *hardly*." Davy yelled across the deck, "Parachutes, men! Prepare for action."

"It's got to be O'Connor," one of the airmen yelled. "Only he's ornery enough to drop an airship without taking the cargo."

"The pirate whose men were in the parts store?" Prism asked as she ran with Davy to the parachutes. Even she'd heard about the pirate Cavan O'Connor.

"He doesn't care for me," Davy answered quickly.

"Captain Bowditch stole his best gunner from him." An airman guffawed as he tossed Davy a parachute.

"Who also happened to be his only son," another chimed in. "Snatched him right off the deck and let him be presumed dead."

"What?" Prism tried to read Davy's face, but he kept his head down as he strapped a parachute on her.

"This is no time for explanations. Peter, is the Escaper ready?"

"Yes, Captain." He handed Davy a parachute.

"Right. Colin *O'Connor's* in charge here. Miss Andrews and I are going over. We'll be back shortly."

"Going where?" Prism asked as Davy dragged her into the bowels of the *Dawn Singer*, down corridor after corridor until she felt the weight of the entire vessel above her. "The pirate ship?"

"Where else would you suggest, Miss Andrews? If pirates are boarding *your* ship, naturally, the safest place to be is on *their* ship."

Prism pursed her lips. Teasing man. "So you're abandoning your crew to fight alone? I'd thought better of you than that, Captain Bowditch." She barely managed not to bump into him as he spun around.

"That's not—" He caught her gaze, which was a touch impish. Frowning, he tugged her forward again. "We need something from the other ship, and I'm the best one to get it."

"That's not much of an answer."

"I'm saving my breath for speed, as you should."

He led her into a hold made narrow by the miniature airships filling it. With a bottom like a wooden boat, each Escaper had two benches and a small shelf in the back, enough seating for five men. It had a propeller in back and a glass windscreen in front protecting the control panel. A folded leather topper padded the craft's sides, ready to be pulled up at need to make a closed cylinder of the ship. A steel beam arced over the craft, forming a spine for a pair of wings, folded and as brightly smeared with color as an oil sheen when the sky crystals were at full glow. The Escaper sat on wheels, making it seem like the decorated toy wagon of a boy who dreamed of flying.

Prism turned her attention back to the hold. Shelves lined one wall, large red buttons the other. Davy grabbed a box labeled "PullLine" off one of the shelves, drew out a metal-and-leather gauntlet and harness and fastened the gauntlet around her arm, leaving her to secure the chest harness. He snatched a crate off the bottom shelf, and Prism spied another of the small machines with the phonograph horn, a few pairs of odd shoes, and a baseball in it before he urged her into the copilot's seat in the craft.

She buckled herself in and kept her hand well away from

the controls in front of her. "I'm quite competent as a trapeze artist, but I'm a touch rusty on piloting."

"Hopefully, you won't need to brush up on it. Hold tight." After stowing the crate under his seat, he handed her the ping reader and hurled the baseball at a large red button on the wall. The baseball depressed the button and fell into a basket below it. The floor underneath them dropped away.

The familiar thrill of a plunge surged through Prism, and for one moment it was the circus's sandy ring below her, her partner's outstretched arms, and the awed gasps of the crowd around her. Then the cries of Chance's victim—and a recording of what sounded like Holy Scripture—blasted her out of her pleasant dream of being at home.

They dropped about thirty feet before wings stretched themselves wide and propellers whirred into motion and sent them through the thick clouds toward the belly of the pirate ship.

"Wind up the ping reader using the crank on its side and watch for it to indicate we're under the pirate ship. I don't want to fly too far past it."

Prism did as requested, though she was able to see the ship's influence on the grays of the cloud cover as well as the reader could detect it. She pointed out the ship just as the reader pinged, earning her a strange look from Davy. He piloted the Escaper just port-side of the pirate ship. Taking one hand off the controls, he launched a line from his gauntlet, attaching it beside a porthole, and then did the same with a line attached to the Escaper's bow. He dove back down, directly under the pirate vessel, and docked the Escaper against the hull.

"All right, Miss Andrews," he said, strapping on the odd shoes. "Here's where you earn your keep. Guard the

Escaper. If I'm not back before the battle's won, well ... there's a manual on how to fly this thing in the box under the seat."

"But—"

He yanked twice on his PullLine, scampered up the Escaper, and jogged up the side of the pirate ship, using the PullLine to reel himself up. His long blue coat flying out behind him, he disappeared around the curve of the hull.

Another boom concussed the air, and Prism got the feeling the captain was walking into more danger than he'd bargained for. And that he had a good reason for doing so. But what was it?

CHAPTER SEVEN

Davy loved climbing. And sneaking into pirate ships. And the fact that pirates didn't bother to guard the bridge and its automaton.

He hoisted himself through the bridge porthole and looked around. The pirate's automaton—programmed with the flight path of whatever merchant vessel they chose thanks to hefty bribes and threats to Time Keeper Station clerks—sat at the controls.

He'd have to explode it before leaving so the pirates couldn't follow them. If he exploded it now, would he be able to find useful parts scattered about the room when he came back through after getting the pirates' parts chest?

"If you're here for an automaton, I'd suggest searching the captain's cabin for ones stolen from captured ships."

Davy spun around, drawing his revolver.

Standing six feet away, hands on her hips, Prism smirked at him. "The highwaymen we've encountered like to keep automatons. I figure pirates are the same, always hoping to discover the automatons' secrets to find a way around paying the bribes."

"What are you doing here?" Davy exclaimed in a shout of a whisper. "You're supposed to be safe in the Escaper!"

She held out a folded piece of yellowed paper. "I found this stuffed into the extra pair of shoes in the box. It smells of nectar, sickeningly sweet. Like a faerie trove. Like that gunnysack Marianna and Bertram guarded so carefully. You're trying to build something for navigation, aren't you?"

In a shoe ... then maybe she is innocent. He frowned to repress the stupid smile that threatened. It had been harder than he'd cared to admit to keep up his guard against her the last two weeks, especially with Philip always trying to drag him into conversation with her. "Are you sure you didn't place it there after ripping it from a priceless book in my quarters?"

Both shock and anger flitted across her face. "I don't make a habit of visiting gentlemen's quarters, Captain, or ripping pages from books." She thrust the page at him, and he took it, noting the dried rice grains stuck to it, which brought another wave of relief. "The question should be why *you* hid this *in a shoe.*"

What would this spunky young woman look like—awake —without those goggles? He shook himself. "Later, Miss Andrews. Now, you must choose to either break a habit or return to the Escaper." Davy spun around and jogged to the door, cautiously opening it.

Seeing no one about, he eased into the hallway and ran lightly down it, both pleased and terrified to hear his co-conspirator's footfalls behind him. *Bring us both safely through this day, Lord, especially her.*

Davy sought back in his memory for the plans of the

various ships his family had designed, and especially to the one O'Connor had stolen years ago. He found the captain's cabin in his mental map and guided them in that direction. He slowed before the hallway to the cabin, gunfire and yells drifting down to them from the deck.

"There'll be a man guarding the captain's room. You distract him"—he tapped her PullLine, and Prism nodded —"and I'll take care of him. Go."

They darted around the corner, and Prism launched her PullLine at the pirate pacing in front of a door and yanked it back as soon as it attached to him. He crashed to the floor. Davy raced to him and cracked him on the head with the butt of his revolver. He shot the lock and kicked in the door.

Empty. No one even opened the door to the inner chamber to take a shot at him. Strange.

Motioning for Prism to stay outside, he crept to the room's center, glancing around. No pirates or chests, only a wardrobe. He waved Prism forward and strode toward the inner chamber. The wardrobe door cracked open. A gun barrel edged out.

"Look out!" Prism yelled. Davy spun around, then lurched back as a bullet pierced his arm. His gun hit the floor as a pirate sprang from the wardrobe. Prism sent her knife into the pirate's shoulder and lunged for the dropped revolver.

"Leave it." The command came from behind. A burly man with a wrist tattoo stepped from the inner chamber. Another entered from the hallway.

Prism stood slowly, raising her hands. Davy pressed his fingers against his wound, stemming the red flow, his nostrils flaring as he forced himself to breathe through the pain.

The pirate waved his gun between Davy and Prism.

"Bandage his arm. We don't want blood all over the floor. In here."

Prism did as directed, using her handkerchief. Davy met her gaze. *I'm sorry.* She gave him a weak smile.

The man from the outer doorway collected Davy's dropped gun from near Prism's feet. Davy pulled Prism to his other side with his uninjured arm, away from the staring pirate.

"Poor Captain O'Connor said you'd come." The burly man pulled Prism's knife from his companion's shoulder and handed the man his handkerchief. "It would've pleased him to know you'd get to see your ship go down before we made you walk the plank—without a parachute. But maybe not the girl."

The blood drained from Davy's face. Prism stiffened beside him, and he cursed himself for not making her return to the Escaper, or at least giving her her own gun. It had more shots than her little derringer.

A weight on his belt came to his attention, but it was on his injured side. He slid his arm from Prism's shoulder to her waist and tapped her hip. She edged away. "Even if you don't care about my men," he pleaded, "surely you want our cargo. Keep the airship afloat long enough to get it. That'll give my men time to escape. *Please.*" He tapped Prism's hip again. This time, she slipped her arm between his shirt and jacket and around his waist, feeling for the gun he'd hidden there. "You have no quarrel against them. Keep me, but let them and Miss Andrews go." *Please let them escape, Lord, and Philip with the clock and ... book.*

"Wait! Let me speak with O'Connor. I have something on board he'll want to know about—I'm working on a machine to help us navigate ourselves."

The pirate's face darkened. "The airship goes down, a funeral pyre to our captain and his son. You think yourself so righteous, Bowditch, but you killed them both before the fighting had even begun. There's no honor in that."

"O'Connor's dead?" Davy sucked in a breath. "*Second Chance!* Your captain's not dead. He's—"

Prism slipped the gun from his belt and kicked him behind the knee, sending him to the floor. Shots rang out above Davy as he crawled for the gun the burly pirate dropped. Before he got to it, three pirates lay on the floor, each with a shoulder and leg wound.

Prism stepped around him and snatched up the gun as Davy gaped.

"We're ... um ... going to have to work on your aim, Miss Andrews."

"There's nothing wrong with my aim, Captain." Prism held out her hand to him, a smug twist to her lips, and Davy almost forgot to take her hand. A bolt of pain when he finally did reach with his right arm did wonders for his focus.

He struggled to his feet, collected his gun, and grabbed Prism's hand. He turned to the pirates. "Captain O'Connor's alive. If you want to keep him that way, stop the bombardment of my airship. Otherwise, he's going down with it. Colin too."

He and Prism sprinted back to the bridge.

"What about the automatons and parts?" Prism asked.

"No time. We'll have to bargain with O'Connor once we stop the fight." Davy locked the bridge door behind them. "We can grab this one though." He and Prism yanked the automaton from its chair and strapped it to Davy's back, then climbed out the blessedly wide porthole.

"You're horribly pale," Prism said as they dropped into

their seats in the Escaper. "What do you need me to do, Captain?"

"Please call me Davy. You've more than earned it." His hand trembled as he wiped sweat out of his eyes and took hold of the controls. "As for what to do, watch the ping reader. We're going just past the airship and picking up O'Connor." He released a lever on the control panel, and the Escaper dropped with a rush.

They leveled out, then rocketed up and over the airships to avoid falling projectiles, then dipped beyond the *Dawn Singer*. "Miss Andrews," Davy said as they slowed and hunted among the clouds for Chance's prize. "I apologize if I was rude and hurtful when discussing your father. I'm building a Star Clock to keep accurate time so we can know something called longitude. That's treason to the Time King and a treasure to those who'd want to replace him themselves. When you had nothing to help with the Star Clock, I feared I'd been duped, that you were a spy, and when that page went missing, I feared you'd taken it. I don't now. There's a mostly reformed old pirate-turned-cook on board whose eccentricity is to steal things and hide them in shoes.

"And the harpoon gun—Second Chance and Redemption, it's called—isn't for killing but for giving pirates a good scare and uninterrupted exposure to Scripture while in a ... uh ... open frame of mind. I did steal Colin O'Connor that way. He chose to stay with me. We both felt it best if his father thought him dead. I'm sorry for the danger you're in, but I'm not sorry your father sent you."

Prism stared at him a moment, her thoughts impossible to guess under her goggles, but then she smiled a sad smile, and covered Davy's hand with hers. "Thanks, Davy. I wish I had what you need, and you can call me Prism. I see more colors than most, and I can see differences in—There he is! Captain O'Connor!"

"Curse you, Bowditch! You're going to get us all killed!" O'Connor roared as they approached.

"Not today, I hope." Davy released him into the Escaper and left the nets dangling as they soared back over to O'Connor's airship.

CHAPTER EIGHT

"And I want my automaton back." Seated in Davy's study, Captain Cavan O'Connor braced his hand on his knee and leaned toward Davy. After a day to see to their ships and injured men, Davy and O'Connor had met again, as agreed, having tethered their airships together so as to not lose the automaton-less pirate ship.

"Not with my route programmed into it." Davy's smile turned into a flinch as he lifted a steaming cup of coffee to his mouth with his injured arm. He switched the cup to his other hand. He felt naked without a weapon—well, something more substantial than hot liquid—in or near his hand at the best of times, but especially with pirates on his ship. But O'Connor had come unarmed, and he was, in some ways, a man of honor. So Davy would have to trust him and suffer through being weaponless.

Of course, neither was alone. A burly pirate stood beside O'Connor. Philip sat beside Davy; Colin stood behind him. Cavan O'Connor cast rather sentimental glances at his son when he thought no one was watching. Davy repressed a smile. So the scruffy old pirate had a heart after all.

A box of parts and a pile of automatons, some whole but most in segments, formed a mound between the two groups. Apparently, if one cut off the head first, they didn't explode when one tried to open them. Who knew?

Prism, back in a rather fetching cobalt blue dress, knelt beside the pile, examining the crystals studding the automatons' chests. He'd convinced her to abandon her goggles unless she needed them. Now he only had to convince her to look people in the eye without them.

O'Connor's arguments plunged into silence as he joined Davy in watching Prism. Her fingers hovered over a particular crystal in the chest of O'Connor's current automaton. Her jaw clenched.

"What is it, Prism?" Davy rejoiced inwardly when Prism looked him in the eye ... and he didn't flinch. He smiled, and she shifted her gaze, which hardened into a glare, to O'Connor.

"You were going to Amezak, weren't you?" she said.

The man actually squirmed. And looked contrite. "I'm sorry, lass. One of your mates tipped us off about you going with the captain and the prince's reward for you. How did you—"

Prism touched a crystal. "You have the Amezak crystal."

"Her bloody eyes," O'Connor whispered, gaping. Prism dropped her gaze.

"There's nothing wrong with her eyes," Davy exclaimed. "They're beautiful. As soon as you get used to them."

O'Connor rolled his eyes. "Besotted fool. I meant, they're exactly what we need." He caught Prism's gaze. "There's a different crystal for each port of call, isn't there?

But how did you know? They're all the same size and shape. We've checked."

"They're slightly different colors." When O'Connor protested, Prism shook her head. "I see more colors than anyone else, even my father. The crystals in the automaton's chest and in the night sky may all be the same to you, but I see faint colors there, differentiating them. I don't know why. A certain kind of faerie blood perhaps; more than a drop of it on both sides.

"I've traveled all my life. I noticed patterns in the automatons' crystals and the sky crystals. Each automaton has a crystal matching the sky crystal for a particular city, a crystal to find a reference point, and one for itself." She hesitated, then met Davy's eye, and he got the feeling she had a bigger secret she was about to share, and he was beginning to suspect what it was. "I can make maps and navigate more than three miles because I use the sky crystals themselves. It's a strain, but I can do it. For a ways, at least."

Davy stared at Prism, then laughed. "Your father wasn't sending me a part. He was sending me you! *Have solution. Prism.* He meant *you* were the solution. He knew we needed you, that you weren't safe in the circus, and he just couldn't bear to say goodbye. He didn't abandon you."

Prism blushed and ducked away from Davy's admiring gaze. "Except for the maps I can make," she said, "I'm not sure how my gift will aid in the long-term solution you're hoping for."

"It will," Davy said with a smile. "The maps too. You don't know how much they'll help."

She smiled back at him, then continued, turning to O'Connor, "Once the port has been reached, or forbidden by the Time Keepers, the crystal cracks and dulls. I imagine it's no longer usable." She pointed to a crystal in a dismembered automaton. "This is for Sheffield-on-the-Sea. It's not cracked. Not being in use, the navigator didn't receive the order against that port."

"What!" With a joyous cry, Philip dragged Prism up and danced around the room with her. Davy rescued her and seated her beside himself, and was pleased when she didn't scoot away from him.

O'Connor alone looked grave. "You're in a hurry to get supplies to Sheffield-on-the-Sea and build the Star Clock"— he paused, picked up Davy's book from the table beside him, and removed the torn page tucked inside the cover—"but you'll need more than that." He stood and handed the folded page to his son.

Colin unfolded it and spent a moment reading over it. "It tells how to build something called a sextant for calculating something called latitude." He paused. "Miss Andrews, can you see Polaris, or the Southern Cross?"

Prism shook her head.

"What's Polaris?" Philip asked.

"With Miss Andrews's help, we might be able to get to places we have crystals for," O'Connor said, "but even with a hundred Prisms and Star Clocks, the Star Veil will still conceal and befuddle." O'Connor turned to Davy. "I think there's something else you're—we're—supposed to do, Captain: take down the Star Veil itself."

The room exploded into questions, with Davy's "How?" being the loudest.

O'Connor's whiskered, weathered face crinkled into an unfamiliar pattern: a smile. "You're not robbing me of all my secrets at once, boy."

"Don't try me," Davy growled, fighting back a grin.

O'Connor barked a laugh. "You captured me fair and square, so by rights I must answer you, I suppose." He shook his head grimly. "And to think I owe this idea to the Vanons themselves." He roused himself, then focused on Davy. "When I was a boy, I knew one of the Vanon family. Each member of the Vanon family meets with their accursed ancestor once or twice a year. I bullied the boy into asking the Rí Am to read a book from his private collection, just to prove he wasn't afraid of the old man. He asked, and Ulrik Vanon gave him one hour with his choice of books. The book he chose was on faerie spells and faerie-created things.

"According to what he read, the Star Veil, if the faerie queen cast it as you say, would have to be a curse-creation, a real thing with magic woven into it, and since it's such a big thing, it would have to be anchored to the earth, likely to a tree, at or near the queen's faerie mound. And it follows that it would be easiest to destroy at its smallest point—its anchor."

"But legend claims the faerie mound's on an uncharted island!" Davy exclaimed. "That we'd only find by chance or curse! Even if we found the island, we probably couldn't see this Star Veil anchor, much less destroy it."

Philip's pinched expression eased, and he leaned over to whisper to Prism. "Aye, so he thinks it can be done then. Davy always points out the biggest issues first in that petulant tone when he thinks it can be done but hasn't figured out how yet. It's as if he thinks whining will make the answers present themselves."

Davy jerked around to glare at his first mate.

"Just giving the girl a lesson on how to understand you," Philip said with an unabashed shrug of his shoulders. He elbowed Colin, who was busy clearing his throat.

A slight smile tugged at the corners of Prism's mouth. She turned to O'Connor. "Could I see it?"

"I don't know about that, lass. Those with a touch of faerie blood might see the Star Veil at its anchor, I suppose, so you might. But as to the captain's other argument, I'm pretty sure it could be destroyed with iron."

"So," Davy said, with more excitement than complaint this time, "we need to find an island that's impossible to find —even if we could navigate ourselves—and destroy a curse anchor we can't see, with iron, which we don't have." He rubbed his hands together. "I've always wanted an impossible quest."

O'Connor leaned back, shaking his head. "*We* can be a narrow or broad term, lad. You're going to need help. You and Miss Prism there must get food to Sheffield-on-the-Sea before those good people starve, and you must let me take you there. And then let me take you everywhere Miss Prism still needs to map out. If the Time Keepers were after you in Dondre, they'll be after you anywhere you stop. It wasn't hard to get crystals to find you—the Time King wouldn't mind if something fatal happened to you, I suspect. Let Colin finish your route. He can tell people you and Miss Prism were taken for her reward. Don't scowl, lad, she'll never get to Amezak.

"I think you'll find I and my brethren can help you finish this Star Clock and keep the two of you safe. Everyone knows I hate you for supposedly killing my son. My airship is the last place they'd think you'd be. We want to be free of the Rí Am as much as you. Let your Sky Keeper network know about all this; they can help figure out the faerie queen's island and so on. Colin, if he hasn't intentionally forgotten, can use my connections to get the iron for the Star Veil."

"I have connections of my own to get the iron," Davy said smugly.

O'Connor's eyebrows rose, then his eyes twinkled. "Of course. I'd forgotten. That's partly why your sister's on the run. You smuggle for the Sky Keepers. Captain Bowditch, I've a new regard for you. You're neither a Pharisee nor a hypocrite."

"The regard of a pirate is a dubious thing, yet I thank you, sir. But I think you're right. Marianna and Bertram need time to study, copy, and distribute the books and equipment they found, traveling and getting help from others for that. Removing the Star Veil before the world's ready with an alternative method of travel would be disastrous. We've got to feed the people of Sheffield-on-the-Sea and figure out how to work the old navigation methods first."

"What about the mine on Sheffield-on-the-Sea?" Philip asked. "I hate to think of those men enslaved there any longer. On *my* island."

Davy frowned. "We can't risk an open assault, even if we could find it. Now that we know the crystals are necessary for automatons to navigate, we know the importance of that mine, or mines if there are more elsewhere. We can't close down production without stopping all trade and travel—and we know that would hurt a lot of people dependent on it. We'll have to strike there last, but we will free them. We'll just have to pray for a miracle, that all plans are ready soon."

O'Connor's eyes twinkled again. "I think it interesting that your miracle involves a pirate."

"Perhaps *that* is the miracle," Davy said with a smile.

PART III
SKY KEEPER

"For as high as the heavens are above the earth, so great is
his steadfast love toward those who fear him;
as far as the east is from the west, so far does he remove our
transgressions from us.
Psalm 103:11-12

CHAPTER ONE

Even for those who knew Scripture, "as far as the east is from the west" was a mystery to them, for all such things as time and direction were obscured by the faerie queen's Star Veil. Long had it concealed and lied. But the time of unraveling had come. Men and women of courage, who loved the Truth, were rising, ready to fight for freedom and true light, and they were call Sky Keepers.

An airship port town of Rìoghachd Criostail
Four months later

"Y
ou've killed the last of the Bowditch line, Colin O'Connor." The man with the balding pate and breath reeking of spirits took a step toward Colin and his first mate, Philip Orren, and shook his fist at them. "We'll not be helping you now, lest it be to a Time Keeper jail or an unmarked grave."

For the third time in as many days, Colin felt as if he'd been shoved over the side of his airship and had just hit the ground. Did everyone still think so ill of him? Three years it'd been since Davy Bowditch's invention, the modified harpoon Second Chance and Redemption, had snatched him off his father's airship, the pirate ship *Breaker*. Since he'd become a new man as Scripture promised. Must his old life try to kill him—and the Sky Keepers' hopes—even now?

"You don't understand, sir," Colin said, too desperate now for the anger that had accompanied the first such accusation he'd received. "You've got to help us find those iron harpoons. We'll pay your exorbitant price, but we need them. For the sake of the Sky Keepers, for everyone. Captain Bowditch's my greatest friend. I didn't hurt him. He even told me to come to you before he left in the Escaper." *He's safe! But only so long as the Time Keepers think he's dead.*

"This is what I think of you and your lies." The smuggler spat on the warehouse floor and advanced a step. Two of his sons, both as burly as their father, did the same.

Philip grasped Colin's shoulder and whispered, "His youngest son was taken by Time Keepers last week and never came back. In his grief, he's looking for a fight."

"But he's the last of Davy's smuggler contacts."

"But not your father's."

Colin swallowed the bile rising in his throat. *Was the iron worth it? It'll tear the Star Veil loose and set us free, you cowardly idiot.* Not getting the iron also meant he'd failed the one task both Davy, his friend and mentor, and his father had given him. He'd do whatever it took to get it. Except return to his pirate ways. But he'd been hiding for three years among the godly men of the *Dawn Singer*. It was time he got over the fear he'd go back to his old ways if around his old companions.

Philip jerked his head toward the exit. Colin nodded. They ran out of the darkened warehouse.

REYDON, CAPITAL OF RÌOGHACHD CRIOSTAIL
ONE MONTH LATER

COLIN DUCKED A BLOW. The third one in as many seconds. "Cavan O'Connor's my favorite cousin and the bravest of all the pirate captains."

Colin dodged another of Latimer Harrison's punches. The middle-aged smuggler liked to finish his speeches before actually pummeling his foes. That didn't stop him from decorating the pontification with foreshadows.

"And you, his only son," Latimer continued with a right hook, "breaking his heart and nearly driving him mad with grief, letting him believe you were dead."

Darting away from a kick, Colin bumped into one of Latimer's sons. The stone-faced man shoved Colin back toward Latimer. Colin jerked to a stop just before ramming the man. He tipped forward, but then rolled back on his heels. He was as tall and almost as broad as Latimer, but he couldn't afford to get into a brawl with a smuggler with four sons and two hired hands. Not even with Philip to back him up. And Latimer's parlor didn't provide a lot of space for maneuvering.

"Please, if you'll just listen—" Colin began, feeling more like a dancer in a boxing ring than a captain trying to arrange a smuggling deal.

"Don't say it's because you wanted to change your ways, for everybody knows how you stole the Bowditch airship for yourself. Cavan would've let you go honest if you'd wanted, but pretending so as you could get a ship, that's lower than even a Time Keeper or drug runner."

Colin's insides went cold.

Apparently finished with talking, Latimer reared back for real this time. Colin braced himself. His father had always taught him to take it like a man. Men like Latimer Harrison were worse on cowards.

"Ahhh." Scowling, Latimer lowered his fist. "You're worse than a stinking maggot, but you're my cousin's son. I'll not strike you. Throw them out, boys." He spat on Colin and turned his back on him. His sons lost no time in carrying out his wish, ejecting Colin and Philip through the front doorway with all the requisite force and expediency.

Having bypassed the steps, the two airmen landed half on the path to the gate and half in the front garden.

"I'll never regain my dignity," Philip murmured, rubbing his hip as he sat up.

"Worry about that after we've cleared the next block." Ignoring his burning cheeks and aching body, Colin stood and pulled Philip up beside him. He wiped the spit off his cheek, unable to find any anger against Latimer. Had he really hurt his father that much? Deserve the suspicion of everyone who knew his past?

Overhead, the sky crystals were beginning to dim, enough that the bland white of the day sky was quickly changing into a faintly dotted checkerboard of neatly arranged sky crystals, the night sky. Colin didn't think it wise to be around the Harrisons' neighborhood after the dimming. They set a brisk pace and had gained the next street when a sharp *psst* arrested their progress.

One of Latimer's sons, the one with the wan, sickly look

who'd stood toward the back of the room, jogged after them. Neil was his name, if Colin remembered rightly from his occasional childhood visits.

"Wait," Neil said, panting.

Studying Neil as he caught his breath, Colin couldn't help but wonder if the wan look was due to a physical illness or something else. There was something not quite wholesome about the young man's eyes.

"Well," Colin said. "What do you want? Your father might not like to see you with us."

Neil huffed. "The old man doesn't like a lot of things." He briefly met Colin's scrutiny before glancing around, his gaze finally landing near Colin's ears. "But his bluster doesn't always last. You still want the iron? You got the cash?"

"No," Philip said under his breath. "We enjoy these excursions with smugglers."

"Yes, but we don't have the cash on us," Colin answered warily. "We figured we'd pay half upfront to go to the ironmonger for supplies and the rest on delivery."

Neil leaned forward. "After the shipment of iron fencing to Sheffield-on-the-Sea went down with the *Dawn Bringer*"—he leered at Colin—"that Bowditch ship escaped you, didn't it?"

Colin narrowed his eyes at him.

Neil leaned back and licked his lips. "Anyway. The ironmonger made a second set of iron fencing to send, but now the Time Keepers have stopped all travel to Sheffield-on-the-Sea. The iron's just sitting in one of our warehouses."

And you want us to pay for donated iron? But the Harrisons were the last smugglers of all Davy's and his father's contacts. "How much?"

Neil's answer made Colin's hands fist. He walked away before he could hit the kid, a more vocal Philip following.

"Wait!" Neil ran around Colin and planted himself in front of him. "You wouldn't have come if you had any other options."

Colin's fingers itched, visions of him grabbing Neil by the shirtfront and slamming him into various hard surfaces bringing a certain amount of pleasure. And disgust.

For as high as the heavens are above the earth, so great is his steadfast love toward those who fear him; as far as the east is from the west, so far does he remove our transgressions from us.

Taking a slow, deep breath, Colin flexed his fingers. He hadn't even known what *east* and *west* were until reading the books Marianna and Bertram had found, and he was still hazy on where they were, but he figured they were a long ways apart. If the Creator had seen fit to separate the guilt of his transgressions from him that far, and by his own Son's blood, Colin ought to at least separate himself and the doing of any further transgressions that far.

"Who's the ironmonger?" Colin ground out.

Neil laughed. "Do you think I'd tell you? Sell what you have to, but bring me the money tomorrow at Hammerhead Pub. I'll fix it with Pa and tell you which warehouse it's in."

"You'll get a modest commission, I suppose?" Philip asked.

The man sneered but otherwise ignored him. A sick feeling twisted Colin's gut. The kid was going to win the bout. But not that easily.

"Half that amount," Colin said. "Take it or keep wasting storage space."

They dickered for a bit, finally settling on an exorbitant

fee, but one more in line with what Colin anticipated. Neil agreed to get the fencing refashioned into harpoons, though it would add a few days to their wait.

They parted, and Colin and Philip made their way to the docks, discussing how they could get the needed funds. They'd collected money from Davy's family and other Sky Keepers in the ports where they'd stopped, but not enough. Some of it went to buy supplies for the printer who'd risked his life printing copies of the navigation books Bertram and Marianna had found, and who'd promised more. They'd sworn to distribute the books to the Sky Keepers at each point-of-call. Colin set his jaw. The *Dawn Singer* herself was the best source of funds.

THE NEXT DAY, Colin and Philip sold the *Dawn Singer*'s remaining Escapers and gave Neil the first payment. What little money they had left from the sale they gave to the Time Keeper Station clerks to put their current navigator automaton's route on hold. They got a return-trip navigator to take them to Hollym, an old sea port town where Latimer had a warehouse. A trusted friend of Davy's had a repair hanger there, providing a legitimate excuse for the reroute, since the *Dawn Singer* desperately needed repairs.

CHAPTER TWO

Vesper Vanon had always admired reformed characters, so it was no shock that seeing former pirate Colin O'Connor came as a pleasant surprise. She'd gone to a lot of trouble to ascertain who he was and that he was such a changed man, and all without raising the Time Keepers' suspicions while doing so. She just hadn't counted on Colin's airship departing while she was on board making investigations. He wasn't supposed to leave for another four hours, at least according to the schedule she'd sneaked a glance at two days ago.

She'd already discovered—along with the location of the kitchen—that the airship had no Escapers. Why not? Well, she had a five-day trip to find out. She set her jaw and tugged her cuff down, pulling it firmly over the leather arm bracer decorated with golden leaves and sky crystals.

Five days assuming no one used her homing crystal to find her before then. That would bring ruin to them all.

"The next time that lummox Nick spills his coffee, it'd better not be on my fresh bandages." The good-humored grumbling of the first mate, Philip Orren, wafted through the air vent from the captain's cabin below.

"That letter was enough to make anyone miss the coffee cup," Colin said.

Vesper inched forward in the ventilation shaft, then raised her night-vision goggles to her hat and peered through the vent grating.

"And better the bandages than my skin with that boiling brew," he continued.

"Yes, but I don't have to change your skin," Philip retorted. "I don't figure the note. How did it get onto the bridge? And the writing is chicken-scratch, as if the writer was afraid we'd recognize the handwriting."

"If it were someone whose handwriting we'd recognize," Colin added, "they would know what happened and there would be no reason to tell us to warn Davy to stay hidden. We've already guessed the Time Keepers are suspicious of him."

"Unless—" Philip began.

A squeal escaped Vesper as the airship hit a turbulence pocket. She slid backwards in the slick shaft and grabbed for the grate, her fingers barely thin enough to sandwich between the slats.

The voices below her stilled, and she held her breath. The grate was pulled from her fingers, and a rush of air hit her as she was dragged through the opening. Vesper allowed herself one scream, then decided playing the affronted party would be her best bet.

"Unhand me at once," she cried as Colin, taller and stronger than her distant observations had prepared her for, set her on her feet. She pushed against his chest, but he merely pinned her arms to her side. "Really, sir. This is preposterous. I can explain everything." But she'd rather not.

Tilting her head back, she bombarded him with her most disdainful glare, but the tall blond simply stared at her, apparently more thunderstruck than pierced by her contempt. Her afternoon was definitely not going as planned. She'd gotten herself stranded on an airship, her glares weren't working, and she couldn't even reach a hatpin, as any proper heroine would.

"Unless," Philip said slowly, looking her up and down, "the writer was trying to disguise a feminine hand."

"Quite probably," Vesper said, turning to him briefly. "But if you'll excuse the intrusion, gentlemen, it was purely unintentional and shan't last much longer." The tip of her polished boot connected with the sensitive spot at the top of Colin's left foot, where it met his leg. His leg bent automatically; his entire body lurched in surprise. She swiftly repeated the action on his other leg, then scooted from his hold. Thankfully, that technique wasn't painful to the victim. There was nothing sinister lurking in Colin's blue eyes to make her want to hurt him, but there was something alarming in his proximity. He'd ask her her name eventually, and she just might be fool enough to give it to him. He'd likely forget he was reformed then.

She darted for the door, her messenger bag flapping against her side. She might need to misplace a parachute to throw them off her trail—once she escaped. The two men dashed after her, but she was already at the door. She jerked it open, slid out, slammed it behind her, lunged into the hallway, and landed on her knees with a shocked sailor in front of her and the tail of her ankle-length smock caught in the door.

"Come back!" The cry carried through the door, causing the sailor's eyes to narrow.

Vesper groaned and touched her forehead to the cold wooden hallway floor. Next time she had a heroic impulse, she was going to stifle it.

The door opened and Vesper was picked up around the waist and carted back inside like a sack of potatoes. Was she the rotten one in the sack? What if she caused the trouble she was hoping to save them from? Cursed homing crystals *and* heroic impulses.

"Why is there never anyone my age to carry about?" Philip groused.

Colin sat Vesper on the bed. With surprising care considering he thought her a spy. She fought a smug smile. Another confirmation she was right. Colin was definitely a reformed character. People used to say he'd be just as harsh and violent a man as his father. As handsome as well. *Focus, Vesper.*

"I noticed you don't have any Escapers." She steadied herself on the mattress, and reminded herself that a kind, intelligent, handsome face did not prove anything. But then, she'd seen enough of the crew's interactions with Colin to know they respected him and yet were still loyal to the Bowditch line. Colin was innocent of Captain Davy Bowditch's loss. "Why don't you?"

Colin pulled up two chairs, placing them diagonal to her, forming a blockade. He and Philip seated themselves, sitting on the edges of their chairs, ready for action. But their feet were tucked out of her reach. Smart men.

"We have parachutes. That's all that's required." Rising briefly, Colin relieved her of her messenger bag, sliding it gently over her head.

"Yes, but—"

"Looks like a warehouse worker to me, in that odd jacket. What do you think, Colin?" Philip rubbed his whiskery jaw, his gaze taking in her coat, an ankle-length gray smock with large pockets and big black buttons. "A ship's mechanic who got lost? There are oil spots on the jacket."

"It's a painting smock," Vesper said with dignity, "to protect my dress, and those are paint spots."

Colin bent over her messenger bag, his rolled-up shirt-sleeves revealing a three-inch gash up his forearm, above his wrist tattoo. The gash had the pink tint of a fresh wound slowly healing. Bandages lay on a nearby table. "There are paint brushes, watercolor pencils, a sketchpad, and a small canvas." Colin glanced up at her, one eyebrow raised. "And a flat-head screwdriver, wrench, hammer, and pocket knife. Ah ... for removing ventilation shaft covers."

Vesper crossed her arms in mock contempt. "I resent the implication that I know of no other use for such tools."

"Perhaps she wanted to apprentice with Captain Davy as an inventor. Or to sneak sketches of the blueprints for his inventions, or the inventions themselves." Philip's perusal was not particularly friendly. The door to an inner room suddenly caught her eye, and she guessed it was Davy's workshop.

That bit of teasing might have been a tactical error.

Vesper shook her head. "Inventions are fascinating so long as I don't have to suffer through the failures needed to reach anything that qualifies to be called such. As for sketching, I've little talent for it. I'm a patroness of the art. I hire artists, or unemployed, artistic-looking persons hanging around the docks, to paint or sketch whatever interests me at the moment." Whatever gave her an excuse to be where she could gather information. Wearing the smock added to her eccentric air; people didn't bother paying attention to eccentric women poking around in places society ladies didn't typically go. "Airships and their crews recently."

"Ah," Philip said. "A different type of work. Time Keeper spy, perhaps?"

Vesper's eyes widened, and she clasped her locket. "No, no. I'm not a spy for the Time Keepers."

"Then you admit spying?" Philip asked.

Vesper paused for one heartbeat. "Of course. Why else would I be in the ventilation shaft?" Actually, she could think of two good reasons—her older sisters. The twins tended to come looking for her when they were tired of fighting with each other. They'd been good enough reasons for ventilations shafts before. And windows and dumb waiters and the back of her father's carriage as he headed off for work.

Both men's eyes widened like the diaphragm of a camera in low light. Vesper bit back a smile. Her father was right then—blunt honesty had a way of disarming one's questioners.

"Great stars above," Philip muttered.

Her grip on the locket tightened. *Stars above.* A rare expression. Did this man really believe in stars? Did she? If she didn't, why was she here? Frowning, she pushed the discussion aside once more and released the heavy locket.

Colin eyed her narrowly, and Vesper forced a serene smile. He cocked his eyebrow again, braced one hand on his knee, and leaned toward her. She resisted the urge to scoot back on the bed, straightening her spine instead. Colin may have inherited the commanding air his father was known for, but she had inherited a few talents from her own father.

"All right, little miss spy," he said, his gaze intense, "who are you and what can we tell you?"

Vesper opened her mouth, then shut it. That was a dirty trick, asking her what *she* wanted to know. Her father had never taught her that one. "I prefer *Snoop* to *Spy*, and I only want to know two things: what's your fare to Rymswell, and why did you leave four hours early? I would've been safely off if you'd left on schedule."

"We're not a passenger ship, Miss...?"

She proffered a generous smile. "I'll happily pay double the reasonable fair, for the inconvenience."

He raised an eyebrow.

"Triple."

He opened his mouth.

"Quadruple. That's my final offer."

"Your name?" he asked again in that commanding tone, leaning forward a little more.

Vesper shrank back. She could feel her family name rising in her throat even now, like a guilt she was desperate to confess. "Please just call me Vesper," she squeaked, heat flushing her cheeks at the panicked edge to her voice. She squirmed in her seat until she managed to get her back straight and her hands still in her lap.

Colin furrowed his brow, then gave a quick nod and leaned away, as if putting up the question for the time being. Vesper was only half relieved.

"How and why did you bother to learn our old schedule, Miss Vesper?" he asked.

All thoughts vanished but that one word: "Old?"

"Yes, our next stop is—"

Three rapid knocks on the door were followed by an equally insistent, "Captain!"

"Come in, Sam."

A man of average build and owning perhaps five and twenty years hurried in. "We've picked up a ping, Captain." He sighed heavily at this cryptic announcement.

Colin stiffened. The tension in his muscles affected hers. Who knew such an unprepossessing word as "ping" could evoke such a reaction?

He sighed. "Thank you, Sam. Sound the alarm and prepare the shield for the hull. We'll be on the bridge in a moment." Colin stood, frowning as Philip, bandages and a bottle of antiseptic in his hands, moved with surprising stealth to his side.

"You're not getting into another scrape with pirates while your last trophy is showing, so think where you're sitting," Philip said.

Colin sat.

Pirates? So close to Reydon? Vesper's heart thumped. Would she witness the famous Bowditch evasions? Or the first defeat?

"I'm sorry you chose this voyage to join us, Miss Vesper," Colin said, watching her watch Philip bandage his arm. "But as a 'fresh' captain in a prize Bowditch airship, I've drawn a considerable amount of undesirable attention to the *Dawn Singer* since Captain Davy's disappearance."

"Seven attacks in five months," Philip said, quickly tying off the bandage. "It's lost the fun and become a drudgery."

So many... And Colin's arm proved the men weren't invincible or able to outrun every fight.

"It's more than that, I'm afraid, Captain O'Connor." She took Colin's offered hand and allowed him to escort her from the room.

Colin spared her a sideways glance as they walked

briskly around a corner, heading toward the bridge. "Do you know something about this, Miss Vesper?"

"Please, it's just 'Vesper.' Nothing specifically. Just a theory." She swallowed hard. It was a little more than that. "The Rí Am could easily stamp out pirates if he wanted. Time Station clerks aren't bribed into giving out navigator automatons to pirates with routes that match the pirate's merchant target's: they're *allowed* to do so. The clerks all have families—the Rí Am makes sure of it—and they wouldn't risk their families by giving out automatons to just anyone. The battle between pirates and captains is a game to the Rí Am. It's a sport he watches to see who's the cleverest, the best fighter. A game he uses to indirectly rid himself of captains or pirates or traveling merchants who might be a threat or nuisance to him, and to quietly punish disobedient towns—giving the pirates all the information they need to better raid the ships taking supplies there."

Colin gave orders to the men they passed, always keeping a portion of his attention on her. "Why are you telling me this? Why leave the note?"

Why? A locket that wasn't really a locket, a new grave in the family plot, the compass rose and triquetra inked over a pirate's mark on Colin's wrist proving the courage to change paths did exist.

"*Why* doesn't matter now. Don't you see? Whatever happened on Sheffield-on-the-Sea when Marianna Bowditch's airship went down displeased the Rí Am. He's suspicious and angry. You're standing in the place of the last of Commodore Bowditch's heirs and in command of the best airship in the skies." *He intends for you to die.* Her voice rose, and she tried unsuccessfully to keep it down. One of the atrocities that normally made for distant, unfathomable newspaper headlines and card party gossip was about to happen in front of her, to people she'd just walked past or talked with and felt an odd liking to despite their short acquaintance. "He *wants* the pirates to take down the *Dawn Singer* and the loyal Bowditch crews and is making sure pirates know your routes. For all you know, he may have put a hit out on you, Colin O'Connor!"

"I wouldn't be surprised." Colin paused, checked the revolver on his hip, then opened the door to the bridge for her.

"Don't you care?" Why did she care so much? Other than the fact she was currently on the airship about to be attacked. She took a calming breath and started through the doorway to the bridge.

Colin touched her elbow as she passed him, and she paused to meet his gaze. "It wouldn't matter if the Rí Am himself *and* the faerie queen wanted this ship, they'll not get it or send it to the bottom of the sea. That's my focus now." His tone softened. "But I appreciate your concern and your information, Vesper. It confirms a suspicion. I feel less responsible for the worn state of the men and ship now. ... And I appreciate more than I can say that you don't think I killed Davy Bowditch and stole his ship."

A deep gratitude shone in his eyes, and for once, Vesper didn't know what to say. She nodded. Colin's lips curved into a smile for a brief moment, then he guided her onto the bridge. Releasing her, he strode to the ship's control panels and his men.

"Will," he addressed a lanky young man with thick blond hair as he adjusted a few dials and checked readings. "Use the intercom to tell Nick to put cargo crates 13a and 13b in the fast release slot."

The ship rocked side to side, and Vesper grabbed one of the tall stools bolted to the floor. Her heart increased its pounding at the alarming hissing and fizzing sounds rolling with the ship. "Uh ... Captain—"

"It's the foam shield for the hull. It hardens quickly in the cold air into a tough carapace, then disintegrates after a day and returns the ship to its lighter weight and better aerodynamics." He picked up the brass bell to the intercom system. "This is Captain O'Connor speaking. There's a ship approaching rapidly, suspected pirate vessel. If confirmed, we're employing Defense Tactic Cargo 13. We can stall only a few minutes. That's Defense Tactic Cargo 13. Also, we've a passenger on board, a lady who's heard of the famous Bowditch crews and their airships. Let's impress her today like you've impressed me the last three years. We're the Keepers of the Sky, and today we'll prove it. Signing off."

He put the bell down and turned to her. "Shall I assign you a room in which to wait out this ordeal?"

So she could twiddle her thumbs and jump at every pop? No thanks. "I'd rather you didn't. Is there anything I can do to help? Load guns, fill water buckets in case of fires, carry messages? I'm near-sighted and my glasses are in that bag you confiscated, so I won't offer to waste your ammunition as a markswoman."

Colin's eyes crinkled at the edges, though his mouth didn't form a smile. "Wouldn't you rather roam the ship while everyone is engaged? You mustn't forget your duties as a spy."

Vesper pressed her lips together, then cocked her head and grinned up at him. "I've already accomplished most of what I came for. I couldn't find evidence of a traditional smuggler's hold, so you most likely don't have one. I did stumble across some suspicious packages amongst your food supplies, but I refrained from opening them," she added quickly at his alarmed expression. "So there's not much more I can get into. Is there something you want to know about your ship that I can find out for you?"

Colin turned hastily away to check a reading, then turned back to her, his mouth a firm line. "Are you brave enough to be in the line of fire?"

Her knees went weak, but she took a deep breath. "I don't know if I'm brave enough, but I want to be."

"That's enough of a start then, to want to be."

"I rather think to love something or believe in something enough to stand for it is the beginning of bravery and courage," she said quietly.

"Perhaps that is what stirs the want." Philip strode to Colin's side. His dark head, bearing only a few gray strands despite the distinguishing silver of his beard, reached just above Colin's shoulder. "Tactic Cargo 13, eh, Captain? Good choice considering the situation."

Colin glanced at her, then exchanged a look with Philip. They both nodded. They were very skilled in talking around her in that silent manner.

"I could use your help, Vesper, out on the deck, if you're willing," Colin said. "But I'm going to need you to take off your smock."

Vesper nodded, quickly unbuttoning the light jacket and leaving it on the stool.

"Pity she doesn't have a parasol," Philip said. "It would've added a nice touch. A baby on her hip even more so."

A baby and parasol... Grinning, Vesper straightened her hat and smoothed her outfit, a deep green corset and skirt with a white blouse and ruffled collar. "Should I faint or just look scared?"

"Ah. Clever lady." Philip gifted her with a grin.

Vesper was soon jogging behind Colin through the ship and out onto the deck. The crisp, cold air kissing her cheeks reminded her of their altitude. Wisps of clouds floated around them, only a slight gray tint differentiating them from the eggshell sky. Could a battle really be nearing when the world smelled so pure? A different breeze blew over her, tangling the wisps and pummeling her with various chemical odors belonging to the protective foam. She could believe it.

They collected parachutes on their way to the starboard bow. The brown hull and bronze balloon shield of the approaching ship blinked in and out of view between the clouds, growing larger with each appearance.

"It's the *Thunder*," Colin said, his mouth twisting in distaste. "She's approaching at a higher altitude. We can't have her shooting down on us." He stationed them next to the starboard bow railing in what appeared to be a mini-bridge outpost complete with gears and levers, an intercom mouthpiece, a speaking trumpet, and a locker with additional weapons. He picked up the mouthpiece and spoke into it, his words echoing around the ship. "Now hear this: This is your captain speaking. Confirm pirate vessel. Cargo 13. Be alert for the signal. May the true Bringer of Light give us victory." After rotating a gear, he spoke into it again, "Philip, we need altitude, about fifty feet, and quick."

Replacing the mouthpiece, he pulled a revolver from the locker. "In case my plans go awry and pirates get on board." He held the grip out to her. "Can I trust you with this?"

Vesper's heart warmed at his faith in her. She was *almost* speechless. "Of course, Captain. I am *your* spy, after all."

Colin huffed a laugh and placed the revolver's grip in her hand. "Just keep it out of sight so we don't spoil our 'lady in distress' ploy." He pointed to leather straps hanging from the underside of the railing. "Put the strap around your waist and step into the footholds there."

After slipping the gun into her pocket, Vesper did as directed, grateful for the restraints as the ship rose in altitude. "Are pirates really that chivalrous? Would they decline to fight for the sake of a lady?"

"No. Not most, that is, and certainly not Redsail. He ... he calls himself after a legendary sea pirate who smeared the defeateds' blood on his sails. We're simply stalling for time and setting up our game."

Vesper shuddered. "Our game?"

Colin winked at her, and the horror knotting her stomach eased away. "You'll see. Be sure to hold on to your hat at my signal."

One moment passed, then another. Wood and canvas and bronze balloon shield broke the monotony of cloud and sky, looming toward them at equal altitude.

"About to make contact," Colin said quietly into the intercom mouthpiece. He set the bell-shaped piece into a hook, allowing the men on the bridge to hear.

"Time to look scared, Vesper." Colin checked her restraints and the straps securing her parachute, then put the speaking trumpet to his mouth. "Captain Redsail, this is Captain O'Connor of the *Dawn Singer*. Give us a wider berth."

A blocky man in a blood red coat stepped to the *Thunder*'s bow and lifted his own speaking trumpet. The glint of guns and the crimson head coverings and dyed beards of some three dozen or so pirates lined the ship's railing. Cranes for moving cargo stuck up like spindly trees beyond them. "No berth and no quarter, O'Connor. You know the rules," he hollered back.

"We've a woman on board, Redsail. We can fight on the next leg of our course."

Feeling oddly like she, as the topic of conversation, should wave, but knowing better, Vesper hugged herself and scooted closer to Colin. She strained to watch the *Thunder's* preparations and started rubbing her arms, her heart beating uncomfortably fast. *Don't get too much into your role, Vesper.*

Were those canons being aimed at the *Dawn Singer?* And a harpoon specifically at her and Colin? Just how much trust did she have in the Bowditch crew and captain?

Have I not commanded you? Be strong and courageous. A line from a forbidden book she'd read long ago spoke to her mind with startling command.

But blood on the sails...

Be strong and courageous.

She forced herself to breathe in. *Inhale one two, hold one two, exhale one two.* She focused on calming her breathing until her heart slowed as well.

"Are you willing to hide behind the skirts of a woman now, O'Connor?" Redsail yelled, the laughter of his men trailing his words. The ship was almost within firing range. "To think your father used to claim you'd be the bravest pirate of all."

"Cavan O'Connor's a wily devil and would appreciate this." Philip's mumbled comment came through the intercom mouthpiece.

"We had to sell the Escapers—she's no way to get off," Colin said. "And the ship's suffered a lot of damage. Would you spoil your sterling reputation by kicking a downed dog?"

Blushing, Vesper wished Redsail's reply unsaid.

"Just give us a month. That's all I ask," Colin said. "We can settle this then."

"After you've dumped your valuable cargo? I'm no fool."

Colin glanced at the control panel as Philip's whispered, "The hull shield's solid," slipped from the intercom mouthpiece. Colin depressed a lever, and the ship shivered. The signal to his men?

"There are worse sins than cowardice. I've got to get the girl to safety and protect the ship, so if you want the cargo, Redsail, you'll have to catch it!"

The *Dawn Singer's* nose tipped up. The whoosh of displaced air sounded from below the ship. The pirates cried out, pointing to something also below the ship. Released cargo crates? Redsail's ship dipped, its cranes and nets struggling to catch the falling crates.

Whack! Whack!

Their equipment hit the crates.

Boom! Boom!

Colin yanked her down to the deck, holding her against him as the *Dawn Singer* shot up and forward, riding the concussed air. Gasping, Vesper struggled to breathe in the thin air. The whole atmosphere seemed to press against her, pushing her against the wooden deck and away from the railing. Then they were falling, the restraints digging into her waist and ankles, her skirt slipping away from her legs into the space between her and the deck. Gradually, her breathing eased, her stomach returned to its proper place, her body to the deck. The ship leveled out. Colin released a heavy breath and let go of her. She scooted away from him, allowing him room to get up. All over the deck the crew likewise stirred and loosed their restraints.

"Captain? Bridge reporting in. Is everyone okay?" Philip's tinny voice flitted about overhead.

Colin hopped up and stepped over her to get to the intercom receiver. "I'm here, unharmed." He looked at Vesper; she nodded. "Passenger well. How's the ship?"

"Looks like she took it okay, thanks to the shield. I'd say she isn't in too much worse shape than she was before, judging by the instruments. Have to look around to make sure though."

"Send Will to inspect the ship. I'll check on the men and then join him. Signing off."

Colin hung up the receiver, then knelt in front of Vesper, who'd sat up but stopped there, deciding to give herself more time to adjust to all the ups and downs. Concern wrinkled Colin's tan face. "You weren't lying when you nodded earlier, were you?"

Smiling, Vesper shook her head. "Just thinking how jealous my friends would be that they missed such a ride—they who're always crowing about how they rode the highest and fastest of the newfangled roller coasters." She paused. "But I'll keep this experience just between us, I think. However, you may tell your men I am thoroughly impressed. The Bowditch crews and ships really are the best in the skies." Tucking her legs underneath her, she reached for Colin's offered hands.

His eyes widened, a flash of something unsettling passing over his face before he stifled it, his jaw clenching. He didn't take her hands, just stared at her.

He wasn't bleeding. Was she? Sometimes shock prevented one from feeling injuries right away. She discreetly cast a glance over herself. No blood. What had horrified him so? *Ah.* Did the fate of the *Thunder* bother him? It'd likely been knocked on its side when the cargo crates exploded. Had its crew been wearing parachutes? How many went flying off the deck? But the pirates had chosen their path, and the *Dawn Singer* was safe, she reminded herself.

Nonetheless, tiredness washed over her. "I'm ready for that room now, Captain." And a hot chocolate and a cheerful book. "I won't keep you from your duties any longer."

His face unreadable, Colin helped her up, then bowed. "I'll have one of my men escort you to Philip's room and bring you some refreshments." He hailed a young man, gave him his instructions, then walked off to see to his crew.

Vesper glanced swiftly around the ship and up at the balloon, searching for any damage. A cold breeze tickled her wrist, drawing her attention away. She tugged her sleeve back down over her bracer and buttoned the cuff, then followed the airman.

CHAPTER THREE

The next two days sailed by, pleasantly as far as Vesper was concerned. After leaving the pirates behind, she'd realized that if her parents grew concerned and used the homing crystals to find her, the *Dawn Singer* would be too far ahead for the "rescue" ship to catch it. Not comforting if she really were in danger. As for an excuse to her parents, she had a recently married friend in Rymsby. She could claim she'd made a sudden decision to visit her and had forgotten to message home. She'd promised her friend a visit anyway.

As for her current companions ... Philip was a darling. She wanted to keep him. And Colin ... She'd almost made him smile three times. She relished a challenge, and he certainly was that. Every time she thought she'd succeed, his mouth would straighten out under a furrowed brow. Still, to *almost* make him smile in only three days, and after the news she'd given him, she'd count that a success. His was a smile that wouldn't lose its beauty if it lost its rarity. Or so she suspected. She still had two days to find out.

Apparently unwilling to let her wander the airship alone, the two gentlemen had resorted to being her constant companions, including her in their duties when necessary. In their free time, she'd bested them at chess, until she taught them a few tricks Grandfather Ulrik had taught her to make her decent competition for him. She'd badgered them into teaching her poker. She'd won her first hand, and as a prize, got to choose the next game—charades. She was certain she'd get a smile from Colin during *that*. But after a few rounds they returned to poker and she never won another hand.

The two had dressed for dinner, kindly ignored her inability to do so, and made themselves quite charming. Their manners were nearly equal to those of her set. Slightly rough around the edges but decidedly more open and genuine. Her surprise at their dexterous use of the silverware and then later at their choice of reading material must have shown, for Philip playfully nudged Colin, exclaiming that Vesper didn't expect much from a former pirate. It seemed Colin's grandmother, while not able to stop her husband, son, and grandson from being pirates, did make certain they were gentlemanly pirates. That explained one mystery about the stoic captain.

She grinned at the memory of Colin's almost-smile at Philip's pantomime of a whistling tea kettle as she fixed her hair for dinner as best she could in front of Philip's shaving mirror.

A knock on the door sent her eyes to the window. A clear sky showed the crystals growing less vibrant, but they were still a ways from the dimming and dinner.

"Just a moment." After hastily finishing her coiffure, she opened the door. The two men outside had red faces. It wasn't their appearance that embarrassed them, for both were quite handsome in their officer's uniforms. The neatly folded man's shirt and trousers resting in Colin's hands answered her question. "Ah." She'd never washed her own clothes before and didn't relish the idea of it, but to have a strange man do it for her was uncomfortable to say the least. But who was she to argue with such kindness? And clean clothes would be wonderful.

Philip cleared his throat. "Old Dan, as the only one with experience in such matters, informed us that in order to have a lady's garments washed, dried, and pressed by morning, he needed them as soon as possible."

"We brought these in exchange." Colin held out the folded clothes. "If you'd prefer to dine in your room tonight, we understand, though we don't feel you have to."

Her embarrassment suddenly turned to amusement. She accepted the clothes, repressing an impish desire to feign great embarrassment to make them turn even redder. "I'll put my painting smock on over them and no one will ever know the difference." If they pretended rolled pants legs and sleeves were the fashion. "You two promised me a concert tonight and to let me play your violin and cello. I shan't let you renege."

Relief eased the tension in their shoulders, and Colin looked as if he wanted to say something but clamped his mouth shut instead.

"I wouldn't want you to," Philip said gallantly.

"We'll return your dress before we land in the morning," Colin said finally.

"Land tomorrow? Oh! We're not going to Rymsby, are we? What is our destination?"

"Hollym. We got a reroute there to repair the damage from the pirate attacks."

The clothes dropped from Vesper's grasp. Colin steadied her with a hand to her arm and guided her to the nearest chair.

"Are you all right?" he asked as she sat.

"It's two days shorter a journey than to Rymsby," Philip said. "Were you trying to get to Rymsby? Is there some danger awaiting you in Hollym?"

"No, I wasn't trying to get anywhere. I was spying, as I told you." Vesper hid her face in her hands. "Oh, you've ruined everything."

A hand touched her shoulder. "Why?" Philip asked.

Stilling her rocking, she took a deep breath, laid her hands in her lap, and uncurled her back until it was straight. "I'd learned that the Time Keepers hoped rather than believed Davy Bowditch was lost for good. They were planning to arrest him as soon as he was located for forbidden inventions and for being complicit in smuggling the iron found in his sister's wrecked airship over a year ago now. I had hoped and hoped he had survived somehow, so I snooped about and finally snuck on board your ship. I wanted to find out what I could about you, Captain O'Connor, and to leave a note of warning for Davy Bowditch, if I thought you were a true friend of his."

Vesper paused, feeling Colin's gaze on her. His mouth lifted in a grateful smile, and Vesper's failed her. She was about to destroy that beautiful curve of his lips.

"That warning was for him," she continued, "but if you're going to Hollym, then it's you who are in danger now. A special Time Keepers unit left for Hollym not long before we did to arrest a band of smugglers who've started dealing in iron. They're to make the arrest the day we will land there. They're expecting the *Dawn Singer*. I'd stake my life on it."

As she expected, Colin's smile disappeared behind a stoic mask.

"How do you know this?" Philip asked, not bothering to deny that they were going there for the iron.

"Oh, you know." Vesper shrugged, her chest tightening. "Parties. People will talk, after all. Walks along the port. Silver to the right person. I come of a wealthy family and have little to do but snoop. It keeps me out of trouble. Usually."

"Won't you trust us with the truth?" Philip asked quietly.

Vesper stared at him, then looked down at her hands in her lap. She tucked her left arm with its distinctive bracer under her right.

"Thank you for the warning, Vesper," Colin said softly. "It won't go in vain." He added under his breath, "I pray you'll not have reason to regret it."

"LET us see you into town, Vesper," Philip pleaded for the third time as they stood at the inner doorway of the busy cargo hold the next morning. The *Dawn Singer* had docked for unloading before it was to move to the repair hanger. "At least see you settled into a hotel if you won't stay with us until your folks get here."

Vesper stood on tiptoe to kiss the man's whiskered cheek. "And have to explain if someone saw me? No, you've been too kind already."

She turned to Colin and held out her hand. "I've relatives here, so you needn't worry. I'll saunter out along with the cargo and no one will notice me."

Colin shook her hand, his expression unreadable. "Thanks for the warning, Vesper."

He made to release her, but she tightened her grip. "You will act on it, won't you?"

He nodded, and Vesper released his hand. "And take care of yourself?"

Colin grinned.

Vesper nearly fell over.

She was off the ship and halfway through the docks before she realized he'd beaten her at her own game. He'd agreed to act on the information she'd given him but had evaded promising to stay safe. He was still going after the iron.

CHAPTER FOUR

C olin and Philip paused in front of Reydon's First
Bloom Florist, then ducked inside. Philip pulled in
a loud breath. The man had always had a fancy
for the smell of lilies.

"Happy?" Colin asked, his eyes crinkling.

"In heaven. This is what I miss most when I'm sailing the
skies—the flowers. It's a pity I can't send any to my Mary
anymore." He stared sadly at the floor a moment, then shook
himself and gave Colin a sideways glance, but he didn't say
anything. No teasing about Vesper could only mean one thing.

"You saw her arm bracer, didn't you?" Colin said, his
voice carefully emotionless.

"I saw your face when you walked onto the bridge after
the attack." Philip gave a cynical laugh. "I've always said
there were no good Vanons. Guess I'll have to take that back.
To think our darling Vesper is a some-odd great-grand-
daughter of the hated Rí Am, Ulrik Vanon, himself. With a
bracer that fine, she's from a favored line."

Colin merely nodded, not bothering to state that she wasn't "our" anything, other than a shining memory. Vanon ladies were paired off to the family advantage, a prize to those the Rí Am wanted to reward. They had money and prestige but not true freedom.

The way to the counter cleared, and they were greeted by a rosy-faced, round woman in a dress made of fabric that looked as if someone had wrapped her in a painter's palette and smeared it. "What can I get for you, dearies?" She glanced between them. "A bouquet for the mum?"

"Not exactly. I need two bouquets." Colin ordered roses for an aunt, with whom his grandmother frequently stayed. It was time they both knew the truth about his "death." The word had gotten out about him in Time Keeper, smuggler, and pirate circles, so they likely knew he was alive, but he figured a note before he showed up would be appreciated. Fortunately for his pocketbook, his aunt Fiona lived just outside the city. Navigators for delivery-based businesses weren't cheap, driving up the price of the goods and services dependent on them.

"And the second bouquet," he continued, "red carnations. I'd like it sent fifteen minutes after the first to a separate location." Just in case they'd been followed and the Time Keepers accurately suspected an attempt to contact the smugglers. He jotted down the address of Latimer Harrison's warehouse, then accepted the card to go with the flowers. He addressed the note "To: TK Target, From: COD," and added, "Please take, with apologies."

The florist stared at the card a moment after Colin handed it to her, then *tsk*-ed and set it aside to ring up the order. "I've seen some unfortunate initials in my time, and

169

COD is certainly one of them, whether you read it 'cod' or 'cash on delivery.'"

Colin hoped they read it the latter, realizing that the one bringing the cash was warning them. He hoped they'd be able to remove all evidence of smuggling and save the iron harpoons for him before the Anti-Smuggling Unit arrived, but he held that hope loosely. He had a suspicion the Time Keepers knew exactly when he was supposed to deliver the rest of the money and collect the iron.

After leaving the florist, they hurried to the fishermen's quarter and joined Nick and Will for an evening of fishing. After renting tackle and an automaton navigator to take a small dinghy out to Six-Mile Island, they set out, rowing.

"Do you think we've lost them, Captain?" Will glanced over his shoulder at the few other crafts in the water.

Colin patted the automaton sitting at the rudder. "Why would Time Keepers bother following us when they know our friend here has locked us into a path?"

Will grinned, then sobered. "I don't envy you your swim. But bringing a self-propelled SCUBA suit onto a row boat *would* have been suspicious."

Philip grunted. "I saw that look ya gave me, youngster. I was born swimming and will be glad to get back to it."

Will and Philip bantered back and forth while Colin watched the shore and Nick pretended to watch for fish. Nick's goggles helped him see beneath the glare on the water's surface, but Colin made use of the spyglass lens on his. A faded blue warehouse along the distant shore finally rewarded his diligence. Unfortunately, the sky crystals would start dimming soon. How long before the planned rendezvous would the Anti-Smuggling Unit arrive?

He flipped the telescopic lens on his goggles up to better see his companions. "Time to go."

Will pulled out two bulging, waterproofed leather bags from under his seat. Philip, Nick, and Colin stripped down to their pants and smeared black grease over their bodies. It would help protect them from the cold water and make them less visible.

The three of them slipped into the water, and Will passed them the bags filled with their clothes and other supplies. "Continue on to the island and then keep flashing the light until morning?" he asked.

"Yes," Colin answered, treading water to warm up his muscles. "If all goes well, we'll be back long before then. If not, well, as second mate, you're in charge of the ship."

"I'm not quite ready for that, so be sure to be there." He paused. "With the smugglers in tow?"

"No, they're on their own. Probably out of town by now anyway. We're only after the iron, assuming Neil didn't hoodwink us about it being there."

The young man blanched. "Good luck. I'll be praying for you—and that the iron's there."

"Thanks." Colin jerked his chin toward Philip and Nick. "Ready?"

"Don't forget the fish for my breakfast," Philip called back as they set out swimming for what Colin guessed was a two-mile swim.

"Just how far is two miles?" Nick asked sometime later, when Colin called a break to get his bearings and rest.

"About two-thirds of the distance before the faerie curse scrambles all sense of direction and distance," Philip answered.

"And how far is it from this warehouse to Six-Mile Island?"

"Twice the scramble distance. The way the coast curves here makes the island six miles from pretty much the entire coastline."

"Ah. And just how—"

Colin kicked his legs and rose back up into a swimming position. "You'll see. Come on."

THEY LOCATED the warehouse by the peeling blue paint and the graffiti of a muscled man with a tattoo of a skimpily clad woman on his bicep. Colin remembered the distinctive building from a visit there years ago with his father. Latimer had been much friendlier then.

A few local workmen walked the dock in the dimming light. One looked a little too neat and alert to be what his clothing claimed.

Sinking lower in the water, they swam along the pier until finding a shadow deep enough to allow Nick to climb onto the pier unobserved. He slipped off into the shadows between two warehouses.

The neatly dressed man walked their way, his steps keeping pace with the waves lapping at the pier's barnacle-crusted pilings. Colin and Philip ducked under the pier and followed it back to Latimer's warehouse. A moment later, when the man promenaded in the opposite direction, Nick stepped from the shadows and slipped back into the water.

"No sign of the Anti-Smuggling Unit out front," he said, shivering. "No lights in the warehouse."

"Good. Let's hurry then. It won't be long." Treading

water, Colin pulled three slender oxygen tanks from the supply bag and doled them out. He slipped the mask over his face, adjusted the fit against his nose and mouth, then lowered the night vision lens on his goggles. Philip took the supply bag and strapped it on his back and nodded in response to Colin's mime of "Stay here while I go down."

Colin dove until a skull and crossbones registered cold and black against the pale green of the warehouse wall. Bright green fish scuttled away from him, stirring debris in the water, which flickered like dust motes as he righted himself in front of the marked wall. The empty eye sockets fixed on him, ghoul-like in their glow and ghost-like in their ability to dredge up memories, shame, and doubt. His stomach clenched, and he touched his doubly tattooed wrist. He was no different than those pirates he'd blasted from the skies a few days ago. He may have tricked them into destroying themselves to save Vesper and his crew this time, but what about all the earlier times he'd fought and killed on their side?

He has delivered us from the domain of darkness and transferred us to the kingdom of his Beloved Son, in whom we have redemption, the forgiveness of sins.

Setting his jaw, Colin pressed the gleaming eye sockets until they sank into the wall. A rectangle about twice his height high and nearly as wide sank back with a sluggish creak, then lifted up.

Colin pushed off the wall, propelling himself to the surface, away from the dragging rush of water into the small pressurization chamber. Breaching the lapping waves, he motioned to Philip and Nick, then dove again. A second black pirate's mark was visible on the inner doors of the pressurization chamber. They swam into the buffer space, and

Colin shifted a lever on the side of the chamber. The outer doors closed. Water spurted away down a drain, and the inner door disappeared. The gaping skull rose into a slit in the ceiling with a muted rattle.

They'd made it to the warehouse. Were they the first?

CHAPTER FIVE

There was nothing like a little art to smooth over a three-day absence. And validate her excuse. Vesper claimed the first artistic-looking vagrant in Hollym Park she could find and sent him out with money and instructions to paint, sketch, or otherwise capture in art, an airship. Any airship but the *Dawn Singer*. Said artist was to send the completed canvas to the hotel where her father stayed when working in Hollym. She had no friend here to visit, so she'd had to improvise.

That done, Vesper headed straight for the dress shop. It wouldn't do to be seen wearing the same gown—albeit clean —that she'd worn the last time she saw her father. Not much escaped him, which is what made him an excellent Chief Officer of the Anti-Smuggling Unit.

A half hour later, armed with a new gown and the promise of artwork, she stepped onto the crowded sidewalk and hailed a horse-drawn cab. "Where to, miss?" the driver asked congenially as he opened the door for her.

"To my father." She tugged her cuff back to reveal the

leather arm bracer with its sky crystals and golden leaves that marked her as a Vanon.

To a certain extent, Vanons could come and go as they pleased, gifted as they were with select navigation crystals that didn't break after each use as most did. Cabbies and a few others could purchase special automatons to make multiple runs on the same crystal, though most people didn't realize it was the crystal that was significant. They fancied it was a program hidden in the automaton, or, as far as the bracer went, that the golden leaves bore spells in their intricate etching that made the automatons go wherever the Vanons wished. If that *wherever* matched one of their crystals. They didn't have quite that much freedom, just a crystal for each of two residences, each member of the immediate family, grandparents, and a homing crystal. She hated the latter.

"Let me see your automaton. I can direct us to my father."

The driver's affable demeanor disappeared like blossoms under a late winter snow. Vesper felt the coldness all the way to her toes. "I'm sorry, miss, but I don't have a navigator automaton. I'm a short-distance cabby."

Vesper narrowed her eyes at him. What had been that doll-like creation sitting up front with him? "Hollym Time Keeper Station then. That's likely where he is." When the driver didn't move, she leaned toward him and said, lowering her voice, "Unless you have some reason to avoid the station?" *That I should report,* her manner implied.

He swallowed hard, then opened the door wider. "As you wish, miss."

With an appropriately arrogant lift to her chin, Vesper stepped into the cab. After the cabby closed the door and mounted the box, Vesper blew out a breath and sank against the cushions. No one would dare treat a Vanon like that in Reydon. No wonder she hadn't left the capital city since her family's last summer vacation.

The butterflies that had been fluttering in her stomach since Colin smiled at her sputtered out. Would Colin's eyes turn cold and hard like that if he knew who she was? Not that she was planning on seeing him again.

The cabby was polite, if cold, when they arrived at the Time Keeper Station. Vesper paid him, and he hurried off. She dodged the main entrance in favor of the small gate between the squat Automaton and Navigation Center and the Constabulary and hurried to the larger warehouse behind them. Given Hollym's proximity to the capital and the sea, it tended to have a fair bit of smuggling, and thus its own branch of the Port Inspection and Anti-Smuggling Unit. Her father and uncle had offices here as well as in Reydon, their main base.

Her steps slowed as she neared the door. She ran her gloved thumb over her locket, ignoring the impulse to open it and stare at the compass rose design in its hidden base, a design she'd only seen two other places. Would the wearer of one be safe? She tugged against the chain. What else could she do for Colin? She'd warned him. It wasn't her mission to see them get the iron! Yet, somehow, she felt it was.

Vesper stilled as she touched the door handle. She stood straighter and resolutely formed a smile. She was Vesper Vanon. The bright, cheerful, careful Vesper Vanon. She walked inside.

"Hello, Donald." Vesper smiled broadly at the middle-aged man who'd sat at the front desk since she was seven, tagging along behind her father at work because her mother was too busily engaged with society matters to bother with her daughters, and the nanny had no patience for a mischievous, energetic little girl when she already had a fussy pair of twins to take care of.

"Miss Vesper!" Donald nodded to a messenger boy, who then darted out of the room. Donald walked around the desk, revealing a little more weight about the waist and a little less hair than when she started coming with her father. He welcomed her with a fatherly hug. "I was just saying how dull the office was without you getting into mischief with your cousins."

Vesper laughed and tried not to think about her cousin Mark, her chief companion in mischief. "Quieter for certain, but not duller. My father has praised your team's excellent work the last year." After a few minutes of chatting and inquiring after Donald's family, Vesper excused herself to see her father.

Donald cleared his throat. "He's in conference about the raid tonight. He did say that if you arrived to tell him immediately but to make you stand on a stool in the corner wearing a dunce's hat until he came for you." He accompanied that statement with The Look of Parents to Children Who've Misbehaved.

"Ah. Of course. I'll wait for him outside his office. Thanks, Donald." Vesper hastily retreated deeper into the building, making her way to the office suite, greeting various workers, including several older cousins, as she went. She paused in front of Dermot Vanon's office. Uncle Dermot had married her father's sister but had been required to take the Vanon name, as well as an arm bracer, when he'd married. His office was dark. Her father's was bright and bearing a "Meeting in Progress" sign over the glass door.

She settled into a stiff chair in the antechamber and rehearsed her story. After a while, the door to her father's office opened. Two guards exited, pulling a young man along between them. That the young man had been crying was apparent in his red eyes and splotchy cheeks. That he was a user of chrurhol, the most detested and dangerous drug known, was apparent in the frantic look in his dark-rimmed eyes and his haggard, yellowed skin. It was also marked by the orange band around his arm standing in contrast to the black-and-white stripes of his jail uniform. Distaste and pity fought for dominance in Vesper's heart, but both were quickly squashed. What had he to do with the raid on a smuggler dealing in iron?

Sniffling, the man sagged between the stoic guards as they led him away. Was it prison or execution for him? He had no Vanon bracer. That made a difference, but not favorably for the Vanons. Blinking quickly, Vesper clasped her wrist, remembering the cheerful smile of her cousin Mark, Dermot's son, as they played together growing up; his solemn face as he confessed to her that he'd chosen the Sky Keeper faith; then the lifeless photograph on a stand near a coffin. But the coffin held no body. Mark was being buried alive day after day in the secret crystal mines, all the while working to further the Rí Am's empire. The perfect revenge for any who dared displease Grandfather Ulrik.

Vesper rubbed her arms, dragging her cuff over the leather bracer she couldn't pry off no matter how hard she tried, and hoped no one found out she'd warned the buyer of the smuggled iron. She caught herself praying that rather than merely hoping it and pressed her lips together to silence her thoughts. She switched her attention to rehearsing her story.

Some time later, the door opened again and several department officials walked out.

Their surprised greetings to her were cut short by her father's, "Ah. Vesper. I'm relieved to see you. Come in my office."

Uncle Dermot patted her shoulder as he walked by. She smiled weakly in return, summoned her courage and her story, and walked into her father's office. He greeted her with a kiss on the cheek and a hug that was tighter than usual. And a frown.

"Sit." Eoin Vanon pulled a second chair behind his desk, placing it next to his. Vesper sat and folded her hands in her lap, feeling his stern gaze as if it were a real thing trying to pierce her soul. "Just where have you been the past three nights and why didn't you at least leave a note? Your mother actually wired me multiple times to ask if you were with me."

Vesper flinched, then focused on her genuine sorrow for his distress. "I'm sorry, Daddy. Truly I am. You know how I've taken an interest in airships and paintings of them landing and departing. I thought it would be perfect to get a painting of an airship leaving Reydon and the same ship arriving at its destination. It was such an enchanting idea. It would be easy enough to hire a sailor to have it commissioned for me." She paused and made a conscious effort to neither fidget nor be too still. Her father knew how to read people. "Well, I went aboard an airship and it took off before I got off! Everyone was quite shocked, especially me."

Her father eyed her narrowly. "Your name was not on any airship's passenger list."

"Well, naturally not. I wasn't a registered passenger until after we were under way." She grinned at him, but not too

sunnily. "Don't worry, Daddy. They treated me very respect-
fully, and I paid handsomely for their trouble." With money
left on her bed so no one could protest it. "And I was able to
hire a painting myself after we landed. It'll be at the hotel
waiting for us."

Seeing the tension lines ease in her father's brow, Vesper
rose and settled herself on the arm of his chair. She wrapped
an arm about his shoulders and leaned lightly against him.
Her guilt increased. He must have been really worried: he
hadn't even asked her the name of the airship! "You can
imagine my relief when I learned they could drop me off at
Hollym. I could've ended up anywhere! But now it's like old
times, just the two of us." She kissed his cheek, relieved he
seemed satisfied with her half-tale.

Eoin huffed a laugh and removed his glasses. Rubbing
his eyes, he let out a deep breath. "I've come to expect unannounced, overnight trips from your sisters, but the thought
that my little bird had taken up the Reydon fashion of
weekend trips with whatever man struck her fancy..." He
cleared this throat, then hurried on. "Your sisters were
laughing at you, saying you'd finally run off with whatever
young artist you'd been patronizing. Your mother wouldn't
let me use the homing crystal to find you, saying you ought to
have whatever fun you wanted before Grandfather Ulrik
married you off." He rubbed his eyes again.

Vesper hugged him tighter, a sick feeling twisting her
stomach. She'd always known she'd pay for the Vanon privi-
leges by being a pawn of the Rí Am's when it came time.
What if whomever Grandfather Ulrik married her off to was
one of the *fashionable*, one of her sisters' companions even?
Or someone like her mother, only interested in society and
gossip and parties, with little affection for a spouse or chil-

dren? Perhaps getting sent to the crystal mine wouldn't be so bad. But before that she was going to take up boxing so she could flatten her sisters with style. "I'll never be so *fashionable* as that."

His half smile of acknowledgement died almost as soon as it was born. He stared at the papers strewn over his desk, but Vesper felt all his attention on her. "And you were always so close to Mark..."

Vesper stilled, her hand on the locket before she realized it. *Mark had the courage to change paths, like Colin.* Mark paid for it as he knew he might. Did she have that courage? Vesper let the locket go slowly, then kissed Eoin's cheek again. "I am sorry for the worry. Can I take you out to dinner or a concert tonight to help you forget it?"

He disentangled himself from her arms and stood. "You know I have a raid tonight. Blasted drug runners. I suspected it was more than a common case of smuggling, even of smuggling iron. I've had the informant locked up for the past few days. He finally broke down and talked today. He turned in his own father because his father threw him out of the house over drug use. I don't know if Harrison knew his son had been using the family smuggling business for drug running or not, but we'll have to assume he does."

She'd been right about the chrurhol. Did Colin know of it? She doubted it. Vesper stood and paced around Eoin's desk as he gathered paperwork. She paused and looked over at him. "Those raids are always so much more dangerous, aren't they?"

"Yes. Drug runners are more likely to shoot at us." His mouth firmed into a thin line. "And we're not as careful about bringing them back alive for questioning and prison."

"Would you ask the guards not to kill anyone tonight?" Vesper asked slowly, her hand clasping her locket once more.

"They're drug runners, Vesper. I can sympathize with iron smugglers wanting to protect their homes and lands from the fey creatures—don't let this get back to Grandfather Ulrik or it will mean the whole family's heads—but not with drug smugglers. You know what chrurhol does to people."

"Would you make sure they're drug runners and not merely iron smugglers before there's shooting?"

He cocked his head to look at her. "What's gotten into you? You don't usually ask about what happens to the smugglers."

Vesper squeezed the locket and let it go. "Just a mood, I guess. Will you?"

There was silence for a long moment while he studied her, his expression worried. "All right," he said at last.

She smiled weakly, then joined him at his desk and kissed his cheek. "And take care of yourself. I'll get a room at the hotel and wait up for you."

Vesper left his office and made a sharp right to knock on her uncle's door. When he didn't answer, she wandered around the building, ending up in the transport bay. Horseless carriages with large beds for holding confiscated goods waited quietly for the evening's run. Before them, closer to the bay doors, were the smaller horseless carriages, her father and uncle's in the lead. Several others for the guards were mixed in.

Vesper ran her hand along the polished metal of the carriages as she passed beside them. There would be no shortage of men to confiscate the smuggled goods, to protect her father, uncle, and cousins. To hurt her friends and doom their mission.

Vesper pushed the thought away and looked around for her uncle. Not seeing him, she climbed into the lead car, beside the navigator automaton, a specialized one allowing the Anti-Smuggling Unit to place crystals in it themselves to get them wherever they needed to go for a raid.

The open-topped car's cushioned seats were just as comfortable as a lonely hotel room, and her uncle was sure to find her eventually. He was responsible for putting the correct navigation crystal in the automaton's chest.

How long before the caravan would leave? Vesper glanced at her wrist, the worldwide symbol for wanting to know the time, though no one knew what connection time and wrists had. She could get up and go to the courtyard to see the Time Keeper Station clock tower—a crystal tree with clockworks visible at its heart and which was typically the only time device in each city besides the more expensive automatons. Or she could sit and worry.

Vesper groaned and pulled a small notebook and pen from her handbag. It was time she brushed up on rhythms and rhymes and bad poetry.

"So you made it out alive, did you?" Vesper's uncle lumbered to the car a moment later. Though alike in disposition and talents, Dermot Norland Vanon and his brother-in-law were opposites in appearance, her uncle being stout and red-faced where her father was trim and pale.

"As you see, Uncle. It was a narrow escape, though, I must say."

"It deserved to be no less." Putting his foot on the runner board, he leaned over the door to wrap her in a tight hug. The carriage dipped under his weight. "You had me worried too."

"Why, Uncle Dermot, I didn't think you cared," she teased as he released her.

"Not at all. That's why Anna and I half raised you."

"Only one-third, Uncle dear. You shouldn't take so much blame on yourself and my dear Aunt Anna."

Huffing a laugh, he leaned, collapsed almost, against the door and rubbed his arm.

"Are you okay?" she asked.

He shrugged. "A bit of indigestion and a twinge in my arm. It's nothing. I'm just tired." He winked at her. "Your father works me too hard. Just because I married his sister doesn't mean he can boss me around."

Vesper smiled in return. Aunt Anna was one of the few lucky Vanons.

Guards and others of the Anti-Smuggling Unit filtered into the bay. Uncle Dermot pushed off the car and stepped away. "I'd better get the automaton ready. Can't have the lead car ignorant of the destination." He opened the door for her and helped her out. "You're traveling back to Reydon with us when we finish with this case, aren't you?"

"Yes."

"Good. We can keep an eye on you." He gave her a serious look before starting toward a small office at the back of the bay, pulling out his keys as he walked. Ten feet away, he stumbled and eased himself to the floor.

"Uncle!" Vesper's cry was echoed by several cousins among the unit, all rushing to Dermot's side. Getting to him first, Vesper helped him lie down, her stomach twisting at the clammy feel of his skin. Despite the coolness of his hand in hers, sweat slicked his palm.

"I feel like a weight's sitting on my chest, Vess." He

snorted, then grimaced. "And like some debutante about to faint."

She squeezed his hand. "Do you have any nitroglycerin tablets? I think you're having a heart attack."

He shook his head, flinching.

"Donald would have some." Jimmy, a cousin only a year older than she was, jumped up and sprinted toward the outer office.

Vesper's father knelt beside her, and she released Dermot's hand to him.

"I'm sorry, Eoin," Dermot rasped between short breaths, "but I don't think I'll make the raid tonight."

Eoin squeezed his brother-in-law's hand. "I'll excuse you this once, but you'd better be at the next one."

Dermot winced as he chuckled. "You couldn't want that any more than I."

Jimmy brought the nitroglycerin tablets, and shortly afterward, an emergency transport carriage arrived. Eoin stared forlornly as the medics loaded his brother-in-law into the red-and-white carriage. Vesper stood beside him and hugged his arm.

"Vesper, I can't call off the raid," he said, a desperate tinge to his voice. "You know what Grandfather Ulrik would do. He hates iron smugglers worse than I drug runners. It looks like these are both."

Vesper hugged him tighter. "I'll follow them to the hospital and send word to Aunt Anna and Robin in Reydon. You do what you need to do and meet us at the hospital later. Aunt Anna will understand."

He stared a moment more, then nodded and patted her hand. "Jimmy, sound the bell. We'll leave as soon as we're ready."

She released his arm, and he walked over to the lead car and examined the automaton.

"He was on his way to get the crystals when he collapsed," she said, following him. If the automaton had no crystals, would that mean they'd have to call off the raid? Her heart sang a tremulous song of victory.

"The crystals are in the loading bay office," Eoin said.

The song stopped.

"I'll go get them." Eoin pulled his keys from his pocket.

"No need. I'll get them." Vesper stepped to his side and held out her hand, hoping she'd not spoken too quickly. "I know you have a lot to do since everything is behind schedule."

"Thank you." He handed her the keys, the dullness of his voice doubling the ache of her heart.

She hurried across the bay to the office. The spot where Uncle Dermot had lain was damp from his sweat; she skirted around it but made a mental note of it.

In the narrow office, a giant, well-organized desk reigned supreme. Rows of little cubbies lined the wall like loyal subjects. On the desk rested three hand-sized velvet pouches, each marked with a location: Warehouse district (Harrison's warehouse), Smuggled Goods Storage, Hollym Anti-Smuggling Unit headquarters. The crystal tool, key-like in shape and wrapped in silver wire, that allowed Dermot to change the crystals without the automaton exploding sat beside the bags.

She stood in front of the desk in the dimly lit room. The commotion of preparations from the bay quieted as the door shut behind her. She cradled her left arm to her chest. The bracer dug into her arm. But the locket pressed against her heart.

Setting her jaw, she snatched up the three pouches and loosened the drawstrings on the pouches labeled Harrison's warehouse and Smuggled Goods Storage. She picked up the keys and the crystal tool, jogged back out in the bay, and slipped on the wet spot left by her uncle. She screamed. The pouches flew to the floor. Two crystals and the crystal changer spun out and across the polished concrete.

"Vesper!" Eoin ran to her side as the guards chased down the fallen items.

Groaning, Vesper sat up, barely able to stop herself from rubbing her aching backside. Cursed heroic impulses. If they didn't work. "I'm all right."

"Are you sure?"

Nodding, she handed him the pouch nearest her. "I'll have bruises in unmentionable places but nothing serious."

Eoin sank to the floor beside her and buried his face in his hands. His few gray hairs seemed more pronounced than normal. "No more scares, please, Vesper."

"I'm sorry, Daddy. For the fright ... and the crystals."

His gaze jerked to the guard holding the two empty pouches and the crystal tool in one hand and two seemingly identical crystals in the other. His mouth twisted in a silent curse. "If we put the wrong crystal in ... No, I'm sure I'll recognize it in time to change crystals, if need be, before we get too far in the wrong direction. We'll catch the smugglers. We've got to."

The Rí Am doesn't long tolerate failure. And if a man falls, so does his family.

Fear and guilt knotted Vesper's stomach. *Please let Colin get the iron and Daddy the other smugglers.*

188

CHAPTER SIX

The drip of water echoed loudly in the pressurization chamber separating the smuggler's hold from the ocean. No sound came from the hold above them or the warehouse above that.

Colin, Philip, and Nick quickly put away the diving gear and dug into the two bags for towels. No sense being cold and leaving telltale watermarks. Colin dried quickly and turned his attention to their secret chamber within a secret chamber. In it slumbered their escape. Sleek as a serpent, with a glass dome front and a spike like a narwhale's, the submarine his grandfather stole off a Vanon sea ship rested on its dry dock supports. His grandfather said it always pointed out to sea, eager to get back to the action. Colin hoped to give it that chance. To use the sub stolen through bloodshed and for vengeance to help bring freedom and light.

He ducked under the sturdy, ornate spike, ignoring the way its open spaces reminded him of the Time King's emblem, and did a quick inspection of the ship. The tension in his shoulders eased as he noted the vessel's stable condition. He joined Nick and Philip as they armed themselves and chose for himself a pistol with a small crossbow attachment, stun darts, and a PullLine from the supply bag. Nick struggled into a black bodysuit shot through with silver lines in an intricate pattern radiating out from his chest.

"Please tell me this thing hasn't got the Banshee wail programmed into it," Nick said of the suit as he hopped around, pulling on his boots. He finally leaned back against the submarine to tug them on.

Philip flashed a grin. "Davy hadn't decided on a *specific* sound for it."

"Meaning?" Nick asked warily.

Philip merely grinned back. Then his grin faded, and he patted the glass window of the submarine's bridge. "Think she'll go after all this time, Colin? No one's used her since your grandfather died, right?

Colin strapped on the PullLine harness and gauntlet, then fastened Nick's for him. "Yes, not for about seven years. But she'll go." *She has to.* "Take care of her, Philip. Refill the air tanks and familiarize yourself with the controls and do whatever else needs to be done." Colin passed the supply bags off to his first mate. "There's a pair of pliers in there. The automaton's head was detached so it wouldn't go to Reydon as programmed. Power up the ship, reconnect the automaton's head so it will be able to get us out of here, then open the cargo hold's upper doors. I'll find the iron. Nick will open the doors to this chamber and then work the lift to get the iron into the sub. We'll join you, then flee like a bird from a storm. When we're near Six-Mile Island, we'll detach the automaton's head and guide the sub in using the fine movement controls. A friend will meet us there with his tug."

"Why exactly does Latimer have a sub he doesn't use for smuggling?" Only Nick's head showed bright green through Colin's goggles. The rest of him was nothing but faint lines matching those of the suit. The helmet between his arm and side would fix the bright green of his head.

The skin around Colin's eyes crinkled. "Grandfather and I were the only ones who could handle tight spaces. Latimer offered this area for storage thinking he'd be able to use the sub when Grandfather wasn't, but he couldn't handle it either."

Nick's quiet chuckle was cut short by Colin's, "Ready?"

With a silent prayer, Colin patted both men on the shoulder, then they went their separate ways. Philip climbed onto the sub and opened the hatch as Colin led Nick to the far wall and up the ladder to the manhole that opened into the smuggler's hold.

The metal plate screeched but didn't budge as Colin pressed against it. He stilled. Had the ambient noise above changed? Well, it was too late now no matter how empty or crowded the space above was. Readjusting his position, he shoved the cover until it popped out of the opening and landed with a clang that rattled both holds and Colin's nerves. So much for a silent entry.

But aside from the cover still rocking, he heard nothing save the water beating against the building's side and some rattling and humming of machinery below.

He climbed out, located the marked barrel about ten feet to the right that hid the hatch to the sub's chamber, and started toward it. Nick crept up beside him, and together, they shifted the barrel back against the wall, exposing the ring in the floor used to open the hatch.

"As soon as you get to the lift's controls—you'll have to

climb that ladder—open this," Colin whispered. "I'll—" The hair on the back of his neck rose. He shoved Nick aside and rolled to the left as shots rang out and bullets dented the walls.

Blast. Colin had figured the Anti-Smuggling Unit would at least have the decency to light up the place and yell for their surrender. But perhaps the ASU treated iron smugglers differently.

Nick had shoved his helmet on, making him almost invisible even with night goggles. That left Colin the only bright spot in that part of the smuggler's hold, if the others had night vision goggles. He was against the side wall near the front, closer to the lift and the hidden stairs leading to the warehouse above than to the rows of crates he needed to search. A center aisle provided space for the smugglers to move goods, dividing the room into two halves. The crates were mostly at the seaward wall on his side and along the opposite side, where the ASU was.

He jumped to his feet, snagged a crowbar and hammer off the tool-studded wall behind him, and sprinted toward the rear of the chamber, ducking behind barrels too short for his harpoons, feeling the cursed breath of bullets shooting past him. They needed more of those suits Nick wore, Banshee wail or not. Beyond the barrels were the first of the crates.

Chunking the hammer across the chamber as a distraction, he darted to and around the nearest crate and stumbled over a lid pried off and left on the floor. Sawdust packing did little to break his crash onto the wooden slats. An unsmiling face stared vacantly at him from inside the crate. Biting back a curse, Colin scrambled back. Had they killed the Harrisons and left them?

But the figure coated in sawdust was too small for one of the smugglers, and the face had a painted look. An automaton. A half laugh forced itself from Colin's throat. So people were still trying—and falling for—that racket? Fake automaton navigators sold at low rates from mobile "Time Keeper Stations."

Shots nearer the manhole they'd come up warned him Philip had probably popped up to see what was going on.

He snatched up the fallen crowbar and ran for the next crate. It was open. Someone was doing part of his work for him. But it wasn't iron inside. A flash of bright green across the hold sent him around the crate's side just before a bullet tried to embrace him.

Lunging back, Colin released the PullLine's grapple and sent it to the ceiling in the center of the hold. He leapt onto the crate and rode the retracting line into the thirty-foot airspace above the crates, counting the brilliant green patches shining around the crates below as he flew upward. Maybe a dozen men, if one or two were hidden from view. Most were at the front of the hold. He sent the crowbar spinning toward the man who'd just tried to shoot him and was about to try again and then flicked his leather-and-brass bound wrist. When he fisted his hand, his upward movement slowed, and he hung momentarily suspended as the line detached from the ceiling and raced back to its reel on his gauntlet.

Pulling the pistol topped with a crossbow from this belt, he sighted the closest Time Keeper and fired the stun dart loaded on the miniature crossbow. The man toppled. Colin plummeted. The retracting line clicked into position, and he sent it out again to where the ceiling met the wall and arched his body. As he swung down and over the crates, a door crashed open above. Yells and the pounding of footfalls beat their way through the ceiling. More ASU men?

Pain erupted in Colin's side as a bullet grazed him just above his left hip. He released the line and followed his momentum onto the top of a crate beside the man he'd stunned. He jerked as the wail of a Banshee blasted through the hold again and again, each echo growing softer and ghostlier. Someone had noticed Nick on the lift then. His protective suit would redirect the bullet's force into vibrational energy, sound waves, and heat. Nick would get a good shaking, a bruise, and possibly a minor burn, but no puncture. But Nick wasn't invincible. How long before he managed to open the doors to the sub's hold?

Ignoring the wet warmth spilling down his side, Colin crawled forward on the crate's top, his gaze searching the open crate about five feet away. Not his harpoons. He loaded another stun dart onto the crossbow and rolled off the crate. He'd not use a bullet on a man doing his job to keep smuggling in check.

Colin landed on a bulging sack and slipped. He jumped back and landed in a crouch amid packets of powder spilled from the sack. A sense of foreboding twisting his gut, he yanked up a packet. White powder. Cursing, he crawled to the downed man and flipped him over. No Time Keeper insignia. A drug runner come to collect a load that idiot Neil had probably promised him and failed to deliver for some reason? The only thing Latimer hated worse than Time Keepers and cowards were the runners of the drugs that ruined his brother-in-law and brought his sister so much pain. It hadn't been Latimer who'd put the chrurhol here. But if these men were drug runners, that meant the ASU—

The door to the hold crashed open.

—had only just arrived.

"I want them alive," a man yelled as heavily armed and armored Time Keepers flooded through the doorway. "Bleeding is acceptable."

Colin ducked out of sight as gunfire erupted at the front of the hold. The drug runners had no qualms about bloodshed, and for once he felt badly for the Time Keepers. Huddling closer to the wooden, useless-against-bullets crate, he rotated a few gears attached to a series of small, removable tubes on his gauntlet, a recent modification. *Please work.* A slight mist puffed between the tubes but blew away. Shifting the tubes further apart, he tried again, this time blowing on them and giving them a good whack. The mist drifted between the tubes again, this time coiling tightly into a rope of silvery air that stretched to follow the tubes as he repositioned two of the three.

He placed one tube on the top of his shoulder and one on his back, at his belt on the opposite side. The line of compressed mist stretched between them. Bringing his gauntleted wrist with the third tube nearly up to his shoulder, he rotated his arm in a cranking motion a few times. There was a soft whir in the tubes, and a Mist Breaker, two circles nearly two feet wide each, materialized between the tubes, one a shield from gauntlet to shoulder, the other over his back from shoulder to hip. Moist air spun in them fast enough, he prayed, to deflect bullets.

Puffing out a breath of relief, he picked up the stunned man's crowbar and dashed to the next crate. He shoved the rope bindings off it, wedged the crowbar into the crate's side, leveraged his weight against it until it creaked open, then repeated the process at another corner of the crate.

A lion's roar shook the room, eliciting a number of curses

and startled cries. Colin worked faster. The heavy thump of a body hitting the floor nearby told him Nick was covering him.

Someone near the front screamed. A young man taking his first bullet. Colin ground his teeth and shoved the crate's lid to the floor. The *crack* as it hit the floor did little to ease the pull to join the fight. *I'm here for the iron, not to protect bloody Time Keepers.*

"Dead is acceptable," the Time Keeper from earlier yelled, anger edging into his controlled voice.

Colin ducked as wood splintered above him, and the Wind Breaker sputtered as it flung debris away from him. He rolled into the aisle, took a split second to note the lack of the Time Keeper insignia on the shirt of the man there, and fired his pistol. He lunged back behind the crate and brushed the sawdust from whatever lay inside.

His hands swept along something cold, straight, and cylindrical with a barbed end. Heart pounding, Colin pulled a magnet from a slot in his gauntlet and held it to one of the slender rods lying black as night amid the green sawdust. The magnet tried to drag his fingers down to the harpoon. The *iron* harpoon. He breathed a prayer of thanks as he scooted out and reattached the crate's lid. He yanked a thumb-sized corked bottle from his pocket, wrenched out the cork, and doused the luminescent blue woad dye along the crate's sides.

Blue. For the true sky.

For Vesper's eyes.

He slipped the rope bindings back in place, hoisted himself on top of the crate, and emptied the remaining dye where all the rope bindings met at the attachment point for the lift. Putting his fingers to his lips, he let out a whistle loud enough to be heard over the yells and shots, waved his arms, then dove off the crate. And none too soon. Wood splintered around him, and the Mist Breaker hissed.

But the lift creaked as Nick swiveled it around to him.

"Stop that lift!" cried the Time Keeper with the loud, cultured voice.

The deafening beating of wings and the screeching calls of a monstrous flock gripped Colin's chest as he climbed onto the next crate, making the air feel crowded with birds about to dive bomb him. He glanced at Nick. The faint lines in his suit glowed brighter from the hit. They wavered, as if Nick were shaking. How much more could he stand? They might have to go back to the drawing board for that design.

The lift's hook swung toward the luminescent blue stain. Colin leapt onto the crate, caught the hook, and secured it. He whistled again and grabbed the rope above the hook as the crate rose into the air, rocking with each of Colin's movements to flatten himself against its top. With his hands secure on the rope, the crate momentarily steady, Colin stilled. His eyes slipped shut by themselves and his body went limp, stealing a moment of rest. Blood, both dried and fresh stained his side and pants. The excitement of the fight would only keep the pain and weakness at bay for so long. Colin forced his eyes open and his body back to alertness. A large black rectangle in the floor not far ahead confirmed that Nick had gotten the hatch to the sub's hold open.

A movement in bright green dragged his gaze to the foot of the ladder leading to the lift station and Nick. A man, trim and not so tall as Colin, with a Time Keeper insignia on his uniform, started up the ladder like a general determined to do what his men had failed to. Despite the bullets still whizzing through the hold.

Leaving one hand on the rope, Colin released his smaller PullLine lead, one with a suction ending, hit the man square in the back, and jerked. The Time Keeper cried out as he flew backwards. Colin released the PullLine. The man hit the floor, sprang up with surprising grace, and fired at Colin.

Colin ducked, then jumped off the crate as it began to lower into the sub's hold. He caught a glimpse of Philip waiting below to guide the cargo into place, then darted to the ladder behind the Time Keeper. He leapt onto the second rung, raced up two more, and grabbed the fast-moving man's heel. The man's kick nearly caught Colin in the jaw. Colin released the ladder, trapped the man's foot between both his hands, and sprang backwards, using all his weight to rip the Time Keeper from the ladder. He crashed to the floor with the man's legs on top of him. The Mist Breaker puffed out. Biting his lip to keep from crying out as pain shot through him, Colin rolled over and lunged forward, pinning the man to the floor as he tried to rise.

Colin lay across him, using his weight against the lighter man, and pressed his arms above his head against the floor. "We're not the ones trying to kill you," Colin snapped as the man attempted to knee him.

The crate disappeared into the sub's hold.

"Tell him to stop the crate," the man ground out, struggling to free his arms. "There are men outside. You won't escape."

"Good thing we're not going out then," Colin huffed, his arms trembling with effort, his side roaring in protest.

"It's the only way any of you will leave alive." There was something familiar in the lines of the man's face, scrunched though it was with his struggle.

"Some deaths are worth dying, Time Keeper." Colin's elbow began to buckle, the man's hand to rise.

Philip whistled a retreat, the crane's rope loosened, and water rushed into the sub's hold.

"Look out!" Nick cried. Colin flattened against the Time Keeper and drew his gauntleted arm beside their heads. A bullet ricocheted off it with a force Colin's arm wouldn't soon forget. Grunting, Colin grabbed the man's shoulders and rolled with him as another bullet hit the floor behind them.

"Don't make me come up there," Philip yelled. As if they didn't know it was time to go.

He pushed off the Time Keeper, but the man grabbed his wrist. Colin's tattoo, vivid dark shapes on his green arm, was turned toward him like the red hour glass of a black widow, unmistakable and always a shock. The man hissed, and his other fist connected with Colin's jaw, sending him sprawling backwards. The man pulled himself up and crouched as if ready to spring, but Philip shoved him away toward the shelter of a barrel.

"Stop!" Several Time Keepers charged their way.

Colin struggled to get his feet under him. Philip grabbed him by the arm and pulled him up. Together, they darted for the gaping hole the harpoons had disappeared into, reaching it as Nick stumbled to it.

"Stop!"

The three men jumped.

CHAPTER SEVEN

esper startled awake sometime before the
brightening and blinked against the light coming
into the hospital room along with a limping man.
Gasping, she jumped from her chair and turned on
another lamp. "Daddy!" She barely managed to keep her
voice down as she hugged her father and helped him
collapse into a seat beside her uncle's bed. Red smeared his
shirt.

"You're bleeding!"

Dermot groaned and Eoin caught his daughter's hand as
she reached for the nurse's bell. "It's not my blood, Vesper. I
wasn't seriously hurt. Please, keep your voice down, for
Dermot's sake."

Vesper stilled, then squeezed Eoin's hand and sank onto
the edge of Dermot's bed. She clasped her locket, the force of
her grip causing the chain to bite into her neck. "There was
fighting then, obviously?"

Eoin nodded, though he stared at his brother-in-law, who
moaned as he woke.

"The doctors think he'll be fine if he takes care of himself," Vesper said.

"Thank goodness for that." His eyes drifting shut, Eoin rested his head on his hand.

"Was ... was anyone hurt?"

He sat up and shook his head slightly. "Four of our men were shot, including Jimmy. They're here. I think they'll be okay. We killed over half the smugglers and captured all but three. One of those three claimed not to be connected with the drug runners."

Vesper closed her eyes, her grip on the locket turning her knuckles white. *Thank you, Maker.*

"They got away in a submarine with a crate," he continued, his voice odd, "but we'll find them."

"Do you think you'll recognize them?"

He sat quietly, rubbing a thumb over his wrist, the one not covered by his Vanon bracer. "Perhaps. Yes, I think so."

"I can't believe we got away, and with the iron!" Nick exclaimed for the third time. He sat in the bottom of the dinghy, propped against the side of the small craft. He'd barely been able to stand after the adrenaline rush ended on their uneventful escape in the submarine to Six Mile Island. A tug boat, its captain a Sky Keeper known for using his tug to fish at night, met them at the island and took over the sub, hauling it beneath his tug to a dock where Colin could pick it up before leaving. Where the Port Inspection and Anti-Smuggling Unit would never look for it.

The sky crystals were beginning to brighten for day as Philip and Will rowed the rented dinghy and the four men back to shore, where a Time Keeper was likely watching for them. Colin prayed he and Nick would have the strength to walk from the dock, or that the smell of the brandy Philip doused them with would be sufficient to explain why they needed help. Fortunately, they'd brought non-bloody clothes to change into.

Once safely in the sub, Philip had forced liquids into Colin and bandaged his side, then stripped the protective suit off Nick and put ointment on several burns. Now, Colin sat opposite Nick, his eyes closed but still feeling the brightening light. He forced his mind from the darkness of sleep and pain to the question of dawn.

Did it really grace the morning with the beauty of a woman's blush as the poets claimed? Would it compete with Vesper's blush? Would he get to see an actual dawn before he died? For the first time ever, he thought he might.

"We may have the iron all right, lads." Philip's voice grated in the silence, and Colin opened his eyes and straightened, determination not letting hope die despite the warning in Philip's tone. "But we don't know where the iron's needed, where the Star Veil is anchored. Our job's not done yet."

PART IV
MOON SONG

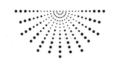

And God made the two great lights—the greater light to rule the day and the lesser light to rule the night—and the stars. And God set them in the expanse of the heavens to give light on the earth, to rule over the day and over the night, and to separate the light from the darkness. And God saw that it was good.

Genesis 1:14-18

CHAPTER ONE

It is said Morgan Unseelie cast the hated Star Veil for the Time King, a ruthless ruler whose descendants had no hope of reigning, for their sire was a man who never aged, another gift of the faerie queen.
But all gifts come at a price.

REYDON, CAPITAL OF RÌOGHACHD CRIOSTAIL AND HOME OF THE RÍ AM, ULRIK VANON
TWO WEEKS LATER

"Only pirates would consider knocking their *friends* senseless all part of a day's job."

"Just hit me, Nick." Colin scooted his knees apart to brace himself as the skiff in which he knelt swerved toward shore. "We've gone seven miles. We can't keep swapping navigators. We've hit the scramble distance for groups." He grabbed the side of the boat as it veered in the opposite direction.

"I'm sorry," Philip yelled over the roar of the engine and

the rush of wind. "I can't keep it on course. It's that bloody curse."

Nick stared at Colin's bare neck, then flicked a glance at Will, unconscious by Colin's own hand, lying in the skiff's floor. For a fierce man in battle, Nick had a soft heart, which wasn't helpful when they were racing Time Keepers to get to the beached submarine.

"But, Captain—" Nick began.

"We can't control the boat again until half of us have lost consciousness, and we don't have time for a nap, so use the brachial stun!"

Colin woke shortly in the bottom of the boat. Philip was pulling Will up and pushing him toward the controls. The wildly veering boat straightened out. The outskirts of the coastal city was easily visible as they sped parallel to the shore toward the city proper with its smoke stacks and glass and metal windows and towers blinking in the bright sky crystal light. Full glow was *not* when he'd wanted to recover the submarine's goods and passengers.

With a sheepish look, Nick offered Colin a hand up.

"Thanks, Nick." Colin let Nick pull him up and onto a seat. Ignoring his headache, Colin pulled out his spyglass. The WACU—the Women's Auxiliary Communication Unit, an association of smugglers' and pirates' wives and daughters adept at sending information to keep their men safe—had alerted his grandmother about a submarine beached on a sandbar some miles from the Reydon port. They ought to be approaching it soon. He'd been planning on getting the submarine's passengers and contents to shore that night, for the *Dawn Singer* had only arrived the previous morning. The sub left a day behind them to give Colin time to prepare.

"What do you think happened?" Nick asked as he too scanned the water ahead for the *Sea Snake*.

"I don't know. I told the Lockleys to keep an eye on the depth reader and time-to-docking readout. When they neared land, they were to sever the automaton's head to keep it from sailing into port like a prodigal son, then settle on the bottom of the bay. There may have been an instrument failure." Water sprayed Colin as the boat jerked around a pod of dolphins playing. "The *Sea Snake* hasn't been serviced in over ten years, so that's not exactly unexpected. There it is!"

A gray spire rose over a length of steel body and glass front like a shark's fin. The forty-foot sub listed to one side, the starboard-side water light brown and shallow.

Beyond it, speeding from the main port, were two Time Keeper Port Authority Vessels, their authority and the power to enforce it displayed in the trees emblazoned on their hulls.

"What does the third ship read?" Will yelled as they crashed over a wave.

"Faerie queen!" Nick hissed. "It's the Anti-Smuggling Unit's boat." His hand hovered protectively above a sore spot over his heart that would have been a fatal bullet wound if not for one of Davy and Colin's inventions. "And I don't have my suit."

"Pity." Philip hefted a portable cannon the length of a man's arm to his shoulder. "You could've sung us a selkie song." Philip backed up against Nick, using the broad-shouldered man as a brace, and sighted the sandbar a few feet from the sub.

"Just none of you sing the death rattle today. Captain's orders." Colin tucked the spyglass back into his belt and activated the ping reader beside it. He tapped out a series of pings the Lockleys could read on the submarine. *Coming aboard. TK on way. Prepare to roll.*

As he stood, his side reminded him it'd only had two weeks to heal since the last encounter with the ASU—and the drug runners—and urged him to caution. He ignored it and strapped on his air tank and pulled on his goggles, but he left the mouthpiece hanging around his neck. Adjusting the goggles to dim the glare on the water, Colin sighted the sub and incoming boats.

The Time Keepers were about thirty yards from the sub, Colin's skiff about twenty. The sub lay silent and still between them. He checked the ping reader. No response.

"Stay clear of the submarine by order of the Time Keepers!" The tinny command blasted their way from the ASU boat.

"Will," Colin yelled, "hold your course. Get me as close as you can to the *Snake* without getting us stuck on the sandbar. As soon as I'm on board, Philip, you fire the charge. Nick, hit them with the Dragon's Breath and Pea Soupers. We only have two each, so choose wisely. Take out those ships' Sea Gazers, if you can, so they can't spot us underwater. If you can't without getting shot, then don't. I have other uses for you all. Remember that."

"Right, Captain."

"Will, do you remember how to work my grandfather's modifications to the skiff?"

Will grinned. "Oh yes."

Colin grinned back, then slapped Nick hard enough to send the farewell to Philip still braced against him. "See you at the bottom." Stepping to the boat's edge, Colin checked the silent ping reader, then glanced up with a brief prayer. *Don't let Darius and Caroline be dead or injured. And help us get out of here without hurting anyone.*

For they *were* leaving with the iron.

Then all they had to do was find out where the Star Veil was and how to get the iron to it before his father and Davy arrived on the *Breaker*. Easy as jumping off an airship...

Ahead, a narrow section of deep blue wove between light brown banks. The *Snake* nestled on the end of a sandbar near the deeper passage but still about five feet back. Colin rocked back and forth on his heels.

"Repeat, stay clear of the submarine. This is your last warning."

"We're gettin'!" Will steered the boat up the narrow passage and whipped the aft toward the sub.

Colin stepped back, then lunged for the gray hull. Metal clanged and water arced around him as he landed on its edge. A dull thud, followed by a whoosh of swirling water, told him Philip's explosive was now buried in the sandbank. *Three hundred steady beats—however long that was in actual time—and counting to get the sub ready to roll.* Crouching, he ran along the rounded top toward the hatch, unease twisting his gut at the gaping darkness where the porthole should be. Had the Lockleys abandoned ship?

The sharp report of a rifle proved the Time Keepers *had* given their last warning. Colin dove belly down into the shallow water sweeping over the sandbar and scooted next to the sky crystal–warmed metal of the sub. The bullet dinged against the hull where he'd been. *Come on, Nick.* Four hisses rent the air in short succession. One hiss ended in a *clunk* as a round, orange-sized Pea Souper Distraction Device hit the sub, concentrated "fog" spilling from it. *Good choice, Nick.*

The *tick tick* of the charge in the sand below him warred

with the continued rounds of ammunition denting the physical cover provided by the sub as the fog continued to spread and thicken. The sound varied slightly as the angle of impact changed, as if the ship was circling his way. How long before the Dragon's Breath breathed? He scooted forward toward the hatch, sparing a brief thought of gratitude for the small blessing that his diving suit kept the sand out of his clothes.

A few feet beyond the periscope, the open hatch formed a dark hole barely visible in the artificial fog. A scream and curses and the report of a fired gun from the ASU boat sent him belly down again, the *tick tick* below charging his nerves. The curses reassured him. No one would dare fire another shot while Dragon's Breath lingered in the air. He leapt up and bolted onto the sub, darted past the periscope, sprang for the hatch, and fell down it to a woman's scream. She sprang back, falling to the floor as Colin crashed down.

"Welcome aboard, Captain," the woman said sarcastically as she picked herself up off the sub's floor a few feet from where he landed. She slid a revolver back into its holster. With her mouth set in a grim line, steel in her eyes, and a revolver for a companion, Caroline Lockley only wanted a wrist tattoo to be a pirate queen. Or a uniform to be a Bowditch captain. It was more than chivalry that made Colin glad he hadn't fallen on her.

"Seal up, Lockley. We're diving." He sprinted past her to the control room.

"We're only one notch above the warning level for air!"

However long the air would last was still likely only half the time of fog and Dragon's Breath cover, if the wind didn't pick up.

"It'll be enough," he yelled over his shoulder.

"With three Time Keeper ships up there?"

"Caroline, seal up! Then strap yourself down some-where." Darius Lockley's bellow sent his niece into motion, grumbling, as Colin entered the control room. "O'Connor. Thank heavens." Darius stepped away from the headless automaton navigator and the rows of dials, levers, and knobs. "The air system malfunctioned after we stopped the naviga-tor, and we had to surface. We ran aground trying to avoid a ship. I can't get us off. I'm a printer, not a sailor!"

"We're taking care of it. Just be prepared to hold on when you hear a high-pitched whine." Colin expanded the strap holding the automaton in the captain's chair and lashed himself to the chair's back, then focused on the fine naviga-tion controls.

"What's that noi—" Caroline shouted.

"Hold on!"

A deep rumble shook the sub, and the ship slid on spreading sand. Colin hit the thrusters on the starboard side and tipped the nose down. The *Sea Snake* rolled down the sandbar as a second charge pounded them, accelerating their flips. Colin felt his stomach dip five times before the sub stilled. Leaning around the headless automaton to reach the dials, he spun the sub's nose around to the open sea and engaged the propellers for forward motion. Full speed ahead.

"Check in!" Colin didn't turn as he watched the depth meter readings and glanced out the two windows wrapping the control room. He may as well have been in a desert sand storm for all the visibility he had.

"Okay." Darius grunted as he hauled himself off the floor.

"No broken bones," Caroline grumbled from deeper in the ship. "I didn't hear a crash, so I guess the cargo straps held."

Colin let out a relieved breath and focused on guiding the speeding sub in the direction he thought was away from the port and toward the cove where his grandmother lived. *Passengers alive. Cargo safe. So far, so good.* Caroline and Darius Lockley had been a surprise cargo from his aunt in Hollym. On their way to Reydon for a Sky Keeper meeting, but officially for a seaside holiday, the printer and his niece had given their train tickets to a couple of Sky Keepers on the run, then went to Colin's aunt's house. They figured Fiona could find a way to smuggle them and the navigation books they'd printed—copies of the books given them by Marianna and Bertram—to Reydon eventually. Colin was always glad to help Sky Keepers, but he quickly discovered by shrewd guesses and a warning note that this pair would come in handy. The Time Keepers hadn't let the *Dawn Singer* out of their sight in Hollym and had searched it three times before letting her leave. Colin hadn't dared shift any of his crew to the submarine to pilot it before he left or even during the voyage. Two Time Keeper ships had flanked the *Dawn Singer* its entire flight from Hollym to Reydon.

He'd had to hand over the precious iron shipment to an ink-covered, bespectacled, lion-hearted printer and his equally lion-hearted niece.

"Good. Air tanks and swim gear?" Colin asked.

"We've got them," Darius said, "but we'll never make it to land with them, not between the curse and the Time Keeper ships. We'd run out of air even if we found our way."

"We won't have to swim the entire way, but we've got to drop the cargo and send the sub off as a decoy. My boat will pick us up."

"Again," Caroline said, "those three Time Keeper ships? Or did you sink them?"

Colin's burgeoning, smug smile faltered. "They won't see us, and I didn't sink them. Did you already put your personal belongings in the crate with the iron, as I told you?"

"Yes, first thing this morning," Darius said with a scowl at his niece, "and we sealed the crates with grease." He picked up the automaton's head from a corner and secured it on its lap along with the pliers to reattach it to the doll-like body.

Colin nodded his thanks. "Then suit up. I'm going to flip the sub again and open the hold. We'll release the crates with my iron and your books and ease them down. The third crate we'll leave."

Darius and Caroline did as bidden, and Darius swapped positions with Colin before Colin reached the Scramble Distance. He checked the oxygen levels as Darius took the controls. Two notches to the danger level, and he was already feeling short of breath. Twisting the ping reader on his belt to face him, he tapped out a message to Philip. *Location? Low on oxygen here.*

At your rear. Fleet approaching. Stop now.

Will do.

Colin rapped Darius on the shoulder, causing him to turn around, and was relieved to see that Darius's skin color was still normal. "Start using your air tank. Slow the ship and steer her toward that rock outcropping."

He flipped on the ship's intercom. It didn't work. Not as important as oxygen but rather nice to have. He stepped into the narrow hallway and yelled toward the cargo hold. "Lockley, seal the flood chamber leading to the cargo hold and prepare for another roll. Start using your air tank."

The ping reader went off again as Colin slipped the mouthpiece to his air system into position. He struggled to catch the words in the series of dots and dashes as he helped Darius slow and guide the sub.

Is that a sunken ship ahead? Will wants to know.

Yes. No time to explore.

Not far to the right, the reef's middle was crushed under an old merchant ship with a broken hull. A perfect cycle of revenge, Colin thought grimly.

Its treasure went into building the skiff.

So pirating does pay.

Yes, and cheaters prosper. Until justice catches up. Signing off.

He tapped Darius on the shoulder again and thumbed toward the restraints hanging from the ceiling. Darius and Caroline gripped them and braced their feet near the wall as if ready to walk up the wall when the roll began. Colin strapped himself to the navigator's chair, took over the controls, and slowly adjusted the spin control.

Out the window, the fish swimming by and the rock jungle beyond them appeared to dive down, their rear fins rising, as the sub rolled gently upside down, then stilled.

"Are those fish belly up?" Caroline laughed, and Colin almost joined her. But the fog would be gone by now, and he didn't know where the Time Keeper vessels were searching.

He opened the outer cargo hold hatch. The sub bobbed up and down as water filled the hold. Colin released the strap keeping him attached to the navigator's chair and flipped backwards to stand on the ceiling. With Darius and Caroline following, he sprinted to the cargo hold flood chamber and ushered them inside. Darius hit the inner door release, and water from the hold rushed in. Cold water pressed against Colin's legs and brushed his fingertips and face as it filled the chamber. Once again, he was grateful for the black dive suit and swim cap that both concealed his identity from the Time Keepers and his body from the chill sea.

Caroline pushed off the inner door and swam up to the two marked crates and untied the straps as Colin and Darius grabbed the sides and slowed their descent through the open hatch and onto the sand. Caroline moved toward the third crate and its basalt harpoons, a gift from the Sky Keeper who'd repaired the *Dawn Singer*, who thought the harpoons might fool the Anti-Smuggling Unit into thinking they'd been tricked about the iron. Colin darted back up into the hold and caught Caroline's heel. He motioned her and Darius to the shelter of the rock forest beside the sub.

He gave her a push in that direction and wafted backward accordingly. She swam between two jutting rocks, Darius following. A series of bubbles floated up, and Caroline darted back out, plowing into Darius and sending him floating off.

Six feet of sleek wonder swam out from between the rocks behind her. Colin ducked as the eel took its curving way above him, between him and the sub. But his awe was cut short as a spotlight caught on his companions. The beam was too narrow to be from the Time Keeper ships on the surface.

Through the dim water, his grandfather's modified skiff motored their way. Upside down, with a propeller on top to keep it under water, the motor and rudder on back to drive it, an air pump to make it breathable, and an expanded metal casing and glass windshield to seal it, *The Pearl* was a treasure indeed. With luck, anyone watching would think it sank when it flipped over and disappeared into the water.

The ship slowed, the metal bottom folded back, and

Nick and Will floated out with a large canvas balloon attached by a hose to *The Pearl*'s air pump. They swam toward the crate of iron but stopped and pointed to large shadows further darkening patches of the sea floor beyond them, then up to the surface.

Colin kicked onto his back and flipped his telescopic lens down on his goggles. A dozen sloops broke the surface a little ways back toward the city outskirts and were approaching quickly. A skull and crossbones leered down at him from the bottom of half of them, a barrel and knife from most of the others. But on one was the design matching his wrist tattoo, a triquetra and compass rose. That craft stayed carefully in the center of the group. He pressed his hand to his heart, then raised it to the ship. They had a way to shore.

Signaling his friends to hurry, he left Darius and Caroline to help Nick and Will secure and inflate the balloons to the two crates while he climbed back into the submarine. After closing the cargo hold and starting the bilge pump running in it, he passed through the flood chamber and, when it had emptied of water, went on to' the dry control room. With a glance around to make sure they'd left no clues, he re-attached the automaton's head and set the sub into motion, programming it to speed up after three minutes. He fiddled with the settings until, with any luck, the submarine would explode at sea before running into any vessels or its port.

He sprinted to the diver release station and plunged into the sea, getting as far from the influence of the sub's forward momentum as possible, then swam back to *The Pearl* with its two jelly fish–like followers floating closely behind it.

After sardining all six of them into *The Pearl*, Philip took over the controls. The metal case expanded again, and the water spewed out. Colin shoved the wooden cover off a skylight in the skiff's bottom—the current ceiling—as they rose to meet the oncoming sloops. Following his directions, Philip brought them even with the compass rose decorating the bottom of Colin's grandmother's ship. She'd had the sloop repainted after his grandfather died seven years ago.

After stopping its whirling, Colin unscrewed the top propeller and lowered it into the ship, slid the expandable rod to its shortened form, and folded the whole thing into its place in the deck's flooring. They righted the ship and retracted the expanded metal casing, covering them all with water.

It was just a skiff that docked under the sloop *Sun Bolt.* Colin banged on the bottom of the sloop as water was pumped out of *The Pearl.* The triquetra disappeared as a hatch opened.

A backlit figure knelt beside the opening and leaned down to cup Colin's face in her hands and kiss his cheek. "Welcome back, grandson."

She released him and scooted back. "Keep *The Pearl*'s motor running to compensate for the extra weight you've brought. I won't come in last, even for you, Colin O'Connor."

CHAPTER TWO

"We got a license for a race a week ago. Paid good money for automatons too." Arms crossed, Bridie O'Connor stood at the edge of the *Sun Bolt*, her height nearly equal to that of the two Time Keepers in the ship pulling alongside theirs. Bright blue eyes, smooth skin, and silver-touched hair, she was a woman age hadn't caught. "You can't just turn us around midway because some piece of sea junk exploded."

Stretched out on the warm, open deck, Colin leaned back, bracing himself with his arms, and glanced around the dozen or so sloops and skiffs of various sizes all rigged out with sails and manned by the fierce woman of the WACU. They'd obligingly moved up the date of the semi-annual race when he'd asked his grandmother for help in getting the iron and the Lockleys to the safety of their cove. Two ships over, Nick's dark skin stood in contrast to the bright dresses and golden hair of the two girls who'd claimed his and Will's attention. His young cousins had grown up since he'd left. He suspected his grandmother was glad to get Nick and Will over to their boat for more than just separating Colin's group in the little time they'd had to change and disperse before the Time Keepers halted the race. Bridie had rather forcefully sent Philip, a not-disinclined Philip, to the girls' mother, his widowed aunt Fiona, who was helping a friend on another boat. That just left the Lockleys and him with Bridie.

"It's more complicated than that, Mrs. O'Connor," the unfamiliar Anti-Smuggling Unit officer said. Colin hoped he only worked locally and hadn't been in the warehouse at Hollym. Nonetheless, he checked that his sleeve hid his tattoo. He had a feeling the man who'd seen it wouldn't forget it. "We're *going* to inspect the ship and reverse the automaton. We'll give all your ladies a certificate for replacement navigators."

Bridie narrowed her eyes at them, arms still crossed in refusal to catch the tie rope and connect the boats. "That's a guarantee about the automatons and license?"

"Yes."

She sighed heavily but uncrossed her arms and motioned for them to throw the rope. "Another day for my win then. I bet the weather won't be as fair," she grumbled, catching the rope and lashing the ships together.

Caroline, sitting close beside Colin, giggled. Colin sent her a warning look, but she grinned mischievously, then batted her eyelashes at him before turning to Bridie. "You'll invite me along next time, won't you, Mrs. O'Connor? I wouldn't miss another day of open Star Veil and crystal glow for anything." She lowered her voice for only Colin to hear. "Another day in the sub and I would've eaten that six-foot eel tip to tail just to see the light again."

Bridie winked at her and fell into line behind the two Time Keepers determined to search the ship. She seemed equally determined to make certain they touched nothing and noticed less. "That depends on my grandson and your uncle."

"You'll invite me, won't you, Colin dear?" Caroline simpered. "Oh, please say you will."

Resisting the urge to roll his eyes, Colin smiled at her. "Would you and your uncle do us the honor of joining us on another day, Miss Lockley?"

"Oh, Uncle! Did you hear? We've been invited for another excursion!"

Sitting beside the automaton at the wheel a few feet away, Darius cleared his throat suspiciously before nodding. "Yes, dear, I heard." He gave Colin a commiserating shrug, as if to say, *You started this charade by sitting next to her. You'll have to put up with it or stop it yourself.*

Not knowing quite what to do, Colin lay back on the warm deck and rested his head on one arm. Almost without thinking, he pulled a small pouch on a leather chain from under his shirt and rubbed the soft leather between his fingers. It held two letters and the key to Davy's study and its inventions.

Scooting away a few inches, Caroline rested on her side, facing him, and released a great sigh. "I should've known."

"Known what?"

"That there was another woman."

Colin's fingers stilled on the pouch. "Where?" he asked blankly, glancing around.

Eyes twinkling, Caroline tapped the pouch. "There. I should've known you'd never fancy a woman of such an advanced age as twenty-five."

Colin snorted and slid the pouch back under his shirt. "I'm twenty-three, Caroline, and I highly doubt any heartbreak on your part. I was under the impression that first time we met that you wanted to shoot me."

"How perceptive of you. I'm embarrassed to admit I *was* contemplating it."

"You wouldn't be the first."

"You're positive you and your father didn't attack the *Dusk Crier* and drop the crew off on some deserted island?"

"The *Dusk Crier* went down in a storm, according to the Time Keepers who found the wreckage." That's not to say he and his father hadn't attacked the *Dusk Crier* on multiple occasions.

Frowning, Caroline lay flat on her back and stared up at the Star Veil. "My brother sailed on the *Dusk Crier*. He was one of the fools loyal enough to go with that arrogant numskull Kingsley Bowditch on his search for the mythical island where men still know how to navigate themselves."

"I'm sorry." Colin could only hope those two words, as deficient as they seemed, carried all the genuine sorrow he felt for her loss and his past. On first meeting Caroline and her uncle, he'd gotten a terrible feeling he'd tried to kill her brother. He certainly had Kingsley Bowditch, a brilliant, daredevil of a captain and the bane of pirates. *Thank you, Maker, for keeping me from some of the evil I intended.*

She let out a long breath and closed her eyes. "Ever since he disappeared I've never been quite certain how to treat a Bowditch captain: with respect or enmity. Since my father died during a pirate attack, I know perfectly well how to treat those."

Colin winced but decided to address only the first issue. "A lot of brave men were lost on that ship. Commodore Bowditch regrets not having tried harder to prevent Kingsley from going."

From the wheel, Darius huffed. "Courage gets a lot of men killed." He nodded at his niece. "She's got the same courage that led her brother astray; only she has the sense not to throw it away on hopeless dreams and impulsive schemes. Foolish loyalties." He added softly, "I pray she holds on to that sense. I worry sometimes."

"I'm still listening, Uncle," Caroline said without opening her eyes.

"I know it."

"And Herschel's not dead," she retorted, sitting up to glare at her uncle. "He's my twin. I'd know it if he were."

Colin touched her arm and flicked his gaze toward the departing Time Keepers.

Caroline's voice turned to a forceful, though quiet, hiss. "The Rí Am imprisoned him somewhere. I'm *going* to find him."

Eyes sad, Darius turned to watch the Time Keepers' boat detach and move away. Colin said a prayer for Caroline's boast to prove true. Somehow, he believed her, that her brother, and maybe even Kingsley Bowditch, were still alive, captives to the Time King.

A dark-haired young woman with a sparkle in her blue-green eyes and a smile that could light the ocean deep filled his memory. A crystal-studded armband choked the wrist she often tried to hide. Frowning, he traced the contours of the pouch again. There were different kinds of prisoners.

"So you prefer a princess then?"

"Huh?" Colin struggled to gather his thoughts as he turned to Caroline.

"You prefer a princess to an older, cynical woman and the eager young flirts your grandmother was shooing away after you stepped on deck."

"There are no princesses in Rìoghachd Criostail, Caroline."

"There are equivalents."

The gold-and-crystal bracelet gleamed as brightly as a crown in his memory. Try as he might, he couldn't deny that royalty of a sort existed there. "You're content to be an old maid. Why can't I be content to be an old bachelor?"

At her uncle's shush, Caroline checked her howl of laughter. "Oh, so you're the noble knight who prefers to admire his lady fair from afar? I figured as much."

"Quit your teasing and let the poor man alone," Bridie said good-naturedly as she dropped a hat on Caroline's lap. "And put this on. 'A hat to keep the skin fresh and a breeze to smooth it out keeps the pirate's wife sleek as his ship.'" She knelt beside Colin and for a moment seemed content to watch him, making up for three years of missed glances. She took his arm and rolled up his sleeve, exposing his tattoo, the pirate one covered by the Sky Keeper's. Colin squeezed her other hand. She smiled softly and met Caroline's gaze. "Even unlikely prayers are answered. Don't give up on your brother."

She released Colin's hand and stood. "Help me with the rigging, Colin. We're falling behind. I don't care who wins this race, so long as it's not that Bessie Gillum. She bet me a dinner *with you* if she beat us, and for the sake of the Lady of the Pouch, I'm not letting her win, even if we're racing back home."

"I'll second you there." Colin hopped up and helped let out more sail, his mind turning over Bridie's words to Caroline. That done, he stood by the mast and looked out over the picturesque horizon, white sails against darker water and a dimming sky. Like a painting.

His lips formed a smile without him meaning them to. She'd used a blocky print script this time and an artist selling a painting of the *Dawn Singer* to get the message to him. He pulled the folded slip of fine quality stationery from the pouch.

Dear Captain O'Connor,

Concerning those kitchen goods I mentioned, they will never pass a careful inspection. Please remove them. It's imperative you do not bring anything of such a quality on board again. Your companions—and you will have two—on your return voyage to Reydon would never approve of them.

Take care and farewell.

As Colin slipped the note back into the pouch and tucked it away, he added one more item to his list of things to do in Reydon: find a way to break crystal chains.

CHAPTER THREE

A charismatically gnarled tree was as essential to any graveyard as ornately carved headstones and dead persons. Vesper Vanon glanced in the mirror covertly attached to her easel and then up to the lumpy, spreading magnolia taking up two plots with its base and covering countless others with its thick, waxy leaves. Leaning toward her canvas, she carefully darkened the shadows under the summer canopy, her eyes darting between the subject, the canvas, the Time Keepers watching this section of the graveyard, and the young woman walking hesitantly toward the gated family plot behind her. Vesper gave the girl another glance. Slender, a shopkeeper's apron folded in her hand, and mousy brown hair under a hat that was respectable but certainly not one belonging to a person likely to be visiting this neighborhood of the dead, where Vanons and other especially wealthy persons were buried.

A heartbroken sweetheart was apparently as essential to

the tragedy of Mark's story as her cousin's own demise. An empty grave; an angry, grieving family; and a shortened lifetime of slavery in a dark, underground world.

Vesper wiped off her paintbrush and waved to the girl. "Claire! Over here." She rose and gestured for the girl to join her. "Claire!" she repeated as she walked toward her. The poor thing was staring at her with the largest brown eyes she'd ever seen and looked ready to bolt. Hardly a wise thing to do when being watched. "I see you brought the apron as I asked. Wonderful." She gestured to the easel, daring a prayer that the girl would catch on. "I've decided on a name for the painting: 'A Shopgirl on Break.'" Vesper managed to make eye contact with her, then flicked her gaze to the gate behind her. She gave her head a slight shake and motioned toward her setup. "It's not terribly exciting, I know," she prattled on, relieved when Claire inched toward the easel, "but it matches the idea. I brought a selection of books for you to pose with since I didn't know which one a shopgirl would be most likely to read on break."

"How do you know my name?" Claire whispered as Vesper took her arm and directed her to the bag of supplies by the easel. She kept glancing around and at Vesper's locket.

"I've always enjoyed snooping, so my cousin Mark used to tell me all his secrets to keep me out of his affairs." Vesper tugged Claire's arm and attention to the easel as the girl glanced at the gated family plot at the mention of Mark. "Stay away from there," Vesper whispered, removing Claire's hat and fluffing her hair in a manner she hoped made her look like an exacting artist. "The Vanon family's power and affluence is dependent on the Time King, so becoming a Sky Keeper is tantamount to treason. They'll want to know who influenced Mark to that decision, even if it means seeing who visits his grave."

Claire's eyes widened even more, and Vesper contemplated the possibility that she was a fae-owl. "But I didn't even know him until after—"

"That doesn't matter." Vesper picked up a book with a light green cover and held it beside the girl's skirt and face, then did the same with two other books of different colors, letting the girl regain her composure.

"Do shopgirls choose their reading materials based on color?" Claire's lips curved slightly despite the moisture in her eyes.

"I wouldn't know." Vesper winked at her. "But it seems logical to me." She chose an adventure with a light blue cover —Mark's favorite color—and arranged Claire under the magnolia. "How long do you have?"

"Not long. I'm on lunch. I just wanted to see—" She broke off, glanced down a moment, then took a determined breath and settled back into position.

Vesper gave her a sympathetic smile. "Wave the book when you need to go. Can you come back a couple more times for me to finish the painting and strengthen this ruse?"

Claire's eyes widened. "You *were* waiting for me then."

"Of course. Why else would I be in a cemetery? Much as I cherish any excuse to avoid attending gossip-filled card parties with my mother and sisters, sitting in a graveyard with Time Keeper spies at my back and the dead all around is not my first choice of excuses. But I figured a sensible young woman such as Mark claimed to have an affection for would wait until about now to visit his grave, so I decided to come each day this week." She added softly to herself, "And it wouldn't be wise to go to the docks now."

"He said that?"

"Something to that effect, yes." Vesper squeezed Claire's hand and returned to the easel to paint and to wish her art teacher was standing over her, sharing her talent just by her presence as she had when she'd tutored her. As it was, Vesper would have to hope the Time Keeper spies didn't expect her to both enjoy art *and* be good at it.

"You're a liar, Vesper Vanon."

"Really, Uncle Dermot!"

"I mean it. You're a much better artist than you give yourself credit for."

Vesper laughed and scooted her chair closer to her uncle's for a better view of the finished painting he held. He was recovering well from his heart attack, but the doctors had told him to rest a while longer. "It did turn out better than I expected. It might even look decent with an exquisite frame."

"I'll have it framed. Your aunt will love it." Squinting, Dermot studied the magnolia in the background. "That tree, I've seen it before. Is it the one just before the—" He faltered and turned wide brown eyes to search Vesper's face. He jerked his attention back to the painting, seeming to study every detail. Dread built in Vesper's chest.

"Uncle, I—" *Think I'd better be going.*

"That's one of Mark's books, isn't it? And the magnolia beside the family plot at the cemetery?"

Vesper gave a tiny nod of her head. Why this of all times must her artwork be presentable? When she both did and didn't want it understood?

He closed his eyes, pain flitting across his face. "And the girl is...?"

Again, she nodded, though he couldn't see, and laid a hand on her uncle's trembling one until he eased the painting down to his lap.

"She wanted to say goodbye," Vesper said. "I had to stop her."

"The watchers were put there for a reason, Vesper."

"She didn't have anything to do with Mark's decision."

"But she might know who did. Or be another useful lesson to wavering Vanons."

Vesper drew back, clutching her locket. "Uncle!"

"*I* didn't hire them, Vess. I can only assume they report directly to Grandfather Ulrik. And I'd rather this shopgirl be turned in than anyone else I care about." With a pointed look at her, Dermot leaned forward, resting his elbow on his unoccupied knee, and rubbed his forehead, reminding Vesper he was both a grieving parent and a man recovering from a heart attack.

Vesper hesitated, then released the locket and touched his arm. "She's very nice," she said softly.

Dermot huffed and sat up. "That will be a great comfort to my son as he labors in the crystal mines, knowing that there's one more broken heart lying at his feet, and a very nice one at that."

Vesper flinched at the acerbity of his voice but remained silent. Dermot contemplated her a moment, then sighed. He rested the foot-wide canvas carefully against the side of his chair rather than depositing it in the nearby wastebasket, which Vesper took as a good sign. He leaned back in the high-backed cushioned chair with an air of putting away their former topic.

"I suppose you know Eoin thinks there were both Sky Keepers and drug smugglers in the Hollym warehouse? That it was the Sky Keepers who used the stun darts and who got away?"

"Yes," she said cautiously. "He told me." *He told me the blood on his shirt was that of a Sky Keeper.* Her gut tightened, and all her mental assurances that she'd seen Colin seemingly hale and hearty giving orders from the deck of the *Dawn Singer* as her father's ships escorted the airship to Reydon couldn't make it relax.

"You might not know that Eoin was here earlier today," Dermot continued. "They found the wreckage of the missing submarine. It wasn't iron but basalt in the crate. Harpoons of some kind. No bodies."

It took all Vesper's control to make sure surprise, rather than fear or hope or the combination warring in her chest, showed on her face. "Basalt? How peculiar. I wasn't aware of a black market trade in whaling goods, other than of unwilling sailors. What happens now? Since it was a bust?"

"I guess we can't keep hunting for iron smugglers when there's no evidence of iron. The kid could've been lying to get us to raid his father's place out of revenge. The men on the unmarked skiff were after the sub though, and they obstructed the port authorities in apprehending it whole. What they wanted, we can't be sure of until we find them. It sank rather too conveniently, Eoin thinks."

"They were quite purposeful about not hurting anyone, isn't that so?" *So why hunt them?*

"Yes, which makes Eoin's job less than pleasant."

Vesper's heart twisted and warmed at the same time. Colin hadn't hurt anyone.

But had he failed in his mission? Or was he that clever?

Her uncle's narrowed gaze made her wonder if he thought the same.

"When is your yearly visit to Grandfather Ulrik?" Dermot asked suddenly.

"Next week."

"What about Cara's and Cait's?"

"Cara's is always around the same time as Mark's. Cait's is a couple of hours before mine. Why?"

"Mark didn't get a chance to come home after his meeting. He was never a good liar, but he wasn't fool enough to give away his change of allegiance easily. Don't take any paintings with you to the meeting, Vesper."

A HANDSOME MAN in possession of an elusive smile was a dangerous foe. Vesper considered herself a sensible woman and a capable conversationalist, but when a certain broad-shouldered, blond-haired airship captain jogged up to her outside her favorite bookstore, she wasn't sure she could manage even a comment on the weather. He was actually smiling ... at her.

"Vesper," Colin repeated as he reached her, his blue eyes sparkling with a light-hearted happiness she'd not seen there before. Philip sauntered up behind him and winked at her, a knowing look about him that piqued Vesper. She *would* pull herself together before Colin's beautiful smile turned into a smug, masculine smirk at her expense.

She stepped from the cobblestone street onto the sidewalk and readied her grin, and wasn't surprised that it came easily once called. "Captain O'Connor. Mr. Orren. This is a pleasant surprise. I didn't know sailors ventured so far from the docks, and to a bookstore!"

"We read too, if you remember," Colin said with another smile as he eased closer to get out of the way of passersby.

"She's forgotten us already?" Philip said with dramatic woe. "Or perhaps it was only a lovely dream and never happened?"

"I remember." Vesper laughed as she shook Philip's hand. "How could I forget—"

"Oh Vesper, darling."

Fighting a frown at the patronizing use of *darling*, Vesper whispered an "Excuse me a moment" to Colin and Philip and pivoted to face the two young women strolling her way. She sighed. The attacks had already begun. She preferred pirates and figured Colin and Philip did too.

She caught the girls' line of sight—it wasn't her—and moved to stand in front of the airmen, her back to them. Her smile threatened to turn smug. That ought to fix things. She couldn't be expected to introduce gentlemen she wasn't talking with.

"Good afternoon, Jen and Margo."

"We're so sorry to interrupt your conversation," Jen said after a brief greeting.

"Think nothing of it." Vesper's smile was polite and resolute. Colin and Philip had defended her from pirates; she could defend them from a different type of assault.

Jen pressed her lips together and eyed Colin again. At least, Vesper assumed he was the destination of her gaze, for it was over Vesper's shoulder. She finally refocused on Vesper and lowered her voice. "I suppose you've heard Cara's off again this weekend and that, well, Cait's not very happy about it? Perhaps you could distract her with an introduction to your friends."

Quickly guessing what Cait was unhappy about and who Cara was going with, Vesper said coldly, "I would imagine she's not." As embarrassment threatened to flush her cheeks, she wondered how far she dared go in defiance of hints for an introduction before the two reported her rudeness to her mother. As Margo opened her mouth, Vesper found she dared pretty far. "It was thoughtful of you to stop and greet me," she said in a clipped tone. "Don't let me keep you from your outing."

The girls' eyes flared wide, then narrowed, but they left, to Vesper's relief.

Vesper saw them off with a polite smile, then turned back to Philip and Colin. Only when she found them still there did it occur to her they could have slipped away, if they'd wanted. The unpleasant mix of sensations the girls brought faded away to be replaced by genuine warmth. "I do remember we share a love of reading. What are you looking for, if I might ask? I shall be quite shocked if Belmont's doesn't have it."

Colin's lips curved slightly as he stared down at her, then flattened out. "We're looking for history on Ulrik Vanon and the faerie queen."

"Oh." Vesper flicked a glance at Belmont's, then up at the crystal clock piercing the air above the Time Keeper station three blocks away. Her neck felt the pressure of her hand tugging on the locket's chain. She forced her hand to her side. "In that case, I don't believe even Belmont's can help you, for I don't believe there are any such works, or any mention beyond that in grammar school histories. The Rí Am carefully guards his privacy."

"I'm not surprised." Colin paused as a carriage with a rattling wheel clattered by. "But perhaps they have books on folklore that would help—"

"O'Connor!"

Vesper jumped and Colin spun around at the angry bellow drawing the attention of everyone on the street and in the shops. The broad-shouldered, gray-bearded man and his three equally robust sons all glared murder at Colin as they marched down the quickly emptying sidewalk. Perhaps spiteful, man-hunting gossips weren't so bad after all. Vesper's legs trembled at the thought of facing a pirate without the *Dawn Singer*'s assistance, for this man had the bearing of one even if dressed like a businessman.

"Why is that fool Latimer not in hiding?" Philip tugged Colin's arm as if attempting to get him to flee. "I don't think he wants to chat, Colin. Come on. If you'll excuse us, Vesper. Colin," Philip hissed when Colin stood rigid, his jaw set.

When this Latimer person added a few choice insults to his hail, Colin turned suddenly to Vesper. "You need to go. Now."

"Not without you both." She took Colin's other arm and unsuccessfully attempted to tug him toward the street. Over the rumbling of an approaching cart, a boy yelled, "Brawl!" A woman screamed for the constables. The four men's stomps vibrated the sidewalk. Still, Colin didn't move. "Oh, for pity's sake, Colin! Move!"

"I'm not a stray dog that I can be whipped and driven away in public and in private, Vesper. Not this time." She caught the pride of his pirate family in his gaze before he gently pried her fingers from his arm. He held her hand out to Philip. "Make sure Latimer doesn't bother her. I have a few things to say to him and now is as good a time as any."

"Col—" Philip began.

"He'd only follow and corner us somewhere else now that he knows we're in town."

Philip shut his mouth and turned to Vesper, his gaze pleading as he took her hand. Vesper squeezed his hand.

Then she darted into the street and slipped on the worn cobblestone. She screamed as Philip yelled, "Look out! Stop that cart!"

Her scream ended abruptly as she thudded to the cobblestone, the breath knocked out of her. Her body went limp and her head dropped to the dusty street. The vibrations of cart wheels and horses' hooves added a throb to her head to match the pain radiating from her hip and shoulder.

Cursed heroic impulses. Would they never cease to cause her pain?

Then a body landed beside her and pressed against her back. Arms wrapped around her waist, and she was rolled into the center of the street.

"Vesper, look at me." Despite her closed eyes, she fancied Colin was now kneeling beside her, a frantic look on his face. Perhaps heroic impulses had their rewards, after all.

One.

How long could a damsel in distress safely remain unconscious before her hero doused her with a bucket of water?

Two.

Would it be long enough to diffuse the situation with this Latimer person?

"Vesper." Colin gently probed her head. More panic

edged his voice. Vesper fought a strange cheerful feeling and kept herself limp.

Three.

Was that snickering?

Unrefined laughter burst from the occupants of the sidewalk. A horse nickered and pawed the stones a few feet over and up from her head.

"Is the lady okay?" asked an unfamiliar voice coming from the direction of the horse. Colin's fingers stilled and retreated from her head.

Vesper cracked one eye open. Colin's jaw dropped as he glanced from the cart stopped ten feet back, to the amused crowd on the sidewalk, to her. Red began creeping up his neck. She shut her eyes.

The laughter on the sidewalk roared again.

"I know it's always a fright to fall in the street, but I wasn't *that* close," the driver said. "Should I get help?"

"I can handle her," Colin said through gritted teeth. He lifted her into his arms and shook her shoulders gently. "I should have known," he said when she opened her eyes.

Vesper thought it best not to grin. "It *was* still a lovely bit of heroics, Captain. I am forever in your debt."

He snorted, but she fancied a smile sneaked past his defenses before being shooed away. "I hope it's worth the ... um ... *dirt* clinging to your dress. Sorry about that." He sniffed, wrinkling his nose as they crossed to the sidewalk.

Dirt... Vesper sucked in a breath. *No!* Not her favorite dress. And not when she'd planned on getting an invitation to help hunt books out of Colin. No one she knew here knew who he was, so there was no reason she couldn't accept ... only she was apparently covered in malodorous piles of horse excrement. She focused on breathing through her mouth as Colin stepped onto the sidewalk.

The crowds began to disperse, more than one familiar face among them. Was that one of her twin sisters disappearing into the haberdasher? No, surely not. Cara would come over to gloat and Cait to share her pain through caustic comments. Or both to meet Colin. Even so, Vesper felt her own face flush red as paint. Her mother would be mortified and angry when she heard—and she would—about this additional evidence of Vesper's eccentricity. Fashionable ladies did *not* throw themselves in the street for any man.

But then, perhaps such a reputation for oddity would keep Grandfather Ulrik from marrying her off. He'd always found her amusing and treated her kindly.

But she wasn't eccentric enough to not be embarrassed. Horse manure. Of all days!

Though biting his cheek against laughter, Philip managed to mouth "thanks" as Colin deposited her on the sidewalk with Philip between her and the well-dressed ruffians.

CHAPTER FOUR

Not caring if he were keeping an angry smuggler and his three sons waiting, Colin took his time brushing off his clothes, his back to the Harrisons. He snuck a glance through Belmont's windows and was relieved to see the Lockleys staring out at him, a mixture of expressions on their faces. At least they'd had the sense to remain incognito inside the shop. The two of them and he and Philip had been to nearly every bookstore and library in town trying to find out where the Rí Am met the faerie queen, but Vesper was right. For a world dictator, Ulrik Vanon was surprisingly quiet about himself.

Colin accepted his hat from a boy who'd picked it up off the street, brushed it off, and then turned to face Latimer Harrison. And was annoyed to find Latimer watching him with an amusement Colin would be more than happy to wipe off his face.

As far as the east is from the west...

Colin unclenched his fists.

That was how far he needed to remove his temper and pride from himself.

Before he really got Vesper or someone else hurt.

Latimer stepped close enough to shake hands but didn't extend his. "Every man has his weakness, eh, O'Connor? I just didn't expect to find yours in front of Belmont's." His chuckle sobered into a contemplative stare that made Colin step in front of Vesper. "But perhaps you're more like your father and grandfather than I thought."

Like Colin's father, Latimer had a certain respect for women, but Colin didn't trust that to be enough when balanced against Vesper's heritage, something he had no intention of letting the smuggler discover. He also didn't want Vesper to question Latimer's meaning.

"And she's a clever one too," Latimer continued, his gaze hardening as he met Colin's. "I've never liked to beat a man whose woman stood up for him. Didn't always stop me though. Won't you introduce us?"

Colin raised an eyebrow in silent refusal. "I didn't expect to see you in Reydon, Harrison, much less on Beaker Avenue."

He huffed. "It's Paul Latimer. Do you think I'm fool enough to keep that name? Or to have only one identity in my racket?"

Colin frowned on behalf of all "Paul" Latimer's deluded neighbors but was surprised by a sense of gratitude that he had a different identity than he once had: an honest captain and Sky Keeper rather than a pirate. The fire in him cooled.

But he still wasn't going to let Latimer accuse him of squealing to the ASU out of revenge. "Speaking of your racket, if you don't like the color of the carnations I sent you, I'm sorry. I had nothing to do with the necessity of them.

And I didn't care for the stench of some of your *trade* goods. Or Neil's. Whoever was responsible for them. He's the one who offered to get me what you refused."

A small, feminine gasp came from behind him, and Colin guessed his guardian angel had just realized who Latimer was. Once again he wondered just who *she* was and why she was so determined to help him.

Various colors reminiscent of heated metal passed over Latimer's face before his skin settled on pink, whether of embarrassment or pain Colin couldn't say. Latimer sons' faces settled on a fiery red, but Latimer held up a hand as they stepped forward.

"He's telling the truth." Latimer turned away briefly before meeting Colin's gaze. His face was carefully expressionless. "So it was you. I thought Neil had gotten wind of it somehow and had done something good for a change. Those *goods* were all his. I was figuring the best way to dispose of them without the dealers killing me when the warning came. Was the kid with them?"

Colin shook his head and spotted Vesper as she scooted slightly out from behind him to study Latimer. When Colin caught her gaze, he thought there was a guilty, sad look in her eyes before she lowered them to study her feet. Her hands briefly crossed behind her back, like a bound man's. She flicked a glance at Colin. He turned back to Latimer. "I think he was the informant. I don't know what happened to him, probably jail. I'm sorry."

A hard swallow was the only indication Latimer gave Colin he'd heard. An uncomfortable few seconds passed before Latimer rubbed a hand over his short, grayish-blond beard and looked Colin up and down. "I'm glad the girl kept me from pummeling you. I hear your father's on his way. If you need anything after the *Breaker* lands, or before"—he pulled a calling card from his coat pocket and handed it to Colin—"I can send carnations too."

Without waiting for a reply, Latimer and his sons marched away, a silent wave clearing the sidewalk as they went.

Colin stared at the card. That hadn't gone as expected. The Maker worked in mysterious ways indeed. Slipping the card into his waistcoat pocket, he turned to find Vesper twisting around, examining her dress.

"There's nothing on my dress," she said to Philip.

"No, you're as lovely as ever, lass," Philip responded, a laugh in his voice.

Clearing his throat, Colin offered Vesper his arm and smiled his most charming smile when she narrowed her eyes at him. "Tea?"

THERE WERE some men who threw punches to get what they wanted and some men whose wits worked just as well. Colin figured the trim man of average height and expensive suit who'd just closed the tea shop door behind him was the latter. His gut twisted as the man's gaze, blue-green eyes keen, moved deliberately to their table. Colin had thought there was something familiar about the commander of the Anti-Smuggling Unit during the raid, and now she sat across from him and Philip. Laughter still sparkled in her eyes as she held her steaming cup of tea, delighting in its aroma as much as its taste.

"Did your grandmother really—" She broke off, turned to

follow his gaze, and jerked in surprise, telling him all he needed to know. "Daddy!" she said, rising.

Switching a silent curse to a prayer, Colin rose. He preferred men who threw punches, but that didn't mean he couldn't block a blow of wits or throw one himself. But if this man was anything like Vesper, he might be in trouble.

That was even if the man didn't recognize him from the warehouse. Between the dark and Colin's goggles, he could only hope the Time Keeper wouldn't. Most men didn't appreciate being yanked off ladders and deprived of their quarry.

Colin stepped away from the petite tea table with its damask cloth and fine china and watched the man who'd just reached Vesper's side and been received with a kiss. When Vesper looked over her shoulder at Colin, there was worry in her eyes. Within a day of meeting her, he'd gathered Vesper adored her father. That the feeling was mutual was evident in their greeting. He doubted the concern was for herself. He smiled confidently at her, drew himself up, and then extended his hand. He was a respectable airship captain. He ought to act like one.

"Eoin Vanon, head of the ASU, I presume? I'm Captain O'Connor of the Bowditch ship *Dawn Singer*, and this is my first mate, Philip Orren. It's a pleasure to meet you, sir."

Vesper's eyes flared wide and fearful and flew to his at the name *Vanon*, but he kept his gaze fixed on Eoin. Eoin's eyebrow arched slightly before grasping his hand firmly. He hadn't bothered to conceal his armband, but the rolled fabric above it indicated Eoin had the same desire as Vesper to be inconspicuous when it suited him. The hammered gold leaves and crystals encircling the leather were similar to those on Vesper's, but the leaves had a bolder, more masculine look.

Philip greeted him quickly, without his usual affable conversationalism. Colin groaned inwardly. Philip's was a voice Eoin might remember too.

"Please join us." Colin motioned for the server to bring another cup of tea.

"I regretted not meeting you aboard the *Dawn Singer* before we left Hollym." Eoin took the chair beside Vesper with an alert type of calmness that impressed Colin. "But it seems we were destined to be introduced, Captain." He speared Colin with a hard look, and Colin's heart skipped a beat at the deliberate use of "introduced" rather than "meet." Suspicion certainly sharpened Eoin's eyes, but questions lurked there as well, Colin fancied, beneath his confidence.

"That was unfortunate," Colin said, resisting the urge to mollify him with an explanation of his whereabouts, "but then you could have come over during our mutual journey back to Reydon."

"So I could have." Eoin let the thought drift like a stray bullet through Colin's mind as the server brought another cup and saucer and Vesper poured her father tea with expert attention to the details of no sugar and one biscuit. Colin could almost swear it was with a smug smile that Eoin caught him watching. His pride flared, but he smashed it back down. He was *not* going to fall into that trap.

"I thought it best to accompany you." Eoin curved his arm around the teacup, scooting it closer to him in an automatic manner, as if accustomed to enjoying the fragrance wafting up with the steam, just like his daughter did. His gaze shot to Colin's with surprising force. "For I've heard you tend to attract undesirable attention, whether traveling by air"—he gave a pointed look at Vesper, at which she blinked innocently, and then pinned Colin again—"or along sidewalks."

"I would never let anything happen to your daughter, sir." It slipped out before Colin remembered he was neither trying to assiduously court Eoin's good opinion or antagonize him.

Eoin's pursed lips and steely-eyed look at his declaration reinforced the idea that the Time Keeper was unlikely to give his good opinion.

"You should have seen him handle the truculent man outside Belmont's, Daddy," Vesper piped up with a bright smile at her father. "There was no fighting, and the man seemed ashamed of ever having threatened Captain O'Connor."

Again, Eoin looked less than pleased. Colin wasn't exactly pleased at being the subject of praise either. Or being in debt to Vesper for a large part of that "handling."

"And when the *Dawn Singer* was attacked by pirates, Captain O'Connor was very clever in keeping his ship and men safe. He—" Vesper stopped suddenly and wilted under her father's glower.

"I should thank you, O'Connor," he said, "for making sure my sometimes exasperating daughter made it safely to Hollym."

At Vesper's indignant huff and glare at her father, who nonchalantly sipped his tea, Colin felt a tug at the corner of his mouth. He could easily like Eoin Vanon if the man didn't hold his and his crew's lives in his hand.

"It was a pleasant surprise to myself and my crew to have a lady on board."

"That it was," Philip added with a chuckle and a look of

fatherly affection at Vesper. "She even made the captain and me join her in giving a concert for the crew. They were right sad when they learned she wasn't going any further than Hollym with us."

Eoin cut him a glance, then indicated the plate of cakes near Colin.

"We were glad to run into her today to learn she made it back home without harm." Colin reached for the plate and picked it up.

Vesper met his gaze with a warm smile, and Colin felt both corners of his mouth trying to tug up. Fortunately, sense prevailed. His mouth turned down, as did his gaze, following Philip's insistent straightening of his own cuffs. He glanced at his wrist, the object of Eoin's interest.

The merest hint of ink peeked out from beneath the fabric of his sleeve as he stretched. Adjusting his grip on the plate, Colin pivoted his forearm so that his wrist faced downward and passed off the plate to Eoin.

"Do you believe in harming your opponents, Captain?" Eoin took the dish, choosing a slice of carrot cake before setting it away. "Vesper mentioned there were no blows against the man in the street, but I understand the pirate Redsail's ship was lost. I won't say that's a pity, but it does make me curious as to your opinion on the matter of violence."

Colin's insides went cold. "I give no quarter to pirates—they expect none—when my ship is in greater danger than I think she can handle. It's my duty to my crew and Commodore Bowditch and to any passengers. Otherwise, I am constrained from killing any man, whether I have a disagreement with him or not. I have tried to break with my family's history—my history—of violence."

"There are non-lethal means of disabling opponents, aren't there, Captain?"

Yes, sleeping potions in tea. Not that he'd use one on Vesper's father, even if he'd had warning enough to do so. "Many. The Bowditch captains prefer them to killing, even to killing pirates, if possible."

Eoin smiled in a catlike way and tucked into his slice of cake, pausing only to ask Vesper if she'd bought anything at Belmont's. Something about that conversation, or that look, had Vesper tugging on her locket, as she had when Colin asked why she'd sent the warning note.

With his questions answered and the cake finished, Eoin rose, and Colin followed suit to shake his hand.

"The case that took me to Hollym," Eoin said, keeping a firm grip on Colin's hand, "is officially closed as the drug runners are where they belong and no trace of iron could be found. But it can be reopened if new evidence presents itself." He released Colin's hand, nodded to Philip, then bent to accept Vesper's kiss on the cheek. "I'll see you at dinner." Instead of leaving directly, he met the server and gave her enough coin to cover the entire table's expenses.

When Colin found himself grinding his teeth at that more than at Eoin's not-so-subtle warning, he purposefully pulled his cup of black tea to his lips and drank. Eoin may not have ordered Vesper home immediately, but he'd clearly intended to emasculate Colin and stake his claim to his daughter. But Eoin Vanon forgot one thing.

O'Connors never paid attention to claims. And rarely to threats at all.

Before he and Philip parted ways with Vesper a few hours later, he'd secured her acceptance to an invitation to a concert two nights hence. His grandmother and Philip would be along as well, providing proper chaperones. While Vesper's eyes sparkled with pleasant surprise, Colin's stomach turned with a sick sensation that Vesper herself might be more helpful than a bookstore's shelves in finding the location of the Star Veil's anchor. He hoped she'd forgive him for mixed motives and a bit of scheming.

CHAPTER FIVE

The one benefit of living in a world where the only way to tell time was by the Time Keepers' crystal tower in the city center was that when you needed to knock someone unconscious, it was difficult for him to know if he'd been out for an hour or had just blinked.

"All right! I'm sorry!" Caroline Lockley glanced nervously around the shaded woods surrounding the cove where Bridie O'Connor lived. Jumping at each twig that cracked underfoot, one would think she'd never been in a forest before. "Quit playing and come out, Colin." She continued up the leaf-and-pine-needle-strewn slope, swatting away annoying insects.

With barely a sound, Colin slipped behind the next tree, about twenty feet up and to the left of her. Raising his modified crossbow, he checked the stun dart, then sighted through the trees. *Just a little further.*

"This isn't funny. I said I was sorry." Leaves crushed to dust noisily under Caroline's boots. Colin could count each stride. "You know your grandmother will never stand for this. She told me herself no child is too old for a whipping, and frankly, you deserve one."

Colin resisted the urge to roll his eyes, keeping them fixed instead on the brown-and-green coat nearly blending in with the forest.

"Colin! Come. Out."

One more step.

Bare neck came into view. Colin fired.

The man in camouflage slid along the pine to the ground, a dart in his neck.

Caroline stilled, likely counting to ten as Colin was. At ten, he moved around the tree and waved at her. "You're forgiven."

She punched a hand to her hip. "But you're not. Do I really have to stay here until he wakes up?"

"Yes." Colin knelt beside the man, yanked out the dart, then checked his pulse. Sleeping soundly. Good.

Once the Intruder Signal Devices had alerted them to a spy, it had taken a good bit of maneuvering to back the man away from the cove and up into the semi-circular ridge of woods surrounding the secluded bay. Caroline had an uncanny knack at driving him. Good thing, because they needed privacy this afternoon. It had been a week since the *Sun Bolt* had released its two crates into a small cave at the edge of the cove, where they had a dry room hidden. It was time to get the books and iron out. The books, copies of *Sun, Moon, and Stars and What They Tell Us* and *Elusive Longitude,* had to be ready to disperse that night and the iron to be ready when the *Breaker* arrived. The pirate airship wasn't watched as closely as the *Dawn Singer.*

He attached the crossbow to his belt and began patting the man's pockets. He pulled a Time Keeper badge from the inside vest pocket. With a grunt, he put it back. It hadn't taken Eoin long to start searching for more evidence. Was he planning on using it or keeping it on hand just in case?

"I have a concert to get ready for, you know," Caroline said.

Grabbing the man under the arms, Colin hefted him back up and leaned him, face-forward, against the tree. "I know. I'm going too."

Caroline's lips quirked into a mischievous grin, but then she crossed her arms and studied him. "Does this princess I saw outside Belmont's have anything to do with you spending most of the last two days diving for rusted iron from the sunken wrecks off the cove?"

Holding the man in place with his shoulder, Colin pulled a strap from his belt and began securing the limp man upright against the tree. "I needed iron, and I couldn't sacrifice the harpoons."

Her eyebrow arched as bark flaked off the tree as the Time Keeper slipped a few inches. "Do you want help? I can find my way back to this spot if you do."

"No."

She shrugged. "Needed iron for what?"

"To counteract a type of faerie chain. I hope."

"But you were shaving the iron, not making a knife or cutting device."

He pulled another strap from his belt and secured the spy around the waist. "I was making a paste."

"Oh."

"I'll explain another time." Colin jogged over to Caroline and handed her two small flasks and a cloth. "If he starts coming to before I get back, use the chloroform on him—only a little. When I give the signal, untie the straps, use the smelling salts on him, and get back into place. Quickly."

She slipped the items into one of the leather pouches attached to her corset. "And he'll really not think something fishy is going on?"

"If you're in the same place and the crystals haven't completely dimmed, why should he think anything other than that his body reacted to a warm afternoon and the soothing buzz of insects by trying to take a nap on him?" He took off jogging down the hill. "I'll try to be back before he wakes. Just pray there aren't any more spies around."

Bridie was fishing and Darius studying the watery horizon when Colin slowed to a stop beside them on the dock. "He's asleep. Caroline's staying with him. Any signs of more?" he huffed out between breaths.

Bridie reeled in her line and stowed the pole in the dinghy tied to the pier next to her. "Will took care of him. Hunting accident."

"He did what!" Colin roared. He'd kill him. He promised Commodore Bowditch he wouldn't lead his men into unnecessary violence. Will would be peeling potatoes and scrubbing decks the rest of his miserable life.

Chuckling, Bridie placed a hand on Colin's heaving chest, as if ready to block him from carrying out his mental threats. "It was a nick on the arm, Col. Will apologized profusely, and right now the man's in the kitchen being fussed over by—and effectively prisoner to—Fiona and the girls. Will went to retrieve the deer he killed with the same shot. I thought it best. It's just us to move the goods. Philip and Nick are readying the carriage."

Jaw a tad loose and rethinking what he'd do to Will, Colin followed Bridie and Darius into the skiff. They paddled quietly to the tip of the cove, anchored the dinghy under the shadow of overhanging willow trees, and set the fishing line in position. Leaving the boat, they scrambled up the wooded ridge until they came to a particular rock outcropping—a semi-circular, disc-like ledge heavily clothed with moss, lichen, and fern. The white blooms and broad green leaves of ransoms covered the rock shelf and filled the wood with a pungent, garlic-like fragrance. Rock, dirt, and a few violets formed the ground under the curving, six-foot-high-at-its-edge shelf. Colin peeled back a particularly large cup-shaped lichen from the ledge's center and swiveled the knob beneath it. A section of the rock floor and lower ledge pulled back, revealing a stone stairway. They quickly descended. Colin lit the torch he'd brought and led them down and toward the tip of the spit of land, toward the cave.

Soon, the damp tunnel opened into a chamber and they were greeted by the lap of water against the rim of rock forming the sea's boundary. The two crates rested at the rear of the chamber, near another tunnel. Other crates, goods stolen by his father and waiting patiently to be sold when the highest price could be fetched, sat around as well. Dollies and hand trucks positioned themselves along the wall as if eager to be of service, as they often were after his father, and formerly his grandfather, returned from a voyage.

Colin traced the tunnel's dark path with his eyes. The cove was such a beautiful setup for pirating and smuggling it seemed a shame it would fall out of use when he inherited the place. He shook his head. He was making use of it now for the Sky Keepers, which was enough.

Darius touched the crate of books as if it were the shoulder of a dear friend. "I really hope all the packing worked and the books survived. I can't abide musty books."

"I hope the iron didn't rust," Bridie added. "It's harder to come by than books."

"Not these books," Darius said proudly.

He and Colin opened the crates and began loading the smaller trunks of books onto the dollies and shuttling them and the iron harpoons along the tunnel. Bridie went ahead of them and opened the trapdoor leading up to the carriage house. It only opened from the cave to prevent inspectors from finding anything in the carriage house.

Using a lift, they quickly raised all the supplies to the stone floor. Philip and Nick packed them away in Bridie's carriage. The old contraption had a kind of unique charm to it, and Colin hoped it wouldn't embarrass Vesper. His grandfather had built it for Bridie when they married. He hadn't told her until later about the particular advantages of its design.

It was a horseless carriage with a high, broad engine casing up front; four short, thick-treaded tires; a running board that looked like an ocean wave caught in wood; panels of a color Colin could never decide was blue or gray; and an unfashionably high cab.

It also boasted an unusually powerful, small engine neatly hidden in the guise of a clumsy, large engine, thus providing space for goods in the "engine parts." It also had smuggling compartments in the usual spaces—in the panels and under the seat. A trunk rack with a trunk on the back, appropriate for goods with misleading covers, was also available for the literary treasures.

For the iron, he and Philip rigged up a fancy top rack above the carriage, using the iron harpoons as the railing. They slid the harpoon tips with their sharp flues into painted blocks of wood that Darius carved to form corners, then covered them with fabric to match the carriage's panels. After stashing another trunk of books up top, Colin hopped down from the coach and scanned the carriage house.

Various mechanical parts, bins of gears, trays of tools, woodworking equipment, and trunks of stored household goods, lined the workshop. A half dozen automatons, pre-programmed for Reydon and a few other places so Bridie would never be trapped at the cove, stared eerily at them from their shelves. Residential navigators were also cheaper in bulk. Mercifully out of sight of their brethren was a collection of dismembered automatons stolen by his father and grandfather.

He lifted one of the functional five-foot navigators from its shelf, placed it in the driver's seat, and brushed off its coat, smiling grimly at the irony that the most obvious sign of the Rí Am's power couldn't tell what it had just witnessed. He ran a finger over the row of crystals decorating its chest in the Rí Am's emblem. Or tell how useful iron paste can be.

CHAPTER SIX

I t was one of those rare nights when Vesper's parents went out together. It was with a stab of regret that she considered the circumstance with suspicion. Was her father still investigating Colin and watching her when she thought he was away? She'd not mentioned her engagement with the O'Connors for fear her parents would forbid it. She knew it was unwise, but after Mark "died," she sometimes found herself angry enough with Grandfather Ulrik to not care if she defied him and was sent away too.

She hesitated before slipping the beloved but somewhat incongruous locket over her neck. What would that do to her family? What would *he* do to her family?

Vesper discarded the thought as she gathered her wrap and handbag and headed downstairs. She wouldn't get sent off for going to a concert with two airship officers and a grandmother. Steeling herself, she popped her head into the library, keeping hold of the door handle for a fast exit. She'd been prohibited from leaving unannounced after the Incident of the Accidental Airship Voyage. With her parents out for the night and Cara away, that only left Cait.

Her older sister was curled up on the horsehair sofa, a book on her lap and a glass of wine in her hand. She paid more attention to the deep red liquid than the book, though from the set of her jaw, Vesper figured she was imagining throwing the drink in Cara's face. But probably the next glass she poured.

"Cait, I'm going to a concert tonight. I'll be back later."

Cait raised her eyebrow and set her glass down long enough to turn a page. "Going to see an opera with those white-haired eccentrics who claim you as their sister? How exciting."

"Actually, no. Would you—"

She finally raised her gaze to Vesper, then arced her eyebrows higher with a touch of displeasure as she took in Vesper's pale blue gown with its gold corset and stitching and sapphire necklace. "Don't you look lovely." Cait's sneer managed to shift the compliment to an insult. Vesper raised her chin and began to spin away.

"What concert are you going to?" Cait laid the book down, her gaze turning sharp. "It's a modern piece playing at the Reydon Grand Theater, and I know you don't like it." She paused. "Or are you sneaking off with that pirate you were making a fool of yourself over outside Belmont's?"

"He's not a—" *Pirate. Anymore.* "Just tell Daddy I'll be back late and not to wait up for me. I'm well-chaperoned and won't disappear anywhere."

"If you wish." Cait's hand found the glass again and her eyes the book.

"Have a good night," Vesper said, regretting that the sentiment was only half genuine, then closed the door. A slow, heavy tread muffled by the Oriental rug stretching the length of the hallway warned her of the old footman's approach.

"Your party has arrived, Miss Vesper."

"Thank you, Johns."

He took her cloak, slipped it over her shoulders with a fond smile, and led her to the vestibule. Colin, his grandmother, and Philip, all splendidly dressed, stood in the center. Philip was spinning slowly in a circle in awed appreciation.

Was it the marble statues and engravings along the walls and stairs? The ceiling worthy of an art gallery? Or the fact that the vestibule alone took up almost as much space as the *Dawn Singer*'s cargo hold?

Colin stood beside Philip, his hat in his hand, his grandmother's arm through his. Vesper did her best not to notice that he looked just as handsome and dashing as she'd anticipated, or how he ignored the impressive mansion around him in favor of her. Mrs. O'Connor seemed un-awed as well. Tall for a woman, with striking blue eyes that were both shrewd and kind, and a regal bearing any governess would be proud of, she could walk into any home in the neighborhood and no one would question if she belonged.

"Good evening," Vesper said. "It's so kind of you to let me join you tonight."

Colin introduced his grandmother, then offered Vesper his arm.

"Vesper—"

She spun around at the hail, her color rising. Cait stopped short at the edge of the hallway. She blinked, then sauntered forward as Vesper introduced her. She smiled a shrewish smile in greeting. "It appears I was mistaken, Vess dear. I half suspected you were running away with one of those scrawny, bespectacled artists you're so fond of." She looked Colin up and down, flicked her gaze to Philip and Mrs. O'Connor, then turned to Vesper. "These are much more interesting associates. I think Father would agree to that, don't you?" She looked Colin over again and stepped nearer to Vesper. "As your big sister, I feel I must warn you, aside from a little matter of questionable heritage you should keep in mind, that men always know when a woman's not used to receiving compliments and take advantage of it. Do be wary."

Vesper wondered what it would take to fall through marble. Or push someone through it. *I don't judge you by your family, Colin. Please don't judge me by mine. She's hurt and angry.*

Colin's eyes turned dark blue, and his gaze hit Cait with all the force of a storm. Something about the rest of his demeanor was also reminiscent of a man who was well acquainted with violence. Cait shrank back.

It seemed there *were* some advantages to associating with ex-pirates. Her lips quirking, Vesper slipped her arm through Colin's. She knew his heart better than to be worried.

"I see little has changed in this neighborhood since I was young." Bridie held her hand out to Vesper. "Come, darling. We should leave—before my grandson tells you how stunningly beautiful you are, inside and out." With a curt nod to Cait, she took Vesper's free hand and turned to the door. "Good night, Miss Vanon."

Cait barely managed a reply. Vesper felt like dancing.

Johns opened the door for them and then saw them to the carriage, holding a large umbrella over the ladies, protecting them from a heavy, misting rain.

Every carriage in Reydon was unique, whether it had smoke stacks on the back—the more, the better, some thought —elegant matched horses, or mechanized horses. The O'Connor's unusually tall contraption sitting in the street was no exception. It was every bit as matchless as they were, and she loved it, the peculiar height and the top rim that made it look like an old mail coach and all.

One of Colin's crew sat on the driver's bench with an automaton. Two more, a dark-skinned giant and a lanky blond, stood beside it, heedless of the rain. Nick and Will, respectively, of the *Dawn Singer*, if she remembered rightly. Apparently, she'd underestimated how well-chaperoned she'd be.

"Vesper." Still standing on the sidewalk, Colin looked over his shoulder at the front windows of her home. A curtain shifted. "Is snooping a family trait?"

Vesper glimpsed Cait's shadow against the curtains before she moved behind the wall. "It's strongest in me, but when properly motivated, or bored, my sisters exhibit it as well." She paused, speculating as to why Colin was inquiring. "I wouldn't be surprised if Cait decided not to stay in tonight."

He nodded, then turned to Nick and Will. "Nick, you were once a bodyguard for some of the wealthy families, right?"

"Yes."

"That position entailed keeping their daughters out of mischief, didn't it?"

Nick sighed, his broad shoulders slumping slightly. "It did."

"If Cait Vanon shows up at the theater, you and Will keep her occupied for a few hours."

"Yes, Captain."

"Thanks. I'll make it up to you." Colin joined Vesper, Philip, and Bridie in the carriage, and it pulled away to the hum of a quiet motor.

Some minutes later, it slowed in front of the Vallendester Theater, one of the second tier of concert halls. It wasn't fashionable enough for her to worry about running into the Rí Am or her mother's friends but into a few of her less-fashionable friends. Colin handed her and his grandmother out while Philip held the umbrella, though the rain was slackening off. Vesper raised her hood, and they hurried inside amongst a decent-sized crowd.

She'd heard that the Vallendester Theater was once the premier theater and that the owning family had never forgotten. She could believe it. Elegantly decorated with vibrant tapestries depicting scenes from famous tales, the vestibule opened up around them with all the breathtaking beauty of a blossoming flower. Its towering ceilings and columns were a creamier white than the Star Veil, tastefully gilded and decorated. Dark, plush crimson carpets marked their way.

Trusting Colin to guide her safely through the crowd, Vesper indulged in a little polite gawking. She stared but kept her mouth closed. Such places never ceased to awe her. She wondered briefly if the night sky—if such a thing existed beyond the Star Veil—would have that effect.

Her gaze slowly swept the room and was caught on a tapestry that wasn't. That one should be there above the curving, broad stairway was so obvious from the exquisitely woven hangings lining up around the empty spot to the faint outline of faded color around it that Vesper could only conclude a tapestry did still hang there. At least in the mind of the owner. All other details of the theater were meticulously decorated and preserved but that spot.

An usher, his coppery hair and stretching frame suggestive of an organ pipe given the location, gave the group a second glance as Colin handed him the tickets. As the man led them up the staircase to their box, Vesper scanned the wall of tapestries again, catching the story building in their scenes and mourning the unknown end.

"Many great works were destroyed in the Time King's purge of *mythology*-inspired art work and musical scores." Colin touched her elbow and gently guided her up the steps. His voice dropped to a whisper as they passed under the empty wall. "But not all."

The usher led them along a hallway and stopped before a curtain of crimson velvet. He held it back for them until they passed by him into an upper box with a splendid view of the orchestra warming up.

After seating her beside himself, Colin handed Vesper a program. An involuntary frown slipped past her watch. She adored all the composers listed except the one responsible for the symphony that formed the highlight of the evening. It was far too harsh and modern a composition for her taste. Was it the composer's birthday that every hall should be playing his works?

"I've always enjoyed listening to the orchestra warm up." Colin leaned back against the plush chair, as intent on the musicians clad in elegant black and white, moving here and there, tightening strings and emptying valves, as the most rapt music lover during the climax of a symphony. Their box fell oddly silent, Bridie and Philip likewise entranced. So Vesper joined them and tried to pick out the notes of each individual violinist.

A minute later, Bridie raised her opera glasses to her eyes and instructed Vesper to note the lovely lace trim on the first violinist's dress. Vesper did as asked, getting the strangest feeling she was playing a part. After that, they chatted for a few minutes about Colin taking up the cello again under Davy's influence and Vesper's desire to further her violin proficiency, all the while watching the stage or the crystal chandeliers and the statues and wall-hangings covering the balconies.

"I do beg your pardon." The usher opened the curtain behind them just as the musicians settled themselves. "There's been some mistake. I've shown you to the wrong box."

"I thought so," Bridie said cheerily as she rose.

Colin took Vesper's hand and helped her up. "I wouldn't be surprised if we came to the wrong concert," he said quietly as she brushed past him. She paused, catching a glimpse of mischief in his eyes. "But you wouldn't mind, would you?" he asked. "I take it you're no more a fan of Hiram Zedock than I am."

Vesper blinked, re-considered her trust in her companions, found it sound, and grinned. "Curiosity forbids complaint." Were they to hear some of the composers forbidden by Grandfather Ulrik? She'd always been interested in them. Or have a secret meeting with Davy Bowditch?

Holding a single candle, the usher led them swiftly along the darkened hallway and then down a carpeted stair. Other softened steps and flickers of light hailed her curiosity. They traveled down, to the ground floor or below. She wasn't sure from all the twists and turns and short sets of stairs.

"I believe these are your correct tickets." The usher

handed Philip a single ticket the size of a calling card and opened a plain door. Moist, warm summer air swept in from a semi-lit alleyway.

"How clumsy of us." Philip took the card and walked out. The carriage sat in the alleyway, driverless. The clop of hooves announced the driver's return as he led a pair of horses from the side door of the opposite building. Colin and Bridie each went to one of the front corners of the carriage and simultaneously pulled out a pin and repeated the act on the carriage's rear. The oddly tall cab shortened, a bar extended from under the front grill, and flaps covered the steering wheel and headlights. The driver harnessed the horses to the carriage before hopping up onto the box. Philip handed him the card and opened the door for them.

"Ronan would never agree, but horses are so much more elegant than steering wheels and windshields." Bridie settled into her seat and patted the leather cushion beside her in invitation. "I hope you won't mind missing Hiram Zedock, Vesper."

"Not at all. But won't someone miss us?" And those scurrying to the carriages waiting behind theirs?

"Harcourt Ladell—owner of the Vallendester Theater—collected enough images of us to cut and splice for the holograms to appear quite realistic for the duration of the show," Colin said appreciatively.

"Holograms!"

"It's Ladell's specialty," Philip said. "He and Captain Davy were tinkering with the things the last time we were together in Reydon. Fixed the major glitch he'd been having trouble with."

Bridie chuckled and took Vesper's hand affectionately, pulling it into her lap, making Vesper's heart swell pleasantly. "You see, my dear, we listened raptly, fidgeted, chatted amongst ourselves, and most importantly, spied through our opera glasses. He caught that on camera. He has all the raw material he needs to cut and splice into holograms for the performance. And *we'll* be in a darkened box, which will help." A delightfully impish chuckle followed as Bridie shared a look with Colin. "He also detests Zedock."

"He's one of Grandfather Ul—" Vesper clamped her mouth shut, not wanting to remind them of her heritage.

"We know who you are, Vesper. It's okay." Colin said it with one of those rare smiles that seemed made just for her. He accepted her as she was. She vowed to always do the same for him.

"You'll get no judgment from us." Bridie laughed and indicated herself and Colin. "The pirate-bride and the pirate-born."

"I might judge you though." Philip thumped his chest. "I come of good sailor stock."

Bridie shook her head. "Do continue, dear. Oh, out of curiosity, might I see your arm bracer? I hear the gold-work on the Vanon bracers is magnificent."

Vesper smiled her thanks and raised her sleeve, though she couldn't help but keep her attention on Colin. "I've never cared for Zedock, but he's one of Grandfather Ulrik's protégés."

"Which means he must be played at least once every season." Colin smiled wryly. "I suspect Ladell is enjoying the fact that many of the audience are not listening."

"But why the risk?" Vesper asked. "And where are we going?"

"You'll understand when we get there."

Vesper narrowed her eyes at Colin, whose expression only grew more teasing.

"Surely a woman who sneaks aboard airships and jumps in front of carriages isn't alarmed at the prospect of an unknown destination?"

"But I might be overdressed."

"In which case we'll all be conspicuous together."

"What my grandson means, dear"—Bridie arranged Vesper's sleeve back over the arm bracer and released her arm—"is that the Vallendester Theater is an easy place to get automatons for. The concert hall we're going to is within three miles of it, so it's convenient to start there. Our destination also prefers to remain inconspicuous—it never plays the Rí Am's favorites." She handed a silver compact to Colin, and he pocketed it, and they continued chatting.

In a dark, old section of town, the carriage stopped. The rain had ceased, but the cobblestone bore reminders of it. Vesper lifted her skirts as they passed through an alley and down an outer stairway. Colin rapped on the uninviting door, and a small window opened at head height. Part of a man's face appeared, and he and Colin exchanged a few words. He opened the door, but instead of letting them in, he let out a stout, middle-aged man and an attractive, petite brunette in her mid-twenties.

"At last! My treasure has arrived." The man slapped Colin on the shoulder, then brushed by, sparing a smile for Vesper. "Welcome, Miss Vesper. I look forward to a proper introduction later, but right now I must attend to some valuables. Come along, Caroline."

Vesper did a double-take on him, then the woman as she planted her feet and put her hands on her hips.

"Your niece, who loves you, who is more to you than seven sons—is not lifting anything in this dress."

"You're opening doors. Come," Darius replied.

Caroline sighed, then curtsied to the group. "Please excuse me. I have a very important engagement as a doorstop. I hope to join you later." Before following her uncle, she gave Colin a pointed look, which Vesper was sure somehow included her, along with the kind of grin that promised mischief. It was such a fond, teasing-sister kind of look that Vesper suffered a pang of envy. Yet Caroline wasn't Colin's sister, so who was she? What treasure was her uncle referring to?

Colin offered Vesper his arm again, and the doorkeeper opened the way for them. Pieces of a puzzle clicked together in Vesper's mind in time to Caroline's steps to the O'Connor's carriage, and Vesper's jaw dropped. She let go of Colin's arm and poked him in the chest. "Did you use me to smuggle goods? And even take them to my father's doorstep!" Of all the nerve!

His eyebrows rose, which was hardly a sufficient reaction. "They're only books, Vesper. And I would have brought them even if you hadn't come."

"But—"

"I followed your advice about the *kitchen goods*. I assumed you had no objection to Sky Keeper smuggling. We never smuggle anything else—nothing for profit—only what helps Sky Keepers in need or books that convey the Truth."

Vesper shut her mouth, her indignation cooling rapidly. She must remember to be more consistent in her objections and approvals. She took his arm again, ignoring Philip's stifled laugh, followed Bridie inside, and immediately caught the discordant but oddly entrancing melody of an orchestra warming up. There was an air of secrecy wrapped about the place as tightly as a dinner jacket but still the familiar sounds of a concert hall.

A short, plain hallway gave way to a brightly lit room with a stately set of double doors and several hallways leading off it, like a spoke at the center of a wheel. Theater-promotion style signs announced the events or exhibits present in the rooms down each hallway.

If only she were close enough to read the signs without her glasses, or without the eclipsing effect of the bustling patrons dressed in a wide array of finery, from the poor shop-girl's cotton frock to the socialite's furs. Beside one sign, a lady dripping in diamonds chatted with a fishwife as if old friends. A variety of accents blended into the mix of voices about her. What had drawn this disparate group of people together?

A gasp to her right dragged her attention from the unique combinations of persons to just one. Claire stared at her. Dressed in a simple dress that was doubtless the best she owned, Mark's sweetheart barely kept her grasp on the stack of programs in her hands.

Vesper froze, then jerked her gaze around the room. Nearly every inch of wall was covered with paintings depicting the mythological sun, moon, and stars, and land-scapes spread beneath blue skies. Her heart beat wildly. Somewhere in this set of rooms was the Vallendester's missing tapestry, she was sure of it. Her skin flushed red, then chilled, then flushed again.

Colin O'Connor had taken her to a Sky Keeper meeting. Her, a Vanon, to a Sky Keeper meeting! If she weren't terri-fied, she'd be fascinated. Blast her arm bracer! If only she could safely stay.

Eyes once more wide as an owl's, Claire shoved programs into their hands and hurried away.

Habit took over where unruly emotions tried to reign. "Claire." Vesper stepped forward, an unsteady smile on her face. She should always be polite.

The girl spun around.

"It's good to see you again."

Claire nodded, a timid smile blooming into genuine warmth. "It's good to see you too, Miss Vesper." She darted away, handing out more programs.

Taking a fortifying breath, Vesper turned around. Colin O'Connor had a lot of explaining to do—as they made a hasty exit.

Why was he grinning at her? And offering her a compact case?

"I don't care if my nose is shiny, and I don't need to go to the powder room to calm down. We need to leave. Now."

"No one followed us. We made sure of it."

"You don't understand. I have a *homing* crystal. What if my father grew worried or suspicious and decided to locate me? He'd have to report this. I don't want these people hurt on my account." *Or for me to end up in the crystal mines.*

A flash of sympathy was overcome by confidence bordering on smugness. He offered her the silver compact again. "We took care of that too. For tonight, Vesper, you are not a Vanon."

Not a... She blinked, then clutched her arm bracer. It was still there under her satin sleeves. "But—"

Bridie took the compact and opened it, revealing an ebony paste and a circular cotton pad smudged with black. "While we were in the carriage I rubbed iron paste on your homing crystal and wrapped the bracer with a cloth so the paste wouldn't rub off onto your sleeve. You can't be traced for a few hours."

Was it possible she was free? Even if temporarily? "But I don't remember you—"

"You were talking with Colin at the time and not paying attention to anyone else."

"Oh."

"I didn't want to interrupt." Eyes twinkling, Bridie held up the program Claire had given her. "Come, there is much to see and hear and read, for this is the Sky Keeper's Moon Song Festival, a celebration of the long-awaited re-release of books on navigation and the heavens. What would you like to see first?"

Recovering her composure, Vesper grinned. "All of it."

"Perhaps you should look at the program before you say that," Colin exclaimed with a laugh. He tapped the crisp sheet Vesper had all but forgotten.

For the next few hours the orchestra played such pieces as Beethoven's *Moonlight Sonata*, Debussy's *Clair de Lune*, and Dvorak's *Song to the Moon*. While she was familiar with the composers, these pieces were strange and beautiful to her. In the various smaller rooms off the hallways were book distributions and discussions led by Darius and Caroline Lockley on the newly republished books *Sun, Moon, and Stars and What They Tell Us* and *Elusive Longitude* and the previously republished *The Building and Accurate Functioning of Clocks*. Vesper vowed to collect at least one of these forbidden, world-changing books before she left.

There were also additional art displays, children's crafts and stories, poetry recitations, readings of Scripture and hymns focused on creation and the heavens, times of prayer and worship, and lectures such as "Linguistic Evidence for the Existence of the Celestial," "What is the Moon Made Of?," and "A Moon God but No Moon? Evidence from Archaeology and Mythology for a Real Moon."

She was introduced to the long-admired Commodore and Mrs. Bowditch, to Harcourt Ladell—one of the major funders of the evening—and to Darius and Caroline Lockley, whom she found delightful, albeit somewhat alarming in their forthright comments and teasing. She shared Philip's disappointment that Marianna Bowditch Orren and her husband, Bertram, were not there, as they were leading a Moon Song Festival in another part of the world. Davy Bowditch was expected soon, with Cavan O'Connor of all people, and had hinted he had a surprise for his parents. Colin and Philip shared a knowing look at this but refused to give away the secret.

They were joined after a time by Colin's aunt Fiona and her two daughters, but they soon fell away into the crowd, taking Philip with them. Other friends and crew members of the *Dawn Singer* flowed against them, chatting for a time before being whisked away in the current of Sky Keepers. Even Bridie slipped away with an old friend.

"Colin. Vesper," Caroline called to them later as they stretched their legs in the atrium between concerts. "There you are. Uncle and I were just debating whether it's wrong to steal a stolen craft." Her voice dipped as she reached them, Darius following behind her. "Does that sub we came on count as the spoils of war or have we added theft to Sky Keeper smuggling?"

Beside her, Colin stiffened. Though her arm was still looped through his, he seemed to draw away from her, and she felt a twinge of guilt. He had been one of those her father had hunted in connection with the submarine.

Caroline's gaze had shifted to her dress as she straightened it, and when she raised her eyes back to Colin, she frowned. Darius cleared his throat.

"I didn't mean to insinuate you'd gone back to pirating, Colin," Caroline said quickly. "I consider it the spoils of war." She smiled cheerily at Vesper when Colin remained silent. "Did you pick up a copy of *Elusive Longitude*? I—"

"It was a Vanon sub," Colin said suddenly.

Vesper's fingers instinctively lifted from his arm, her stomach twisting. She felt more than saw Colin glance at her before fixing his gaze rigidly ahead. Caroline fell silent.

He swallowed hard. "Ten years ago my uncle was betrayed and murdered by another pirate, one he thought his partner and friend. When Grandfather and Father learned of a Vanon ship passing through waters frequented by this pirate, they saw it as a chance for revenge. We took the ship and sank the cargo but kept the submarine that was aboard. We pinned the crime on the man who'd betrayed my uncle."

"The penalty for attacking a possession of the Rí Am's is death." Darius's voice was a whisper of horror. "For the entire family."

"He killed himself before they could question him," Colin said flatly. "His family disappeared ... as we knew they would."

"You say 'we' but surely you weren't a part of this?" Caroline exclaimed. "You would have been too young."

"He was my uncle—Fiona's husband—and thirteen is not too young for an O'Connor."

Vesper's fingers hovered over Colin's arm. Her insides felt as if a rainstorm had turned to ice and pierced her heart. She'd known he'd been a pirate, but ... Her mind raced desperately through all her interactions with Colin and her gleanings about him. Had he really changed? What kind of power could change a man like that?

"I'm sorry, Colin." Caroline reached out as if to touch Colin's hand but drew back. "I didn't—"

"Didn't realize I was just as much a pirate as those who killed your father? 'Twas grace alone that brought me to who I am now, not a hidden nobleness in my youth. It's best any misunderstandings of that sort be cleared up now."

Vesper heard the plea to both her and Caroline and respected his honesty, though she couldn't shake the hollow feeling in her chest. Her fingers found their home and tightened around Colin's arm. A bit of his stiffness drained out. Again, she marveled at the power that could seemingly both forgive and change.

"And the sub ended up dry docked at a smuggler's because no one could handle being underwater in it?" Darius's lightly spoken words mended the silence, offering a hand out from the depths. "I can't say I blame them. The thing isn't much good without an automaton anyway. Seven miles max with a crew."

Colin's fingers brushed hers, then fell back to his side as his posture regained its usual strength. "You can go further than that if you're determined and not afraid of *sleep*."

"Sleep? Why didn't you tell us when we were aboard..." Darius's voice tapered off as the meaning of Colin's stare at his chin sank in.

Caroline's eyes widened before she grinned like a feral cat at her uncle. "Herschel always said I had an excellent right hook."

Darius rubbed his jaw and scowled at his niece. "Just remember that anything you do to me, I can do back to you, young lady. If we're ever stuck in such a situation again."

Caroline opened her mouth to protest, but Colin held up his hand. "I actually recommend a brachial stun instead of a punch to the jaw. You'll only be unconscious a few seconds, and when done properly, it won't do lasting damage. Or leave a bruise people will be asking about at say ... a Sky Keeper festival."

Feeling her own jaw, Caroline said, "You have a point there. A purple blotch *would* have clashed with my dress *and* given Uncle a bad name."

"It's comforting to know my reputation is safe thanks to the color of a dress," Darius replied drily.

As the evening wore on, the crowd grew larger and louder with a kind of joyful anticipation. After the third time Vesper asked Colin to repeat himself as they took refreshments after one of the Lockleys' lectures, he took her by the elbow and guided her up to the roof. In one corner, an inventor displayed a type of extra-powerful spyglass called a telescope. He gave viewings of the sky crystals and explained his theories on studying the heavens, if the Star Veil weren't in the way.

If the Star Veil weren't in the way. At one time, that statement would have elicited a patronizing smile, then serious questions, and now ... There was no doubt these people believed in— that they were willing to stake their lives on—the sun, moon, and stars. No. That wasn't quite right. They were willing to risk and even lose their lives for the One whose Word proclaimed the existence of the sun, moon, and stars. That didn't serve as proof of those objects or their Maker, of course, but it gave her pause. As did everything else she'd seen and heard that night.

As Colin led her to a quieter corner of the roof, she wondered again if these people's courage would prove to be a foolish waste or a fitting tribute to the One who gave his Son for them. If he could change Colin so much, could he change her?

Despite her lingering questions, her heart quieted as the world stilled around them, the noise of the crowded hallways below and its people gone. Just a whispering breeze holding on to spring's chill and the city spread before them as company, a thousand pinpricks of light in a blanket of night. While Vesper tried to find the Crystal Clock Tower and determine her location, Colin settled back against the brick wall encircling the rooftop and stared up at the Star Veil, the clouds mostly having disappeared.

"Why do you think they are so interested in the stars and the moon?" she asked, giving up her geographical pursuits. "Other than as proof of the Word."

"They'll be useful for navigation when the Star Veil falls." He indicated the inventor with his telescope across the rooftop. "And they're a mystery, a place where we can challenge our ignorance and, slowly, win." The skin about his eyes crinkled as he looked at her. "Gran also claims her grandmother said walks at night were once considered romantic, though she didn't know why. I think the stars and the moon had something to do with it."

"There's nothing romantic about a checkerboard sky. What if the stars are just brighter, more distant versions of the sky crystals?"

The unvarying rows of sky crystals against a black background reminded her of the floor in Grandfather Ulrik's home and of the chessboard they made use of on nearly every visit. Was it possible this Maker, or any god or natural process, would have created all the world beautiful but neglected the sky? So that it needed the faerie queen's Star Veil, as Grandfather Ulrik claimed? Her ancestor was clever but not imaginative or artistic, not a lover of nature and its beauty. He would have no qualms about concealing a real sky with the uninspiring Star Veil. She almost laughed. That was hardly good reasoning, but it seemed to unlock a doubt. The sky crystals *were* in a pattern he seemed to favor and did not match the rest of the world.

"You heard the poems and songs earlier," Colin answered. "'I see his blood upon the rose and in the stars the glory of his eyes.' Or 'Had I the heavens' embroidered cloths, enwrought with golden and silver light, the blue and the dim and the dark cloths, of night and light and the half light...'" Even in the crystals' faint glow she could tell his smile was wistful. "No, they'd be beautiful. A stunning wildness in a kind of order, like wildflowers in a meadow. There's an order if we look for it. He made them 'for signs and seasons, and for days and years,' after all. But they're more than mere time makers. 'The heavens declare the glory of God, and the sky above proclaims his handiwork. Day to day pours out speech, and night to night reveals knowledge.' That hardly sounds like the faerie queen's Star Veil, does it? No. *He* can make things orderly and useful and yet glorious and beautiful, as can the artists he's gifted with creative talent. Can you imagine something as insipid as sky crystals inspiring the music we heard tonight? No."

"I'm afraid I have to agree with you."

Something in her tone must have surprised him, for he looked down at her, his eyes wide.

But she wasn't quite ready to discuss what she meant.

"Why did you invite me tonight? Do you hope to convince me to do something for the Sky Keepers?"

Colin's sigh as he twisted around and leaned his elbows on the wall and looked out over the patchwork of city lights was not particularly reassuring to her feminine vanity or his own comfort in what he had to say.

"I asked you for many reasons, Vesper." He gave her a sideways glance and frowned at whatever he saw. He tucked her hand into his, drawing her to his side as if determined she would listen to all his reasons. Perhaps *all* his reasons weren't impersonal then. "The Sky Keepers do need information you might be able to get for us. I don't want to ask you though because it would be a risk, and I don't want to risk you."

"Despite your precautions, wasn't bringing me here something of a risk? For everyone?"

"Yes. And it's not a decision I made lightly. I discussed it with Mr. Ladell and Commodore Bowditch. They agreed it was something of a danger but that you should come. I couldn't just ask you to get the information because—"

"Because not even those belonging to the Rí Am's family are immune from disappearing. I know."

His hand tightened around hers. "If you're to take that risk, and even if you're not, I wanted you to know more about the Sky Keepers and the Maker of Stars. If you believed, the risk wouldn't be the same. It would be greater, but it wouldn't matter in a way. If that makes any sense."

Hadn't Mark told her the same thing?

"But," he rushed on before Vesper could reply, "I also just wanted your company. We're leaving in a week, and I didn't want to count on another chance meeting. Please believe me when I say that."

She'd been right in both her hopes and her suspicions, yet she couldn't muster a smile. Vesper squeezed his hand instead, and the creases in his forehead smoothed in relief. "When will you be back?"

He looked away over the city. "I don't know. Quite possibly never. What we're trying to do, it'll change everything or get us killed, or both. Even after the Star Veil falls there will be chaos until governments are formed and navigation is re-learned, free of the Time King's control." He paused. "It must bother you to know we want to overthrow your relative. I'm sorry for that."

"I realized a long time ago what he was," she said softly. "While there is a certain amount of pain, I would rather stand on the side of freedom and truth, and that is, sadly, not with Grandfather Ulrik." She drew herself up and pulled her hand free. "Now that I know your reasons for bringing me here weren't entirely mercenary, tell me what the Sky Keepers want of me. But first..." She slipped her locket over her head and held it out to him. "Here." Colin looked at her quizzically.

"In his discussion of *Elusive Longitude*, Darius Lockley lamented that the world only had one compass, as they were still working on building new ones." She opened the locket and with her fingernail pried an ancient photograph of a smiling young couple from a layer of glass. "There are two." Beneath the glass, arrows floated over a compass rose design. "You'll need it after the Star Veil is destroyed."

Colin's hand went instinctively to the matching design on his wrist. "How...?"

"I found it behind some old books in Grandfather Ulrik's library when I was a child and begged him for it. It belonged to his grandfather. I doubt he anticipated I'd snoop enough to find out what it was or bother to read a smuggled copy of the Word confiscated by my father."

She dared a glance at Colin. He wore the same thunder-struck look as when she'd first met him, but it was quickly changing to a grin of pure joy. She hurried on. "He read it at lunch 'to better understand the other side.' So of course, my cousin Mark and I would sneak into his office in the after-noons and read it too. Mark took it more seriously than I did ... up to now." Standing on tiptoes, she slipped the compass's chain over Colin's head, then took his offered hand. "So tell me what your spy can find out for you."

CHAPTER SEVEN

An angel, robed in spotless white, bent down and kissed the sleeping Night. Night woke to blush; the sprite was gone, Men saw the blush and called it Dawn. So Dunbar said.

Vesper sighed for the twentieth time as she paced her bedroom, then caught herself humming for the tenth time. She really should be terrified, or somber and calculating—she *was* about to have her yearly visit with the Rí Am. But all she could think about was dawn and moonlit walks and starry skies. They were real, their Maker was real, and she wanted the world to have them back. She especially wanted to share them with a certain ex-pirate.

"This will never do." She gave her head a good shake, then plucked up the sepia-toned photograph of her and Mark playing together as children and stared at it until her mood settled.

Unease instead of butterflies tickled her gut as she put the photograph down. Her hand retreated to her chest only to remember the compass wasn't there. She felt its loss but didn't mourn it. She checked her pocket for the silver compact, gathered her courage, her handbag, her thoughts into a prayer, and went downstairs.

Then fought the impression that the highly polished horseless carriage with well-dressed guards and a Time Keeper symbol waiting outside for her was a prison cart. She was handed in immediately, but no one got out. Cait must have gone somewhere else after her appointment with Grandfather Ulrik. Not that Vesper was complaining. She wasn't certain if Cait was still furious at Will and Nick's forced escort. They'd caught her at the theater and taken her to a garden club meeting, where she'd had to participate in a demonstration of the best way to pull weeds, and from there to a café that was entirely beneath her station. Or if she was appeased at having had the attention of two gentlemen to herself for an evening, plus having been introduced to Commodore and Mrs. Bowditch when they'd all met at that little café after the concert. Either way, she was still Cait and not very sociable.

Vesper's amusement at the image of Cait with her hands in the dirt lasted until Grandfather Ulrik's footman opened the door for her. Since she arrived in his carriage and didn't cover her arm bracer the guards didn't bother checking her invitation. Stiffening her spine and putting a lock on her tongue, she marched down the hallway—her black boots disappearing into every other square—past the library, and into the sitting room. She thought briefly she heard Cait's voice at the entryway, but it faded and she quickly forgot it.

The unfamiliar *ticktock* of a mantel clock, the only one in the world, beat decidedly slower than her heart. The Rí Am rose from a cushioned chair beside a fire that burned year round. A perpetual coldness was the only sign of Ulrik

Vanon's true age. He moved lithely toward her, and she refused to let it bother her that his build was very similar to her father's and his age, seemingly, not much more. There was only enough silver in his brown hair and trim beard to add a distinguished air to his handsome face and strong, natural confidence.

If only he hadn't used his gifts to hide the truth and seek to control the world, he could have done much good. But she couldn't let him see those thoughts in her eyes.

Conjuring images of gifts and fun games played together when she was a child, Vesper smiled, met his gaze, and accepted a hug from her some-odd great-grandfather.

"Vesper, my dear. It's so good of you to come see an old man every year." He took her by both hands and held her out from him as he inspected her appearance with a fond smile that stung her heart. *Traitor.* "As I suspected, you've grown into a lovely young woman. Nineteen already." He swept a glance over her again, and Vesper hoped she blushed appropriately at his praise. *Liar. Manipulator.* Did he care about her at all? Or only so long as she was on his side?

He tucked her arm in his and led her toward a table set with refreshments. "Beautiful, sweet-tempered, *and* cunning at chess. You will be harder to find an appropriate match for than your sisters."

Vesper stumbled.

"I beg your pardon," he said as he steadied her. "That rug is thicker than it seems. I've tripped on it myself."

"Forgive me. I was distracted. Are those almond cakes?"

He answered with a sly smile. "Did I remember your favorite correctly?"

"As always." Was this how he caught Mark? Disarmed

him with kindness until his tongue loosened? Bile rose in her throat.

Ulrik gave her a sideways glance as they stopped at the table.

I knew you were truly ill when you didn't ask questions. Her father's long-ago comment on her curiosity rang like a warning bell through her mind. She schooled her face into what she hoped was an expression of appreciation for sweet things and helped herself from the spread of goodies. She opened her mouth to speak but nothing came out. Not good. She grabbed a chocolate to put in it and said another prayer, one she never thought she'd pray: to be more herself.

"Can I get you something to drink?" he asked, gesturing to a second table. The various bottles, containing wine to much stronger drinks, made a fair imitation of a city skyline against the wall. She definitely did not need their influence, and she suspected her dear Grandfather Ulrik made rather too much use of them on those he invited.

"Might I have some milk? To cut the sweetness?" She indicated the slice of cake and squares of fudge on her plate.

He raised an eyebrow. She shrugged.

"One of the odd consequences of growing older—I now drink milk. And eat peas. But I firmly resolve *never* to like Brussels sprouts."

"Milk it is then." He pulled the cord for the butler and helped himself to cake.

Vesper settled into her usual chair, the one opposite his by the fire, then squirmed to the edge of it. "So ... have you made matches for my sisters yet? I mean, is there something you can tell me?"

He swallowed a mouthful of cake, then laughed. "There

you are! I was afraid my curious little Vesper had *disappeared* in the past year."

Why the emphasis on *disappeared*?

A mischievous grin lit her face. "Well?" Laying her fork aside, she watched him watch her with a self-satisfied smile.

"Cara and I came to an arrangement some time ago." His smile curled in a way that reminded her of a storybook villain's mustache. *Get a hold of yourself, Vesper.*

Why was Cara still running around with a man beneath the appropriate standing for a Vanon then? "Oh?" She let the question hang, but he didn't deliver.

"I'm not so sure about Cait yet," he said after a pause. "She can be useful. She tends to drink when she's upset or anxious and then talks a great deal." His tone conveyed a *tsk* that never passed his lips. "But more than that, I cannot say. Tell me about your past year."

They ate and chatted about family and life until Vesper's head ached. Tomorrow, she was going to resign her life as a Snoop. To be guarded but give the appearance of openness felt like a continual stabbing of herself. How did real spies stand it? And ferret out the information they needed? Somehow, she doubted blurting, "Where did the faerie queen cast the Star Veil for you?" would get the response she wanted.

At last, he laid aside his plate and rose. "Would you mind if we delayed our game of chess until next year? I hear you've made progress in your artistic endeavors."

CHAPTER EIGHT

Ohe could easily drive straight from the street onto the dock and into the *Dawn Singer*'s cargo hold, if one so desired. Colin had paid extra for this dock for that purpose. The familiar hum of his grandmother's carriage wove its way to him through the cries of airmen and the rush of propellers on a departing airship. It was a sound he couldn't miss if he tried, so attuned was he to it from his childhood up.

But today wasn't the day the carriage was to drive aboard and give up its iron.

Colin walked out of the cargo hold with the cargo manifest still in his hand and watched the carriage approach. Fiona's daughters leaned out of its open windows and waved. The carriage was piled with luggage. Bridie parked about twenty feet from the ship. She, Fiona, and the girls got out.

"We're coming with you." Fiona stood with her arms crossed, her feet braced apart. She was definitely her mother's daughter, which meant there was no point arguing the danger.

"We're not leaving for a few days, Aunt Fiona."

"We thought we'd give you fair warning."

"Give it to Philip. He'll get your rooms set up." After *he* tried arguing her out of it.

Fiona nodded, the steel in her posture melting back to mere bone. "Thanks." She kissed his cheek, received a kiss in return, then herded the girls inside the ship.

Colin turned to Bridie, his eyebrows raised in question.

"The Lockleys returned home by train and too many men have been prowling about the cove. Not all are Time Keepers."

His jaw clenched. Not all smugglers and pirates held to the code of respecting one another's goods and women. Not all were above being the Time Keepers' pawns as well. "Stay on the *Dawn Singer* until we leave. I'll send men to board up the house."

"It's done." Bridie pressed her hat to her head and stepped back as a breeze gushed over them like a dry waterfall.

An Escaper with the *Breaker*'s sea blue crest brightening its side alighted behind the carriage. Colin stepped forward. For the first time in three years he felt ready to meet his father. Colin wasn't a pirate anymore, and he knew his father couldn't make him into one again.

Yet it wasn't Cavan O'Connor who hopped out of the tiny winged airship but a trim woman who moved with all the grace of a circus acrobat. A revolver was strapped to her hip, and she left her goggles in place over her eyes. His disappointment was as sharp as the knife also prominent on the lady's belt, but it was dulled by the fact her presence indicated his father had kept his promise to look after her and Davy.

"Hello, Prism."

"Hello, Colin." She met him at the carriage and glanced at Bridie with caution in her posture. Colin introduced them. Prism's face lit, and she lifted her goggles to reveal her crazy, wondrous eyes with their tangled web of colors. "It's a pleasure to meet you at last, Mrs. O'Connor. You'll be pleased to know that Captain Cavan has been a loyal, generous, albeit sometimes surly host these past months." She turned back to Colin. "I hope you'll forgive the intrusion. Davy and the Commodore snuck off to the Clock Tower to check the calibration of the Star Clock, so Captain Cavan sent me to tell you he was here and to ask when you could meet privately."

Colin's heart thumped hard, twice. Once for his father, once for the clock. "It works?"

"We hope so. We've two Star Clocks. We calibrated them at another port, but Davy and the Commodore are checking to see if they're both still running right. If they are, then we're ready to send out blueprints."

Praise the Maker.

Bridie echoed his prayer.

Colin let out a breath and leaned against the carriage's bonnet. Prism's consistent use of "we" reminded him of the surprise Davy's parents claimed he had for them. His lips curved into a smile. "Tell Davy I was given a compass. *You two*"—he gave her a significant look, and she grinned and blushed prettily in response—"Mrs. Davy Bowditch, can check it against those Davy is building. But I want it back— intact—when you're done." He pulled Vesper's locket from under his shirt and off over his head. "I can meet with Father—"

Prism recoiled and drew her gun, aiming it at someone

beside him. Bridie grabbed Prism's arm and pulled her aside, hissing a warning at Colin.

Eoin Vanon snagged the compass as Colin spun around. "Where is she?" Panic and fury fought for dominance in his eyes. His revolver was still strapped to his side, but his posture spoke to him only being a hairsbreadth from violence, or collapse. "Tell me she's here."

Though his heart rate ratcheted up, Colin forced his stance to loosen, his hands to un-fist. "If Vesper is here, sir, I don't know it. ... But I think she'd let me know this time." He fought the panic trying to sweep from Eoin into him. "Why—"

"Then where did you get this?" The locket waved between them like a battle flag. "She's not let it out of her sight since she was seven years old."

Eoin's accusatory glare slammed into him. There was only one way for Eoin to believe him. He'd have to declare his side. And the sooner he did, the sooner he could find Vesper. Clenching his jaw, he began unbuttoning his cuff.

Bridie laid a hand on his wrist. "My grandson, Philip Orren, and I took Vesper to the Vallendester Theater recently. She was wearing the locket when we picked her up, but I didn't notice it when we took her and your daughter Cait home."

Eoin's gaze was still locked on Colin. "Why would she give it to you?"

Colin pulled away from Bridie and yanked up his sleeve, revealing the compass rose tattoo with the triquetra at its center. "Because it's not a locket and she knows it. Take out the photograph."

Eoin didn't move. Colin grabbed the locket, clicked it

open, and peeled out the photo. The compass needle wobbled but stayed true. Eoin's gaze flicked to Colin's wrist and back to the compass. The reaction was immediate, but Colin was prepared this time. He blocked Eoin's punch and grabbed his gun and handed it off to Bridie.

Eoin collapsed to the dock, sitting with his head in his hands. Guilt speared Colin as he wondered if his father had reacted the same way when he'd "died."

Colin knelt beside him and shook his shoulders. "Tell me what happened to her." When he didn't answer, Colin shook harder. "Eoin!" Colin was about to hit him when Eoin stilled and looked up. He swallowed hard, all panic and anger disappearing behind the steady alertness Colin had witnessed at the tea shop.

"She went to her yearly meeting with *Grandfather Ulrik*"—hatred slipped beneath the mask—"and never came back. Just like my nephew Mark. He'd become a Sky Keeper."

Prism and Bridie gasped, but Colin couldn't breathe. *O Maker, what have I done?* He thought she'd ask little old ladies or explore private libraries, maybe ask her father, not talk with Ulrik Vanon himself.

"Cait came to the office earlier crying and half drunk," Eoin continued. "I warned her not to drink when she visited Grandfather Ulrik, but he pushed her too far about her sister Cara's liaison with the man she thought favored her. Cara and this man had been in a relationship for over a year, keeping it secret in part by dallying with others, amusing themselves with their deceit. In Cait's bitterness she revealed Vesper's trip to Hollym. I'd tried to keep it a secret, but Cait must have figured it out and that Vesper went with you. He would have linked that with my partly failed mission in

Hollym and the suspicion you turned Sky Keeper." His face twisted in pain, then settled into a sneer. "He rewards those who expose Sky Keepers in the family. That's how Cara earned the right to marry that swine she's run away with. She turned in her own cousin. She sent Mark to the mines.

"Poor Cait. She, at least, didn't mean to. Grandfather Ulrik kept her until it was too late for her to warn Vesper." He rose, his gaze turning hollow. Colin felt sick to his stomach. "I must get back to my office. I left Cait there."

He turned to leave but Colin grabbed his arm. "Snap out of it, man. We can't abandon Vesper."

Life fired in Eoin's eyes, then flashed out. "I can't. I have Cait, a wife, and a sister and her family. If I so much as question Grandfather Ulrik, he'll take them all. That's how life is as a Vanon." He stared at the compass resting in his palm, then held it out to Colin. "Vesper is lost to us."

Colin hit him. He caught Eoin as he folded and lowered him to the wooden dock.

He pocketed the compass as Bridie knelt beside Eoin and lifted his head to her lap. "Colin—"

"Gran, do you know where the Rí Am lives?"

She searched his face, concern in hers, then nodded, resigned. "I remember."

"Then tell me and go aboard the *Dawn Singer*. Philip will have to unload the iron into it and then leave immediately. We'll follow on the *Breaker*."

Prism knelt beside him and put a hand on his shoulder. "Should I get Davy?"

"Only to get him ready to leave. Tell my father I need his help picking up something in the Crystal District." He handed her the card Latimer had given him. "Ask him to meet me here, if he's willing. He'll understand." He sought her eyes. "The *Dawn Singer's* automaton is set for Rymsby. Can you guide the *Breaker* to waylay the *Dawn Singer* before she reaches port? The Rí Am will be expecting her."

"Yes, if I examine the crystal. What are you going to do?"

"I'm going to jump in front of a carriage."

CHAPTER NINE

V esper's heart had apparently run away without her, for nothing beat in her chest. Her painting of Claire...

"It's time for a new imperial sculptor," Grandfather Ulrik said, "and I'd like your assistance in choosing him."

Her fickle heart dashed back. "I'd be honored." She'd heard of a poet laureate but an imperial sculptor?

A servant cleared away the refreshments and replaced them with a chest. Unloading the chest, Grandfather Ulrik spread out twenty portfolios and statuettes on the table. He indicated for her to sit and then slid a chair under her.

"Each sculptor's portfolio contains a profile, images of his artwork, and a model from a previous project. There's also a score sheet with criteria listed. Consult the criteria, then the portfolio and artwork, and record your opinion. When we're both done, we'll compare."

Assuming a business-like posture, Vesper dutifully perused the list of criteria. Why did family rank so highly? Creativity and ability to work with multiple materials she could understand, but having dependents? A shiver traced its way from her arm bracer to her heart.

She let the semi-silence of rustling pages and critical or appreciative *hmm*'s reign for sixteen minutes according to the only-one-in-the-world mantel clock—fifteen would have seemed calculated and longer not like her. "I am impressed, Grandfather, and almost inspired to study sculpture myself. Any one of these could capture the faerie queen's image without displeasing her!"

The rustling of papers stopped, and the Rí Am stared at her for a full three seconds before blinking back into his normal expression of complete confidence and self-possession.

It was the most peculiar three seconds of her life. He probably hadn't been startled in a hundred years.

"I should hope so," he said at last, returning to the portfolio, "for the honor of Rìoghachd Criostail."

"What was she like?"

"Who?"

"Morgan Unseelie." Giver of Sky Crystals, benefactress to the poor, pitiable mortals. Vesper's heart lurched as she saw for the first time just what the Rí Am had done. He had set up a goddess in place of the Creator God he'd tried to hide along with his heavens. He'd made himself lord of the Earth. He hated Sky Keepers because they refused to bow to him.

"Like a faerie queen should be."

Vesper ignored the obvious "end of discussion" punctuation on that comment. "Have you ever had a painting commissioned to commemorate your meeting with her and the giving of the crystals? Where was it? What was the setting? A ruined castle? A dark forest glen? How old were you? Do you ever return to talk with her? The history book's brief summary is so cold and factual. It could really benefit from the personal angle and an illustration."

"Your task, Vesper."

"Illustrate it?" she asked, as terrified as confused by the idea.

"The sculptors."

"Oh. Sorry." Relieved, she tugged another portfolio in front of her and plucked out the sculptor profile. How far dare she push?

"Oileán Caillte," he said suddenly some minutes later.

"I beg your pardon?" She scooted a portfolio to the pile of finished ones and grabbed another.

"I had gone fishing off the coast of my home island and encountered a storm. I was washed ashore on Oileán Caillte."

"You're not from Reydon?" Her surprise was genuine. She didn't even know her own family history. She'd never heard of Oileán Caillte. But she'd remember it with her life.

"I *built* Reydon. Its grandeur is mine. There was nothing much I could do with the hamlet where I was born."

Vesper held her breath and flipped pages from a slick photo of Isaac Martin's sparse family to one of his stunning work.

"Sheffield-on-the-Sea has its uses but not as a capital."

Her breath collapsed into a muted gasp. *But you cut it off from supplies!* She bit her lip, gluing her eyes with their treacherous anguish on an image of the Norwood Crystal Clock Tower, redesigned and rebuilt after a storm. "Yes. I doubt you could fit Reydon on the island."

They continued in silence, though Vesper's mind roared with two words: Oileán Caillte. But how could they reach it?

She highly doubted she could simply purchase an automaton for it.

A servant brought tea as she finished up. She gave Ulrik her score sheets and fixed herself a cup of hot tea.

"I congratulate your taste, my dear," he said as her tea finished its steeping. "We had the same top three." He laid aside the sheets and pulled one portfolio from the rest. "However, I shall give you the honor of choosing the next imperial sculptor. Isaac Martin, it is."

"I'm flattered, Grandfather. I look forward to seeing the sculptures he'll produce."

The butler and two guards stepped into the room, and Vesper was never so glad to see the stoic men before. It was time to go. She hid her sigh of relief with a careful sip of the piping hot tea.

"He'll only make one, my dear. I'll make sure you see it." He pushed aside the sheets and stood. "Keyes will show you to your room now."

The cup stilled before her lips. "My room?"

"I thought you were cleverer than that, Vesper." He picked up her handbag from her chair and gave it to the guard. "You're not leaving. When a young woman with access to the plans of my Anti-Smuggling Unit disappears and turns up three days later in Hollym, where Sky Keepers evade capture by the same Anti-Smuggling Unit, I was bound to be curious. And then to learn she spent those three days with Colin O'Connor, a man whose drastic change from brutal pirate to honored captain could only mean one thing—he'd become a Sky Keeper—I was bound to be displeased." His voice hardened. "I will not have a descendent of mine a Sky Keeper."

The *ticktock* of the clock echoed in the room. *He controls time, and yours has run out,* it said. *Run out. Run out.*

She'd been caught.

The thing she'd feared since first reading the smuggled copy of the Word had happened. The room about her spun, and a dead calm fell over her. She noted vaguely that her hands didn't even tremble as she laid aside the teacup, and for that she was grateful. "I see."

His eyes narrowed. "Not quite. Every fifty years I take a tribute from the mortal world to Queen Morgan of the Unseelie: a sculpture in her honor. If she is pleased, the sculptor lives. If not, I personally avenge her honor on the worthless sculptor and his entire family." His smile turned Vesper's stomach but firmed her resolve. She'd made the right choice. "Either way, I receive the elixir of youth in return. Let that be your comfort in the next six months. You chose the man whose life and family rests with a chisel and a tempestuous faerie queen."

A guard took her roughly by the arm and pushed her toward the door.

"And you will be the bait by which I finally rid myself of the Bowditch captains, since the pirates aren't able to," Grandfather Ulrik called after her. "Let that be your comfort as well."

Slipping her hatpin back into place, Vesper backed away from the un-pickable door lock and refused another peek at the window with its well-disguised bars and another search for a vent large enough for her shoulders. She took a deep breath and stuffed her hands into her pockets to keep them from wringing together. She would not disgrace herself or the true Giver of Light by going into hysterics now. But the information she'd gained was weighing on her heart, reminding her of her mission. She needed out, if only to get the knowledge of the Star Veil's location to the Sky Keepers.

Or did she?

Her shoulders, which had fallen in resignation, rose again in resolve. *She* didn't necessarily have to get out with the information. Vesper scanned the simple bedroom. A heavy four-poster bed, large wool rug, wardrobe, desk with stationery, dresser with porcelain water pitcher and bowl, a barred window that didn't look barred—the Rí Am would never admit to his home doubling as a prison—and a fireplace. Two indifferent paintings of Reydon, one under a milky-white sky and the other under a checkerboard black-and-white sky hung on the walls. Was he punishing her with poor artwork?

She yanked the night scene off the wall. Her fingers protested as she untwisted the hanging wire tightly secured to the metal loops in the wooden frame. She tossed the wire onto the desk, shoved the painting into a dresser drawer, then slipped into the desk seat and pulled the stationery to her.

New imperial sculptor Isaac Martin to design tribute statue for Queen Morgan to be delivered to her at Oileán Caillte.

Yours most truly,

Vesper

She lifted her pen, then touched it to the paper again, wishing she had some spell of command she could add to it.

P.S. Grandfather Ulrik intends to use me as bait to destroy you. Ignore it. Please. He will keep me around at least until the statue is completed in six months. It would give me great pleasure in my confinement to know you're alive and free—and to see Grandfather Ulrik's frustration that he can't use me against you. Take care of the Star Veil. I'm okay. Truly.

She addressed the note to Colin and folded it into a square. It was a sad comfort that she'd finally gotten to use her normal handwriting and her own name. Secrecy no longer mattered.

Using additional sheets of paper and the wire, she began constructing a small paper lantern, praying it would make it out of the chimney with her note.

The doorknob rattled violently, and Vesper jumped up and shoved the lantern into a drawer, the note into her pocket.

"It's locked from the *outside* as you might recall," she said, seating herself again and pretending to write a poem.

The door burst open and slammed into the wall, rattling the picture frame above her. She whirled around as two men staggered into the room. One was Colin. His face, shirt, and dark brown trench coat were covered in blood and dust.

"Colin!" She darted forward. How was he even upright with all that blood smearing him? The door must have slammed because he collapsed against it or was shoved against it as the guard unlocked it. The brute. She spared a glare for the guard, who looked remarkably like an older version of Colin. Blond hair; blue eyes; handsome, weather-beaten face; muscular build. "What did he do..." Why was the guard grinning at her in that approving kind of way? "...to you?"

"Nothing yet." Colin grabbed her arm and steered her toward the bed. "Get underneath it."

Her heart nearly burst with relief. "You're okay? But how...?"

"Blood" dripping down his forehead, he winked at her and pushed her along. "I jumped in front of a carriage. This is my father, by the way, Cavan O'Connor."

Cavan's eyes twinkled as he nodded at her and brushed by toward the window. "It's a pleasure to meet you, Miss Vanon."

"How do you do?" she managed before turning back to Colin. "You're not hurt? Grandfather Ulrik didn't capture you?"

"Under the bed, Vesper. Explanations later." Her father. "Colin, wipe that muck off your face. You're distressing my daughter."

She found him at the doorway with a gun in his hand.

"Daddy!" was all Colin allowed her before shoving her under the bed as Cavan secured a device of some sort to the window. Colin threw the pillows to the floor, yanked the mattress off and positioned it like a shield in front of the bed, then scooted in after her and wiped his face with his handkerchief.

Cavan darted from the room, and gunshots blasted through the hallway.

Colin yanked the pillows in front of them. "Cover your ears."

"No!" She shoved against him, trying to get out. "My father! We've got to do—"

An explosion rocked the room, spewing shattered glass and brick. A cry came from the hallway, then footsteps.

The bed rose as Colin pushed and Cavan lifted. Her father grabbed her hand, and she scooted out, slipping on shards of glass and coughing up the swirling brick dust. Her knees lost their usual stability as the empty air between them and the nearest building taunted her through the hole in the wall. Shouts and alarms carried in with a clarity she wasn't used to when inside a building, and she firmly decided she preferred outside sounds to remain outside.

"I take it we can't leave the way you came in," she managed, catching the sheets Colin snagged from the wardrobe and tossed to her.

"No." Eoin dragged the dresser to the door as Colin and his father braced it with the wardrobe. "Twist those sheets, Vesper."

As she started on the second sheet, the furious honking of a horn down below barreled in, sounding entirely too loud due to its enlarged approach to them.

"Hurry!" Cavan barked the word like an order to his crew. "Latimer and the boys have had to leave. The rest of the guards will be coming back in."

Colin pulled an elaborate, gear-and-pulley-covered leather gauntlet and chest harness from his trench coat and tossed it to her. "Help your father put the PullLine on."

She caught it, then recoiled, horrified by the crystal-studded leather bracer covering Colin's forearm. One arm, as usual, was covered the Bowditch PullLine gauntlet, but his tattoo was hidden by this new stamp. "Why are you wearing a Vanon arm bracer?"

"It's a smugglers' deception I shall remember to do something about," Eoin said as he and Vesper secured the PullLine.

"It's one of Latimer's many tricks. I needed it to get inside." Colin pulled a polished, wooden bar from somewhere on his person. She hadn't noticed it before, but he did appear considerably bulkier than he should. His father pulled a similar piece from his own coat and tossed it to Colin. Colin snagged it from the air and fitted the two pieces together to form a crossbow. "Latimer and Father arranged an accident outside. I was *hit* by a carriage, and being a Vanon, your father got me carried inside to be looked after."

Colin loaded an arrow tied to a length of rope onto the crossbow and leaned out the enlarged window and surveyed the surrounding buildings. "One guard went for a medic, and several others went to stop the brawl on the street between my friends and the men who ran me over." He raised the crossbow and sent the arrow into the far side of the flat, rectangular roof of the next building, about one story beneath them. Short, decorative metal fencing encircled the mesa-like roof. "The remaining guards we persuaded to let us find you. The Rí Am is out."

Footsteps stormed up the stairs. The door and its furniture rattled.

Colin slung the weapon across his back, leaned further out the gaping hole, and tossed the rope over a gable that still appeared sturdy. Cavan pulled the rope taut and secured its other end to the heavy bedframe, then braced the bed.

Colin motioned for Vesper to come to him. She slung the twisted sheet over the rope and wrapped her arms about his neck. Colin curled each sheet end around a fist.

Then she realized to what building they were going. "Do you really think it's a good idea to go to the guards' hou—"

"Hold on."

They launched into the warm air. Her breath rushed out as they fell like a clipped dove toward the guards' house. They hit the roof at a run and released the sheet. An alarm went off beneath them, rather late considering the recent explosion had served as one. They stumbled to the side, out of the way as Cavan, then Eoin followed.

An odd pair to be traveling together, Vesper thought. She'd have laughed if not for the cries of guards from below and from the bedroom behind.

A warning shot dented the roof two feet away. It seemed the guards didn't know whether to kill or simply detain them as they were all, supposedly, Vanons.

"Do I have to use the stun darts?" Cavan groused as he returned fire.

"I won't check to see what you use." Eoin kept close behind Vesper, shielding her.

Her hand in Colin's, they sprinted across the flat rooftop, leapt over the short railing, skidded down the steep roof, and stumbled onto the narrow brim between two spiked gables. Colin didn't halt but grabbed her round the waist and leapt. His PullLine shot out, securing onto a building across the street.

They plummeted, arcing across the road. A long, open, horse-drawn cart raced up the street beneath them. The PullLine snapped free of the building, and they plunged toward the cart. A man standing in its bed caught them and tumbled with them to the wooden floorboards. Cavan and Eoin crashed beside them, cursing.

"Go, Prism!" the man roared at the woman, clad in loose

pants, riding boots, and a long blue jacket, standing on the driver's seat.

Vesper knocked against Colin as the cart shot forward, lurching into the air at each bump. Vesper had no idea the roads in this area were so rough, but perhaps driving at breakneck speed made a difference.

"Curse you, Davy Bowditch. You almost left me." Cavan rolled to his knees between Eoin and the cart's tailgate.

Davy shrugged as he sat up. "I'm not driving."

Cavan huffed. "You got a plan to get us the ten miles to the docks?"

"Of course."

He grinned wickedly. "Good. Then the chief of the ASU and I can guard the rear." He pulled out his revolver and crawled toward the rear with Eoin, who made a comment about gun wounds sustained at close range being easy to recognize. Cavan barked a laugh.

Vesper struggled to sit upright and attempted to slide backward to lean against the cart's side. Davy lunged across Colin and caught her arm. "Watch out. That's a kerosene lantern behind you."

She froze, then inched forward.

Still leaning over Colin, Davy offered Vesper his hand. "I'm Davy Bowditch, and that's my wife, Prism, driving us," he yelled over the crashing of wheels over stone and the cries of the guards now pursuing them and the pedestrians fleeing them both.

"Vesper Vanon," she shouted, then ducked at the crack of a rifle. Wood splintered from the tailgate. She hunkered down, Colin pressing her against the floorboards.

"Prism!" Davy roared again.

"We're almost there. Get ready," Prism yelled back as

302

Eoin and Cavan made use of the firearms and Pea Soupers conveniently awaiting them near the tailgate.

Flattening beside Colin, Davy turned back to Vesper. "I know. My mother told me about you." A mischievous twinkle lit his eyes as he focused on Colin. "She said she'd make it all right with the Commodore if Colin wanted out of his promise about *taking* a wife."

"Go away, Davy," Colin growled.

"As you wish." Davy winked at her, then bolted up and over onto the driver's seat and leapt off the cart.

She and Colin both eased up. Davy landed on an oddly tall horseless carriage—with no rack on top now—and scurried into the open driver's seat.

They jerked to the floorboards again as Prism swerved to the left and the O'Connor carriage rocketed into traffic alongside them.

"The idiot forgot about the door." Cavan jumped up and sprang onto the carriage, landing on its black top and easing himself down onto the running board. He jerked the door open, stepped halfway inside, and stretched out his hand. "The lady next."

Colin eased off Vesper, and she pushed herself up, refusing to acknowledge the weakness of her knees. There was no time to think about her fear. It would have to get along with being ignored. She put a foot onto the side of the cart, took a deep breath, and jumped.

She landed in Cavan's arms, and he deposited her inside on the leather seat cushions.

Colin followed, then Eoin, who went up top to be ready to relieve Davy at the Scramble Distance.

"What about Prism?" Vesper cried as she bounced across the seat.

"Watch." Cavan grinned and pulled back the window coverings.

Prism flung the reins onto the galloping horses' backs, then vaulted onto the port-side horse. She drew a knife from her belt, swung down, and slashed the straps holding the horse to the pole extending from the cart. She swung back up and stood on the horse, then leapt onto the starboard horse as the freed one galloped away. She slashed the remaining tack and pulled the horse to the side.

Two shots exploded above them. The kerosene lantern in the rear of the cart and another at the front shattered. The wooden cart burst into flames, blocking the road and the Time Keepers following.

Prism pulled herself up to stand on the horse, guiding it alongside the driver's bench as the carriage matched pace.

"Quit showing off and get up here," Davy yelled with a smile in his voice. He leaned over and swept Prism onto the seat beside him.

"You're welcome," Prism sassed.

Cavan leaned back in his seat with a huff and rolled his eyes. "Besotted fools." He eyed Vesper, then surprised her by giving Colin the Proud Father Look. It ended with a silent curse as the carriage leapt a curb.

Vesper yelped as she bounced, nearly hitting the roof. Colin grabbed the door handle with one hand and braced her against his side with his other.

Rubbing his head, Cavan fixed a serious gaze at Colin. "When you disappeared and then showed up with that Sky Keeper Bowditch, I was afraid I would never get to do this. You've made me proud today, son."

Colin's arm fled her side as if burnt. He twisted around to face her, his expression bordering on frantic. "I did not kidnap you, Vesper," he blurted. "You're in no way obligated to marry me. You're free to go wherever you choose. I *promised* Commodore Bowditch and Davy that I would *not* kidnap a wife."

"Why would they even ask for such a promise?" Vesper cried and braced herself as they shot around a corner without slowing.

"It's a family tradition." Cavan said it proudly. Vesper gaped at him, then slammed into Colin.

"It's not like that, Vesper," Colin pleaded, holding her away from him. His anxious gaze tempted her to smile. He really was sweet. "Gran had interviewed with the Rí Am to marry into one of the top families. The potential groom was a brute, in public and in private. When Grandfather offered to kidnap her, she didn't have much choice."

The Rí Am. Vesper gasped and yanked the silver compact with the iron paste from her pocket. *He* would kidnap her.

"An O'Connor would never mistreat his family," Cavan said matter-of-factly. "They're gentle as lambs at home." His lips curved in a smug smile. "Your mother had her bags packed."

Vesper snapped the compact open and snatched out the cotton pad as her hand swayed with the carriage's motion.

"Swap drivers!" her father yelled as the carriage swerved erratically. Her hand swung wildly over the iron paste. It hit once, then bounded off.

"Colin, pull up my sleeve."

Colin complied, though more focused on his father. "Mother's mother was a friend of Gran's and asked for help because Mother was in the same situation Gran had been!"

She rammed the homing crystal with the pad and

smeared the paste, then repeated, trying not to blacken her entire bracer in the attempt.

Cavan shrugged. "She never complained. And the dresses she packed were *my* favorite color, not the man's she was about to marry."

"Knife, Colin."

"It was her favorite color too." Colin held her wrist steady as she worked the blackened crystal out. She wiped the crystal clean and tossed it out the window onto a carriage going the opposite way.

"We don't even need a Justice of the Peace because I can marry you. I did Davy and Prism's wedding. Even gave them a month to get acquainted."

Vesper groaned. Her father and Cavan were not going to get along once the rescue ended. She returned the knife to Colin, whose jaw was hanging open, then lowered the window and lifted herself into a sitting position on it. "Prism!"

"Would you stop already! I am not kidnapping a wife." Colin put an arm around her waist, steadying her.

Prism vaulted onto the carriage top and flattened, peering over the edge at Vesper.

"It's a tradition, boy," Cavan said loudly enough for the entire street to hear. "And a right enjoyable one at that." He snorted. "Never took the father-in-law too though. But he's tough, and fair for an ASU man."

Prism raised her eyebrows. Vesper held out the compact. "Iron paste for my father's homing crystal." Her teeth jarred as they rattled over a pothole. "It's got to come out." Prism took the compact and scooted back to her seat. Vesper tapped on the roof, and Colin pulled her back inside.

"This is not a kidnapping!" he repeated, glaring at his father.

"It'll be awkward if you don't marry her. Gran went after her mother and sister, and clothes and things for Vesper."

Colin sputtered. One would almost think he *didn't* want to marry her. If his arm weren't still around her waist.

Vesper grabbed him by the shoulders. His eyebrows rose as he jerked his gaze to hers. "Colin O'Connor, I consider myself kidnapped. I've not packed a bag, and I have nothing to offer but the ire of the Rí Am." She pulled the folded note from her skirt pocket and grinned. "And the location of the Star Veil. I *am* your spy, after all."

PART V
DUSK CRIER

*Give thanks to the God of heaven, for his steadfast love
endures forever.*
Psalm 1 36:26

CHAPTER ONE

It was taught that the faerie queen Morgan Unseelie gave man the sky crystals to beautify the night and light the day, that she gave the automatons to allow man to safely roam beyond their villages. Whether this was true or not, all knew that the power of the automatons she put into the Rí Am's hands, and he used it to rule the world. Every fifty years the Rí Am sent an offering to the queen, a vain gift for a vain queen, to the secret isle where they'd rendezvoused, where she'd cast the Star Veil for him.

The Sky Keepers, those who still believed the Word—in the sun, moon, and stars and their eternal Maker—meant to use this offering to their advantage. Sending a gift required a crystal for navigation, and the Sky Keepers had sent someone after it, lacking only it to travel to the hidden isle and plunge their iron harpoons through the queen's Star Veil. At long last, the Maker was getting ready to tear down the faerie's Star Veil and reveal his glory written in the heavens once more.

K ingsley Bowditch, captain of the lost airship
Dusk Crier, had been trying to escape for ... His
arm went lax, the chisel slipping away from the
crystal blinking against the coal-black rock wall. One year?
Three and a quarter? Five and one-twelfth?

"No night, no day," he muttered, steadying the chisel.
"Can't give a time then." His grip tightened around the
leather-wrapped handle of the rock pick hammer as a guard
yelled at another prisoner. The guard with the cauliflower
ears and serpent neck tattoo punctuated every sentence with
a flick of his bludgeon rather than a period.

"But time matters now." Kingsley tapped the pick's
square end onto the chisel's head. Black chips flaked off the
wall. He tapped it again, gently, then wiggled the crystal.
"Hurry. Can't be last alone." He coaxed the crystal out and
slid it into the bag at his feet. "Last together." No one got
beat for being last that way.

He glanced back at the hole in the black rock already
beginning to close up, then to his left. The boy Mark worked
quickly now, for he'd watched Kingsley when he'd first come.
Kingsley had told him without telling him how to work the
crystals out faster than the others could. Every day, he grew
faster.

Kingsley's chisel hovered over the rock clinging to
another crystal. *Every day.* Every day he dug crystals from
the wall, but the next day, they were all back. Every day.
Crystals for Dondre, crystals for Bakeston, crystals for his
favorite theater in Reydon. He glanced up at the dust-
covered placard above his section of the round chamber.
"Time Keeper Station, Reydon, city center." He giggled. It
was the biggest wall. They gave it to him because they hated

him the most—and he was the best worker. He had to, "Hurry."

He tapped and pried, tapped and pried. He'd been trying to escape for ... He shifted the chisel to the opposite side of the crystal. *Since I came here.* "Yes, that's how long."

"Will someone shut him up?" a prisoner in the next chamber cried.

"He's gone mad," another said.

"About time."

Time. Since he'd been the captain of the *Dusk Crier*. Before his men had been taken from him, put in other prisoner groups. He had to get them out somehow. His fault. Had to get them out. Keep *them* sane. Keep them kind. Keep them faithful. "Somehow." *Maker, help me. Help us remember.*

"A man can only handle so much," his chamber-mate Tom said, a warning in his tone as he glanced between Kingsley and Serpent.

Kingsley ignored them. He wasn't mad. No one talked to him. Against the rules. So he talked to himself. *That* kept him from going mad.

And he was hot. "So hot." And tired. And sometimes very cold. "Very cold."

"Shut it, Bowditch," Tom growled at him from his wall behind Kingsley's.

"Leave him be." The guard Masked leaned against the barred ventilation shaft in the main tunnel. His voice carried like a sailor's on a windy day. Masked had a mask for a nose and part of his cheek. A piece of machinery for his leg. Like Kingsley's father. Both had lost a leg in a pirate fight. Masked's slightly too white nose pointed toward Serpent. "No trouble, Kev, remember. It costs time."

Serpent sneered. "Yes, we've that extra prize to dig out for our 'guests.'" Serpent stalked through the chambers toward Kingsley. "But when they're gone, we can get back to our normal routine. *Last one to finish is a broken egg.*" Cruel anticipation danced in his voice like a will-o'-the-wisp over a chasm. The Serpent liked to strike the last one and incite the other prisoners to punish the one who made them wait to go up. Not all prisoner groups and guards were like this one. The ones with his crew weren't. He was glad for that.

The prisoners fell silent, like a volcano that had released a little of its steam but wasn't ready to give up more. Kingsley looked to Masked. The former sailor flinched and looked away, the slump of his shoulders suggesting defeat, and Kingsley wondered if the man was a prisoner of sorts as well.

Serpent walked on, reminding them of their quota: All crystals had to be collected from each one's assigned walls before they could return to their cells. No helping. The best prisoner unit earned time out under the sky crystals, a sea bath, a chance to drown themselves. But, the guard accused, they were a lazy lot and would never win it.

Kingsley bit back a yelp as Serpent finished a sentence on his back. Tom growled a warning at Serpent when he got the same treatment. Serpent had finished almost too many sentences on Tom once. Tom had never been the same since. Not that he'd ever been congenial.

Death was the only escape some said. That wasn't the escape Kingsley wanted for his men. No, they needed a vorpal blade or ... Kingsley's gaze fastened on the lamplight flashing in the crystal he plucked from the wall. A light. Faerie magic. A will-o'-the-wisp could bring people in. It could take people out. No one would get hurt then. "Yes, a friendly will-o'-the-wisp. Bring in. Take out too."

A tired breeze slid across his face. It hinted of salt and cool water, perhaps a storm, fierce and free, fighting with the sea. Kingsley blinked and shook his head. Perhaps he was going mad. He clamped his mouth shut and quickened his strikes. He had another wall to finish after this one. There was something happening next to it. A bump in a wall that'd never had a crystal before.

KINGSLEY BOWDITCH HAD BEEN TRYING to escape for ... So why hadn't he?

"No night, no day."

Swaying on his feet, Kingsley wiggled out the last crystal and dropped it in his bag at the same time as the only other prisoner still working pulled his last one.

Escapes were always at night. "No night." No escape.

Masked walked through Kingsley, Mark, Dan, and Tom's chamber and inspected the dust-covered walls for crystals missed by lazy workers. Satisfied with their work, he signaled for them to follow him. They passed through a series of chambers to the Dispersal Point, where the others and the automaton waited. Unlike the usual navigation automatons, this machine looked something like a porcelain child in a barrel on wheels. The doll-like machine had crystals, like the walls did. Only the automaton knew the way to the lift. It only obeyed the guards. They commanded. It whirred along the tunnels. Past endless other tunnels. Past water wells. Past ventilation shafts.

That hint of cool water and salt did little to cool his head. "So hot." It was dark in the ventilation shafts. "Did that make it night there?" The automaton whirred forward. Kingsley hummed and followed. Tom growled at him. Shafts were barred. "Automatons explode."

Tom stopped growling.

No automaton. No bars. Kingsley smiled. "Pop goes the weasel."

"Do they climb?" Kingsley mimicked knocking a hammer on a chisel head, each knock higher in the air than the previous, clicking his tongue for each hit. He shook his head. "No." Would fall. Guards beat to surface. He nodded confidently. He needed a will-o'-the-wisp.

A cool breeze brushed his flushed face, and he shook his head to clear it.

The automaton was too risky.

CHAPTER TWO

Somewhere beyond the land of men, just shy of the isle of immortals, is the place where automatons go to die. Legend speaks of a dark world of peering porcelain masks, broken crystals, and moth-eaten jackets. A desolate land. A haunting land.

And that is where Caroline Lockley was going. *Finally.*

Repressing a whimper, Caroline shifted from her side to her back and pulled her knees up to keep the shortened length necessary for the crate in which she hid. Her legs felt about as useless and stiff as the derelict airship automaton stuffed in the wooden crate with her. The automaton—her "suitcase"—lay on top of her now like a lumpy comforter. Dare she leave her too coffin-like crate for a good stretch?

Her stomach was no longer giving indication of an altitude change, which meant the airship was well underway. Her ears gave no hint of man's activity in the cargo hold, though possibly of the wailing of a murdered cabin boy's ghost, but nothing else beyond the normal creaking and moaning of an airship. Her eyes gave no indication of anything, but she would soon fix that. Reaching behind her head, she untied the porcelain mask most responsible for her passing herself off as an automaton and retied it to hang loosely about her neck.

She scrunched her face, stretched her jaw, and blinked. She still couldn't see anything. Her chest tightened, the darkness pressing in on her. How had her brother stood the darkness of the crystal mines? Had he survived it? Had it driven him mad? It had been four years since the Time Keepers had reported the Bowditch airship *Dusk Crier* and its crew lost in a storm. Caroline and many others were now convinced the *Dusk Crier* had been captured, its men enslaved to the Rí Am's crystal mines for their attempt to free themselves from the Rí Am's tyranny, for a foolhardy search for a land where people still knew how to navigate themselves.

Find the crystal to Oileán Caillte. That's your priority. It's all that will save Herschel, if he can be saved. Find the crystal, then worry about the Dusk Crier's *crew.*

Caroline took a deep breath, reminding herself she could wait to hunt for her brother just like she could wait a minute more for sight. At least she could breathe easily now without the mask.

Reaching around the automaton, she caught the crate lid's inner latch and unhooked it. The lid responded by inching open. *Praise the Maker.* Darius Lockley, her uncle and guardian, had been right: the crate's odd size—too tall and slightly long—had persuaded the dockhands to load it on top of the pile instead of burying it among the other crates of old automatons. She'd insisted on a small handsaw in case he'd been wrong. Her uncle and other Sky Keepers had helped outfit her as an automaton and had supplied her with the necessary tools in another fake navigator, then put her in a crate and dropped her off at the Time Keeper Station office responsible for collecting defunct automatons.

She crawled out around the automaton and all but collapsed onto the stack of crates forming a floor around her. Blast it but her legs were mad about their hours cramped in that box.

She managed to pull her companion navigator out of the crate and lay it beside her. Stretching herself out like a snow angel, she commiserated with her aching muscles, then unbuttoned her blue captain's jacket decorated with crystals —a perfect mimic to a real automaton's—untucked her shirt, and pulled out the blanket and the water canteen hidden in her padding. Also hidden under her shirt—which was a scandalous way of dressing even to her—was her specially designed corset with its stash of things useful in emergencies. She tugged a necklace from under her collar and found the short key at its end, warm from her skin. Working by feel, she located the storage automaton's back, lifted its jacket, and unlocked the compartment forming its chest cavity. After assuring herself the metal chest resembling a large jewelry box was still in its place, she pulled a small Ruhmkorff lantern from the bottom section of the compartment and locked the automaton back up.

She tucked her own shirt back in and buttoned her jacket, then tugged a thin, folded sheet of parchment from up her sleeve. Colin O'Connor had sent her a rough sketch of the ship, and of the ventilation shafts of all things. As soon as her limbs allowed, she'd find the privy and kitchen like a proper stowaway. Setting the lantern on her stomach, she began winding its short crank.

The swish of a well-oil door sent her heart rate rocketing.

She jerked toward the sound, knocking the lantern over. It flickered on, and she switched it off and yanked the blanket over it. Footsteps echoed off the high ceiling. The stream of lantern light exploring the hold made her blink.

"This is most irregular. The captain will not like it."

Caroline could think of someone else who didn't like it either. She inched closer to her crate and quietly lifted the lid. Leaning up, she began packing the blanket, water canteen, and lantern back into the crate, her arms trembling from their half-a-day imitation of a lifeless automaton.

"The question is whether the Rí Am will like his guest gainsaid at every turn."

"Why must you have an automaton? You have a dummy," the first speaker said. A crew member?

"I told you. I want to see the crystals in their setting."

Caroline bit back one of the words her uncle would never admit teaching her. Light hit the roof of the cargo hold and spread over the rim of the stack of crates. The two pole ends of a ladder peered like tiny towers of doom over the edge.

Her legs exchanged their stiffness for a thousand pinpricks of pain and inconvenient clumsiness as she scrambled unsteadily to her knees. She grabbed the automaton and its precious treasure and lowered it into the crate.

The ring of boots on metal grew closer. Light fell on her.

Gritting her teeth, she gripped the crate's edge and pried her tingling foot up and underneath her. One foot in place. Now to move the other ... She fell back, shaking. The crate lid smashed her fingers. *Crystal goddess!*

"What was that?"

Caroline yanked her fingers out from under the lid and

curled up on the floor of crates. She fumbled to pull the mask over her face and her cap down. Just as she tucked her hands back to her side and loosened her muscles, boots thumped onto the stack.

Her ear smacked against the wood as two men marched over the crates to her.

"What's this one doing loose?" The crewmember followed the question with invectives against the dockhands' sloppiness.

"I'll take that one," the other man said suddenly.

No!

"I'll put it in the crate and then operate the lift if you'll stay here to attach the ropes and hook."

"I'll carry it down the ladder myself."

"But—"

"Your habit of saying no is very annoying. I can handle the automaton myself."

No no no. Praying harder than she had for anything but Herschel's return and the Star Veil's fall, Caroline held herself as automaton-like as she could.

The man scooped her up in his arms, struggling a bit but not commenting as he straightened. He laid her down again a few feet away. Was he changing his mind? She'd gladly be considered too heavy.

The ladder's rungs clanged softly then stopped. He dragged her a few inches, then shifted her onto his shoulder like a bag of potatoes.

Apparently, he didn't think her too heavy.

Bracing her with one hand, he moved slowly down the ladder. Her lungs burned. How could she breathe without him feeling the motion of her chest against his shoulder?

His own breathing grew heavy as he stepped firmly onto the cargo hold floor and shifted her to cradle her to his chest. She sucked in a breath too tiny for relief but maybe too small to be noticed.

A few minutes later, she was settled onto something long and firm, though still cushioning. A fainting couch? Footsteps padded away. Her mind sought out the knife in her boot and the revolver hidden in her remaining padding at the small of her back. She didn't want to hurt anyone—not this early in the voyage—but she couldn't keep up the ruse much longer.

There was an exchange of goodnights and a door clicked shut. A lock slid into place. Maybe she could simply knock him out. After she took off her mask, of course.

"Get up."

Caroline froze. How many people were in this cabin?

There was a heavy sigh, then fingers touched the edge of her face and lifted her cap and mask. She flinched against the sudden light and reached for her knife, but nearly toppled.

The man grabbed her shoulders and eased her into a sitting position, holding her firmly. "I wouldn't if I were you. There might not be a need for that anyway."

Crystal goddess. It was times like this when she wondered if the Maker knew what he was doing or cared that the Star Veil was hiding the truth and the Rí Am making a goddess of a faerie queen.

She forced her eyes open in the bright light. Through the rapid blinking, she made out a man with a neatly trimmed, silver-streaked mustache and goatee watching her studiously. He had the strong chin and prominent facial features of a man accustomed to getting his own way. In other words, he looked like her uncle, even claiming as many years. Her gaze centered on the man's mustache—*very* neatly trimmed with thin, curling tips. She'd seen that overly manicured bit of facial hair before, in a photograph of Isaac Martin—the sculptor the Rí Am intended to compel to make a statue of the faerie queen. Yes, this man looked persnickety enough to be a famous artist.

She stifled a smirk. Perhaps the Maker knew what he was about, after all. If there was one person on the airship who might not immediately turn her in, it'd be this man.

Maybe.

"Well? Are you going to stop pretending now?" Martin asked, impatience growing in his tone.

She shook his hands from her shoulders. "How did you know?" she said testily, running her fingers through her mussed hair.

He straightened, huffing in a way that implied someone was an imbecile. "I'm a sculptor. When others see a formless chunk of marble, I see a figure of beauty and grace. When imagination-deprived Time Keepers see a chubby automaton, I see a petite woman." He raised an eyebrow at her. "With a story waiting to be told—one that should include our current destination."

"You don't know?" She looked up in surprise.

His eyebrow went higher in its critical arch. He'd perfected that look of superciliousness.

She paused, then decided answering could do no harm. "Sheffield-on-the-Sea, I hope, is the first stop. After that, I don't know."

"Sheffield-on-the-Sea received the Isolation Judgment

some time ago. Or do stowaways never bother with the news?"

She returned her own expert critical look and held out her hand. To her relief, its trembling was mild. "Help me stand."

He pulled her up and held her hand until she felt stable enough to let go. She would never spend hours in a little box again. Until she was dead and maybe not even then.

"I'm waiting."

Caroline didn't need him to remind her of the penalty of stowing away; she could sense the threat in his voice. She considered it a compliment to her intelligence that he hadn't verbalized the threat. "Apparently, it's not off-limits to the Time Keepers."

"I was told I was going to an automaton disposal and recycling station attached to an important mine. You're telling me that's on Sheffield-on-the-Sea? That backwards hamlet?"

She shrugged. "It's the Rí Am's native home. He was a man of humble beginnings," she said mockingly.

"Is that why you're going there? Visiting his birthplace?"

Caroline snorted, then studied Isaac Martin again. He had a stubborn chin. Who would tire first—her of piece-mealing her answers or him of waiting for a full explanation? She was already tired, hungry, and sore, and there was no reason not to give him all the non-vital information. "Where old automatons 'go to die' is anyone's guess, but it's the Sky Keepers' current theory they go to Sheffield-on-the-Sea—also my home island by the way, so don't slight it. On a hidden section of the island is the mine from which the automatons' crystals come—they and not some program in the automatons navigate. This mine is a slave labor mine. It's also a place where a sculptor known for working with sky crystal would likely be taken to complete his statue of the faerie queen."

Martin's stubborn jaw loosened.

She fixed her gaze on him. "My name, by the way, is Caroline Lockley, and I have a twin brother."

"You think he's there—in the mine?" Martin said after a pause.

She pressed her hand to her chest. "They claim he died, but I know he's alive. This mine, it's a place where dead men live as slaves. Political prisoners, ambitious inventors, explorers, those of the Crystal Set daring enough to become Sky Keepers. Where else would he be?"

"Which of those categories does he fit into?"

"Follower of the arrogant, foolhardy explorer," she said bitterly. *Why, Kingsley? Wasn't losing yourself bad enough? Did you have to convince others to join in your folly? Brave, foolishly loyal men. I'd already lost my parents; did you have to take my brother too?*

The airship rocked as it hit a turbulence pocket, and Caroline staggered with the sudden movement.

Martin grabbed her arm and seated her on one of the two plush chairs. He sat in the other and pulled out a pipe from his jacket and began filling the bowl with tobacco. "Be careful with your titles, Miss Lockley. One could label you the same thing. Trying to rescue your brother would be your doom and that of any fool enough to join you."

Caroline's jaw clenched. "Doom or not, the Maker has called me to it and I will obey." She paused, her throat squeezing out any further words. He'd called her to find the crystal for Oileán Caillte, not to rescue her brother. Not yet.

The Sky Keeper leaders, including Harcourt Ladell, Commodore and Mrs. Bowditch and their children, had prayed long about how to get the crystal that would take the iron harpoons to the Star Veil—and she'd been the answer. They'd made her promise to focus on that responsibility. *Escaping prisoners aren't likely to be killed if the mine is useless—if the Star Veil is destroyed and the crystals of no value,* she reminded herself. And if there was no hope for her brother? Even then, she'd obey. But Isaac Martin wasn't to be privy to any of that.

He puffed harder on his pipe, staring at her with a narrowed gaze. "Tell me, Miss Lockley—"

"Martin!" The bellow and the accompanying pounding on the door sent them both to their feet, Martin swearing at the sailors like one himself.

"One moment," he yelled back as Caroline darted for the adjoining room.

The hallway door's lock clicked, and the door flew open and hit the hall.

"What's the meaning of ordering my men to leave their stations and steal from the cargo hold for you?" A red-faced captain barreled into the room, a pink-faced guard beside him.

Martin's protest and the guard's "Captain!" blended and died as all eyes went to Caroline. The door to the adjoining room was locked.

"It's the automaton!" The bewildered guard pointed at her, his gaze shifting from the mask hanging around her neck to her jacket, then up to her face. "The one he took from the hold."

The captain's response to that was rather longer and more colorful than necessary, but Caroline gathered he was not pleased to have her on board and wanted an explanation. An unfavorable one meant the brig.

It was a pity the Maker insisted his followers not lie. She could have used the practice right then. She opened her mouth, then clamped it shut as Martin stepped close behind her and cupped his hands over her shoulders.

"It turns out my assistant cared for me more than I thought," he said.

Caroline nearly choked. It appeared Martin had had plenty of practice in lying. But she didn't care for the direction of the deception. It was cliché anyway.

She snorted and crossed her arms. "I would've been out on the street with no job if I hadn't come." She skewered him with a warning look. "I will be the model for the faerie queen and *nothing* more, Captain, I assure you."

Silent for once, the captain glanced between them, his arms folded and his feet braced apart. His eyes narrowed as they settled on Martin.

Martin's shoulders sank. Shame laced his voice. "I needed my muse. Her sour temper entertains me." He waved a hand near her face, his voice growing more excited. "Her perfect features inspire me."

Caroline lifted her chin in an arrogant smirk at the captain's doubtful expression.

"And her figure—a perfect miniature for the willowy faerie queen."

Miniature? She was five-foot-one, not two feet!

"Why didn't you ask permission from the Rí Am then?" the captain demanded. "He will not like this."

"He will like it less if my work suffers," Martin said sharply. His tone softened to a shamed mumble. "I did not care to admit to him my need for a human muse." His gaze locked with the captain's. "No more than you would wish to admit a need for drink."

Caroline's teeth hurt in sympathy with the captain's. He released his clamped jaw enough to growl orders for a second plate to be served at the same time as Martin's. "They will dine here since I will not have a woman dressed like a machine seated at my table." He spun on his heel and marched out, the guard following.

"I would appreciate a cot," Caroline yelled after him.

Martin secured the door behind them. "You just cost me the seat of honor at the captain's table."

"You cost me the privacy of the cargo hold. But I thank you for your help just then. Why did you do it?"

He shrugged and began rummaging through a trunk. "I prefer live models to seamstresses' dummies. And I don't like the Rí Am any more than you Sky Keepers do. Thwarting him in minor ways brings a kind of pleasure."

"So you're a man of sense. I'm glad to hear it."

He straightened and stared down at her, his gaze hard. "I am. And don't think because I helped once that I'll do it again, or that I have no one to live for and am willing to throw my life away, or any other such nonsense. I have myself—and a daughter and dependent sister with two kids— to care for."

Pity stirred in Caroline's chest, but she kept her voice hard. "And your conscience would rest better with my death than theirs?"

"Exactly."

"I have a similar issue when it comes to you." Did she? What was the line when fighting for a worthy cause? She prayed she'd not have to find out.

He huffed and pulled a sketchpad and pencils from a

worn leather case. "The Rí Am sent dress suggestions for the statue. I can't imagine Morgan Unseelie wearing any of them, but at least they add an interesting texture and challenge." He pulled an exquisite beaded silver dress from a trunk beside the fainting couch. "Put this on and then stand still or I'll turn you in."

CHAPTER THREE

"Beware the Jubjub bird, and shun the...?" Kingsley swayed on his feet and rubbed a hand over his face. "Shun the ... borogoves?" He brought his right wrist before his eyes. The tunnel lanterns cast as much shadow as light on it. Black marks smeared it, but some were almost legible. There was an *A* and an *l.* That was it. *All mimsy were the borogoves, and the mome raths outgra—*

A guard shoved him from behind. "Down the shaft, Bowditch. And stop your muttering."

A lift like a wooden barrel attached to a pulley system teetered over the shaft dropping to the lowest level of the mine, "The Crusher" the men called it. It was hotter than an oven and a rockfall waiting to happen. But that's where the largest crystals grew. Crystals long as an airship but slender like a man. Wide as a house, short as a mouse. All aglow in the lantern light.

"You two follow when he's reached the bottom," the guard ordered the next prisoners. "The boss wants that twenty-footer out by tonight, or tomorrow at the latest."

So it was day then? What day?

Today, obviously.

Smiling to himself, Kingsley stepped into the lift. It had a small sign: *Wear Helmet. Beware of Falling Rock.*

Beware. Wishing for another breeze to cool his forehead, he pulled the lever to take him down. The lift rushed to obey, jerking down a foot before smoothing out its hurried pace to the bottom. Kingsley went back to rocking. He had charcoal in his pocket. He had his left wrist, somewhat clean under his sleeve, clean enough to write on. A post at the exit to stamp. A right wrist to pick up the reply from the wood on his return. But he needed the next line. "Beware the Jabberwock," he whispered finally, his eyes brightening. That was what was next. "'The jaws that bite, the claws that catch! Beware the Jubjub bird,' Lockley, 'and shun the frumious Bandersnatch!' Remember, Lockley."

The printer's nephew always remembered poetry. Kingsley had already done a hymn for James and another for Johnson. What a memory those two had! But Thomason remembered nothing. He'd been older than the rest; the guards had culled him when he couldn't work any longer. There'd been an equation for Lee. A Psalm for Davis. A list of local capitals for Rogers. Kingsley ticked off more of his crew members on his fingers. He held up a single finger. And now the poem for Herschel Lockley...

And a very large crystal for ... someone.

And, he prayed, a friendly will-o'-the-wisp for him and his men.

CHAPTER FOUR

M odeling as the faerie queen was only slightly less odious than posing as an automaton. But at least the change in her passenger status allowed her to enter the mines on her own feet with her eyes drinking in all the information they could.

Caroline and Martin watched from the airship's deck as the ship descended, stirring up a sandstorm as it landed on a small pad between rock and sea. She couldn't help but smile in appreciation of the setup. The cove was no bigger than the O'Connors' but was just as well hidden. Even within it, little announced a mining operation. Wind-stirred sand over rock left little evidence of the tracks of the carts and lifts waiting to ferry goods to and from the airship and the natural cave opening in the rocky cliffs.

At the captain's signal, Caroline hefted her gunnysack and followed Martin off the ship. She'd made use of Colin's map and the ship's ventilation shafts to retrieve her belongings from the automaton before destroying it. She'd salvaged its clothes and boots for herself. She'd also borrowed a needle and thread from the cook to take up her pants, compensating for the lack of padding. And she'd removed the detestable crystals from the jacket. With leather boots, dusty-brown pants, bulky blue jacket, white blouse, and brown corset, she wasn't the model of feminine grace, but she wasn't an automaton's twin. Nor was she hamstringed with one of the too-long, man-catcher gowns of Martin's.

A horseless cart drove them along a lengthy tunnel with a gentle downward slope. It halted at a pair of heavy, barred metal doors, now currently open and guarded. They dismounted and were ushered into a large chamber of polished rock about the length of a children's playing field, then hurried down the open tunnel on the left, the one just inside the chamber. Nearly walking into the wall to do it, Caroline managed a glimpse of the massive entry chamber— a glass-enclosed control room and crystal sorting station near the outer door, two barred doors on the far wall, and three lifts in the rock floor across from the control room. Just as Marianna and Bertram described it.

She pressed her fist to her chest and lifted it inconspicuously toward the far two doors. *When the Star Veil falls, Herschel, I'll be here.*

A guard led the way down the well-lit tunnel deeper into the cave until they came to a row of doors with removable name plates. Guards' barracks, she assumed. Their stoic guard pointed out a door at a curve in the tunnel, the entrance to a stairwell that led up to a natural courtyard hidden in the rock formation around them. You couldn't view the sea from it, apparently, but you could at least see the sky crystals and feel the breeze.

Around the curve were more rooms, two of which would be theirs. Further on were the showers, mess hall, infirmary, laundry, storerooms, and the studio, which was housed in a portion of the warehouse. Occasional, unlit tunnels opened off the main one, leading to the untamed portions of the cave, and were posted with warning signs: "Beware of Wandering Fae." Another sign added, "Beware of Falling Rocks." Her chest tightened. There was *a lot* of rock above them. *Stop it, Caroline. You're doing this to yourself. Focus on the goal.*

After the tour, the guard brought them back to the housing portion of the cave and unlocked two doors for them, each opening to a suite of rooms.

"The round-toned bell is for meals. You've five minutes to get to the mess hall, unless you request your meals delivered," he said as he lit the lamps in their rooms. He handed Martin the keys. "The shrill bell is not for you. Stay inside when you hear it." Then he left.

"Friendly sort," Martin said drily, giving Caroline a key before going to inspect his own room.

Caroline hurried into hers, locked her door, then made a beeline through the sitting room and the bedroom and into the small adjoining chamber. Her own private bath, complete with tub, water faucet, and commode. She sank back against the doorframe and closed her eyes. *Thank you, Maker, for small favors.* She'd do a lot for the mission, but bathe with who knew how many men in the common showers was not one.

Her eyes flew open and she looked around for another small favor, a rectangular one broad enough for her shoulders to pass through.

There it was. An air vent formed a dark hole in the stone ceiling of each room. It looked like the throat of a dragon. One too small to eat her. "I *love* dark, tight spaces. I am not afraid of rock."

She gingerly set the gunnysack on the bed and pulled out the metal box that had been hidden in the extra automaton and opened it. A mechanical bird was carefully packed inside. She pulled away some of the padding to inspect it. Its gears and metal frame all appeared intact, and she smiled at the beauty of the thing. Davy and Harcourt, who'd made it, had insisted on it being as much a thing of beauty as a practical "winged carrier."

It held three clasps for crystals. In one clasp sat a crystal for the bird itself, a "self" crystal from an old automaton. The second held Cait Vanon's seeker crystal, the one from Eoin Vanon's arm bracer. He had a crystal for each family member, and this one would take the winged carrier to Cait, her homing crystal carefully covered in iron paste for now, aboard the *Dawn Singer* or the *Breaker*, the Bowditchs' merchant ship and the O'Connors' pirate ship now traveling together, outlaws dependent on old crystals and Prism Bowditch's unusual eyes to guide them. And on supplies "stolen" from airships that happened to have extra to share with the pirates who raided them. The third clasp was empty, awaiting the crystal for Oileán Caillte and the Star Veil. Once the winged carrier brought them the crystal, the *Dawn Singer* and the *Breaker* would travel to the isle and destroy the Star Veil with the iron harpoons Colin and the others had worked so hard to get.

After one last look at the empty clasp, she put the padding back in place and hid the box under the bed, against the cold rock wall. Retrieving and opening her notebook, she found Bertram and Marianna's sketch of the caves and added in the guards' quarters and associated chambers and courtyard. Looking at where her and Martin's rooms were, she guessed they were over the mines. If she wanted to get back to the control room and the crystal packaging station next to it, for that was the most likely place for the crystal, she'd have to—

"Lockley." Martin rapped on the outer door, and the familiar sound of knuckles on wood soothed her. She hated to admit it, but the heavy rock arching above her like a wave waiting to crash was a wee bit unnerving. But she'd get used to it. She'd survived a submarine voyage. She could survive this.

She hurried into the sitting room and yanked the door open. "How long will it take to make this statue?"

Martin's eyes gleamed in spiteful enjoyment as he walked inside. "What? No fox in your blood, Miss Lockley? Being as how you've come to steal a man, I would've thought the dark, underground setting would inspire you to sly ventures."

Caroline shut the door behind him and crossed her arms. "And I suppose you feel right at home?"

"Like I'm in a quarry ready to begin work on a new masterpiece."

She tapped her foot. "What do you want?"

Martin laughed. "There might not be fox in your blood, but there's certainly shrew."

"I'm glad you find yourself so amusing," Caroline retorted with appropriate grouchiness.

He tamed his laughter to a smile. "I came to warn you not to engage in any acts of Sky Keeper disobedience until after dinner. I won't cover for you if you miss a meal."

"I never miss meals if I can help it, you can rest assured about that."

"Good. Settle in quickly. We're going to sort crystals until dinner."

"We're going to the control room?" Caroline's heart leapt.

Martin's brows furrowed. "No. There are bags in my studio."

"Oh, of course. No sea breeze there." Caroline bit her tongue. She'd improved in her deception skills over the week-long voyage to the island but had gotten sloppy on sensibly keeping quiet. "I'll join you in a few minutes."

His brow smoothed out. "The Chief Mine Officer is getting me a twenty-foot crystal from the lowest level of the mine. I'd like to use the small crystals from the old automatons for accents as the play of light on them will be different."

"I'm sure it will be lovely," she said genuinely. She'd seen images of his work.

"Lovely? It will be stunning."

For his and his family's sake, she prayed it would be.

"Martin," she called after him as he opened the door. "Call me 'Caroline.' 'Lockley' is a name the guards might recognize."

Martin nodded, his expression turning solemn. "To answer your earlier question, I have one month to finish the statue. Then the Rí Am will arrive and take it. Then you and I are leaving—with or without Brother. Understood?"

CHAPTER FIVE

One week later, after dinner, Caroline repeated Martin's pronouncement to herself and huffed. Before the month was up, she, the crystal, Herschel, and the entire crew of the *Dusk Crier*—except, perhaps, for that arrogant numskull Kingsley Bowditch— would be gone. And Martin would have no say in the matter.

If she could get herself into the ventilation shaft without crashing into the wall headfirst, that is. After learning the routine of the mines, which included a twice-daily vibrating of the caves as transport airships arrived for the crystals, as well as she could while helping Martin, she thought it unlikely she could accomplish anything roaming through the halls. Neither she nor Martin were allowed in the control room. The lifts were always guarded due to some incident a while back, and Caroline suspected she knew the two responsible for that. Her best option was through the vents, which had been carved out of the cave itself and so would be large enough for her to traverse.

Standing under the vent, she tightened her PullLine

harness, then shoved a rope coil, wrapped rock pick and chisel, and a water canteen into her messenger bag and slung it through the vent into the leftward leading shaft. She turned off the lamp in her room, flicked on the headlamp attached to her goggles, and traced her way back to the corner underneath the ventilation shaft. The shaft opening had only been about the length of a man's foot and a handspan wide, but under the cover of the harsh bells and while Martin was out in the courtyard smoking his pipe and admiring the sky crystals—the man was either daft or too ignorant to know what a beautiful sky should look like and what they had wasn't that—she'd opened it up wide enough to get through. A grin stretched her face. No one would think anything about the noise since she was working with a sculptor. She could claim she was adding sculptor apprentice to model in her job description.

She lined herself up with the enlarged vent opening, then scooted to the right until she could barely see the inside-left ceiling of the shaft. She sent the PullLine into it diagonal to her and hit Retract, inching her way up until rock bit into her chest and her head and shoulders were inside the shaft. She pushed the messenger bag ahead of her, then detached the PullLine and quickly reattached it further down. With its help, she wiggled all the way into the shaft. Pulling the bag to her, she took out a reflective square and secured it to the rock next to her vent. Her "suitcase" automaton's boots she'd cut up and fashioned into knee pads.

Rising to her hands and knees, she crawled toward Martin's room, unsteady on the boot-sole pads. Chips of rock scooted forward with her. Whoever had carved this mole hole hadn't bothered to smooth it out, but at least he'd made it big enough for her to get through without snaking through it on her belly. Now, if the shaft followed the hallway, then it'd—

Her knee made an escape for the room below, and she nearly banged her chin on the shaft floor. *Think there was only one vent opening in this shaft, Caroline?* Pressing her lips together, she shuffled to the right, dragging her knee and scraped shin back into the shaft.

Her shoulder pressed to the right side, she crawled forward with her headlamp off. Snores and a few conversations around poker tables in the guards' quarters drifted to her. The shaft sloped uphill as it followed the long tunnel back to the main chamber. She switched the light back on. Ever so often a vertical shaft intersected the tunnel, its shaft rising to the night sky above and descending to the mines below, she assumed. Judging by the airflow and noise, fans capped these shafts at the surface. She eased across the gaps and continued on, pausing only to peer through the vents into the quiet rooms to gauge her progress.

She halted as a tunnel branched from hers at one of the vertical shafts. She figured she'd just entered the main chamber. Across the gap and a ways down would be the control center, and perpendicular to her, the ceiling of the main chamber and the prisoners' quarters. She peered down the way ahead, then to her left. There was no reason why she couldn't do a little research on how to rescue the prisoners.

This vertical shaft was bigger than most, about five feet square, creating a bulge in her tunnel and a gap she couldn't easily cross. She sent the PullLine to the wall of the perpendicular tunnel, tested it, then twisted around until her legs slid into the air. The rest of her following, she swung toward the perpendicular wall, bounced lightly against it with her feet, and pulled herself up into the tunnel. As she crawled along it toward the cell blocks, her heart changed its fast rhythm of exercise and nerves to one that included excitement. The tunnel wasn't spacious, but a man Herschel's size could make it down these side shafts. They could keep the whole *Dusk Crier* crew together or sneak them out a few at a time. They'd figure out a way to disengage one of the fans at the surface or find a shaft without one. She'd have to find a way out for the crystal anyway. The Maker was truly with her. This was going to be so much easier than she thou—

Murmurs and the odor of unwashed bodies drifted to her through the sturdy grating ahead whose metal bars disappeared into the dark rock above and below. Clenching her jaw, she slammed her gloved palm against the bars. They held fast. *Curses on the Rí Am. Curses on Kingsley Bowditch. Curses on Herschel Lockley for being such a fool.* She couldn't dig out these bars without someone hearing.

A bell clamored through the tunnel, vibrating the rock beneath her. She froze, struggling to pick out a single chime. Surely it wasn't the meal signal? They'd just eaten. Yet it wasn't quite the shrill ring of a shift change either.

Scooting back to the nearest vent, she saw guards scrambling into the chamber below. *Curses on Caroline Lockley for being an impatient idiot.* The bars were alarmed.

"It's the ventilation shaft going into the cell block," a guard yelled. "You, check the prisoners. You, search the shaft. Get in at the maintenance hatch."

Caroline, if you're going to be a fool, be a fast one.

"I'm a *clerk*, not a guard," one man whined as Caroline crawled toward the main shaft, her light off.

"Go anyway," the guard bellowed. "Use your gun if it's anything other than a faerie."

A light shone through the vent opening in front of her,

and she crashed against the wall as she skidded to a halt. It moved on. So did she.

She'd not passed a hatch on her way there. The opening must be on the branch going to the control room, which meant she had until the clerk got from that tunnel to the main one to get far enough down the latter that his light wouldn't reach her. She crawled faster.

"It's just a bloody bird or bat or lizard. That's all it ever is." Murmurs echoed up the tunnel, each growing more distinguishable than the last. "Just because I'm smaller than the guards, I always get these tasks."

Caroline changed a curse to a prayer and sent the Pull-Line ahead to the vertical shaft's wall, at the joining of the tunnels, and hit retract. Rough rock threatened to shred her pants as well as the skin of her hip as she was dragged forward, but she kept her focus on the deeper darkness ahead. A light flashed across the gap of the vertical shaft. She could stop in her current tunnel and wait in ambush on the scared clerk who'd be missed, make a visible crawl for it down the main tunnel, or...

The darkness of the vertical shaft loomed ahead of her. Caroline drew herself into a ball. When her feet escaped the rock, she detached the PullLine and fell.

The roar of the mine fans was louder in this shaft. It was a small thing she forced herself to notice as she fought the urge to send out her PullLine and stop her fall. A few more seconds. Then a few more. She needed to be far enough down that the clerk's light, if he searched the shaft, wouldn't catch her, or the sound of her PullLine hitting rock carry to him.

She finally sent out the PullLine attachment and jerked painfully to a halt, finding the wall by slamming into it. A beam of light journeyed into the shaft, sweeping around its walls and moving downward. She descended again, this time using the PullLine to control her descent.

She was fairly certain the mine operated continuously, so somewhere down below, coming through the ventilation shafts, might be the lights of the miners. Perhaps curious or perhaps recognizing she couldn't take the tunnels back to her room any time soon, Caroline decided she might as well see if she could find the actual mine tunnels. See if she could glimpse any prisoners. But she *would* resist doing anything stupid and impatient this time.

Switching on her headlamp, she realized the hewn shaft had given way to a natural, much wider one. After a few more descents and downward glances, she found a glow coming from a barred window on her right. She swung over to that wall, switched off her headlamp, and slowly walked herself down toward it.

When she was about ten feet above and to the right of the opening, voices, then shouts, then a boom joined her in the shaft. Rock spewed from the far corner of the window; debris hit her leg, and the wall vibrated, loosening her attachment. She plummeted, sending the PullLine out wildly as she fell. Its line tangled with the metal bars of the grate flung partway out into the shaft, its ends metal spears she narrowly missed. The line caught on the bars, and they fell with her, leaning further out from the wall, but then they stopped, still supported by stable rock on one side. She swung underneath them, her bleeding leg screaming at her as shouts of violence escaped the mines and echoed around her, chilling her.

But the shouts quickly moved away, and she was able to breathe again. The arc of her swings shortened until she dangled underneath the bars. Trembling, she switched on her headlamp and looked up to her line wrapped tightly around the bars. *Please help me get it loose, and quickly. I just want to get back to my room and curl up in a ball and forget the sounds of hate and violence. Please.*

The practical side of her groaned. She couldn't curl up until *after* she'd taken care of her leg and the blood she'd drip in her room. Gritting her teeth, she started slowly retracting the line, inching up toward the bars, which held. One of the benefits of being short and thin.

"Wait! Come back!" A man suddenly appeared at the blasted opening in the wall and began to crawl out onto the bars.

"No, Captain!" yelled a young man.

"Please!" the first called, his voice familiar. The bars dipped underneath him.

CHAPTER SIX

The crystal peeking through the black rock wasn't fully grown yet. It wouldn't ever be as big as the twenty-footer they'd dug out yesterday—or was that today, or last week?—but it *was* special. Kingsley could tell that. Where would it lead? After working in the mines, he'd figured out it was the crystals, not some program in the automatons, that guided the navigators.

"That one's not ready, Bowditch," Masked said as he passed behind Kingsley.

"No." Kingsley went back to working on his wall.

It wasn't long before they were following the whirring navigator toward the lifts. Serpent walked on ahead, smacking Tom for no reason on his way to the front.

Fresh air, as fresh as they ever got, wafted in from the air shaft before the lifts. The automaton whirred beside the vent, but it wouldn't care about the air.

Kingsley rubbed a hand over his burning face. The bars were too thick. He'd already decided that. He needed that will-o'-the-wisp, one of the mischievous faeries with their lanterns who led mortals astray. If he was astray, would it lead him un-astray? Or maybe he was the will-o'-the-wisp? Hadn't he led his crew astray? To ruin?

A light flashed in the dark of the air shaft. A will-o'-the-wisp! The Maker had sent him one after all! "It's here!" He stumbled forward, dropping his bag of crystals, drawing the guards' attention.

The light vanished, and then time and Tom moved quickly. "Now!" Tom yelled. His chisel flew end over end into the automaton by the vent, puncturing its chest as he ducked.

The mine shuddered, and rock and porcelain flew. Kingsley tumbled to the ground. Men dove for cover, then some rose, rushing for the lifts and Serpent as he tried to push himself up.

"Stop! Leave him be!" Masked yelled, limping forward, his metal leg slowing him just as Kingsley's father's did. The shouts turned his way. There was no reason to yell at Serpent any longer.

Chisels, rock picks, angry men. Masked didn't have a chance.

Neither did the prisoners. Shattered automaton. Guards at lift. Guards above. They would get nothing but blood from this.

Staggering up, Kingsley shook his head. *Help please.* His mind cleared. He sprinted for Masked as several men closed in on him. "Leave him!" He jerked Sam back and shoved Rup into him. "Stop! You'll never get out this way!" Ramming his shoulder into Hammonds, he cleared a path to Masked. As Masked crumpled, Kingsley threw himself on top of him, crashing to the rock and taking blows with him.

"To the lift!" someone cried. The stampede followed that piper.

"Captain!" The young one, Mark-with-the-Vanon-wristband, grabbed Kingsley by the shoulders and dragged him to his feet.

Swaying, Kingsley put a hand to the wall to steady himself. Masked moaned.

"Captain, are you okay?" Mark still gripped him by the upper arms.

Kingsley dropped his hand from the wall but kept swaying. So hot. So much pain.

He'd been trying to escape since...

Light flickered in the night of the tunnel.

"The will-o'-the-wisp!" It had come at last! "Wait! Come back!" Kingsley sprinted for the shaft and hauled himself onto the bent bars. "Please!"

Rock cracked and dusted around him. The metal grate dipped under his weight as Mark called out to him and grabbed him by the feet. The will-o'-the-wisp screamed like an angry woman.

He looked down and saw not a faerie but a woman he remembered, one he always liked to see. The one he most wanted to see. When had he last seen her? The night before he left on the *Dusk Crier* that last time, at his parents' ball. There was something he regretted not asking her then. One of the many things he regretted.

Kingsley reached a hand through the bars. "May I have this dance, Miss Lockley?"

CHAPTER SEVEN

O f all the men from the *Dusk Crier*, she *would* find this one, the once impeccably groomed, confi-dent, witty Captain Kingsley Bowditch. Who now stank worse than a wet dog that had rolled in a dead squirrel. Who was emaciated, bruised, hairy almost beyond recognition.

Who was as mad as a hatter.

Caroline bit her lip and swallowed hard. Who'd asked her to dance. It had only taken four years and an imprison-ment. For a moment, Caroline was too heartbroken to be angry or afraid. But then she reached up with her free hand and caught his dirty one. "The next one, Kingsley. Let's sit this one out."

"Captain Bowditch, come back in, please." A lean young man with an accent similar to Vesper Vanon's—a Reydon elite voice, educated and cultured but not haughty —reached for Kingsley's waist to haul him back in. He wasn't a guard. She didn't see any of those. But then, now that her heart was quieter, she could hear sounds of fighting deeper in the mines. She tightened her grip on Kingsley's hand.

He glanced over his shoulder at the young man, then back at Caroline, as if unsure what to do. That wasn't like the confident Kingsley she'd known.

"What happened?" Caroline asked the young man. "Is it safe for him to go back in? I can take him with me, as soon as I untangle my line." She looked at Kingsley again, and he smiled lazily at her, fever raging in his eyes and flushing his cheeks. "I *will* take him, if the guards won't help him." *I said I wouldn't do anything foolish or impatient, Maker, but I think this is a risk you'd approve of.* It didn't matter Kingsley had talked her brother and many others into the foolhardy voyage that had led them here; he had suffered for it, and he needed her. The Maker had put him in her path. She'd look after him.

"Some of the prisoners revolted," the young man said. "They blew up an automaton, then ran for the lift. Fools. They'll never make it out. There's a guard still here—one of the nicer ones. He's wounded. The other guards will come for him when they can, so we've at least a chance of getting back to the main floor from here. As for other help, they won't give Captain Bowditch any medical care. They're not allowed to. Who are you? He's been murmuring about will-o'-the-wisps for several shifts. You don't look like a faerie, but I'm beginning to wonder, if you could get him out."

Caroline heard the yearning in his voice, but he had a look about him that was some combination of resigned to his fate and determined. Determined not to do wrong by stealing her PullLine to get himself out?

"Kingsley," she said, looking back to him, "help me grab hold of the bars, then lie flat on your stomach and see if you can reach where my line is tangled on the bars. Untangle it and go back inside. I'll follow you in."

Kingsley did as she asked. As she held on to the bars and he worked on her line, she turned back to the young man. "I'm no faerie, but I'll explain later why I'm here. How long has he been like this?"

"Fevered? About a week? It's hard to know since we live by shifts rather than brightenings and dimmings. They won't give him any care. It's happened before, but it's worse this time."

Caroline looked between the two emaciated men. Martin was going to kill her.

"I'm Caroline Lockley, by the way," she said.

"Mark Vanon. Pleased to meet you, Miss Lockley."

Caroline startled. Vesper's cousin? She studied him again. They did bear a certain resemblance. In character as well as in appearance, from what she'd heard. That was a good thing.

"Mark," she said, glancing at Kingsley to gauge his progress, "are you willing to risk being thought dead or escaped? I can't get either of you free of the mines yet, but I can care for Captain Bowditch and get you out of here, but I'll need you to help me."

"I have no reason not to take a risk," he said with a laugh, a slight shimmer to his eyes.

Another explosion rumbled through the mines, and Mark's face pinched. Kingsley looked over his shoulder at something Caroline couldn't see, her free line in his hands. "There were a few automatons at the lift," Mark explained, his expression worried. "They must have blown up one fighting with the guards. Who knows if they haven't blown up the lift too."

A few minutes later, Caroline was inside kneeling beside the wounded guard as Mark strapped on her PullLine harness and gauntlet. The other guard and a few prisoners, none of whom she could help, she did her best to ignore. Getting sick or sentimental wasn't going to help anyone just then.

The guard, propped up against the wall, watched them quietly, wary and a bit hopeful, both expressions dulled by pain. Aside from old injuries that made walking difficult, he had a few deep gashes and probably cracked ribs. Like Kingsley and Mark, he'd been spared the worst of the debris by being toward the back of the group when the explosion occurred. She used strips of his shirt to bind the worst of his wounds and staunch the bleeding.

"This is Masked, or Stewart, if you prefer." Kingsley knelt beside them. He was looking less crazed after she'd given him water from her canteen but more worried, and that worry was focused on her.

She took his face gently between her hands. "Yes, I'm really here, Kingsley. In the mines. I'm not a prisoner. As soon as I do something for the Sky Keepers, I'm going to get you out. You and Mark and as many of the *Dusk Crier*'s crew as are still alive."

His look of growing hope ended with a flinch, and he turned away. Though it came with a bit of guilt, she was glad for that look of pain and shame, recognition of his part in what had happened to himself and his crew. It would make it easier for her to share her room and food with him while her brother's fate was still unknown.

She turned back to the guard. She was pretty sure he was the one Martin preferred chatting with. Martin had lamented the poor color-matching of the man's porcelain nose and the rest of his face and was desperate for paint and permission to fix it himself—he would do it perfectly. He might have a chance now considering the mask was badly cracked.

"I hope you're not the talkative type," she told him.

Stewart shook his head, then said, in the tone of a rehearsed speech, "Bowditch, fevered and crazed, went after the will-o'-the-wisp he's been muttering about for days and disappeared into the shaft, taking Mark Vanon with him as he tried to stop him." He added quietly, "Bowditch saved my life. I wouldn't rat on him. I'm not like Kev and some of the others."

"Caroline," Kingsley said, looking between her and Stewart, "if they've damaged the lift—"

"I'll hint at Martin, the sculptor I came with, for him to hint to the guards to come through the air shaft, if necessary. They can get Stewart and the other prisoners out an easier way than through a hole in my ceiling. They can also get him care I can't sneak." Caroline handed Stewart her water canteen. "Don't let anyone see this."

There was a hint of fear in his eyes, but he nodded firmly. "Thank you."

"Don't mention it." She stood, grimacing as her leg throbbed and wrinkling her nose as it remembered the smell of Kingsley as he rose beside her.

She turned back to Stewart with a bright grin. "How about a deal—my canteen and the promise to come back if I haven't heard of your rescue by the next meal bell for some clothes and a shaving kit from your room?"

"You drive a hard bargain, Miss Lockley." There was a faint dawning of hope in Stewart's eyes as he drew a key from his pocket. "Three down from Martin's. Name's above the door."

"Thanks." She and Kingsley joined Mark by the window, and she and Kingsley both tried to check the harness and explain the gauntlet's gears and mechanisms to him at the same time. "Kingsley." She gently pushed him away. "This one has modifications you're not familiar with. Please let me do the honors."

She thought he might have smiled, but it was hard to tell under the fur on his face. "Of course, Miss Lockley. I will listen with interest instead."

"Just don't listen too closely," she said as she tightened the straps. "Being around two such handsome men at one time might make me nervous."

"One of us is all you can stand to smell at a time, you mean?"

"Now that you mention it, you do have a certain aroma about you. But it could be worse—you could smell like the faeries." From pouches on the back of the harness, she pulled out additional lines. "This one comes with two rescue belts and extra attachments for the wall to bear the weight. Kingsley and I will be attached to you, Mark. It will put a great deal of stress on you as we go up, and we'll have to walk the wall some of the way, but I think it's better than us separating and taking two trips. It may not be long before the guards start coming down. Ready?"

Mark and Kingsley nodded, then climbed onto the bars.

SOMETIME LATER, after a long ascent and a brief recounting of the welfare of Kingsley's family, her uncle, and to Mark's great surprise, that of his own family, Caroline, Mark, and Kingsley dropped, one by one, into Caroline's bedroom. It was lit, and that should have been a warning.

Just before Mark gasped and Kingsley pushed her behind him, she caught sight of Martin standing across the room, his arms crossed, his gaze burning with such anger she was glad for Kingsley's lean but work-hardened presence between them. Nonetheless, she stepped around him to face the sculptor.

"Martin," she began, "I can—"

Martin held up a door key—his own. "If not for the recent explosion, Miss Lockley, I would have thought you entirely too scrupulous and trusting. I always try my key on every door around to know who might be able to get into my room. I've been knocking on your door for some time, since the *first* of the alarm bells went off. I didn't care," he continued through gritted teeth, taking a step forward, "if you went snooping around looking for your brother, but this was an explosion! Men are trapped, Caroline! Some are likely dead."

"Martin, I—"

"She had nothing to do with that." Kingsley put himself between them again, for a moment looking his old self, the fire in his eyes not fever. "Some of the prisoners revolted and exploded an automaton. Mark and I were two of those trapped men you spoke of. If you *do* care for them, then you should be thanking Miss Lockley, and the Maker for bringing her close enough to help but not close enough for serious injury."

Martin's eyes widened, and he examined each of them again, his gaze halting briefly on Caroline's bloody pants leg. Some of the tenseness drained from him, but not all.

"He's not your brother," he said, indicating Kingsley, then Mark, with a sharp jab of his finger. "Neither is he."

"No," Caroline admitted. "I haven't found my brother yet. I found them, and they needed me. The guards will think they died, Martin. I have no intention of hurting anyone."

"Where are the others?" he said after a pause, a sarcasm to his tone indicating he was tempted to relent but wasn't quite ready to. "Why didn't you just bring them all?"

"I know Kingsley Bowditch," she said patiently, "and I know Mark Vanon's family. They were also the only two not involved in damaging the lift. And speaking of door keys." She held up Stewart's. "The guard Stewart was injured, but not by them"—she put a hand on Kingsley's arm and on Mark's—"and I told him I'd suggest to you to suggest to the guards to go down via the air shaft to get him. He said we could borrow some clothes and a shaving kit from his room."

Martin's eyes widened further, then his expression softened. "And I suppose you want me to get them for you?"

"I could, but I'm not fit to be seen at the moment."

"With that, I agree." He stepped to them and took the key, his nose wrinkling. "I'll pass along the hint." He marched to the door, stopping just short of it to glare over his shoulder at her. "And I don't care who they are or what they did or didn't do, you will not bring lice into my studio. Or a putrefying wound. Do something about your leg." He left, letting the door slam behind him.

"Lice!" Caroline gasped, glancing down at herself and then over to Kingsley, his long, greasy hair tied back but suddenly seeming to crawl with bugs before her very eyes. He shrugged under his dirt- and sweat-stained jacket as if in apologetic confirmation. "Oh no," she murmured. *Not my hair. I'll dress up like an automaton, eat hardtack and dried meat for weeks, but don't make me cut my hair. And I hate bugs!* Her lament was cut short by chuckles from both Kingsley and Mark. "What?" she demanded.

"This is a working mine, Caroline," Kingsley said, a faint smile to his voice. "We have to be able to work, and the guards and clerks don't want to suffer with us. They know exactly how far they can degrade us with our own stench and filth before disease breaks out. So we do bathe on occasion, and some are given medicine when the need arises. We don't have lice."

"Oh, thank goodness." She almost sank into a chair but remembered her own filthy state and shooed the men toward the bathroom. "Well, baths then. And don't say, 'ladies first,' because just looking at you two would make me feel dirty again."

The men didn't argue, and by the time Caroline had gotten them both hydrated to her satisfaction from the water pitcher in her room and sent Mark off to bathe, Martin had returned not only with clothes and shaving kit, but with medicine for Kingsley, bandages, and the news the guards were already on the way down the air shaft to look for Stewart and the others. He didn't linger, just said he expected the men to behave themselves and Caroline to be in the studio at the usual time.

With Martin and Mark both gone from the room, Kingsley sank to the floor and leaned back against the wall. For a moment, Caroline feared he was sinking into that crazed state again, but he shook himself and his eyes cleared, except for a troubled look. He glanced at her, then down at his dirty hands, looking as if he wanted to say something but wasn't sure where to begin. She could help with that.

She sat beside him and pulled her knees up to her chest. She might as well get it over with, for both their sakes. "You're an arrogant numskull, Kingsley Bowditch."

He grimaced, then said with feeling, "I know, Miss Lockley. You don't know how sorry I am. And not just for my own sake but also for the crew I led with foolishness and pride and for all the families I hurt when they were lost. Yours among them."

"It was Herschel's choice too," she said softly after a moment. It had been easier to blame Kingsley than her beloved brother, but in the end, she had to admit Herschel had followed Kingsley against her and her uncle's advice the same way Kingsley had gone against his family's.

"He came because he was loyal to me. I bear the responsibility as a leader for leading astray."

"You weren't leading them to something bad, Kingsley, just something pretty much doomed to failure and the Rí Am's wrath." She sighed. "You were the only one who couldn't see it."

Kingsley was quiet, then said, his voice heavy, "Actually, I knew the rumors of a place where people could still navigate were likely false, but I've always felt I would play a part in the end of the Rí Am and his Star Veil, so I went, confident we'd find something, somehow. I was impatient, and in a way, trying to force the Maker's hand. I'm sorry I talked your brother into joining me and so hurting both him and you and your uncle."

She smiled sadly, then asked the question she'd been both eager and afraid to ask. "Is Herschel alive? Is he ... okay?"

"As far as I know. We're not in the same cell block." Kingsley rubbed his palm but didn't say anything else.

Caroline winced, knowing how much the Bowditch captains loved their crews and tried to look after them, how much harder this must be for Kingsley than even for his men. Kingsley had always looked after Herschel, even paid for his medical care the two times he'd brought him home wounded. He'd also insisted on staying with them during those times, hiring a housekeeper and cook to help out, both of whom taught Caroline the things her uncle couldn't. Caroline had always hoped, and half suspected, she was part of the reason for his visits and help, but Kingsley had left that final time without even a goodbye. "Well, you may have your chance at helping defeat the Rí Am now. Let me show you the winged carrier I spoke of." She pushed herself up, but Kingsley didn't follow, just gaped up at her.

"Caroline, you ... you sound almost as if you've forgiven me."

She froze. Maybe? Mostly. But she didn't exactly want him to know it, which wasn't a true forgiveness. "Do I have a choice, if I want to be obedient to the One who forgave me?" she asked, a question to herself spoken aloud.

Kingsley's eyebrows rose, but then his expression fell, and by some grace of the Maker that bothered her. "Come to think of it, you don't. The Maker commands it. That is to my advantage, isn't it?" he said bitterly. "I can be as slowly, begrudgingly forgiven as the worst of the guards." Flinching, he looked away, as if recognizing the self-pity trap he was digging. He sighed and his gaze flicked up to her, then away. He added in a hollow voice almost too low for her to hear, "But even the obedient don't have to restore the relationship."

"Well," she said, kneeling beside him, "I'm not *always* obedient, but maybe in this case I will be. ... And maybe I'll go further than that." She smiled at him, and his face brightened, and that strengthened her resolve to be obedient. She poked him in the chest, "And don't forget to apply that forgiveness to yourself, since you've obviously repented of your arrogance, and don't go do anything foolish to try to undo the foolish things you've already done."

His smile brightened more, and he caught her hand against his chest. "Yes, Captain Lockley."

While Kingsley was bathing, Caroline managed to sneak to the control room. Through the vents in the crystal sorting room, she spotted an ornate box sitting to the side with an open note on it. Using the telescopic lenses on her goggles she read enough to realize the box was for the crystal to Oileán Caillte and that the crystal needed to be collected by the time the Rí Am arrived for it and the statue.

That meant the crystal was still in the mines, and from what she'd briefly seen there, the crystals grew from the walls. She didn't have three weeks before the Rí Am arrived to complete her mission and get the crystal away. She only had a brief window between when the crystal was fully grown and when the Rí Am arrived, and she didn't know when the former would be.

CHAPTER EIGHT

Kingsley's body, being worn and ill and suddenly having no push to rise with each shift cycle, went on strike, and he slept most of the next week, waking only briefly to eat, take his medicine, and bathe. Mark slept a good bit as well, and when he was awake, he seemed to want to help Caroline by doing things about the suite, but he had few domestic skills, so Caroline taught him to wash clothes and gave him the map of the mines Marianna and Bertram made and told him to add what details he could and make them each a copy. Caroline, as a promise to the men, did not go back to the mines to hunt for the crystal in case the one rebellion incited others and made the mines especially dangerous. While Caroline chaffed under the restriction, Kingsley promised her a surprise if she acquiesced. Mark had a knowing look about him that suggested Kingsley's boast wasn't pure fever, so she hoped a search on her part wouldn't be necessary. She kept busy helping Martin as model and sculptor apprentice, playing nurse and nanny to Kingsley and Mark, and trying to figure out how to get extra food without arousing suspicion. Unfortunately, the air shafts near the kitchen were quite warm and too small for her to fit through anyway. With the rotating shifts, there were always people about it.

THERE WAS a sewing kit in Stewart's shaving kit. While Caroline was working with Martin, Kingsley, who had skill in a great many areas, made use of it to take up his and Mark's borrowed uniforms as best he could without ruining them.

"How would you like to visit an old friend, Mark?" Kingsley asked as he handed him his jacket on the eight day since their semi-escape. Mark was slouched in a chair, staring at nothing, with an air of melancholy about him Kingsley well understood. It was time they did something about that tendency of theirs, and about other things. They'd spent enough time sleeping; to continue that or sitting around all day would not be good for them. They'd talked about themselves and their hopes and plans, even made emergency plans if things went wrong with their escape with the crystal. Now it was time to *do*.

Mark's look of alarm was amusing, fully preparing him for Mark's response. "We promised Caroline to stay put." He looked at the jacket but made no move to take it.

"We promised to stay out of trouble. I'm not proposing trouble but good. Look at me, Mark. Would you recognize me?" Kingsley tossed Mark the jacket, then tugged his hat down and pulled his shoulders back. "At a passing glance in the hallway? I'm not suggesting we go to the mess hall or try to inveigle our way into a work unit. Just a short trip, four doors down."

"Not at a passing glance," Mark admitted, unsure. He glanced at the jacket, then added with more confidence, "We're not likely to meet anyone anyway. We rarely hear anyone in the hallway except after the bells."

"Right. I'm going to check on Stewart—he's just four doors down, apparently—and ask him some questions. He'd probably appreciate getting his shaving kit back too. You don't have to go. I'm just letting you know where I'm going." He added in a low voice, unconsciously, "But I think it'd be good for you too. It's rough staying in here."

Mark's eyebrows rose, then he gave a half smile. "I'll go."

"Wonderful." Kingsley fetched the kit, put on his jacket, and headed for the door, murmuring, "This isn't leading astray, is it? There's a risk, but it's slight and the reward sure and high. Stewart likely needs company too."

"He probably does, though I admit he's not likely expecting it from us. Let's go."

Kingsley froze, and when he looked over his shoulder at Mark, the young man had a kind of "oops" expression on his face. Afraid to let the crazy man know he was crazy? Kingsley sighed heavily. "I still talk to myself, don't I?"

"Yes." Mark hesitated. He was the polite sort and sometimes needed goading to full honesty, the kind that could be painful but also helpful.

"Go on. You don't have to baby me."

"You do, and it's ... it's sometimes amusing, sometimes annoying, somewhat concerning, but mostly okay. It's only been a week, Kingsley."

Only a week. Kingsley took a deep breath, straightened, and double-checked that his lips were pressed together. His father was right. Scars came in different forms. He'd heal how he could and accept what showed, just like his father and others had. "Thanks, Mark."

Mark shrugged. "My brother used to complain that I talk in my sleep. If I make it back to Claire and we get married, I hope she'll have the grace to overlook my unconscious ramblings. I should do the same to others."

Kingsley didn't think the two quite the same, but he accepted it with a grateful smile and continued to the door. "She sounds like she would." He listened at the door, opened it a crack, peered out, then started down the hallway, mumbling, "Four doors to the left. At least I don't talk in my sleep. I don't think even Caroline would forgive me talking incessantly day *and* night. She's really not as prickly as she sometimes appears, but—" *even she has limits.* He groaned as Mark chuckled. He glared at him as they stopped in front of Stewart's room. "You have full permission to punch me, you know. Or throw things at me, clear your throat relentlessly, whatever it takes to keep me from embarrassing myself. Or someone else."

"Aye aye, Captain Bowditch."

"I'll hold you to that." Kingsley knocked on Stewart's door, and when Stewart called out for them to enter, he pushed it open and strolled in. "Good afternoon, Stewart," Kingsley said brightly. "I hope you're recovering well."

The guard, mask-less and a bit scruffy and seemingly improving in health, was propped up on a couch, with books, refreshments, and blankets within easy reach. After a brief look of confusion as they entered, Stewart's eyes went quite wide. Alarm was by no means absent from them.

Kingsley held up the shaving kit. "Thanks for this, by the way." After a careful scan of the table by the couch, he laid the kit down beside the cuff with the controls to the automaton. He gestured to the seats arranged to face Stewart. "Do you mind if we sit?"

Stewart shook his head. His eyes darted from them to a table across the room, where his mask lay. A lingering odor of paint pervaded the room, pleasant in the way of something rich with old associations. It smelled of family and freedom.

Kingsley grinned at him and continued in a conspirator's whisper, "We snuck away from our matron for a few minutes to check on you and information gather. You look better. Do you feel better?"

"Yes," Stewart said, his unease diminishing at their untroubled reaction to his face. "You two look better too. I'm glad of that."

"And more sane." Kingsley gave him a knowing look.

"That too," Stewart admitted with a wry grin.

Kingsley leaned back in his chair and stretched his legs out in front of him. "We were wondering if you could settle a dispute for us."

"Oh?"

"Yes, the crystal growing in the wall that's always been empty before, when will it be ready to collect? Later this week or not until right before the Rí Am arrives for it and the statue? I'm for sooner and Mark is for later."

"Bowditch..."

"Would you believe me if I told you it was professional curiosity?"

"Frankly, no."

"Sheer nosiness?"

"No."

"A plot to overthrow the Rí Am?"

"N—" Stewart stared at him, uncertainty clouding his expression.

"That's rather ridiculous, isn't it? What could one crystal do? Even if we could get down to the mines to take the crystal, the wall would only grow another one. The walls always grow more crystals."

"I'm not so sure about this o—"

A knock on the door stole everyone's attention, and Kingsley had just enough forethought to clamp his lips together before his thoughts escaped.

"Stay seated and keep facing me," Stewart whispered. "Leave if they stay, which isn't likely." He added, more loudly, "Come in."

The door opened, and Kingsley was hard put not to turn around or bolt. If they were caught, he wasn't sure what he feared more: being put back in the mines, getting Caroline in trouble, or getting into trouble with Caroline after just getting out of it. Any of those were bad. He needed the safety of her little room. No guards, no taunting fellow prisoners, no endless walls of crystals that always grew back. His knee started bouncing, and he pushed it down with his hand. "Don't panic, Kingsley. You're fine."

Mark laid a hand on his arm, and Kingsley clamped his lips shut.

"I came to see if the paint was dry," the man said as he entered. He paused just inside the doorway. "Oh. You have company."

Martin's voice. The sculptor already knew about them. But Kingsley still needed to be back in Caroline's little room. He forced a deep breath, and Mark's grip on his arm tightened. Kingsley patted his hand and managed to rise slowly and hold out his hand for Stewart to shake, though everything in him was screaming to run. "Ah, well, now that you have other company, Stewart, we'll be on our way. We'll come by again later." Tugging his cap back on his head, he spun around and strolled toward the door, Mark mimicking him.

Martin stood solidly between them and the door, pipe in hand, gaze moving over them with expert attention to details like ill-fitting clothes and calloused hands. A faerie curse on the man. "You two clean up well."

Something about the man's unflappable expression calmed Kingsley, drove his thoughts from hiding in a little room to Caroline and how he wanted to stay in her good graces. But that involved hiding in her little room. "Thank you, Martin. If you'll excuse us, we'd better be running along." He made to move around Martin, muttering, "Before Caroline discovers us gone and skins me alive."

Martin backed in front of the door, jammed his pipe into his mouth, and crossed his arms, looking as formidable as a marble mountain. "There's no rush."

"Oh yes there is." Kingsley wasn't sure why he did what he did next, unless he was just desperate and figured the man would follow his pipe, but he seized Martin's unlit pipe and tossed it to Stewart. As Martin lurched forward, Kingsley scooted behind him. He grabbed for the door handle, but Martin pitched himself backward, pinning Kingsley against the door with enough force to make him appreciate the brawn of sculptors.

"You and I, Captain Bowditch," Martin said deliberately, pressing in just a bit more with his elbow, "are going to have a little chat about Miss Lockley."

"I assure you," Kingsley managed to huff, trying to wriggle out, "that I would never take advantage of Miss

Lockley. I have been a perfect gentleman, as Mark can testify." The sculptor suddenly released him, and he stumbled back into Mark.

"I have no doubt you are, as Miss Lockley would demand it of you even if you didn't demand it of yourself, but I was referring to the matter of your *sharing* of meals."

Kingsley got an unpleasant sensation in his gut, which perhaps had been enjoying more food than it should have been lately. "She hasn't been taking her meals with you, has she? And getting an extra one delivered to her rooms?"

"No. Unless you call sneaking of hardtack and dried meat meals. Her *only* meals are delivered to her room."

"Where she divides them between us," Mark said slowly, his shoulders sinking, "claiming to be eating with you."

"Yes. I had wondered why she'd grown so pale these past few days, until I remembered you two."

Kingsley returned to the chairs by Stewart and sank into one. "Any chance of getting another set of meals delivered?"

"No."

"I don't fancy our chances of making it in the mess hall unrecognized," Mark said, sitting down beside Kingsley and propping his chin on his palms. The tip of his Vanon arm bracer showed beneath the slightly too-short sleeves, catching Stewart's notice.

"You're a Vanon and a Bowditch," Stewart added, shifting uncomfortably. "They hope rather than believe you two are dead. They're looking for you in the mines. They tried your homing crystal, Mark, but luckily for you, it didn't work." He gave him a curious glance, at which Mark blinked innocently.

"Wonderful stuff, iron paste," Kingsley muttered. Mark kicked him, and he cleared his throat. "Given that we're on their minds, they might recognize us in the mess hall. Any hidden food stashes we can raid?"

"There's the mushrooms," Stewart said with a shrug. "There were some locals who got into the cave system a while back, and the guards found a crop of mushrooms while hunting for them. We're allowed to gather the mushrooms and cook them over a fire there as long as we don't engage with any of the fey creatures who occasionally turn up. I've gone a time or two, but I'm not a huge fan of them."

"I hope you two like mushrooms," Martin said firmly, his gaze steely.

Kingsley hated mushrooms, but Caroline needed to eat, and there was a challenge in Martin's eyes, and he never backed down from a challenge. Straightening, he returned Martin's gaze before looking to Stewart. "Can you tell us how to get there?"

"Yes. It's not so far that you need a navigator."

Stewart drew them a map, and then Martin escorted them back to Caroline's room. Fortunately, she was still in the studio waiting for Martin to finish his smoke break. Probably sneaking hardtack.

When they'd gained the privacy of Caroline's room, Mark pulled up his sleeve, the one free of the unremovable Vanon arm bracer. He pulled off Stewart's automaton-controlling cuff and handed it to Kingsley with a sly smile.

"Well done, Mark. Well done." Kingsley took the cuff and held it up to the light, studying the glittering crystals and examining the mechanism that moved them. "I always knew you were the devious kind of quiet."

CHAPTER NINE

A stolen crystal-studded cuff wasn't exactly the surprise Caroline had been expecting. Or hoping for. "Thank you, Kingsley." She pasted on a smile and searched his eyes for signs of fever or madness as he flourished the gift before her. "It's ... um ... uh ..." *hideous. And where did you get that? Please tell me it wasn't from the dead guard.*

His expression fell from excited child to forlorn so quickly she forgot to ask where he'd gotten it. "She doesn't like it," he said to Mark in a mopey voice, worrying her further.

It wasn't until she'd pressed her hand to his forehead, which wasn't at all warm, that she caught the gleam of mischief in his eyes and Mark's attempt not to laugh.

"Really, Kingsley," she protested, dropping her hand from his forehead. "Where did you get that? And why?"

Laughing, Kingsley slipped it into his pocket. "Don't worry about where. And it's for controlling automatons. We might need one when we're back in the mines."

"Oh!" Caroline cried, looking toward his pocket.

He backed away, as if she might try to steal it from him, that teasing gleam in his eyes still. "No, you rejected it. You'll just have to go to dinner without a pretty bauble for your wrist."

"Go to...?" Her stomach rumbled at the thought. How she wished it were possible!

"Dinner." Kingsley and Mark straightened and pulled back their shoulders as if for inspection. "Do we look fit to take a lady to dinner?"

Fit? They were gaunt, with ill-fitting clothes and poorly cut hair, but they had hope and eagerness in their eyes. Caroline couldn't help but smile, though it was bittersweet. "You'll do."

"Excellent. It's down the hall then." Kingsley winked at her as he handed her a map. "No one will notice us with you walking before us."

Laughing, Caroline glanced at the map, remembering the mushrooms Marianna and Bertram had mentioned as well as the treasures nearby. "They likely will be too distracted by my hideous attire to notice you, you're right."

"Given that it's not permissible for a gentleman to contradict a lady, I won't," Kingsley replied as he filled her canteen with water. Mark collected the dinner left outside Caroline's door earlier and the extra silverware they'd scrounged by simply not returning it when the empty tray was put out.

"You made an admirable automaton in that outfit, I'm sure," Kingsley continued. "Misleading with fashion is one of your talents, after all."

Caroline looked at him strangely, sure from his expression there was something she was missing in that statement.

"The first time we met, just before Herschel's first voyage on the *Dusk Crier*," he proffered, "at the dance my parents hosted for the crew and their families, I asked you to dance. I got my ears boxed for that."

The admission didn't help her confusion any. "Well, I was fourteen at the time, but—"

"Exactly!" he cried, startling her. "But how was *I* to know? Herschel introduced you as his sister, not his *twin*. Your style of dress and your coiffure plainly said you were out in society. I assumed you were at least sixteen, maybe a young-looking eighteen given your confident air and boldness in speaking your mind. Thought it was a perfectly appropriate thing for me to do to ask you to dance. Rude not to, actually.

"When Mother realized you were fourteen, she boxed my ears, and while Marianna was laughing at me, Davy and Father were busy 'resurrecting' a family tradition of us dancing with every lady, from cradle to cane, to prevent a scandal. All because of your unorthodox fashions!"

She gaped at him. "You mean all those dances with giggling toddlers and Bart's grandmother were for *me*?"

He capped off the canteen and handed it to her, his eyes twinkling. "You have been trouble from the start, Miss Lockley, and very well worth it."

When Caroline was finished with her burst of laughter, she put away the map and canteen, collected her satchel—the PullLine, iron knife, and her lamp already in it—and gestured toward the door. "Sorry, Kingsley. Consequence of being adopted by a bachelor uncle. He practically threw me at the dressmaker and told her I'd had a birthday and was going to a ball. The poor woman must have thought he was referring to a coming out ball and took pity on me, for she outdid herself on the dress and even taught me how to fix my hair."

"You were rather striking that year, and every pre-voyage ball afterward. Always. Well..." He looked her over. "You still look unnervingly like an automaton now that I think about it. You said Martin had dresses for you to model in, didn't you?"

"Yes, and no to what you're about to ask. Do be quiet, Kingsley. It's time to go." Caroline gave a fond shake of her head. Turning her back on him, she stepped to the door and peered out. Kingsley, having as much sense as mischief, did as bidden. The hallway was empty, and they managed to make it to the path that led deeper into the caves without being seen. Very near the opening into the "wild section" was an entrance hatch to the ventilation shafts, and they made note of it. There was also a stash of lanterns, which they made use of.

They stepped off the polished floor of the mining operation onto the uneven gray floor of the caves and continued on, thoughts of dinner carrying Caroline's feet along at a pace that made even Kingsley and Mark, with their long strides, hurry a bit to keep up.

"You'll cook the mushrooms for us, won't you, Caroline?" Kingsley asked as he fell into step beside her, obviously having decided the moratorium on speaking was over. "What was it you cooked the last time I invited myself over for dinner? I don't remember what it was, just that it was good. You're an excellent cook. Your husband will be a lucky man."

"Yes, and I don't remember," Caroline said, intending to ignore the last comment. It stung: for the past, for all the times he could have asked to be that man and hadn't, and now, because she wasn't sure it was even reasonable for him to ask. She intended for them to leave alive, but she couldn't guarantee it. "If it weren't for you, I wouldn't even know how to cook. You—" She sucked in a breath and turned to glare at him, deciding she didn't want to ignore that husband comment, after all. "Wait a minute. Those times you brought Herschel home wounded and sick and insisted on staying with us until he was well and on hiring a housekeeper and cook for the duration—ladies who made it a point to teach me how to cook and keep house properly—you did that for more than our help during those few weeks, didn't you? You wanted to make sure I could cook for you if we got married! *Not that you ever bothered to ask me.* I thought you were just an altruistic gentleman fond of creature comforts! How many other women did you pay for cooking lessons for?"

Kingsley looked a bit abashed, but he quickly recovered. "You make me sound like a plump old doffer fond of pipes and slippers! And I'll have you know my family *employs* a cook. I simply didn't want Herschel, or my dear friend Darius, or you, to die of food poisoning. I've had Darius's cooking. And I *never* paid for anyone else's cooking lessons."

Caroline scoffed. "I'll have you know *I* know the Commodore believes young couples should start out living within their means and not dependent on family income, which means we likely would not have started out with a cook, if you'd ever gotten the courage to propose to me."

Once again, he appeared abashed but quickly recovered. "You've thought about this, have you?" he asked.

"For about five seconds, as we've been walking." That wasn't strictly true, but it was better for Kingsley to think so, at least until after they were safely away from the mines. Then they would have a nice, *long* chat.

"Well, that's something. A start anyway. Keep thinking about it, if you want to."

"And if I don't?"

"It's better than thinking about what the Rí Am would do to us if he caught us."

"I'm not so sure about that."

"Well, I think it is."

"Have either of you noticed a flickering light ahead?" Mark asked suddenly.

Caroline stilled, Kingsley as well, and that was when she noticed her arm had somehow ended up tucked in his. She could deal with that later. A twinkling of light that disappeared around a boulder ahead created a sinking sensation in her gut. She glanced at the map, the chamber, and the path at their feet. The latter had a faerie glamour on it. They were going in the wrong direction.

So the faeries wanted to play, did they?

Clenching her teeth, Caroline grabbed her iron knife and sprang forward, flourishing it and singing, "Iron that bites, blossom of the rowan tree, that's what little faeries hate!"

The glamour disappeared, and an ugly imp that only came up to her knee darted from behind the boulder with a frightened cry. She gave chase.

Mark and Kingsley watched in stunned silence as the glow of the imp disappeared with all possible haste into a faerie tunnel those not from the island wouldn't be able to see. That is, those who didn't have a drop or two of faerie blood in their ancestry. She wondered about Mark; his eyes were very keen in noticing things Kingsley didn't. And

Kingsley usually noticed everything. While Kingsley was clever, confident, and vocal, Mark was clever and silent, but no less confident for that quietness, she suspected. Fortunately, Mark was better at paying attention than either she or Kingsley, when they were together at least. *Keep your focus, Caroline.*

"You're quite frightening when you want to be," Kingsley remarked as she returned to them, feeling triumphant and rather smug.

She put away the knife and turned her attention back to the map and their path. It shouldn't take them much longer. They were only a few feet off, and she quickly put them back on their path. "Yes, and don't you two forget it."

"Never." Kingsley snatched the map from her and walked on, leaving her side for the first time since they'd entered the caves.

After a surprised stare and an indignant huff, she took Mark's arm and started them walking a few feet back from Kingsley. "If you're determined to lead, Mark will escort me the rest of the way."

"That's the general idea," Kingsley called back before veering to the left into a narrow cleft in the rock wall. "He'll keep you from antagonizing any more faeries. Against the rules. And *that* is an important rule to follow."

"Oh." She looked up at Mark, and he gave her a rueful smile, a kind of apology for not stopping her earlier threats in his shock. *Nice work, Caroline.*

Fortunately, they made it to the mushroom grotto with no further incidents and were able to cook—everything needed having been left there for the guards' use—and eat without incident. For the first time in a week, Caroline ate her own food, as well as some cooked mushrooms, and felt wonderfully, shamefully full. She also watched with rather gleeful delight as Kingsley suffered through the expectation of eating mushrooms only to discover after a few bites they weren't so bad after all.

"Is this water safe to drink, do you think?" Mark asked of a little pool they'd discovered behind a crop of mushrooms.

"It's safe enough to wash the dishes with, at any rate." They'd finished eating, and Caroline was strolling the perimeter of the chamber. Her leg was healing nicely, but she still wasn't keen on clambering over all the boulders and stalagmites littering the place to find the small tunnel Marianna and Bertram had escaped through.

"She walks in beauty, like the night, of cloudless climes and starry skies."

Caroline turned to give Kingsley a quashing look, but he merely winked at her and went back to collecting the dishes and silverware.

As soon as she resumed her walk, he continued, "And all that's best of dark and bright, meet in her aspect and her eyes; thus mellowed to that tender light, which heaven to gaudy day denies. One shade the—"

"Kingsley!"

As if equally surprised to hear Mark shouting, Caroline and Kingsley both turned to stare at the young Vanon. He was near the wall opposite, beside the pool, pointing at a shifting shadow filling the chamber's entrance. As it moved, it seemed to solidify into a fire-eyed black dog the size of a carriage.

"Barghest!" Mark shouted. "Move, Kingsley!"

"The knife!" Caroline cried, crouching behind a thick stalagmite. "It's in the satchel!"

"No iron! That will only bring more!" Mark darted for a group of boulders further along the chamber wall.

The barghest growled low and sprang forward, spittle flying, rocks and mushrooms sizzling at its liquid touch, toward the center of the chamber and Kingsley.

Kingsley snatched up the satchel, spun around, skirted a boulder, and tripped over a three-foot-high mushroom with a sizable slice missing, the short outlier of a thick grouping. He scrambled to his knees and crawled into the forest of mushrooms as the barghest leapt over the remains of their fire and the boulder they'd used as a backrest and landed in a crouch before the fungi.

Instead of springing again, the barghest's nose lifted and its head swiveled Caroline's way and then Mark's, and she wondered if the scent of the mushrooms was covering Kingsley's or if it didn't want to destroy the fungi. Kingsley had disappeared, possibly into a depression in the uneven floor. Her relief lasted only until the creature stalked her way.

Well, this was all her fault, after all.

Making herself as small as possible, she studied the base of the wall up and down the chamber, as much as she could see, desperately looking for that short tunnel. The sound of sizzling rock grew closer.

Please, Maker, this is not how I want to go. Can it wait until after we've sent the crystal and saved Herschel?

"Yes! It worked!" Kingsley whooped in a voice of such triumph it sent a tremor of horror through Caroline. She peered around her cover. Kingsley stood amidst the brownish, umbrella-sized mushroom caps, waving at the fey creature. "Go on, boy! Go get her!"

The barghest froze. Growling, it studied Caroline and Kingsley both.

"Go on! Get her!" Kingsley encouraged, back at his waving. The man only needed a moon to be a lunatic. "Don't want her? How about me then?"

The barghest turned its growl on Kingsley and advanced a step.

Well, she wanted the moon, didn't she? Caroline swallowed hard, stood, and whistled. "Here, boy! C'mon! Got a nice treat for you!"

Her voice cracked, but the creature must not have noticed, for it stilled, then glanced around as if unsure if they hadn't set some trap for it.

She whistled again and slipped around the boulder toward it, holding out her hand invitingly. "Come on. I won't hurt you." *Please don't hurt me, or any of us.*

"That thing you were looking for, it's over here." Mark's soft statement floated across the chamber between calls to the faerie dog.

Kingsley nodded and waved at Mark to go on. Caroline began working her way around the perimeter toward Mark, keeping close to the mushrooms. The creature would advance toward one of them, then Kingsley would shoo it toward her or her toward him, and it would inch away.

Caroline gained the wall near Mark, and when he saw that she saw the two-foot-high tunnel entrance, he disappeared into it, quickly making way for her. Going down on her knees before it, she called to Kingsley, who was still closer to the chamber's center than she liked. "Kingsley—"

"In."

She crawled in, the sound of his cooing following.

"You're going to like your new home, boy. Lots of toys and treats. Squirrel!"

Scuffed boot soles in her face, she followed Mark further

along the ancient faerie road, all her attention focused on the sounds behind her and on resisting the urge to go back.

"Hurry up." The impatient order from behind, quickly followed by a tap to her feet, was among the most welcome greetings of her life.

IT WASN'T fast or comfortable, but the three of them made it to the throne room using the PullLine, and while the men were exploring, Caroline sought out the hidden faerie pathway to retrieve the books Marianna and Bertram had stashed there. She sincerely hoped the barghest would not come barreling through it tracking them. Since the hidden pathway was concealed to most humans, it might still be used by the faeries occasionally, unlike the smaller tunnel they'd taken. She quickly spotted it, slipping in while the men were poking around a busted chest.

"What's that?" she heard Mark ask Kingsley as the trove of contraband tomes reeking of the faeries greeted her senses.

"I don't know," he replied. "Looks like a top made of loops. It was under the remains of the chest broken by the man Caroline tells me is my brother-in-law. We'd better keep it." He added in that lowered voice, "I hope this brother-in-law is something we should ke—" He cleared his throat, then began in his normal voice, "I don't know where we are, but I have a terrible feeling it's best if we returned the way we came." He sounded as if he were near the largest of the tunnels leading from the chamber. "I imagine we're more than three miles from the mining operation. Haven't a clue how to get there from this tunnel either."

"Agreed," Mark said.

"Caroline?" Kingsley asked as she finished piling the books into her arms.

Following a rather impish impulse, possibly strengthened by her physical proximity to the realm of the faeries, Caroline stayed silent, hidden just inside the faerie tunnel.

"Caroline? ... Caroline, where are you?"

After two more hails from different parts of the chamber, Kingsley's tone shifted from wondering to distressed, and her conscience pricked her.

"Here I am." Arms laden with books, she stepped from the tunnel.

When he'd recovered from his relief, his eyes bounced between her, the books, and the wall, and narrowed. "Don't do that to me, you sprite!"

Laughing, she joined him and Mark near the throne at the center of the chamber. "You would do it to me. And no, that's not any different, so you can't complain."

Kingsley started to say something in that low mutter of his but bit it off at a swift movement from Mark. "Thank you, Mark," he finished in a pinched voice.

Mark's look was one of mixed amusement and guilt. "We should wait here awhile, then go back the way we came." He helped Caroline settle the books onto the floor and then stuff them into the satchel. That done, he took a volume on astronomy and walked off, sitting down beside an ancient wardrobe.

Kingsley looked down at her, his mouth opening. She shoved a book at his chest, startling him into taking it. "Go read somewhere." She moved away and sat near the largest exit, the obscured faerie tunnel in view.

"I thought I could sit with you and read," Kingsley said, following her. "We'd only need one light that way. Conserve our lamps and all that." He added in that lowered voice, but she suspected he realized it this time, "And no, I don't want to sit with Mark."

When she didn't respond, just chose a book on the history of flight, opened it, and tried not to let her smile show, he sat close beside her, inched a little closer, turned off his lamp, and dutifully began to read on nautical navigation. As Caroline turned the first page of her own book, she struggled with a delightful confidence in being able to comprehend the material of either book better than Kingsley could since she'd read and helped print copies of the volumes Marianna and Bertram had already taken. A boast of that sort could be very useful in keeping Kingsley out of trouble should he became bored or melancholy. It would prompt him to greater mental exertions.

By the time Mark suggested they return, Caroline had to nudge Kingsley to gain his attention. As he stood and offered her his hand, her eyes caught on the gray sock where his left shoe should be.

"What happened to your shoe?"

He pulled her up and tucked her arm through his. "I imagine it's either been eaten by a very large dog or become an object of abject terror to one. I threw it at the barghest before escaping into the tunnel."

Laughing, Caroline hugged Kingsley's arm and then took her place in their tunnel-traveling pattern. "You really are insane, Captain Bowditch."

To her surprise, he didn't reply or speak again until they'd been struggling down the cramped faerie path for some ways. "We are definitely going to find more PullLines before we go after the crystal," he said. It was half grumble, half consideration.

"I know where the storage and equipment rooms are," Mark said over his shoulder. "I was on repair duty for a while."

"Sounds like the perfect ending to our dinner date," Caroline said. "Let's go."

CHAPTER TEN

I t wasn't that Kingsley didn't trust himself to go out alone, he simply didn't think it wise. He was noticeably tall, and, he had to admit, still prone to conversing with himself aloud if no one was around to stop him. Mark, on the other hand, was average in height, quiet, and had come to the mine young enough to have grown up a bit during his year and a half there, enough to look surprisingly different now that he was cleaned up again. That meant Kingsley got the task of crawling through the shafts to the storeroom while Mark walked the halls.

The previous night—or day or shift or whenever it was they went to dinner with Caroline—they had used the access hatch and vent shafts on their return to avoid the hallways with the books they'd retrieved. They hadn't ended up going for the harnesses. It had been a shift change and was too crowded by the time they'd returned. They had finished their evening by reading more, praying about their mission, and playing silly games they didn't need cards or boards for.

They still had two weeks, as best they could determine,

before the Rí Am was due to arrive, but they'd decided they needed to get the crystal now anyway, as well as establish a way out. Kingsley had an idea about the latter. But first, the harnesses, while Caroline was working with Martin.

After a brief, blessedly uneventful trip back to the mushroom grotto, during which they ate breakfast and conducted a successful search for Kingsley's shoe—still intact—Kingsley and Mark had separated. Mark continued through the hallways toward one of the storage rooms while Kingsley made his way through the air shafts. The shaft they'd come up through from the mines was open, though it bore evidence of its time as a temporary lift station for guards and prisoners. *It's open again, so the lift is working.* Kingsley got a terrible sinking sensation in his gut, one that almost took him straight down the shaft. What if, having fixed the lift, they'd sealed the opening from the shaft into the mines?

"Mark?" he whispered through the foot-sized vent into a large room lit only by a light moving about it, hopefully under the impetus of his young friend. Assuming he'd followed his directions properly.

"You made it," Mark answered pleasantly.

"Of course. See if you can find any boxes labeled 'Dusk Crier.' They stripped me and my crew of our PullLine harnesses after they captured the ship."

As Mark made a brief inspection of the stacks of boxes and stuffed shelving units, Kingsley lay on his stomach to better peer through the narrow vent. "Do you think that cuff we took from Stewart will control the automatons in the lower level?"

"I think the guards got a special one when we went down to work on the big crystals," Mark said after a pause. He collected a crowbar from near the door and began prying open a crate. "Why? The Oileán Caillte crystal is next to our old stations."

"Because there has to be a lift straight from the lower level to the surface in order to get those giant crystals out. I never considered that the lift we loaded them onto wasn't merely the freight version of the one that took us back up to the mines, but it can't be. They need an easier way out for those monsters we dug. We have to figure out where it goes."

"You're right," Mark said, hope and surprise in his voice. "I don't think it's so far as the scramble distance from the miners' lift to the freight lift. I think they sometimes use the automatons to make us think we couldn't make it back without them."

Kingsley huffed. "They would. Let's hope so. What did you find?"

"Other than mouse droppings?" Mark asked, laying aside the crate lid and crowbar.

"I don't suppose the Maker would approve of us finding a way to put those in the Rí Am's tea, do you? Because that's the only use I can think of for them."

"I don't know. If I recall rightly, Elijah mocked the priests of Baal pretty badly before dispatching them, and King David had some pretty strong requests regarding the fate of those who set themselves against our God."

"Hmm. Good point. However, since my motives feel more vengeful than pure at the moment, we'd better leave the droppings."

"If you say so. He prefers whiskey anyway. Perhaps you can find some use for this?" Mark thrust something that glinted in the lamplight toward him, and Kingsley pulled it through the vent. It was definitely metal and leather.

"Oh beauty!" Kingsley wiped off the PullLine gauntlet

with his sleeve and kissed a gear. "How I've missed you! Are there more? And goggles?"

"A boxful."

"Hand them up." He reverently put the PullLine into the sack he'd brought along. "They'll need a good cleaning and oiling, but I think they'll work. Better get two for each of us in case one fails. And see if you can find one that's a little fancier than the others and has *KCB* on it."

SOMETIME LATER, after admiring their haul and going back to the grotto for lunch, they picked up Caroline's meal from outside her door and sauntered down to the studio.

Guards on opposite shifts don't always know one another, Kingsley reminded himself as they passed a guard. He made sure to keep his reminder in his head and his feet on course for the studio rather than back to Caroline's room.

When they quietly entered the studio after a longer walk than he anticipated, his rapidly beating heart slowed its pace. They found themselves in a large warehouse, part of which had been sectioned off for Martin's use. To his right and further into the chamber were large equipment, a lift station, and—he paused to thank the Maker—loading bay doors that almost certainly led to the beach. Ahead and to his left was the partition delineating the sculptor's studio.

Not far from them were a changing screen and the bags of broken crystals Caroline had mentioned. Beyond that, Martin chipped away at a familiar, giant crystal and occasionally glanced at Caroline. And she, frocked in an elegant gown that trailed down to the stool on which she stood, well, he would happily gape at her all day, and if he could think of a useful reason for that, he would. But as he was concerned for her safety as well as the Sky Keepers' mission and his crew, he might have to forego that pleasure. Unless he could think of a reason, of course. He ducked behind the changing screen before either sculptor or model noticed his and Mark's entry and pulled one of the bags of crystals behind it with him.

Mark's steps grew heavier, and Martin said in that unflappable tone of his, "I forgot to mention earlier, Caroline, that your tailoring skills are passable."

There was an intake of breath, and Caroline exclaimed, "I didn't do that! I didn't want them roaming about all day!"

"Hello to you both too," Mark said with a bit of a smile in his voice. There was a dull thud, as if Mark had set Caroline's meal tray on a table.

There was no return of that smile in Caroline's voice when she asked, sharply, "Where's Kingsley?" Kingsley did the smiling for her and dug through the crystals until finding a handful that looked like they might be a good match for the one still growing below. "He didn't go down to the mines, did he? I know he's been eager to go."

"I don't know. He was right behind—"

"Where are you going?" Martin demanded as the sound of rustling fabric indicated at least one person was moving. "You'll trip getting down in that dress. Stay put."

Laughing to himself, Kingsley pocketed the crystals and tied off the bag.

"I'm going after that crazed captain before he gets himself killed or re-taken. He promised he wouldn't do anything foolish. I should have known our definition of *foolish* would be different. Help me down."

"Why, Miss Lockley!" Kingsley stepped from behind the

changing screen. "You do care!" Grinning mischief at her, he strolled over to where Martin was trying to keep Caroline on the stool while she was trying to get down.

Caroline stilled and sucked in a breath. When she released it, her jaw clenched. "You! Why—"

"Now, now, Caroline," Kingsley said, shaking a finger at her. "You did the same thing to me." Out of the corner of his eye, Kingsley saw Mark quirk a smile and slowly resume his walk further into the studio-warehouse.

"I—oh! Why were you hiding?"

Kingsley swept his hand toward her in an upward motion, the gesture including the crystal-studded, alluring gown to elegant coiffure, then brought his hand to his chest. "You're absolutely stunning. I needed a moment to recover."

Caroline crossed her arms and glared at him, her cheeks flushing crimson.

"It's true," he said with a helpless shrug.

"Don't fluster my model, young man," Martin said sternly, indicating him with his chisel, and Kingsley wasn't sure if that was a threat or just Martin talking with his hands and whatever sharp implement happened to be in them. "Your position, Miss Lockley," the sculptor said, turning back to her.

Deciding Martin simply talked with his hands, Kingsley situated himself a few feet in front of Caroline, where she could see him, and stared up at her, his smile mischievous. "I wouldn't dream of it." He also wouldn't dream of allowing his eyes to follow Mark about the room in his study of the lift. He didn't trust Martin that much. He didn't trust himself to keep his thoughts to himself either, and they really needed to stay put. His gaze straying despite his effort, he snapped it back to Caroline. He put a very tight guard on his lips.

Caroline huffed but re-assumed her position. "Go away, Kingsley."

"Impossible! The faerie queen wouldn't be the faerie queen without admirers. I'll stay right here."

To his right, Martin paused, something between shock and illumination on his face. "He's right. The lunatic is right," he breathed in awe.

"He's not crazy!" Caroline protested, and Kingsley was pretty sure his heart would have journeyed to the moon if the Star Veil weren't in the way. As it was, it still leapt pretty high.

"But I am!" he cried with a sideways glance at Martin. "The line between madness and genius is a fine one. One Martin understands as well as I do."

"Young man," Martin warned, glaring at him.

"Shall I keep my pose? I don't mind." Kingsley winked at Caroline and relished in the obvious fight against a smile playing out on her face and lighting her eyes.

"I'll attend to you later, Bowditch." Martin scowled at him. "Right now I need to figure out if I should adjust her expression and the tilt of her head. She wouldn't be returning the admiration, merely accepting it. Hmm." He shifted from a study of the queen taking shape out of the crystal in front of him to the bags of crystals Kingsley had raided to Kingsley. He jabbed his chisel toward Kingsley, then Mark, making Kingsley's nerves fray a bit. The young man quickly leaned on the lift controls as if observing the statue from a different angle. "You two, if you insist on being here, make yourselves useful. Bring those bags of crystals over here."

He continued as Kingsley and Mark went to do his bidding, "I'd considered making her out of thousands of small crystals, but decided that would suggest frailty, and she wouldn't like that. She must be solid crystal and the mortals not. You, Mark, I'll teach you how to start forming the statue's core. Bowditch, you'll model."

After he got Mark started, Martin arranged Kingsley how he wanted him, then turned him away from Caroline. Behind him, he caught a quiet snicker.

CHAPTER ELEVEN

"My, you're both looking ... well-built today." Caroline studied Mark and Kingsley again. The two had just emerged from the bedroom after suiting up for their gathering of the crystal. Kingsley had gained a little weight since his rescue, that mostly due to the curing of his illness, but Mark none, since extra meals weren't plentiful. But they looked fuller now.

"We doubled up on the harnesses," Kingsley explained as he finished cleaning the lenses of his goggles and slipped them on. "One beneath the clothes and one over the jacket. In case of a failure or if we meet any friends, as you did."

Caroline's heart twisted, and she forced herself to say, "The crystal gets out first. With no Star Veil the mine will be useless. There'll be no reason to keep or harm the prisoners."

"We know," Kingsley agreed and handed Caroline the box with the winged carrier.

As she checked the mechanical bird and carefully put the box into her satchel, Kingsley continued, "You don't want to take along that dress you were wearing in the studio, do you? Or any dress? I find it eerie how much you resemble an automaton."

Caroline cleared her throat, trying very hard not to laugh at Kingsley's expression, which was almost the equivalent of a wrinkled nose. "Dresses are not appropriate attire for repelling. Especially not *that* dress. And I am not leaving with you two. You and Mark pack the mushrooms and cooking supplies."

The plan was for the two men to leave the mines when they released the winged carrier—though Kingsley wanted her to come rather than stay as an inside agent—and try to make it to the villages to get help for the prisoners when the Star Veil fell. They'd managed to find the guards' supply room and had raided it and the grotto's cooking supplies, so the men would be okay if it took them a while to get to Robert and Lydia Lockley's house.

"What about a riding costume?" Kingsley persisted, stuffing toiletry items into the bag between extra clothes and a blanket. He pulled out another bag and added the food supplies to it. "One of those with the pants that poof out around the thighs? I've always found the pants a little strange, but the jackets and blouses are becoming."

"Thighs!" she exclaimed in mock horror. "Kingsley, a gentleman does not speak of such things."

He snorted, a strange sound coming from him. "I've heard the things that have come out of your mouth, Caroline Lockley. You've quite shocked my mother on multiple occasions. Your uncle should be ashamed." He added quietly, and Caroline wasn't sure if he was aware he was speaking aloud or not, "And much grief it's given me from my mother."

A pang went through Caroline's heart. Mrs. Bowditch

was different now—loss has a way of changing one—but Caroline had long suspected the woman had never considered her acceptable for her son and that was why Kingsley's evident friendship with her had never gone further. Why he didn't ask her to dance that last night when he always had before.

Caroline struggled to put a smile in her voice. "How about this: excuse the admittedly hideous costume I now wear and at the next Bowditch ball you may choose the style of my gown? Not buy it, mind, but choose the style. You've always had more fashion sense than I have anyway."

"Deal." He sealed up the bags. "Have the fashions changed? Oh. You probably don't know, do you?"

"I pay enough attention to get by, thank you very much." Tired of the conversation, she handed him her satchel. "Put this into the ventilation shaft so I don't have to squeeze both it and me through the vent."

He did as she asked, and they all climbed into the air shaft. Earlier, in order to get out of trouble with her about their little jaunt to the studio, Kingsley had admitted he knew where the Oileán Caillte crystal was growing, which was the gift he'd promised her. The cuff had been something extra. His ploy had worked well.

Mark and Kingsley had also studied the shift changes and were certain they knew when the group that worked where the Oileán Caillte crystal was growing would be off shift. Unfortunately, it was during her own shift with Martin. She felt rather guilty about not telling him she wouldn't be there, but it would be better for him if he knew nothing.

"So *east* is where the sun rises and *west* where it *sets*?" Kingsley began, speaking quietly, shortly into their crawl through the ventilation shaft, taking her thoughts back to their earlier discussion of a book they'd found. "I thought *set* things were placed things, things that stayed put. I always assumed the sun disappeared so the stars and moon could be seen. 'The greater light to rule the day and the lesser light to rule the night' and all that. Does it just sit on the horizon and brighten and dim like the sky crystals? But if the sun was always visible, you wouldn't need a compass, would you? Because you'd always know where east and west were. But you wouldn't know exact degrees or north or south, or anything on a cloudy day. Or at night. Compasses are useful then. I'm glad Davy made a blueprint for them. You'll have to add compass directions to your map of the mines, Mark."

"Good luck with that," Caroline said.

"Maybe in a few days," Mark answered mildly.

"Actually," Kingsley said smugly, "we could make a simple compass ourselves. Your iron knife is too large for a conveniently portable one, but we could glue some of that iron paste you brought to a bone needle, find some cork, a shallow dish for water, and all we would need is a bit of lodestone to magnetize the needle. We let the needle sink and see where it points."

"Really?" Mark asked with genuine interest.

"I'm impressed, Kingsley," Caroline said quietly, conscious of the open vents they were passing, "and I'd say let's keep an eye out for lodestone, but let's save that for the map of Sheffield-on-the-Sea we do when we leave. And, Kingsley, I realize you haven't talked to a friend from the outside in several years, but we should probably be quiet. We can talk later."

Kingsley immediately fell silent, and strangely, something about that silence bothered her.

"Kingsley?" she whispered, glancing over her shoulder at him, careful to keep her headlamp focused on the shaft floor.

He didn't respond for a moment, and she was about to call his name again when he said softly in a voice that wrenched her heart, "I haven't talked to *anyone* in years, Caroline."

"What?" she exclaimed, barely remembering to keep moving.

"The Rí Am doesn't like the Bowditch family, and he doesn't like what I was trying to do. When we first came, the guards tried to turn my crew against me. When that failed, they separated me from them. I was trying so hard to help them however I could. ... It's hard for a captain to be without his crew. I don't know how they are, who's dead, who's alive, who's still himself and who's changed ... how Herschel is. I pray for them every shift—for there is no brightening or dimming, just shifts and rest—and I try to leave them messages. But I rarely even glimpse them. And no one is allowed to talk to me or me to talk to anyone else."

And Kingsley had always been a talker, friendly and outgoing, as well as a good listener. He thrived around others.

"Then talk, Kingsley. I'm listening. Just keep your voice down."

"I don't tell you for pity," he said quickly, quietly, "but so you'll know. I talk to myself, like a proper crazy person. It helps. Sometimes I have nightmares. Sometimes fits of melancholy. Sometimes I want to be back in my 'safe,' dark cell. I don't think any of that's going to change any time soon."

She smiled ruefully. He wasn't telling her anything she

hadn't figured out already, but it was a relief to know he recognized it. "It's okay, Kingsley. We can work on that."

"We?" he said hopefully after a pause.

"Your family and friends. That includes me."

"Ah." He was silent a moment, then said, more his old self, "How much further? The view back here is rather distracting, and I'm tired of watching my hands to avoid it like a proper gentleman. I like to see where I'm going."

Sighing, Caroline scooted to the side of the tunnel. "Come alongside then. Sorry, Mark. There's only room for one more up here."

"That's okay," he answered in an amused tone from the rear.

Kingsley wormed his way forward, putting them shoulder to shoulder with each brushing the wall. "Oh, this is much better."

"You only say that because you like to be in the lead," Caroline groused as she bumped into Kingsley going forward.

"I won't deny that, but I have no intention of taking over this expedition, Captain Lockley. And you forgot one reason: I can see your face this way."

Caroline turned to him, aware that her headlamp was on.

Squinting in the sudden brightness, Kingsley faced forward again. "Ok. I'll be quiet and just crawl."

Chuckling, Caroline set them going again at a fast pace.

As they neared the vertical shaft, vibrations, a bit stronger than normal, moved through the rock under her hands, and they all paused until the rock stilled. "The second airship for the daily shipment must have landed. I'm fairly sure the loading will be done and them gone before we get back up. No need to worry about them seeing you two slip away."

She started forward again, but neither Kingsley nor Mark responded, and it took a moment for Kingsley to regain his spot by her side.

They made a slow descent down the large air shaft. The old PullLines—tested in the mushroom grotto—worked as surely and silently as Caroline's. They found the mine entrance by the light weeping into the dark shaft. The gaping hole had been crudely boarded and the bars pulled back up. Being down a few guards and prisoners, repairs on anything other than the lift seemed to be considered non-essential, fortunately for them. After ascertaining that no one was around, Kingsley and Mark pulled the bars back out into the chamber, and after they'd all slipped through, put them back in place.

They stood in the passage, glancing to the left, where the lift and navigator automatons would be—and those guarded —and to the right, where countless tunnels branched deeper into the cave.

"I don't remember the way," Mark said hesitantly.

"We weren't meant to." Kingsley, the serious captain once again, took in the branching pathways and then studied Caroline, as if she were his muse. Finally, he sighed and brushed a hand through his hair, which she'd trimmed again to make a little neater. "Unless I'm mistaken, the row of automatons left at the lift station are emergency ones. They have all the routes programmed into them, as well as homing crystals for the guards. The cuff we took from Stewart, since its last route was the one we need, might let us activate one to get us to the crystal."

"How are we going to get a navigator away from the guards?" Caroline asked.

"You and I, my dear, have proven how dangerous distraction is, so I say we distract them. We can get close enough without them seeing us to activate the automaton, but we need them closer to knock them out. Otherwise, they'll deactivate the automaton. Mark, you take charge of the cuff. Caroline, you can render the guards unconscious. I'll—" He swallowed hard, and Caroline thought there was a bit of a tremble to his hand, so she clasped it in hers. "I'll distract them," he continued, giving her a brief smile. "Should I stumble from a tunnel and collapse on the floor, or attempt a ventriloquist's routine to lure them into a tunnel beyond us so you can take them down on the way?"

"Ventriloquy." Caroline tightened her hold on his hand. "You're not getting anywhere near them again."

He squeezed her hand in acknowledgement or thanks. "Right. That's settled. Let's go."

They crept along the passageway, the sounds of tapping carrying faintly to them from some of the paths emptying into it. When they could hear the footsteps of the pacing guards beating against the stone floor at the lift station and thought themselves at risk of being seen, they ducked into a side tunnel.

As Mark pulled out the cuff and began rotating gears on it to activate an automaton, Caroline checked the stun darts loaded into her gauntlet. Kingsley pressed himself against the wall at the end of the tunnel and said in a loud whisper that seemed to come from somewhere else and echo past them into the lift chamber, "Do you really think it's gold? Not fool's gold left by the faeries to tease us?

"Do you think I'm a fool? And keep your voice down. You want the other guards to know?"

"What's that?" a young man asked as the guards' pacing ceased.

"Relax," another said. "It's just an imp at his mischief. There's no gold here, and no guard stupid enough to mention it in our hearing."

"Oh." He didn't sound relieved.

"Look," the older one said, "if you're to make it here, you're going to have to learn to deal with the faeries. Don't engage with them. Just show them the Time King's emblem on your cuff, and they'll leave you alone. Now, go find the imp. Show him your cuff and ask if any of the faeries have seen Bowditch or the young Vanon. Their bodies weren't at the bottom of the shaft. It's possible the faeries caught them to play with."

Kingsley groaned and began to mutter something, but Caroline elbowed him.

A noisy mechanical whir and click overshadowed the younger guard's protest. "That's not the faeries," he cried. "Someone's called the automatons. *All* of them."

All?

"Deactivate as many as you can and stay with the lift," the older guard said quickly. "If any prisoners try anything, activate the barrier pulse. That will keep them away from the lift. I'll follow these."

A nervous guard with access to the alarms and the lift was not what they'd wanted. She handed Mark a stun dart and motioned for him to take care of the young guard when the older one was out of sight.

Kingsley scooted back and waved for them to crouch out of the guard's line of vision. He clamped one hand over his mouth and took Caroline's hand with his other, and they waited, a whirring that grew louder and louder approaching, and Caroline had the dreadful image of a swarm of hornets heading their way.

The wooden bodies of five automatons passed by, then the cautious steps of the guard. Caroline, ready to release the stun dart, watched as the guard peered down the tunnel, his gaze staying above their heads, then moved on. Just a little further, and the other guard wouldn't see him collapse.

Summoning her courage, she tugged her hand from Kingsley's, leaned around him to peek at both guards, then scooted out and around the dividing wall into the next tunnel. She stalked the older guard past one more tunnel, then pierced his neck with a stun dart. As he fell, she caught him and dragged him out of sight. He was *very* heavy. Colin had made hefting unconscious Time Keepers around look easy.

"That was marvelous, Caroline!" Kingsley whispered as he snuck up to her, making her jump.

"At least I don't have to hang around until he wakes up this time," she grumbled, trying to cover her start. Kingsley hadn't laughed for once, so it must not have been intentional.

Or perhaps, she thought sadly as he gazed beyond her, where sounds of hammers hitting rock were echoing up the passageway, he hadn't even noticed.

"Deep into that darkness peering," he muttered in that low voice, his eyes searching the tunnel depths, "long I stood there wondering, fearing, doubting, dreaming dreams no mortal ever dared to dream before; but the silence was unbroken, and the stillness gave no token."

"Move him." Her tone as commanding as any Bowditch captain or commodore, Caroline pointed to the guard, directing Kingsley's focus, making him momentarily straighten to attention. He shifted closer to her and slid his arms under the guard's. When she wouldn't relinquish the man to him, he looked at her questioningly.

"Aren't you going to ask me when I had to do that?" she asked in an offended tone. He blinked at her, then looked toward the main passageway and back down the tunnel, his shoulders hunching as if against a remembered blow. "Kingsley..." she pleaded.

He turned to her, held her gaze a moment, and nodded, swallowing hard. Giving him a half smile, she released the guard to him.

"When did you have to do that?" he asked, dragging the man easily down the tunnel.

"Never mind." She said it sharply, in a tone that begged to be questioned. "It was for a friend, and no one was hurt."

"It was to help Colin O'Connor, wasn't it?" He looked up at her suspiciously as he lowered the guard to the stone floor, its surface covered in black dust smeared by many boots. "You know the last time we met he was trying to *kill* me. I was tempted to reciprocate."

"He was a pirate then. What would you expect?" The grin Caroline had anticipated fighting when Kingsley finally asked her about Colin—for she may have talked a good deal about Colin, whom she loved like a brother, without talking as much about Vesper—was one of relief and gratitude rather than teasing pleasure.

His eyes narrowed. "What I didn't exp—"

"Don't be the prodigal son's brother, Kingsley. That's not like you." She took his arm and hurried him back into the main passageway just as Mark jogged up to the opening.

"I took care of the young one," he said, then walked on

after the automatons. Despite Mark's seeming calm, there was a tenseness to his shoulders, a cautiousness to his steps indicating a readiness to fight or run. She might be Kingsley's distraction, but *they*, she suspected, were Mark's.

"And you were 'dead' for four years," she continued to Kingsley, settling them into a quick pace a few feet behind Mark. "Did you expect me to mourn you forever? Especially since we were *only* friends."

"You seemed to know Herschel was still alive. That meant I was too," he protested, walking a bit straighter.

"Not necessarily—"

"And if *you* thought of us as only friends, you wouldn't have expected me to ask you anything or been offended when I didn't."

Caroline snapped her mouth shut. "Not necessarily still alive," she admitted a moment later, not quite meeting his eye as he glared down at her. "Anyway, Colin is or very soon will be married to Mark's cousin. My affection for him is purely *brotherly*."

Kingsley's eyebrows rose, and then his eyes lit. "Well, that changes everything. I am always happy to see a new brother adopted into the family. And the fact he nearly killed me could be useful if I ever want anything from him or need to liven up a family gathering."

"I've already claimed teasing rights on Colin," she said as the automatons disappeared down a side tunnel a few feet ahead, Mark following. "You'll have to find someone else to bug."

Both she and Kingsley froze as a crunch and a distressed whirring came from ahead. *Mark. Guards and angry prisoners.* Had they mistaken the shift schedule?

"It's okay," Mark called back to them, and after letting

out a breath of relief, they jogged around the corner to him. The passageway narrowed suddenly, and the automatons, all five at once, had tried to go forward together and gotten stuck and could do nothing but whir their discontent.

"I believe, Caroline dear," Kingsley said with a bit of a laugh as they stopped behind the row of navigators, "that as a near victim of his, my claims are stronger."

"Colin is mine." Caroline gave his arm a gentle squeeze. "You can tease Mark."

"That's very generous of you," Mark said drily as he gripped the barrel of the center automaton.

"But first you must help him," she said.

Mark and Kingsley pried the navigator out of line, and the others whirred forward. They set it down, and it continued on.

"I don't think it's far now," Mark said stiffly as he watched it. Kingsley's expression was grim.

"Let's not dawdle then." Her short legs forcing her to resort to jogging, Caroline overtook the straggling automaton and then fell into a walk behind the vanguard. "Ready to steal a crystal?" she asked, looking back over her shoulder at Kingsley and Mark. She waved at them. "Come along, men. We've a Star Veil to destroy."

With only a few long-legged strides, Kingsley caught up with her and took her arm. "Yes, Captain Lockley."

"Aye aye, Captain Lockley," Mark echoed, taking her other, proffered, arm.

"Stop calling me that."

"Commander Lockley?" Kingsley suggested as he and Mark kindly matched their strides to hers.

"It's *Miss* Lockley to you two."

"I've never liked 'Miss Lockley,' Kingsley said, looking

down at her with an alarming level of both mischief and nervousness in his eyes. "The name that is. I've always thought 'Caroline' would go very nicely with ... ah ..."

"'Bowditch' is what you told me," Mark whispered to him over her head. "Should I take the rear guard for a moment?"

Caroline, embarrassed by how red her cheeks were turning and feeling this distraction business had gotten out of hand, said rather crossly, "You're exactly where you need to be." She turned from Mark to give Kingsley a quelling look. Those looks tended to be more encouragement than anything else with him, and she honestly wasn't sure if she was glad about that at the moment or not. This was hardly the time for proposals, not when she needed to keep her focus off dreams and wedding dresses and on getting the crystal and the men out.

"You did mention in a remonstrative way my earlier negligence," Kingsley whispered in her ear, the desperateness of his tone tugging at her. "I don't want to be guilty of that again."

While Caroline tried to gather her dazed thoughts, the automatons suddenly stopped. They were in a rounded chamber with a narrow air shaft and a water cistern.

Kingsley straightened away from her. "The Dispersal Point," he said, and Caroline wasn't sure if it was with relief or trepidation or both. He hurried down the center tunnel, ushering them along through domed chambers glittering with crystals in the lamplight.

When they came to a patch of wall that had but one crystal, they stopped. Their guide to Oileán Caillte blinked at them.

"Is it ready?" Caroline asked, and held her breath.

"Close enough. Do the honors, Mark. I'll be right back." Kingsley gave him a significant look, then spun about and disappeared through the chambers, her water canteen in his hand.

Caroline dug out the pick and chisel from her satchel and handed them to Mark.

As Mark tapped gently and slowly at the rock around the crystal, creating echoes that bounced back at them from the other chambers, Caroline noted something she'd missed earlier: it wasn't the crystals that lit the mines but lanterns. After Prism said she could match automaton crystals with sky crystals, Caroline had assumed they were the same thing.

"Why do the sky crystals glow and these don't?" she asked.

"My theory is that the crystals and Veil are actually using the sunlight, not merely blocking it. They don't produce light themselves," Mark said without hesitation, giving her the feeling he'd already thought about that.

"And at night?"

"According to the astronomy book, we're in shadow, the earth itself between us and the sun." He stopped his tapping to wiggle the crystal, then tapped lightly on the opposite side. "So no sunlight then. They wouldn't be at the right angle to reflect it, as the moon is said to do. It might be possible to store the sun's light, however, and give it back later. That's how the sky crystals work at night. I think."

He wiggled out the crystal and began meticulously cleaning the gem.

She was beginning to worry about Kingsley when he sauntered back into the chamber, hands in his pockets and the canteen slung about his chest. He had a pick and chisel tucked into his belt.

"What have you been up to, Kingsley?" she asked warily, watching as he pulled his hands from his pockets.

"Getting souvenirs." He held up a crystal similar to the one Mark had plucked from the rock. "And decoys." He lunged to the wall and shoved the crystal into the hole Mark had formed, which Caroline realized with a shock was shrinking. "Keep it, keep it," he muttered, pressing his palm against it. When he finally stepped back, the crystal was as snugly set into the rock as the ones being birthed.

"Do we put the Oileán Caillte crystal in the carrier now or just before we release it?" Mark asked, hand curled around their treasure.

"Now. The carrier won't activate until I switch it on." Caroline turned away to rummage through the satchel for the box containing the winged carrier and the pliers to secure the crystal in its clasp. When she looked up, Kingsley was holding the crystal.

"May I?" he asked, handing the water canteen to Mark. She gave him the box, and he knelt on the dusty rock and opened it. As he pulled out the mechanical bird, he jerked his chin toward the canteen. "Drink up. It's hot in the lower level. I've drunk my fill and replenished the canteen. You two should do the same."

"The where?" Caroline asked, her voice rising to an embarrassing pitch.

"The lower level. Fortunately, it's near enough to not need the automatons."

"Why?"

"Sometimes you must go down to go up," Mark said with a wry grin and a knowing look at Kingsley.

"Mark," she said sternly. He had been spending too much time with Kingsley, apparently. "I do not wish to have any more rock above me than strictly necessary. Our goal is to have sky above us."

"Yes," Mark agreed, his smile even more amused. "But first, we're going to the lowest level of the mine, where we get the large crystals for the clock towers and statues. There's a lift there that will take us straight to the warehouse."

She glanced from him to Kingsley, who nodded as he checked the clasps holding Cait Vanon's homing crystal, the one that would allow the mechanical bird to find Davy's ship. "Why can't we go back the way we came? We can take the carrier to the guards' alcove at the surface and release it there."

"There are very fine wires preventing anything getting in, or anyone getting out, there," Kingsley said. "Many guards are sent here as a warning to themselves or their families. The guards know what will happen if they displease the Rí Am, in this or any future position. And the families, they'll know that one slip from them will move their son, nephew, or grandson from guard to prisoner. The transition is very easy. I've seen it happen. They end up in the work unit Mark and I were in. They don't last long no matter how nice they were before the switch of their role.

"We need a quick route to the loading bay doors in the studio, and this is it. I'm sorry, Caroline," he finished, looking up at her.

Caroline nodded, her heart squeezing for all those unfortunate enough to be within the Rí Am's notice.

"I'll hold your hand if you're nervous," Kingsley volunteered, holding up a dust-blackened hand. Like Mark, his face was dusty now too.

She stiffened and lifted her chin. "I'm not—touching your filthy hand." She took the canteen from Mark, who'd finished drinking from it. "I'm going to replenish this. Follow me when you're ready."

Caroline had drunk as much as she could hold, replenished the canteen, and had time to wonder about the cleanliness of the water in the cistern before Kingsley and Mark trudged up to her. The three took the next passageway to the left and soon came to a lift with several warning signs, none of which reassured her about their course. But she didn't complain, even though the descent was quite long and the lower level, as Kingsley warned, hot.

But he hadn't warned her about the crystals. She'd seen the one brought up for Martin to work on, seen the lofty crystal clock towers at the Time Keeper Stations, but seeing whole crystals shooting out from the walls of an enormous cavern that seemed to stretch the width of the entire island, was something else entirely. Seeing Kingsley dwarfed as he passed by one and led her up the gently sloping face of another, was something else entirely. She was *walking* on crystal like a road.

Some of the crystals were single pillars, straight with perfect facets; some twin columns, each a piece of the other; some a grouping of radiating spikes longer than Davy's airship; some spears so covered with shorter crystals as to be almost invisible beneath them. And they were all, in some unreal way, the enormous twins of palm-sized crystals she'd seen in gift shops. They were beautiful and strange, like many of the Maker's creations.

"I feel very small," Caroline said quietly.

"Awe will do that to one." Kingsley handed her off their crystal walkway and pointed to one of the broken crystal faces creating jagged patches in the wall. "Martin's faerie queen."

"Poor Martin. All his hard work will be for naught. Though I wouldn't have it any other way." Caroline smiled sadly, blinking against the sweat trying to slip into her eyes. She wiped her forehead on her sleeve and caught Kingsley doing the same, smearing the covering of black dust there. Kingsley had always been fastidious in his appearance, and Mark had even commented that Kingsley's determination to walk upright and keep his hair and person as neat as possible, his silent order to Mark to do the same, an encouragement to maintain his dignity, had been tremendously helpful to him. When Kingsley was dirty or disheveled, something wasn't right.

"I don't think he'll mind, too much, in the end," Mark said. They followed him into a smaller, but still vast, chamber and past what appeared to be a workshop for shaping crystals. To her relief, the freight lift was at the center of the chamber.

At her side, Kingsley slowed, the sudden change in pace nearly causing her to trip. He stared at the lift, his expression more lost than she'd seen it since rescuing him, and it worried her.

"Why is your face so dirty? How many crystals did you dig out?" she asked by way of distracting him. "Clean up," she said sharply. She gave his arm a little shake, and that seemed to help, for he straightened and resumed his normal pace. "We don't want to dirty the studio. Martin would not appreciate that."

Eyes alert once more, Kingsley complied, briefly wiping his face with an appropriated handkerchief. "Yes, dear."

Caroline froze, gaping at him. When she finally got her mouth to open in protest of that endearment, though why she felt the need to protest something that didn't bother her at all, she wasn't sure, Kingsley interrupted, putting away the cloth, "I can't call you 'Captain,' and I don't care for 'Miss Lockley,' and I don't want to overuse 'Caroline.' Precious things like names should be taken care of, after all. So unless you prefer 'sweetheart' or 'darling' or some like term, 'dear,' it is."

For a long moment, Caroline tried to fight a ridiculous grin with a scowl and lost. "Do be quiet, Kingsley," she managed at last.

"Why?" Kingsley asked, tucking her arm through him. "No one else is in the lower level. And names are of utmost importance, you must agree."

"Because we're about to leave the lower level." Caroline gestured to the lift, whose controls Mark was already inspecting. A crane was part of the far end of the large, railed rectangle. A safety cage with another set of controls stood near it. Their pace slowed.

"Caroline," Kingsley said as he turned her to face him, suddenly serious, "would you consider staying down here while Mark and I take the carrier? I know it's hot, but just in case Martin's not alone, I'd rather you not be involved if there's fighting."

"But I'm the one with the weapons," she protested, somewhat bewildered. "The cargo airship should be gone and the warehouse empty except for Martin. I'm the best one to handle him too."

"That's not—"

"The guards or faeries will find her even here, Kingsley," Mark interrupted, his expression both firm and understanding. "Or when she leaves to get food and water, which she'll have to do eventually. I say we stick together, come what may."

Food? How long were they wanting her to stay? Or were they really wanting her to stay at all?

"Kingsley," Caroline said, stepping away from him, irritated at both men, "are you still trying to convince me to escape with you instead of staying with Martin? By using reverse psychology this time? And Mark's conniving with you?"

Kingsley's fleeting smile was pained, and that gave her pause. "No, Caroline." He walked past her to the lift and sat his bag on the floor at his feet and turned to Mark. The young man left the controls as a clanking announced the ignition of the lift's mechanism. He joined Kingsley on the lift, leaving the gate open after him. With a sorrowful glance at her, Kingsley latched it shut, even as she approached it.

Stunned, Caroline stopped, glancing between him and that space far above that was Martin's studio. Kingsley, really and truly, wanted her to stay—which meant he and Mark were going on a foolish venture. And this time, he wasn't trying to rally others to his cause for company and justification.

Her eyes fell to Kingsley again. Captain Kingsley Bowditch wasn't so straight and confident and brimming with energy as he used to be, but Caroline had always understood why her brother and others had followed him voyage after voyage, against pirates, against storms, against Time Keeper Anti-Smuggling Units. Against the unknown. The Rí Am himself. But she'd always had more sense than they. She wasn't some foolishly loyal pup always following him around. Even if, well ... even if she'd always been waiting for him to come back.

Her gaze shot from the lift to the crystal-pierced cavern to Kingsley, still watching her, sad and a bit lost, but still resolute. Still one men would follow. But not sensible women.

Still, she didn't fancy camping out in that hot, eerie place by herself.

Caroline ran for the lift, and Mark opened the gate and handed her in. She planted herself in front of him and Kingsley. "I don't know what you two are up to, but you're not getting into trouble without me."

"That would be too much to hope for," Kingsley muttered.

She narrowed her eyes at him, a sharp reply forming, then tipped forward with the shuddering movement signaling the lift's departure. Kingsley caught her from behind and pulled her upright. Despite his earlier grumble, he kept hold of her upper arms, letting her lean back against him as they made a slow ascent, and Caroline decided that was as good a place for her to stand as any.

"Caroline," Mark said after they left the cavern behind. "There's something we should tell you. That airship we felt the vibration for earlier, that wasn't a cargo ship. That was the Rí Am's airship and his two escort ships."

As Caroline sucked in a breath and started to protest their withholding of information, her own mind protested itself. She knew as well as they did there was no getting out of the mines with the Rí Am there. There were too few exits and too many guards. Telling her wouldn't have made a difference, not in convincing her to stay. She'd love to punch the Time King in the face. Maybe this way she'd get a chance.

She leaned back against Kingsley, and he hugged her tighter. "Now is the time for madness," he said. "For cowering. Trust us."

CHAPTER TWELVE

"The dead do rise, don't they, Grandson? In a more literal fashion than you claim to believe."

Mark's expression hardened as the lift shuddered to a halt in the studio, which was anything but empty. Caroline didn't bother to count the guards, mostly noting those with guns aimed at them and the two Martin glared at, who flanked a young woman with Martin's eyes. Those packing up Martin's unfinished statue. And those beside the Rí Am, the ever-young Ulrik Vanon, standing before the lift, arms crossed as if impatient for their arrival. Caroline was tempted to put a sleeping dart in him but didn't think it would help matters. Kingsley, who'd moved away before they'd breached the studio, had warned her against heroics or even too much defiance.

"Grandfather Ulrik," Mark said coldly as guards swarmed them and hastily removed their PullLines, bags, picks, chisels, and her boot-knife and revolver, then bound their hands. Caroline was struggling with fear and too much anger at the Rí Am, whom she'd never seen in person before, to even give a smug smile when the guards, deceived by the obvious and in a hurry to get out of the Rí Am's way, missed the thin knife and other things hidden in her corset, and the extra PullLines hidden under Kingsley's and Mark's thick padding.

"When my miners revolt," Ulrik said, eyeing the three of them closely as the guards stepped away, "and my favorite captain and beloved grandson go missing, having only *presumably* died—when my imperial sculptor gains an unexpected model—did you think I would not investigate?"

"I've never thought you lax," Mark said, a defiant edge to his voice, "though I stopped letting it stop me."

"Proof that knowledge without proper application is folly," Ulrik said, his words crisp.

"The wise of heart will receive commandments," Kingsley murmured, his eyes a bit unfocused, his forehead drawn in worry, "but a babbling fool will come to ruin. Whoever winks the eyes causes trouble, and a babbling fool will—" He bit his lip as Mark cleared his throat.

Ulrik shot Kingsley a warning glare, and one of the prison guards spoke up, "Captain Bowditch has gone a bit crazy, sir. Talks to himself."

"In that case," Ulrik said with evident enjoyment, making Caroline want to punch him even more than usual, "I shan't let it bother me." With another inspection of the slump-shouldered Kingsley, which seemed to please him, the Rí Am turned to Caroline, and she lifted her chin. Her brother wasn't in the room, so she didn't think the Time King knew of him. Doubtless, he didn't consider anyone other than a Bowditch captain and one of his own descendants worthy of being rescued.

"Who are you?" he asked in a musing way that reminded her of Kingsley, and she wasn't sure if he was mocking Kingsley or enjoyed allowing his prisoners to follow his train of thought as a kind of building of suspense or a display of his cleverness. "Cara suspected Mark had a sweetheart, but you're obviously more interested in Captain Bowditch, for you drew closer to him rather than to Mark when the guards took your things."

One corner of Kingsley's mouth curved up, and Caroline was tempted to kick him. The man had no proper sense of danger. But at least he'd regained his proper mind, for however long that would last. She forced a calming breath. Hitting anyone at the moment would not be useful or wise.

"The question is, is this a recent development or a planned rendezvous? For I made certain the captain was believed dead."

The loading bay doors opened, and a cool, damp breeze rushed in, smelling of the sea and reminding her of her early childhood, before she and Herschel had gone with Darius to the mainland.

When Caroline didn't answer, the Rí Am's gaze flicked to Martin and then to the pretty nineteen-year-old woman Caroline assumed was his daughter, Prissy. Caroline fancied the Rí Am wasn't perturbed she hadn't answered since he had others he could establish his power over by threatening.

"Her name is Caroline. I found her in the cargo hold," Martin said quickly, understanding that look. "She was dressed as an automaton. I don't know why she came, something about her family. She said she was from Sheffield-on-the-Sea. Maybe she thought she could steal an automaton for there, since you can't buy one now? I thought if I took her as a model I could redirect her from a life of crime. She does have fine features."

"I've always thought so," Kingsley muttered. Caroline elbowed him and then glared at Martin for good measure. *Bless you, Martin.*

Ulrik rolled his eyes and turned to the guards searching their belongings. Beyond them, the statue of the faerie queen was being carefully shuttled out toward an airship big enough, elaborate enough, and well-armed enough for a world dictator. "What have you found?" he asked.

The guard gestured to the floor on which he'd laid their things. "An iron knife, revolver, stun darts, cooking supplies, mushrooms, and a mechanical bird—with crystals. All three PullLines have the Bowditch Shipping Line emblem on them."

"Perhaps your father will be joining you at last, Bowditch." Ulrik indicated the mechanical bird, and the guard brought it to him.

"Those were from the *Dusk Crier! My* ship, bought and paid for," Kingsley cried, and would have stepped forward had Caroline not blocked him. "We found them in the storage room."

Ulrik ignored him and studied the winged carrier. At some point when out of her watch, it had acquired in its center hollow a makeshift pouch of white fabric likely ripped from Kingsley's shirttail. Ulrik pulled the pouch out and opened it onto his palm. Several crystals tumbled out. He turned them over in his hand, tossed them to the floor, then focused on the three in the clasps. "These crystals, they are arranged so that they will direct the bird. Where will they lead?"

Kingsley pressed his lips together, and Caroline raised

her eyebrow in an insolent manner. Mark wore a look of fake innocence, at which Ulrik narrowed his eyes. The Rí Am seemed to particularly dislike any of his own family who didn't submit to his tyranny. Her estimation of Mark's courage for becoming a Sky Keeper to begin with doubled.

"Please remember," Ulrik said, "that there is a threat behind everything I say: The girl will go to the mines; I'm sure the guards wouldn't mind, as she does have fine features. I'll give you to the faeries. You'll be thrown off the airship over Calandra—the plank is old fashioned but effective. I'll send all your families here. The possibilities are endless."

Kingsley glanced at Caroline, his expression distraught. "There's a self crystal and crystals for Sheffield-on-the-Sea," he said quickly, hanging his head.

"And?" Ulrik gestured at their strewn belongings until the guard handed him the pliers for placing the crystals in the winged carrier. He caught Kingsley's gaze again, then gave Caroline a significant look.

"Kingsley, don't—" she began, sensing it was her part to protest, though why they were telling Ulrik anything she wasn't sure.

"I can't send my family to the mines, Caroline. Or you." He gave her a desperate look, and she shut her mouth, praying whatever mad plan he had would work.

Kingsley faced the Rí Am again. "There's a homing crystal for Cait Vanon. She's aboard my brother's ship."

Caroline gasped and turned to glare up at Kingsley. He wouldn't meet her eye, and she forced herself to remember his warning to her. His madness had saved them from a barghest; she'd trust him now, even if he seemed a broken coward. She *would* trust him. She glanced at Mark, and his expression was defeated as well.

Just like the two of them to scheme without her. And after she'd given up her meals for them!

"Cait's crystal isn't functioning." Ulrik's irritation turned to a warning look at Mark. "Like many others of late."

"I used iron paste on it," Mark said smugly. "They did the same for Cait's and were going to remove the paste when they thought it was time for the carrier to be released. They wanted the crystals."

Ulrik studied him a moment, then without acknowledging Mark's answer, examined the intricate, beautiful mechanical bird in his hands without the least appreciation for it. "So Davy Bowditch and the pirate are wanting directions to Sheffield-on-the-Sea, are they?" he said at last. He plucked the Oileán Caillte crystal and the self crystal from the bird and tossed them to the floor. The bird followed. He smashed it under his foot, and Caroline didn't know why that surprised or angered her so much, but it did. Her fingernails dug into her palms as she struggled to keep her mouth shut. It was a small thing, that bird, but in a way representative and so much easier to fight for.

"We can navigate for ourselves, you know," Kingsley snarled, his attention on his brother's ruined invention before settling with a frightening fierceness on the Rí Am. "The world doesn't need you."

Ulrik's eyes flashed with nothing more than irritation before one eyebrow arched, almost in unconcern. "So you've discovered an Autumn Eyes, have you? That would explain the knowledgeable choice of crystals."

Is that what Prism was? She wasn't unique?

Kingsley cast a questioning look at Caroline, but she made no response.

"I shouldn't get my hopes up if I were you," Ulrik continued. "One turns up every generation or so, the right mix of faerie and human blood to give eyes that hold all the colors of autumn, and see more than that." His expression turned spiteful and smug. "But they usually don't last the day. Apparently, the midwives are getting lax. You can be assured this one too will die soon, and then you'll be left with nothing—all your dreams of using the crystals to navigate yourself dead as an autumn leaf. It's happened before, but I'll see that it doesn't happen again."

Caroline clamped her bound hands over her mouth, nausea threatening. Mark's look was one of horror and shame.

"I wish we'd saved the mouse droppings for your whiskey." Kingsley's mutter came out in a low growl.

The Rí Am gave him a look of disgust and turned to a man beside him in the uniform of his personal guard. "See the prisoners to the ship. We're going to rendezvous with the inventor and the pirate." He handed the guard, who proudly displayed an arm bracer as fine as Mark's, Cait's crystal. "Put this into the ship's navigation system." He smiled at Mark. "Your cousin is going to be more useful than I ever imagined. I also imagine we'll find our dear Vesper with her. It will be a touching family reunion. While it lasts."

The head guard of the mine, a young guard with him, stepped to Ulrik's side and cleared his throat, giving them the time they needed to regain their composure. The young guard, covered in black dust, tremulously held out a small, ornate box. "The crystal for Oileán Caillte, sir."

Ulrik looked the man over, then flicked a hand at the

guard with the arm bracer, who took the box. "Let's go. We'll pay a call on Davy Bowditch and the pirate, collect any of my family with them, then go on to Oileán Caillte. Martin can finish the statue on the way. He'll have plenty of inspiration to do a surpassing job on it."

Martin's eyes flashed dangerously before he submissively bowed his head. Caroline wished she could catch his eye and apologize.

"On the way back to Reydon," Ulrik continued, addressing no one and everyone, "we'll stop here so the prisoners can return to their work and the new can begin theirs."

Beside her, Kingsley and Mark stiffened. *Hold on, Kingsley. Just a little longer.*

Ulrik gestured to the guards, and they ushered Martin and his daughter out, then prodded Mark, Caroline, and Kingsley to follow.

"Hey, diddle, diddle," Kingsley began in that low voice behind her as they walked toward the loading bay doors, his singsong tone alarmingly nervous. "The cat and the fiddle, the cow jumped over the moon—"

There was the sound of a hard whack, and Kingsley stumbled into her, the muttered nursery rhyme shifting into a stifled cry. Glaring murder at the guard, Caroline caught Kingsley's arm and towed him after Mark onto the airship, unimaginatively christened *Crystal.*

Caroline, Kingsley, and Mark stood on the deck for some time, a strong breeze blowing a bit of the sea into their eyes. Storm clouds were brewing in the distance, and Caroline vaguely wondered if the Rí Am intended to set them up as lightning rods by way of amusing himself.

When the Rí Am finally came aboard and the airship lifted off, he took them down to a large room being converted into a studio for Martin. The sculptor was already at work, his daughter in Caroline's place as model. Ulrik talked with him about the statue and reminded him of the importance of it and the honor for himself in being chosen to honor the faerie queen. Caroline found it immensely gratifying that although the beautiful Prissy was wearing the same stunning dress Caroline had been, Kingsley didn't give her a second glance. Unfortunately, Kingsley's expression was still worrisomely haunted.

After following the Rí Am down to the studio for the apparent purpose of following him down, they followed him back up to the deck. A portion of the deck appeared separate from the rest, set slightly lower into the ship and not having any of the cables that held the ship to the massive balloon overhead. Three mine navigator automatons sat near the far end of the recessed portion. The space gave Caroline the impression of a children's playpen, an impression solidified when they were shoved down the three stairs leading into it and no guards followed them. They were left there, hands bound, but still left.

"Grandfather Ulrik enjoys besting his descendants at chess during our yearly visits. He has boards of many kinds," Mark said as he looked about them, more in distaste than surprise. Remembering his voyage to the mines? He drew himself up. "Sometimes you have to sacrifice a pawn to take a queen."

"You aren't pawns," Caroline retorted, tightening her grip on Kingsley's arm.

"But we are." Mark nodded at Kingsley, whose lost expression was still feeding both her heartache and her anger, before focusing on her, apology in his gaze. "This game is between us and Grandfather Ulrik, Caroline.

Kingsley and I agreed to the risk, but not you. I'm sorry I didn't try harder to make you stay in the mines."

"So I could face the Rí Am alone? With him there to inspire the guards they would have searched my room and figured out how I was getting around. They would have alarmed the shafts and searched, probably even sent the faeries, until they found me." She inched closer to Kingsley at the thought, but he didn't respond. *Snap out of it, Kingsley. Please.* "So no regrets. What's our move?"

"Be amusing?" Mark said, sharing her worried glance at Kingsley. "He leaves us here to see how we respond, to give us a false hope of escape or revenge. He's seen so much over the centuries he wants to be surprised but also wants to think himself clever. For every move we make, he already has a counter. A man wants to jump overboard to save himself from whatever fate the Rí Am has for him? The side looks low enough, yet invisible wires will stop him. He thinks he can attack the guards and they'll kill him quickly? They'll restrain but not kill. Revenge or escape by damaging the ship? Grandfather Ulrik knows about the explosion in the mine—he left automatons to mock us, to see if we'd try it again."

"You're my queen, Caroline," Kingsley said suddenly, turning to her.

Startled, Caroline stared up at him, but his eyes were clear, his posture straight. *Thank you, Maker.* "Your best defense, you mean?" she managed after recovering from her relief.

He winked at her. "Against all other admiring women, yes."

She scoffed. "I see so many of those."

"Because you do your job so well. Would you like to sit down?"

"Are you offering me your lap?" *I really wouldn't mind a hug.*

"That would be rather scandalous, don't you think?"

Caroline's smile fell. "I'd hate to make a scene in front of all these people," she said with a hint of sourness.

"My thoughts exactly. If you'll excuse me a moment?" Kingsley walked away toward the three automatons, the doll-like navigators in barrel-like bodies from the mines. He adjusted the position of one, pulling it out from the others and turning it slightly so that its porcelain face faced him, then he stepped back and very precisely kicked off the head. It flew to the deck, porcelain face shattering. He ripped out the doll-like body and repeated the action on the second automaton. With a glance over his shoulder at her, then a narrow-eyed look between her and Mark, he moved those two automatons side by side and dragged the third to the corner, as far from the couple as possible. Where if it exploded or caught fire, the damage would spread the fastest —if the Rí Am had left them explodable, that is, which she doubted.

Or did the Rí Am think they would know they weren't explodable, and so he left them explodable so he could scorn them for having what they needed but not using it? Or would he think they'd think that and so make them non-explodable? She shook her head and refocused on Kingsley.

He returned to the shattered automaton heads, selected a shard half the size of his palm, and rejoined them.

"Cut my bonds for me, won't you, Caroline dear?" he asked, holding out the shard. "Or shall I do yours first?"

Cut...? Gaping at him, Caroline held out her wrists. Humming, he began sawing through her ropes.

"Don't you think he's going to send the guards to re-bind us? With chains?" she asked, staring at the fraying ropes.

"Oh, I don't think so," Kingsley said lightly.

"We won that move," Mark explained. "He'll leave us alone until he thinks we've outmaneuvered him."

"How will he counter?"

Mark shrugged. "He'll change out the board when we stop moving or if he gets bored. He might send us to a cell, give us time to strategize." He glanced over the side of the ship. They were approaching thick clouds. "He may go ahead and put us up since he can't watch in the mist, or he might put up fans to keep the deck clear."

"Pity that." Kingsley tugged the rope strands from her wrists and handed her the broken porcelain, his mouth curving in a slight smile. "I rather fancy the cover of a misty deck."

She rather fancied not being on the deck—or the ship at all. She cut the rope binding his wrists, then Mark's, still not convinced they'd be left free.

"Push up my sleeve, won't you?" Kingsley asked as she tossed the porcelain shard to the wooden deck. He held out his arm, and Caroline, not bothering to ask why and listening for guards, unbuttoned his cuff and folded up his sleeve, which took effort due to the tight stuffing of the sleeve with white handkerchiefs.

"There's plenty for each of us," he said cheerfully as she tugged one out. The whole bunch fluttered down, uncovering the gauntlet of the backup PullLine he'd worn. He slid that gauntlet, which was marked with a *KCB*, down into position, tightened it, then pulled his cuff back down. He picked up a handkerchief from the deck. "You might want to clean your face, my dear. You've got mine dust all over it." Taking her chin gently in his hand, he began wiping her face, and she felt rather ridiculous. Despite having tricks up their sleeves, they were likely to all die and to take the Sky Keepers' hopes and their friends to their graves with them, and she was being cleaned up like a toddler caught playing in the mud.

"Have I ever told you how beautiful your eyes are?" Kingsley asked softly, gently wiping her cheek. "Especially when they're all shimmery with a mix of fear and hope?"

An ache settled in Caroline's heart, and she swallowed hard against a sudden burning in her throat. "No."

"How remiss of me." He met her gaze briefly, an earnest apology there, and continued, "I should have. Shall I tell you every day from now on? Or would you get tired of it?"

"Perhaps not *every* day," she said, trying to smile but failing.

"I'll alternate compliments then. Eyes on Tuesday, hair on Wednesday, courage on Thursday, and so on."

Despite her fear, the nervous pull of her attention to the stairs where the guards might come for them to separate them and lock them up, a smile won out. "I'd like that."

This time as he briefly met her gaze, he smiled, warm and hopeful. "You'll have to do the same for me, of course. Only you can't repeat compliments in the same pattern lest it appear you're only returning them in a tit-for-tat type of thing."

"I'll do eyes on Friday then."

"Perfect." He caught her hand, kissed it, and then picked up a clean handkerchief from the deck and handed it to her. "Would you return the kindness?"

After she'd wiped his face, which he'd done a poor job of cleaning earlier, he offered her his arm and led her toward the automaton "chairs." Looking over his shoulder at Mark, who'd been left to clean his own face from his own pile of handkerchiefs, he called back to him, "You can pull up your own chair. Or you can make something out of those two." He gestured to the two headless automatons on the deck.

"I figured." Mark smiled in amusement, then followed them. "I'll tinker instead."

When she and Kingsley reached the disemboweled automatons, Kingsley lifted her onto one of the empty barrels, and she nearly fell into the hole left by the automaton. As she steadied herself, he sat on the other, draped an arm over her shoulders, and pulled her to him. "Comfortable?"

"Not really," she mumbled, still trying to avoid falling in. "You left a hole. I'm smaller than you, you know."

Laughing, Kingsley pulled her into his lap. "How's this? What do we care for scandal?"

She leaned back against him as he wrapped his arms around her. "Much better."

"I thought it would be."

"You know some people would call you arrogant, right?"

"Only the jealous. To everyone else, it's a refreshing lack of false modesty."

She laughed. "I guess I have to agree with that."

"I thought you might." He hugged her a little tighter, then stiffened. His hand ran lightly, questioningly, over her corset at her side, and Caroline struggled to repress a smirk. "Caroline," he whispered, his hand ceasing its inspection, "what manner of unladylike things did you secret away in your corset? A few things from my brother, I hope?"

"I was wondering when you'd consider the abilities of your queen," she said, truly smirking now. "I've a thin blade, the iron paste, and a miniature Dragon's Breath and Pea Souper. I have to put those last two together though."

"I take back everything I said about your outfit. Though if you want to wear that corset over the other dress, I wouldn't complain."

Laughing softly, she snuggled back against him.

"Would you like to dance?" he asked.

Dance? *Now is the time for madness.* She wanted it to be the time for snuggling.

"Last time I asked," he continued, "you did say later. And it *is* later. And we have all this lovely space."

And guards and a cold-hearted dictator watching. And Mark quietly pulling pieces from the two automatons and putting them together into something remarkably scary looking. Was he *building* a bomb?

"I just got comfortable," she groused, delaying the inevitable for another coveted moment.

He hugged her tighter and whispered, "While I would happily stay here with you the entire voyage, we mustn't get boring. The mist is coming, and Mark is nearly done."

Sighing, Caroline nodded and hopped down. If Mark was doing what she thought he was doing, then moving away was a good idea.

Kingsley positioned himself a few feet from her, straightened his dusty prison guard uniform, drew himself up, and held out his hand in invitation, looking regal despite everything.

If he could manage that, so could she. Caroline's manners might be a bit rough in general, but no one could say she wasn't a graceful dancer. Holding her head high, she gave him her hand, and he settled it on his arm just below his shoulder, took her right hand in his left, and placed his right hand firmly against her back. Humming softly, he started them waltzing around the deck, past Mark still tinkering, past the untouched automaton near the ship's side, through the light mist of the cloud top that swirled about their feet.

"How do you fancy being a pirate queen?" Kingsley asked as they neared Mark a second time. "The Rí Am took my ship. I'm of a mind to take his."

It's a nice dream, but ... But they were currently unbound, free on the deck.

She dredged up a conspirator's grin. "I've always thought my talents were wasted as a printer. What's our plan, Captain?"

He winked at her. "I'll convince them I'm the true Time King and then they'll hand over the ship."

Scoffing, she glanced at Mark in the thickening mist, still fiddling, only a few pieces remaining in the pile beside him. "You mean you plan to convince them to leave it to our care. Hence Mark's little building project?"

Kingsley's smile was sly. "Hence Mark. Do you think you could get that Dragon's Breath ready?"

When Caroline nodded, he shifted his hold on her right hand, indicating a turn, and as she passed underneath his arm, she slipped her free left hand behind her back and under her jacket. Grasping the tab on the shirt side of her corset, she tugged and released a tube of fabric and the discs previously secured inside. Four sections of a sphere and a pin slipped into her palm.

Kingsley drew her back to him, and she held the Dragon's Breath parts in her hand against his arm as they moved toward Mark. Over Kingsley's shoulder she could see movement on the upper deck.

"Hurry," Kingsley whispered, dropping her hand and blocking her from view. Footsteps beyond them told her several guards were hurrying toward Mark and the machine, now alive and clicking.

She snapped the slices together into a sphere, a small hole visible at their juncture, and used the pin to puncture the compartments and activate it. She dropped it to the deck, and a pale, almost unnoticeable greenish mist rose from it to join the white of the clouds and spread about the deck.

"Get away from that," one guard ordered Mark as the others formed a semi-circle in front of him.

Kingsley stilled, pulling Caroline to him. Mark rose away from the clicking machine at his feet but didn't retreat.

"I'm not going back," he said, his posture tense.

"You don't have a choice." The guard raised his gun, and Caroline realized the pistol in his hand was a stun gun. His real weapon was strapped across his back. "If you want to remain conscious and free, step away." He gestured again with the stun gun, and Mark, jaw set, glared at him before finally walking slowly from the machine, hands raised. Another guard, the one with a fine arm bracer, hurried to the machine and knelt beside it.

While he examined it, Caroline traced the progress of the light greenish Dragon's Breath, their protection against a second shot. How she wished it was for the first! It was wisping against the sides of the ship and riding a gentle breeze onto the upper decks. *Keep going.*

"This isn't a bomb," the kneeling guard exclaimed. "It does nothing but make noise." He stood, sneering at Mark, who was still slowly backing away. "The Rí Am overestimated you, it seems, cousin."

"Did he?" Mark's smile was grim. "Or did I break his nerve? I am the winner of this round."

The guard with the arm bracer scoffed. "If you had any sense you'd be offering information on the Sky Keepers. You might be able to save at least yourself, maybe your family."

Mark halted halfway to the automaton in the corner near the ship's side. "Our definition of sense was never quite the same, Gerald."

"So it seems." Gerald spun away and headed for the upper deck. The guards backed cautiously after him, eyeing the prisoners warily.

"I meant what I said," Mark yelled after them.

"I'm sure you did," Gerald called back.

"Can you still scream in high C?" Kingsley whispered to Caroline as he pulled his sleeve back from the PullLine gauntlet.

"Yes."

"Get ready to do so and hold on." Stepping away, he repositioned her for dancing, then started them waltzing again, keeping an eye on Mark, who was walking toward the intact automaton.

A few feet from it, Mark glanced over his shoulder at them, then broke into a sprint.

"*Now,*" Kingsley hissed.

Caroline screamed, and the guards turned to them as Mark leapt onto the barrel of the automaton and used it as a springboard to catch the edge of the upper deck and swing himself up and onto it.

"No, Mark!" Kingsley shouted. He opened his arms for her. While the guards turned to Mark, Caroline jumped into

Kingsley's arms, wrapping her arms around his neck and her legs around his waist as he sent the PullLine up to the balloon's bronze shield nearly hidden by the clouds.

As guards shouted and Mark vaulted over the railing and barely visible wires into the clouds, they flew up to the balloon. A shot followed them, but it missed and the Dragon's Breath crackled across the ship, screams and sparks following.

A heavy mist dampened Caroline's hair as they slowed and bumped to a halt next to the shield, water droplets streaming along it with the wind.

"It's a pity I can't reach the rescue straps on this one," Kingsley huffed as they hung, watching the guards below scurry to put out the small fires caused by the sparks from the combination of Dragon's Breath and gunfire, "though they are second rate compared to the ones on your fancy new PullLine."

"I'm not letting go so you can take your jacket and shirt off to reach them." Caroline didn't slacken her death grip as he looked up to study the balloon. It was broad in build, and she figured they could walk along the top, if needed. "By the way, what did you pad yourself with?"

"Bedsheets. Oh, Caroline!" he exclaimed, breaking away from his inspection to beam at her. "You have no idea how wonderful clean bedding is!"

"I can imagine. I got a good whiff of you when I first found you and Mark, remember? But stay focused. We've got a good bit of cloud cover, and I can use the Pea Souper if we want more. What now?"

"Wreak a bit more havoc and open a way into the ship for Mark—I don't think you can see him, but he's making his way along the lower portion of the hull now, and I don't imagine he wants to hang around there all day. As for havoc, personally, I'd like to plunge your knife into the side of the balloon and go ripping our way down it in very dramatic, swashbuckling fashion, but since I want to keep the ship intact and afloat, we'll have to come up with something else."

Caroline gave him a wicked grin. "We have your sheets. They only have to *think* the balloon's not intact."

Kingsley's eyes brightened, and he returned her grin. "You are a pirate queen."

CHAPTER THIRTEEN

K ingsley got them to the top of the balloon near the forward end, and Caroline, praying for courage as she did so, managed to convince herself to let go of him and stand on the bronze shield. Kingsley quickly divested himself of his jacket, shirt, and padding, handing them to her and exposing the PullLine harness. Kingsley, being Kingsley and very proper, had on another shirt under this harness. He'd probably even pressed out the wrinkles too. Not that it mattered since the shirt was currently drenched in sweat and sticking to his thin frame.

"Did you and Mark leave anything in the guards' store-room?" she asked, amused, as she secured the sheets under her foot and he wrapped a simple rescue line under her arms. It was attached to the harness at his side, giving her ease of movement to be behind or before him without awkwardly wrapping him up.

"Not much." He attached an anchor line to the top of the balloon, and they both let out a breath into the mist nearly cloaking them even from each other. "We both had a bad feeling about how easy it sounded to get the crystal and get out. I was hoping we were both just jaded, but apparently not. Knife?"

After putting on Kingsley's delightfully warm jacket, Caroline carefully wiggled the thin blade out of her thick corset and gave it to Kingsley. Together, in the convenient cover of a cloud, they noisily ripped a sheet in two. They stuffed one end underneath the rim of the bronze shield, where the shield ended and exposed the sturdy balloon. Caroline released the free end of the sheet, and the wind caught it. If the sound of ripping hadn't been heard before, the sound of flapping fabric would. If only they could make the airship lurch violently to add to the illusion.

But the wonderful snapping of fabric was soon joined by a different sound of air dancing with a moving object, and her stomach sank. It had a very mechanical sound. Sort of mobile and deadly. "They sent the Escapers after us," she said flatly.

"I'd hoped they would," Kingsley answered with maddening cheerfulness as he detached the anchor line. A sheet draped over each arm, he opened his arms for her again, then wiggled his fingers. "Come on."

"Those things have guns," she protested, yet she quickly complied, saddened by how thin he felt now without the jacket and padding, "and the Dragon's Breath didn't reach this far."

The cloud beyond Kingsley billowed and spread, bright lights and a crimson body showing through. The whir of propellers came from it and rose from both the starboard and port sides. Great. From those angles, the Escapers could run them off the balloon or shoot at them without fear of damaging the balloon.

"All the more reason to leave now!" He tossed one bedsheet into the breeze blowing toward the port Escaper, stuffed the corner of another into the back collar of her jacket, stepped on its end, and scrunched it between his feet.

"Leave it!" she cried as he started hopping toward the balloon's sloping edge, taking the sheet with them. "Sheets—even torn bits of balloon—don't plummet, which is what we're going to do!"

"Exactly! By the time they realize what strange thing they're seeing, we'll be below their sigh—"

The Escaper fired, Kingsley slipped, and they tumbled off the balloon.

The sheet slipped from her collar, but Kingsley caught it, and it billowed out behind her like a sail. As they fell past the balloon's cover, he freed the sheet. It rode an updraft and caught in an Escaper's propeller. He released the PullLine onto the belly of the balloon, retracting it and arcing his body, reattaching as necessary, so that they swung across the breadth of the ship.

"Compensate for the ship's forward movement!" Kingsley yelled at himself as they narrowly missed one of the balloon attachment cables on the opposite side.

They missed it, but the loosed and retracting PullLine did not.

Their plummet over the ship's side ended abruptly as the line wrapped around a cable and they slammed into the side of the ship just shy of a window. They jerked further down as the tangled line slid along the cable to its attachment on the hull.

"Fiddlesticks!" Kingsley cried, yanking on the PullLine. "Let go!"

It didn't.

"There's a window up and to the left." Caroline poked him to make sure he was listening as he began retracting the PullLine, dragging them up the side of the ship toward the knot.

"I don't want to go—"

A bullet hit the hull just to the right of Kingsley's head. An Escaper dove toward them, enough guards in it to either shoot a ring around or through them or yank them from the air, depending on what the Rí Am wanted done with them at the moment.

Or the shot could have come from the escort ship closing its distance to them.

"Window!" Caroline yelled.

Kingsley pulled his feet up to the hull and shoved off, sending them flying out and to the left, arcing toward the approaching Escaper. Caroline wasn't sure how the guards in the Escaper responded, but she screamed, right until they crashed through a window and landed in a basket of laundry. The basket toppled, and Kingsley's elbow ended up in her stomach at least once before they made it to their knees and scrambled on broken glass and through dirty towels to the hallway. Only to be jerked to a halt by the PullLine as it reached its extension limit.

Splattering blood from a cut on his arm, Kingsley detached the line using the emergency release on the gauntlet as Caroline removed her safety line. They fled out the door, shots following through the window. They hadn't taken three steps into the hallway when Kingsley pushed her ahead and then sprinted back into the laundry room. Before she could catch up with him, he came flying out with a shovelful of hot coals and a clothes presser.

A guard ran out of the nearby crews quarter, and

Kingsley took him down with a well-aimed throw of the hefty clothes presser.

"There's going to be a fire shortly, hurry!" He pushed the shovel into her hands, picked up the clothes presser, and ran on, leaving Caroline to struggle to keep pace with his long strides. Or, as he probably saw it, strides that encouraged her to run faster than she thought she could.

Her heart returned to its falling-from-the-sky beat as the yell and heavy treads of guards came from ahead. She dragged Kingsley through a doorway, which turned out to be a stairwell. Sticking his head back into the hallway, Kingsley shouted in his most commanding tone, "Fire in the laundry! Secure the engine room! They're trying to scuttle the ship!"

They ran up the stairs until out of sight, and by some miracle, the guards going down toward the engine room never looked up, only kept going, and so did they.

Regaining a hallway, Caroline panted out, "Well, we're in. Do we take the bridge now? We should be close." She wasn't sure how, given they had no weapons to speak of and no backup, but if anyone could do something so insane to try, it would be a madman, and that she had.

"I didn't want the bridge yet!" Kingsley cried, rather petulantly. They rounded a corner sharply, and he stumbled against the wall, pressing his temple with his free hand. "I wanted the Escaper hold!" he continued, shaking his head when she reached out to him. "The purpose of going up to the balloon was so they'd send the Escapers out after us, opening the hold and allowing Mark a way into the ship right where he could steal the Rí Am's Escaper, plug in Cait's real crystal, and be off, taking you and the Oileán Caillte crystal with him."

Without you? Ignoring the twist of her heart for now,

Caroline asked, "But weren't we going to send everyone to the Escapers to abandon the airship for the escort ships? So we could take this one? They'd be going to the hold too."

"We were going to beat them there and lock them out until you and Mark were gone. Part of the reason for causing a panic was that we needed an excuse for Escapers to be out so the escort ships wouldn't fire on Mark as he left." Dropping the clothes presser, he fell against a door and cradled his head in his hands, reminding her his injured arm was dripping a crimson path after them. "This is what happens when you're not properly dressed," he muttered in that low tone. "If I'd had the proper hat and a cutlass, this wouldn't have happened. I'd be a pirate king by now. You'd be safe."

"Kingsley, please," Caroline pleaded, shaking his arm gently. "Hold on just a little longer." When he didn't acknowledge her, just kept muttering, she put the coal shovel down, took a handkerchief from his jacket pocket, forced his injured arm down, and bound the gash in it to stop the flow and hide their trail. She noticed another cut on his leg and did the same for it.

"How would I stop a madman from taking my ship?" Kingsley murmured. "How would I save myself from him? Which would I do? Murder, escape, destroy? What does he want? How do I stop him?"

The hallway looked like a guest wing, which meant there would be alcohol around. Leaving Kingsley for a moment, she searched the room opposite the one Kingsley blocked and secured a bottle of whiskey, a chair, and a blanket, and moved them out into the hallway with the blood trail. Reclaiming the coal shovel, she blew on the coals to heat them, dumped them on the blanket-covered chair, and poured whiskey over the whole thing, leaving some of the golden-brown liquid for Kingsley. After forcing several mouthfuls down him, she reclaimed her shovel and dragged him, coughing violently, along the hallway in the general direction of where she assumed the Escaper hold was—the other end of the ship. Behind them, smoke rose in search of a fire alarm.

The alarm pealed through the ship as they rounded a corner at high speed. Her eyes registered people and weapons, and she'd just released Kingsley and raised the shovel when Kingsley cried out, rather too happily, "Martin! Mighty Thor! You've still got your hammer!"

Her mind finally registering the important detail of their "assailants" being her friend and his daughter, Caroline lowered the shovel as Martin lowered the hammer and Prissy a familiar iron knife.

The footsteps of others echoed down the hallway, and Martin pushed open the nearest door and barged in, dragging Prissy with him. Caroline, towing Kingsley, followed them into a storeroom.

"You got free?" Caroline asked in surprise after the pounding of feet had passed them by. Her relief didn't make it into her tone, unfortunately.

Drawing himself up and looking affronted, Martin gestured to Prissy. "I object to my daughter being imprisoned and threatened."

Prissy, clinging to her father's arm, the elegant gown puddling at her feet, grinned, her eyes wide with excitement and wonder. "He convinced the guards he had explosives in his tobacco pouch."

"I'm impressed, Martin." Kingsley's tone was the appreciative one of a fellow artist.

Far from being flattered, Martin bristled. "The mystery is that *you two* got free."

"I object to having my future wife threatened," Kingsley said proudly as he draped an arm around Caroline's shoulders. He added in an exaggerated, hoarse mutter, at which she smirked, "Even if she is thoroughly ruthless."

"Caroline, are you really going to marry that madman?" Martin exclaimed, gesturing alarmingly with the hammer at Kingsley.

"Yes," she and Kingsley said together.

Martin stared at them a moment, then sighed and shook his head.

"He must like you." Prissy, bright-eyed and seemingly as friendly as her father was grouchy, grinned admiringly at Kingsley. "Otherwise, he'd be sneering."

Martin shot her a look. "I do not like the madman."

"I am very likeable," Kingsley said smugly, just before Caroline, hearing nothing in the hallway, grabbed his arm.

"We need to keep moving," she broke in. "We need to join Mark in the Escaper hold and make sure he gets off okay." She checked the hallway and started out.

"Won't they suspect that?" Martin cried, he and Prissy following them as Caroline dragged Kingsley out the door.

"The Rí Am won't be sure if we're trying to destroy him —most likely by taking down the entire ship—escape, or take control of the ship and use it to complete our mission," Kingsley said, finally moving of his own accord. "Are we bold revengers or runners? He'll play it safe by sending for an Escaper from one of the escort ships to land on the deck. He won't risk going to the hold for his own or not being prepared. And he'll try to save the statue and secure the engine room and Escaper hold, just in case."

"If he's trying to secure the Escaper hold," Martin protested, "then how can we possibly get in?"

"I was thinking of going out and coming back in, but I had to give up the main line of my PullLine."

Prissy's gasp was cut short by Martin's warning, "Prissy..."

"Daddy's got a PullLine on. He always wears one while working, has ever since having a bad accident with a defective ladder—"

"Broke my arm *and* the statue," Martin muttered.

"And I found the things they took from you boxed up with our stuff!" Huffing as she ran, Prissy lifted a sack Caroline hadn't noticed before. At least it explained her having Caroline's iron knife. "I only brought one PullLine though."

"You're a marvel, Miss Martin!" Kingsley took the sack as Martin sputtered about the absurdity of the idea. "One's all we need. You go with your father, and Caroline comes with me."

"I'm not risking our lives by swinging about on the hull of an airship!" Martin protested as Kingsley changed out PullLine harnesses, putting on Caroline's, which Prissy had wisely chosen, and giving Caroline his old one.

"What's your risk of choice then? You abandoned the statue."

Martin snapped his mouth shut.

"Won't the hold be closed now?" Caroline asked as Prissy handed her the iron knife.

"Oh, I shouldn't think so," Kingsley said, unconcerned. "The Escapers will still be out looking for us, just in case we go back out."

"But—" Martin sighed, shook his head, and kept his forward motion. Caroline and Prissy did the same.

"You didn't destroy the statue by any chance, did you?" Kingsley asked of Martin, his expression suddenly serious.

"Destroy it? Do you think me a barbarian that I would destroy something so beautiful? Your future wife was the model, after all."

Kingsley frowned and yanked the harness straps snug, his jaw tightening. He glanced at her, and she remembered his earlier comment about sending her away with Mark.

"Kingsley," she said softly, running closer to him, "I've known for a long time it would be 'till death do us part' for us. You're not sending me away."

Sighing, he closed his eyes briefly, then caught her hand. "It was unfair for you to get stuck with me, but I'm glad you did." With a rueful smile, he lifted their clasp hands to his lips and kissed her knuckles.

"Besides," she said, squeezing his hand as he tried to release her, "once we take this ship we can return to Sheffield-on-the-Sea and be ready to rescue Herschel and the rest of the *Dusk Crier*'s crew when the Star Veil falls."

Laughing softly, he released her hand. "My thoughts exactly, darling, which is why I collected a Sheffield-on-the-Sea crystal. We've got to take the ship before the Star Veil falls so we'll at least be going in the right direction for it."

"Where are we going now?"

Kingsley's lips quirked. "The Vallendester theater, Reydon."

Taking down a few guards on the way, they made it to a room with a sizable window. Martin, after giving Prissy his jacket, secured her in his rescue line, and Kingsley did the same for Caroline.

They made it out the window, into the mist, and Caroline, clinging to Kingsley again, remembered how cold, damp, and heart-poundingly high it was outside. How unfortunately not-alone they were.

They were only a dozen feet beyond their window when the whir of an Escaper coming up from behind preceded a stirring of the clouds they were quickly leaving. It was open sky after that.

"Martin," Kingsley yelled, and Martin, a half-dozen feet away preparing for his next cautious swing, looked over his shoulder at them. "I didn't mention it earlier, but I'm fairly certain the Rí Am is going to use the Escaper from the escort ship to go to his own Escaper hold to wait for us."

"What!" Martin bellowed.

"Thought you should know."

While Martin cursed and Caroline sighed in a confirmed suspicion, Kingsley leaned close and met her gaze, his brown eyes bright. "Caroline?"

"Yes, Kingsley?"

"Don't scream."

"Wh—"

He detached the PullLine. They plummeted, and he sent the line to the bottom of the approaching Escaper. It bobbed as their weight hit it and they swung underneath it, arcing toward the escort ship.

As asked, Caroline didn't scream. She yelled instead. "I never should have given you that whiskey! I should have slapped you back to your senses!"

Kingsley's deep laughter only confirmed her opinion. "Oh, how I've missed this!"

"You've done this before?" she shrieked as they attached to the escort ship and swung back out, reattached, and swung.

"Almost every pirate attack!"

Groaning, she squeezed her eyes shut, her stomach close to reaching its motion-tolerance level, and hung on.

"Look out!"

They hit something, human by the sound of the cries, human and non-human by the combination of sensations, many of which involved pain. She opened her eyes to find them in an Escaper, both guards knocked insensible by them during their landing or by Kingsley immediately after. The winged craft lurched violently, and she took hold of the controls, sending them down and away from the airships as Kingsley moved the two men to the rear seats. That done, he took over the controls, and she searched the side of the Rí Am's airship for Martin and Prissy.

"I don't see them," she said worriedly as they flew underneath the escort ship. As she shifted to look around, she noted how comfortable the cushions were, how posh the Escaper was compared to those of the Bowditch ships. "Do you think they went back into the ship after your revelation?"

Kingsley's gaze followed hers briefly before he took them up to the starboard side of the starboard escort ship's balloon. "Martin's too angry to hang around and let them get killed or go inside and let them get caught. I showed him how to get an Escaper and flee and made him angry enough to do so. They'll be fine."

Caroline's sputter ended in a moan and a prayer as she pinched the bridge of her nose. *Not everyone is as crazy and brave, or as heedless of danger, as you, Kingsley.*

"And if he takes the other Escaper," Kingsley continued, "it will be a few minutes before they realize and get more out after us. Still have that knife?"

She nodded and held out the stiletto blade. He jerked his

chin toward the white balloon fabric. "Stab it and keep hold. I'll take us down enough to make a good rent."

Grateful for the seat straps that would help keep her in place, she thrust the knife into the fabric and struggled to keep the blade sliding through the tough fabric as they lowered. "It's not wanting to cut!"

"I should hope not, or no airship would survive a pirate attack. It's a big enough gash for the Escaper's grappling hook."

Air hissing out in her face and shouts rising from below, she yanked the knife out and secured the grappling hook into the fabric. They dipped down, the Escaper straining against the taut line, but it won out, and the fabric ripped. More air whooshed out, and the balloon lurched away from them, yanking them with it.

"We'd better go before they decide they can't do any more harm by shooting this way," Caroline yelled over the noise.

"Agreed. We still have one more escort to take out."

They ascended enough to wiggle out the hook, then sped away from the ship, disappearing into the clouds and taking the long way over to the Rí Am's ship.

"What did you mean about you doing acrobatics between ships every time you were attacked by pirates?" Caroline asked as clouds blanketed them. She climbed in the back to check the guards, who were still unconscious. She pulled out more of Kingsley's handkerchief collection from his jacket pocket and began tying them up.

"Didn't you know that the best place to be during a pirate attack is the pirates' ship?" Kingsley asked in a teasing voice. "Unless you're attacking Cavan O'Connor's *Breaker*, of course. That's when our dear brother Colin almost killed me and Herschel."

"Herschel went with you on these circus stunts!"

"Herschel always came with me. Divest those two of their weapons while you're back there, won't you?"

Already collecting the weapons, Caroline gave him a hard glare, which he didn't see. And her own brother never told her! It's not as if she'd have stopped him. It was just something she would have liked to have known.

"While the crew was fighting, we'd sneak over to the pirate ship, mess with their automaton, and rescue whatever stolen cargo they had. We'd return what we could to the proper owners, of course, but the *Dusk Crier* got payment for delivering the rest, and usually some for returning the claimed cargo. Didn't you wonder how I became owner of the *Dusk Crier* so young? My parents didn't give Davy, Marianna, and me our own airships—we had to work our way up to commanding a ship and then pay them back for the ship." His tone lost its teasing, and he continued, seriously, "I took ridiculous risks trying to make the *Dusk Crier* my own as soon as I could. The risks mostly paid off. I grew to think nothing could touch us, the *Dusk Crier* and me, that the Maker had marked us for invincibility. That we could even challenge the Rí Am and get away with it."

"So as soon as you bought the *Dusk Crier* from your parents, you sailed off and lost it," Caroline said with more sadness than scoffing. After slipping a revolver into a loop on her corset and another into the pocket of Kingsley's jacket, she climbed back into her seat and set the remaining weapons at her feet.

"Yes, I—" He turned to her briefly before staring ahead again, his hands tightening on the controls. "Caroline, my mother was after me to marry a particular young woman. I've always tried to honor and obey my parents, and mostly that was for the best and saved me much regret, but I knew my mother's reasons for ... uh ..."

"Trying to keep you away from me? I wasn't socially acceptable, I know," Caroline said, a mix of shame and sadness tugging her gaze down. "She didn't approve of me for her darling son and picked out someone else for you to marry."

He flinched. "Yes. That voyage to find a way to navigate, that was, in part, me rebelling. It was, I thought, a temporary act of rebellion to show my independence from them. I would come home a hero to a changed, better world, and then I would commit a lifelong act of rebellion by marrying you. I was going to ask you to marry me at that last dance, but I lost my nerve. I'm sorry."

Caroline's gaze snapped up to stare at him. Since when did the daring Kingsley Bowditch ever lose his nerve?

Perhaps at times like this, since his white-knuckle grip on the controls didn't convey his normal ease.

Caroline's mood improved despite herself and the whirring of approaching Escapers. "Who'd she pick out for you?" She pulled the Pea Souper from her corset, put it together, and activated it. She tossed it to the rear of the airship, and as it began generating a thick, cloaking fog around them, she rotated a few gears on the control panel and a turret gun rose in front of her. She felt around under her seat until she found a pin. She pulled it out and swiveled experimentally in her seat. She grinned. This was a *very* posh Escaper. Just her kind of posh.

"Ah ... I don't remember."

"Kingsley..."

"It's not like I spent the last four years dreaming of *her*."

"And who did you spend the last four years dreaming of?" she asked, studying the gun and the amount of ammunition they had. Kingsley would rather outwit and temporarily disable opponents than kill them, and now she imagined he rather feared turning into a vengeful brute like some he'd been imprisoned with. She was not so scrupulous when it came to protecting herself and others.

"Mostly I dreamed of steak and kidney pie and ginger-snaps. Ouch! But I dreamed of you cooking them!"

"Well, that's different," she said, removing her heel from the vicinity of his foot and scooting onto the wooden console between them to kiss his cheek. "By the way, Mark's not in the hold, is he?"

"No," Kingsley said, his smile cunning as he made a sharp change in course. "Grab us both jackets and caps from the guards so we won't look so suspicious when the fogs lifts. And open that console. Mark's long gone. Being in possession of a PullLine, a naturally quiet manner, and a devious mind, he would've sneaked into the Escaper hold from the outside while we caused the distraction above, dropped down from the roof onto the unsuspecting guards, and flown out in the Rí Am's Escaper while the other Escapers were out chasing us.

"The Rí Am kindly gave me a tour of the airship on my first voyage with him," he continued as Caroline took the controls while he slipped on a guard's jacket. "His airship bridge and personal Escaper don't have automatons since no deception is needed about the true navigator being the crystals rather than a program in the automatons. They just have slots to put the crystals into. Since the crystals directly link to the ship's navigation system, all Mark had to do was plug in

Cait's crystal and fly away on the finest Escaper in the world."

"He didn't wait for us?" she asked, regaining her seat and pulling the wooden slat of the console up. A small navigator automaton popped up like a jack from the box. Not that she wanted Mark to wait. She wanted the Star Veil torn down more than her safety, but she was rather surprised.

"I told him to wait as long as he could or until the fire alarm went off."

"Oh." She pointed to the automaton. "Does this explode?"

"Yes and yes. He knew I wanted the airship, and he was waiting for you, not me, and—"

"And he knew I wouldn't have gone without you anyway, so he'd have left." She carefully removed the automaton from its seat. "Davy and the Star Veil can't be far, which means we only need to keep them distracted until the Veil falls and Davy comes to get us."

Kingsley didn't respond, just veered sharply toward the balloon of the remaining escort ship, the other having limped away to the nearest port for repairs.

"You weren't actually planning on taking the ship *by yourself*, were you?"

He shrugged, bringing them low over the top of the balloon. "If I could. I'm not sure how we'd get back to Sheffield-on-the-Sea unless we put the crystal in the ship's controls before the Star Veil falls so we'd be heading in the right direction. Waiting could mean losing the island." His shoulders sagged, and he added quietly, "You know as well as I do that if the Rí Am survives he'll find a way to return to Oileán Caillte, remove the iron from the mound, and get the faerie queen to avenge her honor and redo the Veil. But if he and the statue never come, if the Veil falls and the iron harpoons stay buried in her mound, she'll be affronted, but it won't be worth her while to come out to do anything about the foolish mortals."

Caroline squeezed his hand. "We'll take the ship then. After this one. If anyone can do it, you can."

Giving her a half smile, he pointed to the rim of the bronze shield. "Throw the automaton about there, then get ready to shoot it."

She complied. The automaton slid a little further from the rim than she wanted, but it would have to do. Kingsley, who knew her marksmanship, took them as far away as prudent, and she, after slipping the telescopic lenses of her goggles into place, made very good use of the turret gun. The automaton exploded, and they soared off and circled above the Rí Am's airship. Between the clouds, fog, and the danger of mistaking one of their own crews for them, the guards hadn't made much of an effort at chasing them. She hoped that was the reason anyway and not some scheme she hadn't thought of yet.

Caroline wasn't sure how the scramble-distance part of the curse worked when they were circling targets that just happened to be moving forward, but when Kingsley suggested changing seats, she agreed.

"We seem to be traveling faster than we were earlier." She settled into his seat, glancing at the instrument panel before looking down through the clouds for the bronze of the *Crystal*'s shield. It was far leftward of where she expected. Had it changed direction?

"Yes." His voice was grim, his jaw set, and she suddenly wasn't sure if she liked him taking a serious situation seriously. It worried her. "Do you still have the iron paste? I'm going to need war paint if I'm going to take the ship. And I'd like my own PullLine back. We've been through a lot together."

Maybe he wasn't taking it entirely seriously.

She took off the guard's jacket, exchanged PullLines with him, put the jacket back on, and handed him the compact with the paste.

"By the way, when exactly did you and Mark plot all this out?" she asked as he used the iron paste to fingerpaint the Sky Keeper symbol on both cheeks.

"We had to talk about something while you were working." War paint on, he slipped the compact into a pocket and began examining the turret gun.

"What else did you talk about? Or do I want to know?" She glanced over her shoulder at the moaning, shifting guards. "Unless you want to be thrown overboard," she snarled, "I suggest staying still." They ceased their movement.

With an amused glance between the guards and her, Kingsley answered, "Well, we argued over what will happen to the Rí Am's body when he finally dies: Will it turn to dust to match his true age? Undergo normal decomposition? Or has the faerie queen's elixir so well preserved him that his body won't decay at all and we could put him in a glass box for our descendants to revile and take as a warning lesson? I'm for normal decomposition once any faerie protections have been removed."

"I'm for dust."

"That's what Mark said. Take us down. That extra speed —they've figured out what truly happened to Mark and are going after him. I forgot there's likely a tracker on the Rí Am's Escaper. We're going to have to do something rather less imaginative than I'd hoped, but perhaps that's good. He won't be expecting that of us."

Caroline repressed a few of those expressions that had so shocked Mrs. Bowditch and took them down. They broke the cloud cover, and she discovered where all the Escapers were. They'd formed a loose ring around the *Crystal*, and she and Kingsley had just descended into the middle of it. Two of the five crafts rose into the clouds to cut off a vertical escape. The others started to close in.

"Give yourselves up or we'll fire." The order echoed through a loudspeaker to them. The Escapers had to be careful not to hit each other or the *Crystal*, but Caroline had no doubt they could manage to hit them if they wanted to.

"Dive for the bridge!" Kingsley yelled. Caroline tipped the Escaper's nose for the windows rising above the deck and put all the craft's speed into their descent, swerving tightly to make them a harder target to hit.

Bullets dented the hull just before a boom came from below. They banked left as a cannonball shot toward them. It sheared off one wingtip, and they hurtled downward more wildly than before.

"Skim the deck and be ready to jump!" Kingsley shouted as he flipped down the telescopic lenses on his goggles and swung the turret gun around toward the bridge. "And avoid any more of those things if you can!"

Caroline spared him a glare as she struggled to keep the craft somewhat on course. They dodged the next projectile by a hairsbreadth. Kingsley fired at the cannon, hitting both it and the two Escapers grounded on the deck. The Rí Am and a few guards, running between them for the bridge, ducked under them. The windshield of the Escaper nearest the cannon shattered, clearing a path to its automaton. The navigator exploded, and the vessel itself soon followed, blowing the cannon beside it into the side of the *Crystal*.

"Hit the other Escaper!" she yelled.

Kingsley swiveled the gun toward it as roiling, smoke-filled air slammed into them, shoving them toward the balloon's connection cables and throwing off his shots.

"Watch where you're going!" One of the guards reached around her to grab the controls, bruising her hands as he added his strength to her attempt to turn them away from the cables and out of their nosedive. The craft flipped to its side, the cables skimming the wings.

"Pull up and abandon ship!" Kingsley yelled as they soared over the lower deck. The two guards jumped just before Kingsley grabbed Caroline and leapt after them. The Escaper hit the ship's raised side and spun off into the clouds.

Pain, exhilaration, and fear all flared through Caroline as she hit the deck, Kingsley beside her. "Trust me, love," he whispered just before guards surrounded them and he scooted away.

"Put down your weapons and remove your PullLines. All of them." Gerald-with-the-arm-bracer had his rifle rather than his stun gun aimed at them now.

Moving slowly to avoid alarming any trigger-happy guards, Caroline laid both her knives on the deck, removed the guard's jacket, and began unstrapping the PullLine. A hint of the acrid smoke billowing from the wreckage of the destroyed Escaper burned her throat, but most of it was blown away from them over the stern as the airship sped forward. Ulrik, standing in an anxious crowd of crew members and guards in front of the wreckage, his clothes blackened and torn, accepted a drink but gestured for the physician in a crisp white uniform to leave him alone. The rigidness of his posture as he tossed the canteen aside and stormed toward Caroline and Kingsley did not bode well for a second match of wits.

Please hurry with the Star Veil, Davy. Caroline dumped her PullLine on the deck and said a quick prayer. She was ready to die but preferred waiting a while to do so.

"Hurry up," Gerald snapped, kicking Kingsley in the side and knocking him over.

"Hey!" she cried, scrambling over to Kingsley. He ignored her and crawled back to his PullLine as the guards shooed her away and encouraged her to stand with a wave of their rifles.

"It must have a proper burial," he muttered, piling the PullLine so that the gauntlet was on top of the harness, the raised square with *KCB* emblazoned on it pointing toward the second Escaper and the bridge behind it. Toward their failed hopes? He rubbed his thumb over the polished letters as if in final caress, and Caroline almost thought the letters shifted closer together.

"Up!"

Kingsley scrambled up just as Gerald aimed another kick his way. She scooted closer to him, and they both raised their hands as the Rí Am, a barely contained fury in his eyes, snatched a gun from one of their guards and pointed it at Kingsley.

Kingsley gave him a lazy smile in return. "That's hardly sporting," he said in a mildly remonstrative tone, cutting off whatever Ulrik had started to snarl. "Don't you want to finish the game? I was rather enjoying it, and we wouldn't want to ruin your reputation as a sportsman."

The tip of the revolver trembled, though not enough to

miss Kingsley's heart, as Ulrik struggled for his usual cool composure. "Bind them and take them below!" he barked at last, lowering the gun. "You'll live to see all your family in the mines, Bowditch!" An oath escaped him as he handed the gun off to a guard and pressed a hand to a gash on his arm.

"We're going back to Sheffield-on-the-Sea then?" Kingsley asked, his voice blank despite the sharpness of his eyes. "There's a lot of faerie blood in some Sheffielders, isn't there?" he continued as the guards patted them down. He nodded toward Ulrik's bleeding right arm. "Enough for a faerie queen's elixir to have undesirable effects."

Ulrik stiffened, and Caroline, as well as some of the guards, looked closer at his arm. There was a blueish tint to the blood seeping from the wound.

"Started looking for your own faerie mound yet?" Kingsley pressed.

Ulrik slapped Kingsley hard enough to knock him into the guards. With a strangled cry, Ulrik doubled over, clutching his hand. Angry welts broke out across it in a smudged Sky Keeper symbol.

"Wonderful stuff, iron paste," Kingsley muttered as the guards seized his arms.

"Throw them overboard!" Ulrik roared as he straightened, clutching his hand to his chest. He stumbled off toward the bridge as his guards shoved Caroline and Kingsley toward the bow. One guard ran ahead to remove a portion of the railing there. He hit a lever and a plank extended from the side of the ship.

"Wait!" Caroline cried as she tripped up the stairs from the lower deck onto the bow. "The Rí Am lied to us all about a barren sky! He hid it, but the Star Veil is going to fall any minute. If you'll just wait, we can prove it!" Unheeding, they pushed her onward. The wisping top of a cloud partially hid the wooden deck at her feet. The end of the plank now only a dozen feet ahead disappeared into a wind-streaked fluff of grayish white. It was too thick. She didn't want to lose Kingsley in it. They were supposed to go together. "Kingsley!" she cried, struggling to find him behind her.

He was watching over his shoulder as the Rí Am passed between the smoking wreckage and the second Escaper. "Kismet!" he cried.

A hiss sounded from the lower deck, and a disc shot from Kingsley's gauntlet into the automaton of the remaining Escaper. A second disc followed, and the Escaper blew. Flames shot between it and the wreckage, setting the smoldering ruin ablaze again.

Kingsley pivoted, thrusting one of his guards into one of hers. As that one stumbled and loosed her arm, the other slung her toward the open section of railing. Something heavy slammed into her from behind, knocking her flat, with one hand dangling off the side of the plank, the edge of the deck digging into her chest. The plank began to retract. She and the guard on top of her scrambled backwards.

"Stop him!" someone yelled as her head cleared the lip of the deck.

Set into the wall just beside the open portion was a compartment with a heavy set of manacles and a pole for prodding slow plank walkers. She grabbed the manacles and slammed them into the face of the guard reaching for her. As he reeled back, she snatched up the pole and brought it into the outer thigh of the next nearest guard, then his head as he tumbled to the side. She raised the pole again, but the other two guards were already down. *Kingsley...*

"He's still alive!" someone cried as she searched the deck for him. Her gaze jumped up to the burning wreckage and the shadow of movement in it, then to the tall, thin figure racing between her and it.

Chased by gunfire, Kingsley sprinted across the lower deck toward their abandoned belongings. A bullet dinged off his gauntlet. He skirted to the right, dropped into a slide, snatched up her iron knife, and sent it into the Rí Am's chest as he staggered from the flames, a whitish glow of faerie magic about him. Reeling backwards, he shrieked in a mix of pain and fury and clutched the knife as if trying to pull it out. The glow flickered and vanished. His hands fell limp to his sides, and he buckled and fell back into the blaze.

Dropping the pole, Caroline ran for Kingsley as he collapsed onto the deck. She fell to her knees beside him as the Rí Am's remaining personal guard surrounded them. Gerald wore the look of one determined to sit in an empty throne and was yelling at her.

"Kingsley!" she cried, shaking him, not caring about the guard's warnings.

Wood splintered around them, and she and the guards alike ducked as bullets battered the deck. Kingsley twisted around, grabbed her, and pulled her over his side, tucking her to his chest with him between her and the hovering Escaper firing a line between them and the guards.

Above the shots, she heard a young woman cry, "Not so close, Daddy!"

Caroline broke from the shelter of Kingsley's arms to look over his shoulder at the hovering craft and nearly fainted, mostly in relief but partly in shock. The normally cheerful, wide-eyed Prissy was handling the Escaper like a trained pilot as Martin continued firing a ring around Caroline and Kingsley, dodging in toward Kingsley then back out toward the guards, making the guards back away. From his expression, Caroline got the impression Isaac Martin had no qualms about sending bullets through the deck alarmingly close to Kingsley. He'd never send them through him, but certainly close enough to make Kingsley wonder. Beyond them, the remaining guards and crew stood mute, as if unsure what to do, who they wanted to win.

Apparently unperturbed by Martin's show, Kingsley slowly uncurled and rose, pulling her up with him. Martin ceased firing. "The Rí Am is dead," Kingsley yelled, swiveling to make eye contact with as many of the guards and crew as stood on the deck or were peeking out from safer places. "His reign—the Star Veil itself—is ending. You'll see the truth of it in the sky soon enough. You've nothing to fight for now." He gestured to Gerald. "Except another dictator. Put down your weapons and choose freedom!"

Before the guards could reply, Martin bellowed, one hand waving for attention, one still prominently on the gun, "There's also a very large pirate ship heading this way at top speed. Like it or not, Captain Bowditch is in charge now. I suggest you do as he says and surrender before it gets here."

As one, they turned in the direction Martin indicated. A battle-scarred and toughened airship with a cresting blue wave painted on its hull was breaking through the clouds.

All around the ship, men began dropping their weapons. Gerald jerked his up so quickly Caroline almost missed it, but Kingsley didn't. He knocked Gerald flat with a beautiful punch and kicked the gun away.

"Bind him and any like him," Kingsley barked to one of the guards, who was actually smiling in stunned hope. The young man jumped into action. "The fighting is over."

"I'm not sure how O'Connor will feel about taking all of you aboard," Caroline added her own command, "so you might want to put out those fires and stabilize the airship."

"Use the Escaper PullLines to drag the wreckage off," Kingsley continued, giving more orders as Martin and Prissy landed and the crew scrambled to save the ship and ready it for boarding.

As Kingsley quieted and looked at the smoldering wreckage of machines and men, Caroline slipped her hand into his.

"If Mark asks," he said, nodding toward the blackened Escaper being lifted off the deck, "it was normal decomposition."

"Looks more like dust to me."

"That's normal under the circumstances." Wincing, Kingsley turned away, pressing a hand to the gash in his arm, which was dripping blood again. He had another bloody line above that one, likely from a close shave with a bullet.

"Oh, Kingsley! I forgot!" She took his arm and searched the deck for the white uniform of a ship's doctor, and finally found the man tending to a guard with a burn on his arm.

"Send the physician over here after critical cases are attended to!" Caroline yelled.

"You're getting pretty good at this pirate queen business." Kingsley smiled down at her, then took in the ship again, his smile fading.

A pirate queen. Despite Kingsley's somber mien and the wreckage being cleared away, Caroline found a giggle rising to her throat, and another and another following. She spun around, taking in the ship—their ship—the surrendered men, their friends drawing alongside them, the Star Veil that was soon to fall, and let the giggles build. Ulrik Vanon's reign had ended. They'd survived. They were free. Time had begun again. And Kingsley was quibbling about a bet with Mark and worrying about the scarred but operational airship.

Throwing her head back in laughter, Caroline spread her arms wide, the sleeves of Kingsley's ridiculously large jacket swallowing her hands. "Does it really matter? Let Mark win and the ship be scarred. We're free, Kingsley! We're alive!" Caroline threw herself into Kingsley's arms and kissed him. Judging by his reaction, Kingsley decided he had better things to think on after all. They ignored Martin's strident clearing of his throat, and it wasn't until they heard Mark's quiet laughter and a gruff, "Besotted fools," that they realized the pirates had arrived.

CHAPTER FOURTEEN

Kingsley Bowditch had been trying to escape for ... long enough. For it was done. By the Maker's grace, it was done. "And hast thou slain the Jabberwock?" he whispered to himself as he looked around the bridge. When Caroline elbowed him, he pulled her to him and leaned down to whisper in her ear, "'Come to my arms, my beamish boy! O frabjous day! Callooh! Callay!' He chortled in his joy."

She elbowed him again, but it was hardly a serious protest, so he held her tighter, finishing the poem for the pleasure of annoying her, all the while watching as the ship's captain, who like many appeared more relieved than distressed by the end of the Time King's rule, deftly switched out the Reydon crystal for the Sheffield-on-the-Sea crystal and set them on a quick course back. The two escort ships, the captain explained, had receiver crystals that let them travel with the *Crystal*, using its navigation crystals to guide them. After the damage done to them however, they had chosen from a store of emergency navigator automatons and sought out a port.

Kingsley hoped they made it okay, though he doubted all those crowded onto the bridge of the newly rechristened *Dusk Crier* thought so. They were an odd group: a mad Bowditch captain; a surly, printer-bachelor uncle; an O'Connor pirate and his mother; a couple of Sky Keeper Vanons; an almost-mad sculptor and his daughter; and, of course, Caroline, his beautiful pirate queen. It was a good group, despite its oddness, and one soon to grow. Mark and Cavan had promised him that Davy was eager to see him and would follow them to the mines as soon as the Star Veil fell. Davy, Colin, Vesper and her family, and his Autumn Eyes sister-in-law, Prism, were mapping out the path to Oileán Caillte for their return journey. They had all the tools they needed to navigate themselves!

After ascertaining the ship was in stable condition and on course, Kingsley led them all to the deck, where the crew had placed the crystal faerie queen.

"Not bad, Martin," Cavan O'Connor said appreciatively as he looked the statue up and down. Caroline immediately elbowed Kingsley.

"I wasn't going to say anything," he muttered, rubbing his side. That had been a serious protest.

"That would be a first," she whispered. Beside them, Darius Lockley chuckled.

Cavan continued to praise the statue with considerably more knowledge of art than Kingsley would ever have guessed the pirate to possess. Had he raided an art gallery at some point? When Cavan, Eoin and Mark Vanon, and Martin finished their discussion and praise, Kingsley met Martin's eye. The sculptor sighed and nodded.

"Overboard she goes," he said with a gesture of tossing something.

All of the odd group, Caroline, Prissy, and Bridie included, lifted the image of the crystal goddess, carried her to the edge of the airship, and flung her over the side. She tumbled end over end until finally crashing into the darkening waves below.

As they watched her disappear, the earth itself began to shake, the dimming Star Veil to waver. The sky crystals, dizzying in their shaking, went out, and what had been the dull black of the Star Veil between the crystals slipped away, curling back on itself. It vanished, and was replaced with ... Kingsley blinked against a warm wetness to his eyes. ... With dusk.

A domed sky of darkening blue overhead reached down to the horizon, lightening as it did. Soft clouds of vibrant purples and pinks robbed from a summer meadow guarded that meeting of sky and water above the glowing orange sphere disappearing for the night.

"The sun descending in the West, the evening star does shine," Kingsley said softly as someone cried out and pointed to a brightly shining point higher in the sky, another to one with a reddish hue, another to a crescent of blinding white. "The moon, like a flower in heaven's high bower, with silent delight sits and smiles on the night."

SOMETIME BEFORE THE stars had crossed the sky—and what a strange, wondrous thing it was to watch after a lifetime of stationary rows of lights!—land was sighted, and Kingsley was called to the bridge. After a frustrating but wonderful-in-its-freedom search of the coast of Sheffield-on-the-Sea, he and the captain managed to find the cove where the mine was and coordinate the landing of the *Dusk Crier* and the *Breaker*, saving room on the beach for the *Dawn Singer*.

But when they marched out of the ship prepared for another battle, they found themselves surrounded by guards and prisoners alike, all staring at the stars and the sliver of moon.

So Stewart had read his parting note, taken to heart what was going to happen when the Star Veil fell, and warned the guards to free, bathe, and clothe the prisoners. *Thank you, Maker.*

"Kingsley!" A petite brunette—the only woman to rival Caroline for beauty—burst from the group of stargazers, two men following her, and launched herself at him.

"Marianna!" he cried, catching her.

After his sister had nearly squeezed the life out of him and reminded him of his injuries, she introduced the two patiently waiting men as her husband, Bertram Orren, and Robert Lockley, who was both Bertram's and Caroline's relative. An inspection of Bertram—from his fond gaze at Marianna to his air of confidence, kindness, and sense—had Kingsley deciding his brother-in-law would neither cower before his sister nor cow her. According to Caroline, they were equally matched in their bossiness and mature enough to handle that. Bertram would do.

He turned to where Caroline had been only to find her, not surprisingly, in the arms of her brother. Darius hovered nearby, his glasses off as he rubbed his wet eyes. Martin, passing by, pointed to Herschel and said, "Now *he's* her brother. Yes, you can meet him, Prissy, but *later*."

When Herschel, a little shorter than average, with golden-brown hair and a muscular build, was finally released from his relatives, he stepped up to Kingsley, and before Kingsley could apologize again for involving him in his foolish voyage, Herschel slapped him on the arm—and Kingsley was half convinced Caroline had told him exactly where to slap due to the immediate pain—and embraced him.

"It's about time you proposed to my sister!" he scolded. "I was beginning to think there was something you feared, after all." Stepping back, he thumbed toward the airship. "She tells me the new *Dusk Crier* is a step up from the old one. I look forward to sailing her with you."

When the rest of his crew gathered round and said the same thing, Kingsley just about cried. When the birds began to sing and the sky to change colors, silhouetting an approaching airship with a familiar outline, he did.

PART VI
STAR SKY: AN EPILOGUE

EPILOGUE

There were those who claimed if the Star Veil unraveled, the world itself would follow. Yet when the Star Veil thinned to nothing but a shred of memory, the world did not collapse with it, though it did fray. There were struggles and hardships and wars, but it held together, and a new pattern, an old one seen anew, emerged, and most considered themselves better off than before. After a while, governments formed and families settled once more, some with new responsibilities and new members. Nowhere was this more evident than at the estate of Commodore and Mrs. Bowditch in Calandra, where friends and family were plentiful.

Marianna and Bertram spent their summers on Sheffield-on-the-Sea, or traveling, and their school years at a newly established university near Calandra, teaching and enjoying family life. Davy and Prism went back to captaining and inventing, though they did spend a good portion of time with, and doing some of that inventing on behalf of, Cal Andrews's circus. Colin and Vesper were happily traveling the world on their own airship, more often than not taking Eoin Vanon,

*Dermot Vanon, and even pirate-turned-statesmen Cavan
O'Connor, wherever the men's new positions in the trade and
transportation and military departments took them. Bridie
made frequent trips with them as well, for her daughter,
Fiona, as Philip's wife, was sometimes with Colin and
sometimes with Davy. Harcourt Ladell kept his theater open
—all its tapestries back in place—despite his busy schedule as
leader of the land to which Reydon and Calandra now
belonged. Mark and Claire, Nick and Cait, Will and Fiona's
oldest daughter, were all happy and working hard in their
respective professions. All but Mark—an astronomy professor
—were still officers on the Bowditch airship line. Darius went
back to printing but moved his business closer to his friends
and family in Calandra and to the university, where he
sometimes taught on the art of bookbinding. After marrying
Prissy and discovering a talent for designing ships, Herschel
got a job at the Bowditch Shipping Line main office in
Calandra and settled down. Stewart did the same, marrying
and working at the Bowditch office; he and Commodore
Bowditch also arranged programs to assist those who'd been
injured in combat get whatever healing they needed or just a
new start in life. Isaac Martin had to switch to a new medium
for his sculptures, but he quickly became as well known for
his work in marble as he had been for crystal. If he regretted
never finishing his statue of the faerie queen, he never said so.
As for Kingsley and Caroline...*

"Who is teaching *whom* to change a diaper?" Mrs.
Bowditch exclaimed in as polite a volume as
possible when most of her family and, by
extension, Colin and Vesper's and some of the crew's too,
were in her drawing room, chatting, playing games with each

other or the many young ones with great enthusiasm, and enjoying tea and cake. The grandfather clock in the corner, the cuckoo clock collection on the mantel, and the little decorative clock on the bookcase all added a pleasant background rhythm to the sounds of friends and family.

The Commodore, who was bouncing Marianna and Bertram's three-year-old son on his good knee, replied with a grin, "I believe Kingsley is teaching *her*, using Colin and Vesper's Sadie for practice. Cavan and Eoin are both overseeing, so I don't think any harm will come to the wee one." He added with a chuckle, "Can't say the same about Kingsley and Caroline though. Those two are pretty protective."

Mrs. Bowditch turned to glare at Darius. He raised his tea cup as if to hide his face, but then, as if not thinking that protection enough, turned away to Bridie, whose mouth hinted at a smile.

"I knew I should have taken that girl in hand years ago," Mrs. Bowditch said with a sigh, "so I suppose it's my fault." She added sternly, ignoring Darius's ignoring of her, "Darius, as you will be the other grandparent of Caroline and Kingsley's child, you should learn how to change a diaper yourself."

"Now, Lily—"

"Upstairs." Mrs. Bowditch rose and brushed a hand over her cream-colored corset and skirt to remove any cake crumbs left by herself or the grandchildren.

With a resigned sigh, Darius put aside his teacup and pushed up from his chair while the other gentlemen of the room laughed at him. "So much for the benefits of being a bachelor," he muttered.

"You might want to take little James up with you," Colin

suggested with a nod toward Marianna and Bertram's youngest, the one-year-old busy playing on the floor at his feet with Davy and Prism's daughter of the same age.

"Yes." Vesper, comfortably curled up on the sofa next to Colin, wrinkled her nose. "And don't wear out Sadie. I'd rather her not be cross, or at least unusually so, when next we have to change her."

"Feel free to check Abi while you're at it," Prism added, looking up with an amused smile from her seat at the table in the corner of the room, where she and Marianna were admiring her new revolver as Davy and Bertram tinkered with a new PullLine.

Darius looked from Colin to Mrs. Bowditch to James, then with another sigh, picked the surprised boy up under the arms and, holding him out in front of him, started for the stairs.

"Thanks for changing James," Bertram called after him.

"Not like that," Mrs. Bowditch protested, quickly checking Abi. The little girl not needing attention, she hurried after Darius and took James from him. "Thank heavens Caroline and Herschel were seven before they fell into your less-than-tender care," she said as she settled James onto her hip.

"Agreed," Darius said, wiping his hands on his jacket.

But he dutifully followed Mrs. Bowditch upstairs, and for all his protests, did an excellent job changing the diaper, his expression less grumpy and more tender than he intended it to be, Mrs. Bowditch suspected.

"You'd better be careful, Darius," Kingsley said with a grin, "or we might actually let you babysit."

Darius started to protest something, but Caroline interrupted, "Leave him alone, you two." She took her uncle's arm and kissed his cheek, which won a fond smile from him, and Mrs. Bowditch decided the child would be reasonably safe with the printer. Sadie had survived well enough when babysat by Cavan O'Connor, ex-pirate though he was, so perhaps impeccable manners weren't required for the job.

"It's time," Eoin called from his position at the window. Little daylight swept in through the open curtains.

"Come on then." Cavan scooped up Sadie and started for the door. Mrs. Bowditch handed James off to Darius, telling him to carry the boy properly, and followed them out and down the stairs. Behind her, she heard Kingsley gallantly ask Caroline if she wished to be carried too, an offer that was soundly rejected as she had "waddled her way up just fine and could waddle herself down just fine." Mrs. Bowditch sighed delicately at this, but her smile was fond, nonetheless.

Once downstairs, they gathered those not already outside and strolled to the back garden, where chairs and blankets had been set out. Evening had come, and the sun was setting, and as Kingsley had quickly realized, the sun wasn't *set* on the horizon so much as *it* set the clouds on fire with color. Purple and pink tonight, as it had been that first night, though it had been gray clouds and an apricot horizon the night before. He was keeping a list of the variations of sunset. It was a short beauty, sunset, like a sweet treat to be enjoyed in small doses, but it was one for every day. And it always gave way to another pleasure. To stars and moon, things of beauty, mystery, and patterns that could change the world, that could guide one through months and seasons and around the world itself, that spoke of the Maker.

Bundled in blankets as the night's chill grew, they watched as the colors faded and the moon rose and the stars did their slow swirl through the heavens, a few birds and the rustling of leaves in a gentle breeze all the orchestra the show required.

"Twinkle, twinkle, little star, how I wonder what you are! Up above the world so—"

"Kingsley..."

In a galaxy of shapeshifter magicians and magic-altering eclipses, anything is possible.

When Torin Argenti is sucked into an ancient horror movie featuring three children with a remarkable resemble to his boss, Lady Azura, he has until an eclipse ends to break the spell on the children and get them out, or they'll all be caught on film —permanently.

"Caught on Film" is a humorous, light-hearted novelette set in space and birthed of a love for classic films. It is available for free when you sign up for my newsletter at www. elizabethjanekitchens.com/newsletter-signup/.

ABOUT THE AUTHOR

E.J. KITCHENS loves tales of romance, adventure, and happily-ever-afters and strives to write such tales herself. When she's not thinking about dashing heroes or how awesome bacteria are—she is a microbiologist after all—she's enjoying the beautiful outdoors or talking about classic books and black-and-white movies. She is a member of Realm Makers and lives in Alabama.

May she beg a favor of you? You've already kindly read her book, would you also leave a review? Those gold stars can power more than fictional worlds: they encourage, inspire, and help authors through hurdles so we can seek out the people looking for books like ours. It's a daunting quest, and without you, fearless reader, it would fail. Will you join it?

To learn more about E.J. Kitchens and her books, visit her website and sign up for her newsletter.

www.ElizabethJaneKitchens.com

ADVENTURE AND ROMANCE IN A FANTASY WORLD

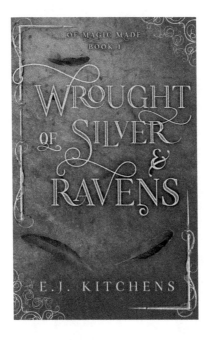

Book 1 of OF MAGIC MADE

With a malevolent prince stealing her kingdom and her magic one dance at a time, Princess Thea must win the loyalty of a mysterious guard to save her kingdom.

Wrought of Silver and Ravens is an adventure-romance retelling of "The Twelve Dancing Princesses" and is set in The Magic Collectors story world.

A CURSE KEEPER, CURSE BREAKER Fairytale

Belinda Lambton knows a curse when she sees one. She also knows the wisdom of agreeing with a powerful enchantress. So when she gets mixed up with a cursed Beast and his enchantress, she finds herself tasked with the role of Curse Breaker. That's not an easy position, for Beast has reasons of his own to keep his curse. There's also someone determined to break it by whatever means possible and claim Beast for herself, and she doesn't take competition well.

With wit, clean romance, and a touch of danger, *Midnight for a Curse* is a retelling of the beloved "Beauty and the Beast" tale.

Adventure and Romance Are Only a Page Away

E. J. Kitchens

CPSIA information can be obtained
at www.ICGtesting.com
Printed in the USA
BVHW031112140121
597831BV00005B/45

9 780999 350973